PRAISE FOR MIKE SHEVDON

"*Sixty-One Nails* is *Neverwhere* for the next generation. The pacing is spot-on, the characters engaging, and the world fits together beautifully to create a London that ought to be. I stayed up too late finishing it."
— *C.E. Murphy*

"Mike Shevdon strikes sparks from the flinty core of English folklore, as a hero every reader can relate to finds he's part of an incredible and scarily believable parallel realm. If you've been thinking urban fantasy has nothing fresh to offer, think again."
— *Juliet E. McKenna*

"Here is the very best of urban fantasy... A highly believable page-turner of a quest."
— *Aurealis Magazine*

"By the end of the novel, I was hanging onto the pages, drawing every last scene out as though I were sucking it out through a straw. I really did enjoy the ride."
— *Lateral Books*

"It's a tale that will keep you gripped... Get this now before the hype hits."
— *Falcata Times*

"This book is magnificent in every way. *Sixty-One Nails* is a novel I will remember for a very long time. 5*****"
— *SciFi & Fantasy Books*

ALSO BY MIKE SHEVDON

The Courts of the Feyre
Sixty-One Nails

MIKE SHEVDON

The Road to Bedlam

THE COURTS OF THE FEYRE
VOL. II

ANGRY
ROBOT

ANGRY ROBOT
A member of the Osprey Group

Lace Market House,
54-56 High Pavement,
Nottingham
NG1 1HW, UK

www.angryrobotbooks.com
One step beyond

Originally published in the UK by Angry Robot 2010
First American paperback printing 2010

ISBN 978-0-85766-061-9

Printed in the United States of America

9 8 7 6 5 4 3 2 1

For Sue

ONE

Kayleigh was running out of places to look. It wasn't like Alex to skip lessons like this. Well, OK, just that once, but they'd done it together, scaring each other with the prospect of getting caught in town when they should be at school. This was different. They had arranged to meet before Geography so that they could swap ideas on the homework, so where was she?

She went through the outer doors, peeping around the wall in case a teacher lurked there. The playground was empty; no teachers and no Alex. She was about to go back into the building when she heard a noise from the gym block. It was more of a yell than a scream and it wasn't Alex's voice, but there shouldn't be anyone in the gym block at this time.

She checked the playground again and ran across the tarmac, praying the teachers in the rooms facing the playground were now engaged with their mid-morning classes and too busy to be looking out of the windows. She reached the side door to the gym and slipped through, breathing hard. The echo from her school shoes on the wooden floor where outdoor footwear wasn't allowed made her walk around the edge rather than crossing the open space. She stopped and listened. There were voices in the girls' changing room.

She tiptoed quickly down the passage and stopped. The voices were louder. She leaned on the door, pushing it open slightly, and recognised Tracy Welham's voice and the unmistakable smell of cigarettes. She was about to ease the door closed again and leave them to coat their lungs with tar when she heard Alex.

"I won't tell anyone, honest, but you have to let me past."

"Have to, do I?" challenged Tracy. She was in the year above them and had a bad reputation.

"You'd better let me go now," Alex asserted, "or something bad is going to happen."

"Yeah," Tracy said, "something bad is going to happen. Grab her."

It was the sound of the scuffle that drove Kayleigh into the changing rooms. Two other girls, mates of Tracy's, were holding Alex, forcing her into one of the cubicles. At the sound of the door, Tracy turned to face Kayleigh.

"You'd better let her go or I'm gonna get the teachers." Kayleigh raised her voice, keen to make sure the others heard her.

"Get out of here now, horse-face," said Tracy, "or you're getting the same."

They crowded Alex into the cubicle and she could hear the grunts and shoves as Alex struggled against the two older girls.

Tracy tossed the cigarette into one of the sinks and made a grab for Kayleigh's long hair. Kayleigh evaded her, slipped back past the changing room door and pulled it behind her. Tracy's arm came through the gap and Kayleigh trapped it in the door.

"You little sod!" Tracy's hand grasped for Kayleigh. "I'm gonna rip your hair out."

"Kayleigh!" Alex's voice sounded hollow in the tiled room. "Tell them to stop, tell them I can't hold it. It's getting free. I can't hold it!"

Kayleigh's mind raced. "You have to let her go," she shouted through the door at Tracy. "She's not herself. You don't understand. She's really going to lose it."

"Yeah, we're really scared about that." Tracy shouted to her mates, "Drown the little bitch." She pulled her arm back and slammed the door closed on Kayleigh.

Kayleigh shoved at the door, her shoes sliding on the smooth floor as she pushed against Tracy holding it shut from the other side.

"You don't understand. You have to let her go!"

From behind the door came the sound of burbling and then coughing and retching.

"Drown the bitch!" Tracy urged them.

The sound of burbling resumed, but underlined by another gurgling sound. Kayleigh hammered on the door, screaming for them to stop. The gurgling deepened to a low rumble, the sound vibrating in Kayleigh's bones, making her teeth ache. The temperature dropped suddenly. The chill sent goosebumps down Kayleigh's arms.

There was a moment of silence.

Then the rumbling returned, building to a crescendo until everything burst at once behind the door. Kayleigh hammered on the door, screaming to them to open it before it was too late, pleading with Tracy. Water started streaming out from under the door, pooling around Kayleigh's feet. Suddenly Tracy was trying to pull it open.

Water crashed into the gap, the weight of it against the door pressing it shut. Tracy was screaming to her to push, her hands white against the edge of the door as water and sewage from the drains put pressure on the gap. Kayleigh tried to wedge her foot in it but the flow was too strong, it was thrusting her aside. The door slammed shut on Tracy's fingers. Kayleigh heard her yank them free with a bone-popping wrench.

The screams turned to hammering as the changing room rapidly filled with foul-smelling water. Kayleigh could hear them shouting and yelling as the water swirled around them. Water was pouring under the door, spraying round the edges as the pressure built. She could see the door handle rattle and then jerk as hands were dragged away, screams gulped off as they lost their footing and were swept under. Their cries echoed, rising and fading as the water began to turn, the screams turning to gasps as they tried to swim against the swirling current. Her imagination conjured the vortex, tugging at their clothes, pulling them into the centre, dragging them under.

Kayleigh turned and ran down the passage and out through the gym screaming for someone, anyone, to come and help. She ran across the playground, tears streaming down her face, shouting until her voice cracked, knowing it was already too late.

The pool of light was no more than twelve feet across and, for this critical moment, defined my world. Beyond its boundary circled my attackers. They would not kill me, at least not on purpose, but they would hurt me if they could.

The blade in my hand was heavy, a training blade made of dark wood, the handle worn smooth by calloused hands and burnished with sweat. I held it level, two-handed, keeping my grip light but firm, giving it the potential for movement in any direction and leaving my assailants no clue as to how I would react.

It had been a long day, both physically and mentally. I was already aching and sore from earlier sessions and I was unlikely to leave this circle without further bruises to add to my collection.

I took a slow breath, rejecting the distraction of consequences. I had to stay in the moment and not let my mind wander. I had to deny them an opening, an opportunity to step into my circle and attack.

This was my circle. It had been made for me to define the space I must defend. Every day the circle got smaller, sometimes by a little, sometimes a lot – giving me less time to manoeuvre. I'd given up trying to predict how it would change, only acknowledging that it would not grow in size, only shrink.

A shift in the air brought me round as a dark figure danced into the light, blade arcing down at my head. I stepped forward and around, sliding my own blade upwards so that his cut glanced off my blade with a clack and swished down over my shoulder. I spun and sliced my blade where the shadow had been but it just whistled through empty air, the figure once again merging with the shadows.

'Too slow,' chuckled Tate, his deep voice rumbling from the darkness.

I stepped back into the centre only to have a figure leap in front of me launching a series of short diagonal strikes. I used my own blade to deflect each one, slowly giving ground, only to realise that her intent was not to hit me, but to drive me backwards out of the circle. Once outside the pool of light I would be at the mercy of anyone already accustomed to the shadow. I deflected the next cut and shoved the attacking sword away, using its momentum to break my attacker's balance and letting my own point drop. I reversed my grip and punched the pommel hard into the attacker's midriff.

There was an answering grunt as my blow sank home and the figure folded over, at the same time trying to tangle my wrist in her grip. I wrenched the sword away, lowering my stance to give me posture and drawing the blade up in a long slice. It found only shadows.

11

"Good. You remembered." This was the voice of my tutor and I smiled at the rare praise. It was he who had taught me that both ends of a sword were a weapon.

I circled slowly, regaining my position at the centre. This would not end until someone went down. The fight wasn't over until it was won or lost, another maxim from my lessons.

I barely saw the next attack. The figure emerged at my left flank, almost casually. He cut downwards in one clean strike, my ears registering the whistle of the blade even as I stepped sideways to avoid it, no time for a deflecting blow. It glanced painfully off my shoulder, but I used the angular momentum to launch a horizontal cut that would part his head from his shoulders.

My slice whirred through empty space as I felt something hook behind my ankle. It was whipped upwards and I sailed over backwards landing with a crunch on my shoulders. The air was driven from my lungs in a great whoosh, my blade bouncing out of my hand across the floor.

A point pressed against my throat, just hard enough to make breathing difficult.

"How many times have I told you not to let go of your weapon?" Garvin paused, literally pressing home his point, and then withdrawing it, allowing me to respond.

"I couldn't hold it."

"No wonder. You went down like a sack of gravel."

His form blended and shifted from the indistinct shadowy figure that had decked me into a lean wiry man in a charcoal jacket and turtleneck shirt. The style was austere and it suited him.

The fluorescent lights flickered on and the circle vanished in their glare.

I lay on my back, trying to catch my breath. Amber was by the door, switching the lights back on. She showed no indication of being winded after the punch in the midriff, her quiet eyes observing me as she observed everything.

Tate, the other assailant, grinned at me in the harsh light. Garvin collected my sword from the floor and then walked across the tiles to the wall-mounted rack where the weapons were stored. He checked down the length of each blade carefully before stowing his sword and mine in their appointed places.

Then he took another practice blade from the rack and paced back towards me. I recognised it immediately and sagged at what the heavier, longer blade meant.

"Two hundred," he instructed me.

Sitting up, I took the heavier blade from him. It meant two hundred practice cuts against the car tyre that hung at chest height from a chain in the corner before I could leave for the evening. I sighed deeply, knowing that I could tell him no, but that if I did, he would instruct me no further.

I nodded and he turned and walked away towards the door. Tate stood, leaning on the end of his sword, his grin widening at my misfortune.

"It's a sword, not a walking stick, Tate," Garvin reminded him as he came to the door. "Clean and check the weapons."

The smile vanished from Tate's lips and he lifted the end of the sword from the floor, saluting in acceptance of the rebuke and of the chore that went with it. Though I rated Tate as a fighter, I also knew that he would do whatever Garvin told him, almost without question. It was a matter of leadership. Garvin led and Tate followed.

I pulled myself to my feet, careful not to use the practice sword for support in case that earned me a further two hundred cuts. A glance towards the door showed that Garvin had left, Amber in tow.

"He had you clean there, Niall." Tate's rumbling chuckle made the hairs on the back of my neck stand on end.

"That's true, but a few weeks ago he would never have had the opportunity because either you or Amber would have been there first."

His smile widened. "You're coming along, sure enough," he said, nodding, acknowledging the progress I had made, "but I could still take you in an even fight."

I let the wooden sword swing gently back and forth in my hand and looked him over. He was taller than me and heavier. His dark brown hair fell in long waves to his shoulders, adding to the impression of bulk. He was certainly stronger than me and I knew that for all his muscled bulk he could move like quicksilver when he wanted to.

"With one of these, maybe," I indicated the heavier practice sword, "but with something lighter? I'm not sure that's true any more, Tate."

It wasn't a challenge. A challenge implied ego and that had been knocked out of me in the months since I'd started my training as a Warder, at least as far as swords were concerned. But part of mastering a weapon was knowing how good you were, who you could take and who you couldn't. A few weeks ago, I wouldn't have speculated, but now? I really didn't know who would win.

"Some other time, huh? I've the weapons to check over."

It was my turn to grin.

He nodded and turned to the weapons racks to carry out his chore. I knew that he would inspect every blade carefully, rather than have Garvin find one later with a chip out of it or a crack along the grain. Garvin had told him to check them and he would, because that was what Garvin expected.

14

I went over to where the tyre hung from its chain. I knew that cutting at the heavy reinforced rubber built strength and stamina, but that didn't make it any easier. In a real fight it wouldn't matter if I was tired, bruised and sore, but this wasn't a real fight.

My first two cuts set the pace and after that I let my body take over, varying the cuts each time as I'd been taught. Overhead down, left side, inside left, slide and cut, turn and slice. My body followed the rhythm of it, the heavy thwack of the sword against the rubber punctuating the turns and twists, my brain counting down the cuts to zero.

After fifty strokes I broke the rhythm, preventing my imaginary opponent from guessing the timing. The whistle and thwack of the blade accelerated and slowed, doubled and paused. I tailored my movements, becoming sharp then smooth, elaborate then direct, spurring myself to find new ways of hammering the swinging rubber.

I missed the time on one, sending shock waves vibrating up my wrist, and reacted by turning and sliding the blade through the centre in a long thrust designed to impale before spinning around, letting the blade whistle out in a flat blur that whacked the tyre into a spin. I spun back to intercept and then let it spin.

I had reached two hundred.

The tyre wound down, turning one way then the other, as I went through a series of stretches and stances, letting my muscles recover slowly, using the effort to ease the tension between my shoulders and the tingling in my wrist.

Tate had waited for me and took the practice sword with a grin. He wiped it over with a cloth and then inspected it for damage before returning it to its place on the rack. We walked in companionable silence through to the changing rooms. I stripped off gingerly

15

and inspected the livid bruises I had accumulated through the day. My fey genes meant that they would be gone by tomorrow, only to be replaced by a fresh set.

Tate shed his clothes and was already in the shower by the time I had my towel ready, his gravelly voice singing a song I didn't recognise about a fair maid whom he was trying to tempt with a variety of unlikely and sometimes grisly gifts.

"Did you make that up?" I asked him, stepping under the cascade of hot water.

He stopped singing. "Mostly not, though some of the verses are mine."

"It's an unlikely courtship," I suggested. "What kind of girl wants a severed head as a betrothal gift?"

"It's the head of her enemy, so I suppose it has its attractions." He shrugged.

"It doesn't seem much like a love token."

"She's a fey lass, so who knows what she wants?" Tate stepped past me, grinning, grabbed his towel and wrapped it around his waist.

I had to admit, he had a point.

I stayed under the hot water, letting the percussion and warmth ease my muscles while Tate went back into the changing room to get dry. After a few moments, his deeply resonant tone resumed the song.

I thought of my own fey lass, waiting for me. I didn't think that she would welcome a severed head as a gift, but then she wasn't truly fey any more than I was. The true fey were altogether more strange.

Not for the first time I shook my head at the turn my life had taken in the last nine months. My first encounter with the Feyre had been only the previous September when, having had a heart attack on the underground, I had been rescued by an old lady who had woken the fey magic within me to heal my failing heart.

I shook my head and smiled. The old lady had turned out to be a lot older than she looked, though she had changed now so that she appeared to be in her mid-twenties. She had become my guide, my mentor and eventually my lover and I had gambled my life in a trial by ordeal for her safety and that of my daughter.

My daughter, Alex, had taken to Blackbird. I had hoped that they would get on well enough to bear each other's company, but I had found myself prodded into jealousy by the way they bonded. They would sit on the sofa, heads together, whispering to each other, and when challenged would tell me that it was nothing to concern me.

When I'd asked Blackbird what they were talking about, I'd been told to mind my own business.

"She's my daughter," I had protested.

"All the more reason that you shouldn't ask."

"Have you told her about me being fey?" I asked her.

"No. You're her father. When the time is right, you should tell her."

Blackbird left me with that thought. I'd held off telling Alex about the gifts I'd inherited from our unknown fey ancestor and the possibility that she would also inherit them. I reasoned that it was partly because I didn't really know whether it would happen or not, and partly because I dreaded what it might mean if it did.

My own gifts came from my affinity with the void, an element that the Feyre believed separated one thing from another, preventing matter from collapsing in on itself. If Alex had inherited that from me then she would inherit the female form of the gift, an ability to become incorporeal, a ghostly shadow of herself, invulnerable to physical harm. She would also inherit darkspore, a corruption that she would be able to spread at will on any surface, allowing her to consume other beings and feed on their flesh.

It wasn't the best news a father could give his daughter. I imagined her reaction, the curling of her lip in that peculiar way as she elongated '*eww*' into a whine. I smiled at the thought, but it had kept me from telling her.

It wasn't certain, though. I had also been told that humanity had introduced a random factor into the inheritance. The Feyre had long had problems with fertility. When they did have children they bred true, each to their element, their forms reflecting their differing affinities. When they discovered that the union between fey and human was fertile it caused a rift between those who believed that the union would save the Feyre from extinction and those who saw human-fey hybrids as an abomination, a corruption of their bloodlines. What neither the pure-bred Untainted nor the remaining factions of the Seven Courts had realised was that the human DNA somehow altered the mechanism of inheritance, meaning that there was no way to be sure what fey traits would be inherited. My hope was that maybe Alex would inherit some other gift, possibly fire and air like Blackbird rather than the grisly gifts of the void.

In any case there was no way to tell. She would either find herself one day gifted with uncanny power, or she wouldn't. If she did, she would live an unnaturally long life. If she didn't, she would live a human lifespan and age and die long before I did, assuming that no one broke my neck with a wooden sword first.

I dried myself and pulled on my jeans and T-shirt. I was not allowed the charcoal uniform of the Warders. Garvin would decide when I could wear grey and he would make sure that I would not disgrace the reputation of the Warders before he would allow that. His decision was final.

I looked forward to that day with a degree of trepidation. It would mean that he thought I was worthy of it, which was a huge compliment, but it would also mean

18

that I was available for duty. Being a Warder meant being ready twenty-four hours a day, seven days a week. The Lords and Ladies could request our assistance or assign duties whenever they felt like it. That was the job.

In practice, it wasn't an onerous schedule. Mostly the courts kept to themselves, dealing with their own internal issues. It was only when something affected all of them that the Warders were involved. Then the Warders would be called upon to carry out the will of the Seven Courts of the Feyre, which could be anything from delivering a message to carrying out an execution. The will of the courts was absolute, and the Warders were there to ensure it was enacted. I had heard that a job rarely took more than three of them.

There were six of them and me, one from each of the seven courts. I had bargained for my life by threatening to expose the High Court's weakness. Their solution had been to make me a Warder, ensuring my loyalty and my silence, sworn under an oath bound by magic far more powerful than my own. But I wasn't an active Warder until Garvin said I was. It was his call.

I clipped my phone to my belt. Amber called it my boy-toy and had told me to drop it down a well. She spurned all the trappings of technology and connected with no one outside the Warders as far as I knew. Even then it was a cold relationship. My phone was my connection with my human life and the means by which other people, human people, could contact me. In truth it had its limitations. If I used power with it near me then the battery would drain, sometimes beyond recharging. It had been through five batteries in its short life, even through I carried it only when I needed it. It wasn't allowed in the practice hall where it could distract me from my training but it meant I could check for messages when lessons were done for the day.

It beeped twice when I turned it on. That would be Blackbird wanting to know what time I would be home. She had only partially settled into domestic life and felt vulnerable without the magic that her pregnancy denied her. I was assured it was quite natural and that it was to protect the baby from the raw power of fey magic. She accepted it, but she wasn't happy about it. It was the first time she had been without magic for hundreds of years and she felt the loss keenly.

I grabbed my bag. The phone beeped again. What was the matter now? She knew I couldn't be contacted until the session ended, so what was the point of sending me multiple messages? Or was it simply that she wanted me to get some milk on the way home?

I unclipped my phone from my belt and pressed the button to read the messages. The phone beeped again as I held it. What was the matter with it?

The first message was from voice-mail saying that there was a voice message for me. The second message was from Blackbird. It said, "Call me, URGENTLY." The third message was from voicemail again. Another message beeped as I dialled Blackbird. What was going on?

The number rang twice, then picked up.

"Hello?"

"It's me. You wanted me to call."

"Thanks goodness, Niall, I've been trying to reach you all afternoon. Katherine rang. There's been an accident."

"What kind of accident?"

"It's Alex. She's in hospital."

My stomach clenched at her words. "What happened? Is she OK?"

"I don't know. There was some sort of incident at school. They called Katherine. She called me when she couldn't reach you. She said they were going to the hospital."

"Is Alex all right?"

"I don't know, Niall. She said to meet her there."

"Give me the name of the hospital."

Blackbird read out the address of a London hospital and gave me directions.

"If Katherine calls, tell her I'm on my way."

"I'll tell her."

"Are you OK?" I asked her.

"Yes." I could hear the lie clear down the phone line. Blackbird had once told me that magic was too close to truth for the Feyre to be able to lie convincingly.

"What's wrong?"

"I'm fine." She must have known I'd hear the lie. "Go see to your daughter. She needs you. Call me when you have news."

"I will." I ended the call and headed for the basement. It was a two-hour drive to London, but I had no intention of driving. The house had another exit for those that could use it.

The Ways were lines of elemental force that criss-crossed the landscape allowing the Feyre to travel quickly from place to place. While the High Court had no Way node of its own, it did have access to the Ways. I went down a set of stairs to a room below ground.

Garvin had told me that the room I entered had been created by the Luchorpán, the Court of the Maker, to connect to the Ways without actually joining them permanently. The floor was marked with an intricate pattern, marking the points that could be accessed with radial lines terminating in silver stars, mirroring no constellation I knew.

The Ways were held open by a smoky clear stone which, if you looked into it, was threaded through with tiny filaments like complex wiring. While it was placed in the centre of the pattern the Feyre could come and go, but once the stone was removed the connection collapsed and the house was isolated from the rest of the Ways.

I only used a couple of the connections, the one that would take me to the house where Blackbird and I lived, and the one terminating in central London. There were eight or nine other connections I had never used. I once asked Tate where they went, and he said, "Everywhere."

I found the star that signified the connection with London. Standing over it, I reached down with my power. Beneath the floor, the power of the Way swelled up to meet me. I took a step forward and it swept me into the stream, bearing me through a depth of blue-black night, swirled with streaks of unearthly light. On other occasions I would have exhilarated in the power of it, but now I only wanted it to carry me to my daughter. I shimmered into being in another basement, many miles away, stepping off the line and mounting the steps to the ground floor two at a time.

My training made me leave the house cloaked in magic. This was one of the places that could connect directly with the High Court of the Feyre and Garvin would not thank me for revealing its secrets. I wrapped myself in power, cloaking myself with misdirection before unsealing the wards of protection holding the front door and exiting to the street. I walked away from the square where the house stood without looking back. Only when I was clear did I let the misdirection fall away and start hailing black cabs.

The driver knew where the hospital was. I asked him to hurry, but with the evening traffic the progress was frustratingly slow. My impatience must have shown because he turned in his seat and leaned back to speak to me.

"Do you want me to try another route? It'll be longer and cost a bit more, but it might be quicker."

"Do it."

He waited until the traffic moved forward, then turned sharply into the other lane. He reversed and then completed the U-turn to go back the way we had come. Shortly after, he turned into a narrow alley, taking us down the access roads between the backs of buildings, swerving around wheelie bins and badly parked cars. When we came to other main roads, he went straight across, halting only to wait for a gap so that he could drive over to the next back alley. We navigated up and down one way streets, taking odd turns and driving right around squares to get to rat runs that crossed the main routes. I held on to the grab handle to stop myself being thrown around in the back of the cab as we swerved around obstacles. Finally we juddered to a halt.

"The hospital is down there, about fifty yards or so. I can't get any closer because of this bastard." He nodded at a huge truck parked in the middle of the road. "It'll be another twenty minutes if I take you round the one-way to the door."

"That's great," I told him. "I'm really grateful." I paid him, adding a substantial tip.

"Ta muchly," he grinned.

I got out of the cab and the driver began backing down the street away from me. I could see the problem now. Someone had parked one of those enormous trucks that you usually only see in Europe in the middle of the road and left all the lights on. It looked new, the paintwork bright and clean. On the back there was a row of hazard warnings, the familiar sign for radiation, one for biological and another two that I didn't recognise.

As I walked past it I felt something I almost didn't recognise. There was faint emanation from the truck, something that was only familiar because of what had happened the previous autumn. It wasn't strong, but it was the unmistakable taint of cold iron.

Cold iron was anathema to fey magic and having it close set my teeth on edge, but this was only a trace, an echo of that sensation. There was no signwriting or logo down the side of the truck to identify it. If I had more time I would have investigated, but I needed to get to the hospital.

As I passed, I noted the driver sitting inside the truck reading a newspaper. He looked settled, as if he'd been there some while. It struck me as odd because he was blocking the entire street and the police would normally insist that something like that was moved to clear the access, especially this close to a hospital.

At the end of the street was the Accident and Emergency Unit, just as the cab driver had promised. I trotted past the entrance where ambulances were parked, their crews waiting on standby, to the public entrance and went straight to the information desk.

"I'm looking for my daughter, Alexandra Dobson?" Alex had taken to using her mother's maiden name instead of my surname when Katherine and I divorced. It made sense, but somehow it still hurt.

The man consulted his computer. "You'll need to go through that door and take a left. Head right down to the end and then take the lift up to the sixth floor. She's in the Tesla Wing. Ask at the nursing station when you get up there."

I thanked him and followed his directions. I had to wait for the lift and nearly went for the stairs instead. It was six floors but I was a lot fitter than I used to be. The lift doors opened just as I had decided to take the stairs.

On the sixth floor, I followed the signs to the Tesla Wing and went straight to the nursing station. As I started to speak, I spotted Barry, my ex-wife's new husband.

"Never mind," I told the nurse. "I can see them."

I went to walk past, but she stepped into my way.

"I'm sorry, sir. You can't go down there."

"I'm Niall Petersen, Alex Dobson's father."

"I was told her father was already here," she said.

"He's not her father." I told her. "He's her stepfather."

24

"I see." Her attitude was brittle. "You may come with me then."

She walked ahead of me down the corridor to where Barry was waiting. His expression was grim. My stomach clenched when he didn't smile.

As we came near, Katherine, my ex-wife, appeared. The nurse was about to speak when Katherine ran forward and threw herself at me, hugging me close. Barry looked on, embarrassed.

"Oh, Niall, thank God you're here. We've been trying to get hold of you all afternoon."

The nurse looked nonplussed and then turned and walked back to the station, apparently happy that I was indeed Alex's father.

"Where is she? What's happened?"

Katherine took a deep breath, stepping back. "There's been a terrible accident."

"Is she OK?"

"They're treating her now."

"Can I see her?"

"No one is allowed in. They won't even let me in."

"What happened?"

"She was at school. No one knows what went wrong. We were told an hour ago that three girls are dead."

"Dead!"

"They were found in a changing room. Kayleigh, Alex's friend, raised the alarm. There was some sort of biological contamination. Everyone who had any contact with it has been brought here."

"What in hell happened?"

"They've quarantined the school, no one is allowed on site. Some sort of specialist unit has been brought in to deal with it all. The doctor came by half an hour ago and told us that they were doing everything they can to save Alex, but it's touch and go."

"What does that mean?"

"I don't know, Niall. That's all they would say. The doctor said they were specialists, the best in the country, and they were doing everything they could."

I held my hand up to pause her, then went back to the nurses' station.

"Excuse me. I would like to see my daughter, please?"

"It's Mr Petersen. Is that right?"

"Yes." She knew perfectly well who I was.

"I've asked the consultant to come and see you. He asked me to notify him when you arrived."

"Fine. I'd like to see my daughter."

"I'm afraid that's not possible at the moment, Mr Petersen."

"Why not?"

"I don't know if you're aware, but this is a specialist isolation unit. We treat everything here from the ebola virus to smallpox. We have very strict protocols which must be followed absolutely to the letter for public health reasons. I'm afraid you will only be able to see your daughter when the consultant gives the all-clear. I'm really sorry, I know this must be hard for you, but that is the way it has to be."

"I want to see whoever's in charge."

"The consultant is on his way."

"Good."

I turned away, angry at being thwarted but anxious not to show my anger. It would get me nowhere in this environment. I walked slowly back to where Katherine and Barry waited. They were holding hands, but dropped them guiltily as I turned towards them. In a moment of clarity I could see that the only reason Katherine wasn't throwing herself at the walls was because Barry was being her rock.

I went to stand with them.

"They won't let me see her either; it was worth a try, I suppose. Barry, I can't tell you how much I appreciate

26

you being with us. I know Alex would want you here." I offered my hand and he took it, pressing it long and slow.

"I couldn't bear to be anywhere else. You know she means a lot to me."

I nodded, conscious of the relief on Katherine's face.

"It's the same for all of us," I lied, and pressed Barry's hand into mine, offering what little comfort I could, knowing that his pain was so much less than my own.

"What else do we know?" I asked him.

"A consultant came to see us, but he wanted you to be here."

"So we wait?"

"We wait."

Katherine went back into the waiting room and sat on the edge of the vinyl-covered armchair biting her nails. Barry and I sat in the corridor, watching the hallway for signs of movement. It occurred to me that I could break into the area where Alex was, if I wanted to, but that I had no idea what awaited me there. This was unknown territory for me and my training had taught me caution.

We didn't have long to wait. A man in a dark suit appeared at the nursing station. He glanced at us and then turned away, speaking at length with the nurse in quiet assured tones. Then he nodded to her and came to meet us. I stood, as did Barry. Katherine appeared, warned by our movement.

She spoke first. "Is there any news?"

"I'm Mr Phillips." He offered his hand to me and answered Katherine's question. "No, I'm afraid there's no change."

"I'm Alex's father," I told him.

"I'm glad you're here. I need to explain what's happening and obtain your consent."

I noticed the sheaf of papers in his hand. The close, tight printing spoke of indemnity clauses.

"Consent for what?" Katherine beat me to the question.

"I'll explain it all. Shall we sit in here?" He glanced at Barry. "I… ah… only need Alexandra's genetic parents' consent."

"Barry is staying with me." Katherine caught his hand as he turned away and drew him into the room with us.

The doctor caught my eye.

"It's OK," I told him. "Barry should hear this too."

"As long as you're comfortable with that."

We sat on unsuitable chairs around a table that was too low.

The consultant adopted an official tone, presumably reserved for moments like this. "Your daughter has been involved in an incident at her school, as you know. This type of incident is very unusual, but fortunately we have protocols in place that can be applied. There has been some degree of biological contamination…"

"What does that mean?" I interrupted him. "What is biological contamination?"

"It's a term used to describe a range of incidents, but in this case it means that your daughter has been affected by a dangerous pathological contaminant. I don't want to get too technical, but you must understand that this is a most serious situation. We were unable to save three of the girls involved and I have had the unpleasant duty of informing their families earlier. Your daughter's condition is… uncertain at best. In cases like this we have been most successful when we have intervened, but we need your consent to do that."

There was something in his tone. My Fey senses told me that he was telling the truth as he saw it, but there were undercurrents in his words that left me uneasy.

"Why won't you tell us what's wrong with her?" I asked him outright.

"Mr Petersen, I have a duty to your daughter and to some extent also to you. I also have a duty to the public not to cause unnecessary panic. We have the situation contained and there is no cause for public concern, but I am unwilling to divulge the exact nature of the contamination as it might draw unnecessary and unwanted attention. It is difficult enough for the families concerned without the press becoming involved. Believe me, there is nothing worse at a time like this than having reporters camped out on your lawn. So far, the nationals have been satisfied with the press release. They have been offered an explanation that there was a hazardous build-up of pressure in the sewers and that the resulting explosion caused the fatalities. This isn't the whole truth, but it is sufficient for their purposes. They are concentrating on the human interest aspects of the story."

"Is this the school's fault?" I asked him. "Did they do the proper maintenance?"

"I can assure you, Mr Petersen, that there will be a formal investigation but our initial findings indicate that there is no way that the school could have prevented what happened. Thankfully, this is a highly unusual occurrence involving a rare form of biological contamination and quite beyond their capacity to prevent or predict."

"But you won't tell us what."

"You understand my position. My priority is with your daughter."

"Just give us the damn forms." Katherine's voice cut across us both.

Mr Phillips spread the forms out on the coffee table. The print was tiny and I guessed that even if we were legally trained we would be there until dawn if we truly wanted to understand the implications of what we were signing.

"Where do we sign?" I asked him.

"Let me explain firstly that you are giving your consent for us to take whatever action we deem necessary to save your daughter. I am not asking for this lightly. Once we intervene things could move quite quickly and we can't keep running back to you to ask if it's OK to proceed. I am asking for this in the knowledge that we were unable to save the other three girls."

He paused, letting the words sink in. I nodded, accepting his case.

"If you would sign this general release here and here and initial it there," he marked the points with an X, "and these specific releases here and here." He offered me his ballpoint.

I took the pen and signed the forms. Katherine waited until I had signed all of them and then took the ballpoint from me and signed them too.

"Can we see her now?"

Mr Phillips looked surprised. "I'm afraid that's completely out of the question. She's in total isolation."

"Dammit!" My fist smashed on to the table. Katherine started at the noise. The sound reverberated in the small room. "We need to see her! We're her parents! We have rights!" It was only then I realised I was shouting.

The consultant raised his hands, half defensively, half placatingly. "Not until the all-clear is given, I'm afraid. This is a very serious matter."

"Steady, old chap," said Barry. "The man's only doing his job."

"You don't…" I ran out of steam as I caught Katherine's eye and she shook her head minutely. "Sorry, Barry. Sorry. I just wanted…"

Mr Phillips stood up, relieved to be rescued and too obviously wanting to be gone before I started shouting again.

Katherine stood and held out her hand to the consultant. "Please do everything you can," she told him. "Bring me back my girl."

He shook her hand and then offered his hand to me and then also to Barry. "We will do everything in our power," he said, his words ringing with certainty for once, and then turned and walked out. I listened to his footsteps fade down the corridor.

I sighed and collapsed back into the chair. I felt so helpless. I had consigned my daughter into the hands of the professionals in the blind hope that they knew what they were doing. My fears were reflected in Katherine's eyes as she hugged Barry's chest close to her, all the while watching me over his shoulder. We had both made our decision but neither of us was sure we had done the right thing.

The next few hours were torture. Initially I went to the nurses' station and asked for news every ten minutes. It was a discipline for me to wait the full ten minutes before I went to ask her again. Eventually the nurse asked me as gently as she could to stop pestering her. She promised to come and find us all as soon as there was any news.

I drank coffee. I tried to focus on the ancient newspapers and tatty magazines that were spread around the waiting room but I found myself reading the same sentence again and again without comprehension.

"I'm going outside to phone Blackbird," I told Katherine. "She'll be worried too."

"If anything happens, Barry will come and get you straightaway, won't you, Barry?" Barry nodded his agreement.

I stopped at the nurses' station and told her where I was going. She promised to send someone for me if anything changed.

I went back to the lift, descended to the ground floor and walked through reception out into the heavy night air. It was cooler, the sort of night when the light haloed around the street lamps. I used the speed dial on my mobile to call Blackbird. She picked up on the first ring.

"Hello?" Her voice sounded thin and reedy.

"It's me. Were you asleep?"

"No. What's happening?"

"I don't know. They're treating her now. The waiting is driving me crazy."

"It was on the six o'clock news. They're saying that it was a sewer gas explosion."

"It's more complicated than that. They say there's been some sort of contamination. They're being very closed-mouthed about it. They're trying to keep it from the press. Whatever it is, it sounds serious."

"Did they say she was going to be OK?"

"No, just that they would do their best."

"That's all you can ask for, Niall."

"I know."

"How's Katherine holding up?"

"She's OK. Same as me really. She has Barry with her."

There was a pause.

"I'll come if you want me to, Niall."

"No, it's OK. You'll never get a train at this time and a taxi would cost the earth."

One of the things I had discovered about Blackbird was that she had never learned to drive. With her magic she had never needed to, but now that she was pregnant and her magic had failed her, she found herself marooned by lack of transport.

"I'll call you as soon as we have news," I assured her.

"Do, please." She sounded small, but the depth of feeling came through, despite the tinny line.

"I'd better get back in case there's news."

"OK, give Katherine a hug for me."

"I will. Take care."

"You too. Bye."

I clicked the phone off and took a deep breath and walked back into the fluorescent brightness, making my way back up to the isolation unit.

As soon as I appeared, the nurse said, "No news."

I smiled weakly and went back to join Katherine and Barry.

They roused themselves as soon as I appeared, then fell back into their chairs as they realised that it was only me. I returned to the armchair, the vinyl cushions wheezing as I sank into it. We sat apart, each with our private thoughts. I suspected that, like me, they were each thinking of the things they would have done differently had they known it would come to this.

When the man appeared in the doorway we all started. None of us had heard him approach. It wasn't Mr Philips, the consultant, but another man, grey-bearded and wearing a shabby jacket over a grey sweater.

"Mr and Mrs Dobson?" He glanced at the three of us.

"Yes?" Katherine answered.

I stood up. "I'm Niall Petersen. I'm Alex's father."

"And you are?" he said gently to Barry.

"I'm her stepfather. They're divorced." He nodded to Katherine and me. It sounded vaguely like an accusation.

"Have you heard?"

"Did it work?"

"Is she OK?"

Our three questions clashed as we searched his face for answers.

He came in and sat down between us.

"My name is David Beetham. I'm not a doctor. I'm a grief counsellor."

He watched us process that information.

"There's no easy way to say this, but I'm afraid I have to tell you that your daughter died a short time ago."

TWO

The worst thing was that they wouldn't let us see the body. Both Katherine and I wanted to see her, just to say goodbye and to be able to believe what had happened. Barry was mute, unable to find anything to say that would touch the grief in Katherine and me. He had been fond of Alex, perhaps he had even loved her, but she wasn't his daughter.

The grief counsellor was kind but firm. "It's out of the question, I'm afraid," he said. "The protocols that come into force in these circumstances are very strict. There is to be no risk of contamination."

He paused, seeing that there was no recognition of his protocols from either me or Katherine.

He tried again. "It is a terrible tragedy that your daughter is dead. It would be a much greater tragedy and a gross neglect of responsibility if anyone else died because we had not been as careful and as cautious as we possibly could be."

"We just want to see our girl," Katherine wailed, and then dissolved into another bout of helpless sobbing into Barry's chest.

I stood alone, my fists clenched into tight wads of

flesh, the tendons on my wrists standing out like wires as I tried to contain the anger that welled up within me. The need to see her, one last time, was raw in me. I knew that I could reach her despite anything they could do to stop me, but also that if I even so much as acknowledged the dark hot core that dwelt within me, it would feed on my anger and release a power that would be beyond my ability to control. No one would be safe, not the counsellor, not Barry and not Katherine.

"Is it such a lot to ask?" I ground my teeth, biting down on the anger that wanted release.

"Mr Petersen, I'm truly sorry. If we had a choice then we would allow it, but we do not. The wider safety implications have complete precedence. Is there someone to take you home, perhaps? Is there someone waiting for you?"

"There is someone, but…" Wiping unwanted tears from my eyes with the heel of my hand, I tried to breathe. I wasn't sure I could tell Blackbird. What explanation could I give? Alex was dead, but saying those words would somehow make them more real.

"Would you like me to call them first and talk to them, to make it easier?"

I hesitated and then shook my head. "I have to tell her myself."

There was a hand on my arm. It was Katherine. "We'll come with you," she offered. "Barry can drive you home."

"It's hours away. It's not even in the same direction."

"That doesn't matter. It's not like we'll be sleeping, is it?"

I hugged her to me and kissed her hair. Using the Ways I could be home within half an hour, whereas in the car it would be a long drive. I could use the time to think of something to say.

"Thanks," I told her, then nodded to Barry. "Thank you."

"The least I can do," he said, shaking his head.

The counsellor escorted us all the way to reception. He gave us a card with his contact details and said that we could call him night or day. He warned us that the next few days would be hard but that we would come through it. He told us to speak to our friends, our families and our loved ones and that they would help us come to terms with our loss. He asked if we were religious and offered to put us in touch with the chaplain for the school. He told us we might find some comfort with the other families that had lost their girls. It all sounded like good advice as it drifted past me like smoke. How could he possibly understand?

The car journey was long and dark. Katherine sat in the front while Barry drove. They barely spoke to each other. I couldn't help wondering whether their relationship would survive this. It brought Katherine and me closer than we had been in years, whereas it placed a barrier between her and Barry that was going to be there for a long time. I wondered if he was strong and patient enough to deal with that. Katherine was right; he was a good man. Sometimes, though, that wasn't enough.

The motorway lights streamed past like a pulse, echoed by the road noise. Barry drove and Katherine stared at the road ahead while I went through all the ways I could think of to tell Blackbird what happened. Most of the time I never got as far as saying it, even in my head. Just the thought of meeting her eyes with that knowledge in my heart was too painful. I shied away and began again until I felt numb with it. The pain was still there, knotting my gut and clamping my throat, but I was dead to it. I could no longer feel.

The lights died away as we transferred to country roads, leaving me in welcome darkness. The trees closed in and shrouded the road, slowing us so that we wound through the tunnel of leaves while my heart grew heavier as I recognised the twists and bends, and then we were there. As soon as the lights hit the front of the house she was in the doorway looking fragile in the harsh light. I got out of the car and walked towards her. By the time I reached her I was dumb. The pain I had locked away welled up in me, knotting my throat, spilling hot tears down my cheek. She simply opened her arms and held me while I shook with sobs.

"Oh, my poor love," she said. "My poor, poor love."

She led me inside, leaving Katherine and Barry to follow hesitantly into our tiny thatched house amid the trees. They stood inside the door looking lost while Blackbird guided me to the big settee where Alex had loved to slouch, her head lost in a book, shoes kicked off, feet up, idly twisting her hair around her finger. The memory made the pain sharper until I could feel sharp metal in my gut. I curled around it, hugging it to me like an unwelcome friend.

"Come in, please, come in," said Blackbird, "It's not much but you're welcome here."

Katherine and Barry edged in, and then Katherine started crying again and Barry was holding her and then we were all in tears. It was some time before order could be restored.

Blackbird disentangled herself from me and went through into the adjacent kitchen to put the kettle on. Then she returned and guided Katherine into the chair by the small log fire while Barry knelt beside her holding her hand and stroking her hair. Then Blackbird returned and sat with me, holding my hand in both of hers.

"What happened?" she said.

Between us, we managed to convey what had occurred, though it was mostly Barry who did the explaining. I was grateful for that. It was hard enough to hear those words, never mind say them. Blackbird was quiet, squeezing my hand hard when we came to the part where the grief counsellor appeared. There were more tears shared and then she made everyone tea and talked with us until we calmed. Finally, Barry suggested that they should be making tracks.

"It won't be the same without her," said Katherine.

"No, it won't," Blackbird agreed.

"The house is going to feel so empty."

"I know."

"Oh God, I'm going to have to go through her things, aren't I? Someone will have to."

"I'll help you," Blackbird offered.

"Thank you, but I think maybe you shouldn't be upsetting yourself in your condition. They pick up on these things. You have to be careful. How long until you're due?"

Blackbird looked suddenly uncomfortable. "I'm… not sure."

"Not sure? They must have got better at this since I had Alex… Oh, Alex." Her eyes filled again and I thought that there would be more tears, but she straightened. "It catches you out, doesn't it?" she said, brushing her eyes with the back of her hand.

"It's going to be like that for a while, I think," said Blackbird.

"She was so looking forward to the baby." Katherine fished into her pocket for a better tissue and then blew her nose noisily. Barry was at her shoulder, slipping his arm around her waist, squeezing her close.

"We'd better head off," said Barry. "I can contact the hospital tomorrow for you, or later today, and find out what the arrangements are. There'll be the funeral to get through."

I took a deep breath and let it out slowly. "Call me tomorrow, and thanks. You've been a rock. I don't know how Katherine or I would have managed without you."

"You do what you can." He shrugged, shaking his head in resignation.

Blackbird and I stood outside on the edge of the light that spilled from the doorway while Barry reversed his Toyota back down the narrow bumpy drive, though the gateway and out on to the road. We waited until the headlights vanished and the sound of the car was drowned by the susurrus hush of the night wind through the branches.

"Are you coming in?" asked Blackbird.

"In a minute."

"Don't be long. You'll get chilled."

"OK."

Blackbird went inside, leaving the door ajar behind her so that a fan of light faded across the grass into the edge of the trees. Clouds scudded across the circle of sky above me in the first glimmerings of dawn. The moist smell of leaf mould and woodsmoke lingered in the clearing around the house. I stood for a long while, thinking. Alex had been my world. I had fought to protect her and risked my life to keep her safe only to have her snatched from me while my back was turned. How could that be? The pain welled up in me again and made it hard to breathe.

I swallowed hard, forcing down the lump that formed in my throat. In truth, I wanted the pain. I wanted to immerse myself in grief. Would it be so terrible to ignore everyone and everything else and wallow in selfish sadness? What would it achieve? Nothing. It wouldn't bring her back. It wouldn't even help to keep the memories sharp so that I could hoard them like some jealous serpent, coiled around and squeezing them for the bitter milk of sorrow. I took a deep breath and let it out in a long sigh. I was dog-tired but not ready to sleep. Maybe if I went to bed, Blackbird would sleep for a while. She looked like she needed it.

Once inside, I locked the door and drew the inner curtain across the porch to keep the warmth in. The fire was the only heating in the house, so I banked it with logs and put the guard in front of it, knowing that it would still be burning by the time we needed to be up again. Then I turned off the lights and climbed the switchback staircase to the high vaulted room above, finding Blackbird huddled in a nest of quilts, waiting for me. I undressed, crawled in alongside her and let her ease in under my arm, resting her head on my chest until her breathing deepened and she finally slept. I lay awake and drifted, unable to sleep but badly in need of rest. The sun rose outside our circle of trees but within the dappled clearing our house creaked and settled in shade, fostering my shadowed thoughts.

I must have slept eventually because I was woken by heavy banging on the door. I left Blackbird pulling the quilt back over her head and went down in only sweat pants to see who was disturbing us. It was Garvin.

"You're late," he said without preamble, "and you look like shit. What's up?"

"You'd better come in."

I left the door open and went back into the sitting room, tugging back the long drapes from the small window to allow the filtered daylight into the room. It was never light in this house, but Blackbird liked it that way. I poked the fire into life and tossed another log on to the embers. The wood sizzled and cracked as the heat blistered the bark.

"What's wrong, Niall?" He never called me Niall. He always used my fey name, the name I had earned in a trial by ordeal. He always called me Dogstar.

So I told him. I started from the beginning and didn't stop. I told it like a story, as if it were something that had happened to an acquaintance; nobody close, no one I cared about. It made it easier.

He stood initially and then sat on the battered settee and listened. He didn't say anything at all and his silence let me speak. I got as far as telling him about returning to the house in the early hours and then Blackbird appeared in the doorway looking wrung out and pale, the soft skin under her eyes bruised with exhaustion and worry.

"I'll make tea," she said.

I started to finish the tale but he raised his hand and stopped me.

"Enough, I've heard enough. Is there anything I can do? Is there anything the Warders can do?"

"No. There is nothing to fight."

"Fighting isn't all we do, Niall. If you think of anything, even a small thing, you only have to ask and it will be done."

"Thanks."

"You have my deepest sympathies. I had no idea or I would have come earlier."

"We were sleeping, or trying to sleep."

"Then you have my apologies for waking you."

"It's not a problem. We would have to be up soon anyway. There are arrangements to make. We have to organise a funeral."

"Once again, Niall, I offer my services and that of your fellow Warders. If there's anything you need, just ask."

"It's something I have to do myself."

"I understand. I should go."

"I think Blackbird's making tea."

"Don't worry, I'll go. You know how to reach me if you need anything?"

"Yes."

He stood and faced me, placing his hand upon my shoulder.

"Anything at all, you'll let me know?"

"Yes."

41

He released me and went to the kitchen door, where he spoke a few soft words to Blackbird and then turned and left, easing the heavy wooden door shut behind him. I sat in the armchair and watched the fire. Blackbird brought me tea, but it went cold in my hands before I stirred.

It was Barry's call that raised me. We spoke at length and then I threw myself into the arrangements. I had to liaise with the school, the church, the hospital; everyone seemed to have some claim on my daughter's death.

I didn't bother attending the opening hearing of the inquest. We were told that the Coroner would order an investigation, that the bodies would not be released until the investigation had delivered its preliminary findings, and that the proceedings would be adjourned. Apparently it was over in ten minutes.

Katherine and I were invited to a meeting with the head teacher from the school, which we thought a little strange. The school found themselves caught between the appalling guilt at what had befallen our children and the awful thought that we might sue them for negligence. I hadn't even considered the possibility after the remarks made by the consultant. We had been told that the cause was a freak accident and that there was no way that the school could have predicted it. It wasn't until I met the other girls' parents that I realised why they were being so cautious.

Katherine and I were guided into an orderly office to meet the head teacher and the chair of governors. They were in a sombre mood and greeted us with courtesy and obvious sympathy.

"The whole school is in shock," the head told us. "I never realised that such things could happen anywhere, never mind here. Obviously the whole of the PE Block has been sealed off and we are not accepting the children back on site until we have assurance that it's completely safe."

She sighed. "That doesn't help you, though does it? I can't tell you how sorry I am for your loss. Alex was a joy to have in class and a pleasure to teach. Her loss will be felt keenly throughout the school for a long time to come."

"Thank you," Katherine answered.

The chair of governors, a quiet man who sat to one side throughout the conversation, leaned forward. "We'd like to suggest a joint memorial service, as soon as we can allow the people back on site. We think it would help the children and the families to come to terms with what happened. Would that be OK?"

I looked at Katherine and she nodded.

"The families will obviously have their private funerals, once arrangements can be made, but this has affected everyone in the school. The whole community is in shock."

"I think we understand that," I said, while part of me was thinking that it was nothing compared to losing your child.

"We'd like to bring everyone together, if that's OK?" said the head. "To help the children and the staff. The school will be closed for the day of the service and I think most of the staff are planning to come along, if that's all right with you?"

"Yes, they'll be welcome, of course," I told her.

"Please let us know if there's anything we can do."

The head stood and offered her hand to each of us in turn. She had a firm handshake and a steady grip. We turned and left, with me still wondering what the meeting had been about. In the anteroom were another couple. The mother had bleach-blonde hair in a scraped-back style and big gold hoops dangling from her ears. She wore a white denim jacket that matched the white knuckle grip she had on the big brown leather handbag on her lap. The chalk-stripe suit and slicked-back hair of the man next to her made them an oddly matched couple. He looked uncomfortable, styled somewhere between city trader and used-car salesman. He was out of place.

She stood as we took our leave and I heard the conversation start behind us. The head greeted the parents with the same courtesy she had shown us.

"Mr and Mrs Welham, I'm glad you could come and see me at such a difficult time."

"You needn't give me none of that," said the woman. "He en't Mr Welham and you're responsible for this and no messing."

"We talked about this on the phone, Mrs Welham."

"Yeah and I en't finished yet. Now you listen to me…" The door into the head's office thumped closed behind them and Katherine looked sideways at me. She winced as shouting started beyond the door, underlined by the calm tones of the head.

"I do have some sympathy…" said Katherine.

"I don't think it helps," I told her, "and it won't bring any of them back."

"What I don't understand is what they were doing together. Alex never mentioned this Tracy Welham or the two other girls before. It's not like they were friends or anything. Kayleigh was the only one she ever talked about."

"I feel sorry for Kayleigh. She must feel like a lost soul without Alex. They spent their lives in each other's pockets."

"Her Mum rang me last night. She said Kayleigh's done nothing but cry. She doesn't know what to do with her."

"It's tough on all of us." I glanced back to where the shouting escalated further.

"Mrs Welham, if you would just sit down for a moment." The voice cut through the histrionics in full

44

head teacher mode. There was a lull and we made our exit. On reflection, perhaps it was better to have these meetings privately, rather than in front of the whole school at the memorial service. I was grateful that the head had chosen to have this confrontation here rather than at the service.

In the meantime I had to go and see my parents. This was not the sort of news I could pass on over the phone.

I asked Garvin and he arranged for the loan of a car. The long drive down to Kent gave me plenty of time to consider what I was going to say, but when I arrived I was no closer to finding the words. When I drove up unannounced, my mother knew there was something wrong immediately and did what she always did in a crisis. She made tea.

We sat in their overheated lounge and I told them what had happened. Initially they did not believe me. They could not conceive of such a thing. Then my mother ran to her bedroom, locked the door and wouldn't come out. I could hear her crying, but she wouldn't speak to me. It made it seem like it was all my fault.

When I went back to the lounge, my father had poured himself a large whisky. It was only eleven o'clock. He poured me one as well, though I couldn't drink it because I needed to drive. We sat in silence, unable to bridge the gap between us. My mother didn't reappear. When I left, my dad came out with me to the car. He kissed both my cheeks, which he hadn't done since I was a boy.

"Will Mum be all right?" I asked him.

"I don't know," he said, in a moment of candid honesty. "I don't know."

A mile down the road I had to pull over and stop, unable to cry and drive at the same time.

● ● ● ●

The memorial service took over two weeks to arrange. I was surprised by the number of people who offered help or support or just wanted to be there. I dreaded the service and spent days obsessing about the arrangements and trying to anticipate every possible eventuality.

When the day of the service finally arrived, there were only two things that really surprised me. The first was the press. Only local journalists had shown any interest in the story up until then. There had been some big events in the national news that overshadowed our tragedy, and for that I was grateful. On the day, though, we received a barrage of phone calls from people wanting to speak to either Katherine or myself.

How did we feel about the loss of our daughter? Did we think the school was responsible? Were we taking legal advice? Weren't we interested in justice for our daughter? I wasn't sure what sparked off the assault but I had a suspicion that Mrs Welham was involved. The police liaison officer who had been assigned to Katherine screened all the calls and we spoke to no one who wasn't part of the arrangements.

At the service, the press were bunched around the school gates, held back by a couple of harassed-looking police officers, one male, one female. A group of photographers and journalists clustered around the school gate, thrusting microphones and lenses in the faces of anyone trying to enter the site.

The other surprise stepped forward to greet us. Garvin, Amber and Tate, all in dark grey, stepped between the reporters and the car and cleared a space while I helped Blackbird out of the car and Barry waited with Katherine.

"Is there a problem?" I asked Garvin.

He stepped in close while the other two prevented incursions.

"Stick with us and we'll keep the press back from your group. Don't worry about the photographers, none of the pictures will come out."

"Won't they think that's odd?"

"Probably. But without pictures the story will die. What can they do about it?"

We were escorted through the gates amid a blitz of flashes and allowed through. Amber and Tate came with us to the main doors and lingered as I allowed Blackbird to enter ahead of me. Once inside, I heard one of them challenge the liaison officer.

"You can't exclude us. The public have a right to know."

She answered, "There'll be a formal statement later if you would like to hang around." There was a chorus of protests, but with Tate looming behind her, no one tried to push past.

Inside there was a hubbub of low voices from the main assembly hall. A teacher walked forward to greet Katherine.

"Mrs Dobson, I'm Sally Helter, Alex's form tutor." She stumbled. "I mean, I was her…"

"I remember," Katherine told her, and squeezed her hand.

"Please come with me. There is a separate entrance for family."

She led us around the side of the hall down a corridor and through what must be the dining hall. There was another teacher waiting who nodded to us sombrely. He held open the door and we were shepherded into a hall filled with people. There was a lull as we entered and then the hubbub resumed as people spoke quietly to each other, exchanging news and rumour on the events of the past days. People were standing around the back and to the sides of the hall. There weren't enough seats. I looked around while Alex's form teacher guided us to reserved seats at the front. Garvin accompanied us and then fell back to the side to a small group gathered there. The other three Warders were there with someone else, someone I had not expected to be here. I exchanged a look with Blackbird, and she shrugged.

"Katherine, will you give me a moment?"

She nodded, distracted by something Barry was saying about all the flowers.

I slipped to the side to meet the group where the four Warders flanked a tall woman with long curls of blonde hair falling around her shoulders. She was the most beautiful woman in the room by far, but she attracted no attention. I doubt they even saw her.

"Lady, I am honoured that you would attend."

I was about to offer the formal salute of a Warder to Kimlesh, Lady of the Nymphine Court and one of the seven most powerful Feyre in existence, when she stepped forward unexpectedly and embraced me. I half-returned the embrace, completely unsure of the protocol for such a situation. Garvin watched impassively, offering no guidance or advice.

She kissed my cheek and then stood back, holding my shoulders to look me in the eye.

"I am here to represent the Seven Courts of the Feyre at the memorial service for your daughter, Dogstar. I bear their condolences and their sorrow at the passing of your daughter, whom we had hoped to welcome into our courts. You have our deepest sympathies in the knowledge that the death of a child, any child, is the deepest loss that one can bear."

"Thank you, Lady."

"Now go and be with your family who need you at this time, in the knowledge that we too are here with you at her passing."

"I... thanks. It's appreciated."

I left her with the Warders and returned to my place

beside Blackbird at the end of the short row set aside for the families, in time to see the head teacher mount a low dais at the front. Alongside us were a couple I didn't know with a younger boy dressed soberly in black. Across the aisle I could see the Welhams and another couple with several children, older and younger than Alex, at the far side of them. None of the children looked as if Alex would give them a second glance. The older girls all had black eyeliner and too much flesh showing while the boys had tattoos and buzzcuts. It was strange that Alex would have anything to do with them.

"Thank you, everyone, for being with us here today to remember four of our children, Alexandra Dobson, Jennifer Longman, Natasha Tolly and Tracy Welham. Our hearts go out to their families and their friends who feel their loss more keenly than any of us. Whatever your faith or beliefs, we ask you now to lower your heads while the Reverend Tim Meadows leads us in prayer."

The service started and I was only half-listening to the vicar who mounted the dais and led prayers for all the girls. The other half of me was listening to the people around us murmuring the words of the prayer, sniffing into handkerchiefs and comforting each other. There was a tension in the room that was unbroken, a dam that was yet to burst. I mimed the words, following the service through a photocopied handout while hymns were sung and prayers offered. Then it came to the part I had been dreading. The head teacher came back to the dais.

"I asked all the parents whether they wanted to say something at this service and it was understandable, I think, that most of them declined. Alex's father, though, said that he would like to say a few words about his daughter."

I stood. Katherine and I had talked about this and she was OK with it. I felt at the time we were asked that something should be said and that it was my responsibility to say it. I wished now that I had kept my mouth shut. Katherine reached up and squeezed my hand and I looked down at her. She gave me a smile and nodded. Now was the time.

I stepped forward and up on to the newly empty dais at the front. I had the words I wanted to say written out and I unfolded them on the lectern in front of me. It was brighter on the dais than I thought, but I could still see the crowd spread out in front of me. I cleared my throat. They all looked at me, expectant. I remembered advice about focusing on one person to make it personal, and my eyes found the one person I should not have looked at. I found Kayleigh.

As soon as I noticed her, her eyes brimmed and she turned and buried her head in her mother's midriff. I could hear her sobbing from where I stood on the dais. I looked down at the words and they blurred. No matter, I knew the opening words by heart. I had been through it enough times.

"I…" The lump in my throat became a stone.

I tried again. "I jus…"

Tears ran down my face. Suddenly I couldn't breathe. A hand was on my shoulder and then an arm. I was shepherded to the side by Fionh who guided me into Blackbird's arms, while Garvin gently pried the notes from my hand and stepped up the dais.

"My good friend, Niall, wanted to read these notes for himself, and for his daughter," he said in a clear voice that rang across the hall, "but he finds himself momentarily indisposed. So I will read them for him and, if you will, I would ask you to imagine that it is him speaking rather than me."

He paused and then started to read in slow measured tones.

"Alex was my only daughter, the child of my marriage to Katherine, her mother, who grieves with me.

50

She was a normal girl in ways that were entirely special to us. She was bright and creative and full of passion and determination. While she claimed not to like school, she found it stimulating and challenging, a place to grow. She liked her teachers and was doing well in her work. She made some friends; I'm thinking of one in particular who is here with us now and grieves every bit as much as we do.

"It is hard for me to believe that she is not still at home, leaving her clothes and belongings strewn in a trail of detritus around the house, texting her friends after lights out with secrets and speculation, waking late on weekends with her curly hair in a messy halo around her face, her mood terse and monosyllabic until she'd had some coffee.

"She could be argumentative, rude, moody, and then all in a moment full of affection and love as if nothing had been said and all was forgotten. Her mother and I struggled to cope with her moods until we were finally forced to accept that it was just the way she was; a normal girl.

"At the time, I viewed all of these as irritations, bumps in the road to perfect parenting. Only now do I see them in their true light, as treasures to be kept in my heart. How will I manage without her turning up on my doorstep unexpectedly, bags packed, swearing that she's left her mother for the last time? How will I function without text messages about things I barely recognise, written in words I can't decipher?

"For those of us who knew and loved her, this is the burden we must carry, but we will carry it in the knowledge that it is ours and without it we would be diminished, we would be lesser people.

"Alex, wherever you are, my own sweet daughter, we love you."

The only sounds in the hall were Kayleigh sobbing and me sniffing. Then a solitary hand-clap turned into a pattering and the room filled with a sound like rain falling on a roof. It expanded, rippling from person to person until the room reverberated with it. Then slowly, softly, it faded away. There was a collective sigh, a deep and profound release and the tension in the room finally dissipated.

There were things said after that, but I don't remember any of them. The memorial service was over. Fionh handed me a tissue, pressed her hand to my cheek and told me how sorry she was. Garvin brought me back the notes, pressing them in to my hand. "Words that are worthy of her, Niall," he said. "Keep them."

Fellstamp patted my back and Tate pressed his hand on to my shoulder, squeezing gently. A lanky man in a dark suit stood before me and bowed slightly and put his hand over his heart. It took me a moment to realise it was Slimgrin and that this was the form he took to pass amongst humanity. Most surprising of all was Amber. I had never seen her show emotion, but she came to me with tears in her eyes and hugged me long and tight. She kissed my cheek and brushed back the tears. "Be strong," was all she said.

Lady Kimlesh reappeared when the Warders had paid their respects and took her leave. She took my hand and assured me once again of the heartfelt condolences of the High Council. Then she left by a side door, Fionh in front and Slimgrin behind.

Katherine was talking to the vicar, who nodded solemnly and spoke in low tones. She smiled weakly and then captured Barry's hand in hers and turned to me.

"We should go," she said.

I nodded, still unsure of my voice.

She stepped forward and hugged me tight, then hugged Blackbird. "Look after him," she told her.

Blackbird smiled and said she would try. Fellstamp and Amber escorted them out.

The Welhams stood up and hurried out together, per- haps to some other gathering more to their liking. The Tolly clan followed in their wake, the girls noisily com- forting their mother while the boys followed, hands in pockets, stares sullen. The Longmans waited until they had all gone and then left quietly, Mrs Longman's face a blank mask while her husband laid his hand over his son's shoulders as they walked away, more for his own comfort than for his son's, perhaps.

I was left with the remnants of the gathering, the head teacher, the staff, a few stragglers.

Garvin turned to me. "We've brought the car round to the side entrance. Tate will deal with any remaining press. Any time you're ready."

Blackbird caught my arm in hers. "We should go too."

I nodded and was about to let her lead me out when the vicar caught my eye. He looked expectant.

"Would you ask the driver if he'll wait a few mo- ments?" I asked her.

"Will you be OK?"

"Yes, just give me a moment."

I nodded to Garvin and he walked Blackbird to the side door, escorting her out.

The vicar stepped forward, hands clasped at his waist, expression calm and solemn. "I wanted to say how much I appreciated your words, Mr Petersen. They were a comfort to everyone here."

"It didn't work out quite how I'd planned," I told him.

"Nevertheless, you managed to put into words what everyone was feeling, and provided a focus for their grief."

I nodded.

"The death of a child is the hardest to bear," he said. "In my line of work we do births and deaths quite a lot." He walked towards the side entrance and I walked slowly with him. "A child, though, that's the hardest."

"My daughter was so precious to me."

53

"The hardest part will be the weeks to come. She'll be in your thoughts when you least expect it. You'll find yourself looking for her at the oddest times. Our hearts, they trip us up sometimes."

"I'll bear it in mind."

"If you find yourself in need of someone to talk to, someone to share a thought or a memory with, you can always call me, night or day." He pressed a slip of paper with a phone number on it into my hand.

"I'm not a religious man," I told him.

"I didn't say you were. But sometimes a stranger can offer you something that those who are close, those who share your grief and your loss, cannot. Think about it."

"I will. Thanks."

"God go with you, and bring you comfort." He pressed my outstretched hand between his. "Safe journey. Think about what I said."

"I will, and thank you for the service."

"Goodbye, Mr Petersen."

"Goodbye, Reverend."

I turned and left through the side door. The car was waiting and I climbed into the back beside Blackbird. Garvin was in the front with the driver. Blackbird held my hand and we were driven home. Hardly a word was spoken. There was nothing left to say. When we reached the house, the driver drove really slowly to avoid the potholes in the muddy track, stopping short of the house where the ground was more solid. We thanked him. Garvin spoke to him for a moment while Blackbird and I went inside. Within minutes, Blackbird had rekindled the fire and the log she had placed was steaming and crackling.

Garvin appeared. "The driver has gone. He offered me a lift but I said I would stay a while. I can stay for a while, if you want?"

I shook my head. "Thank you for all you've done today, Garvin. Especially for the reading."

"Anything for a friend."

"We'll be fine." I was sure he could hear the lie in that.

"I'll go then. Take care of each other."

"I'll contact you in a few days. Maybe we can start training again?"

"When you're ready, Niall. Give it time."

He surprised me by hugging me, and then Blackbird, and then leaving without another word.

"Just us then, love," she said.

We sat on the battered sofa for a long while, huddled together, her head on my shoulder, me stroking her swollen belly. Eventually she had to move.

"I'm getting stiff," she said. "I need to walk round."

"I'm going to change out of my suit," I told her, "maybe have a shower."

She stretched and relaxed, "Why don't you do that. You might feel better."

Upstairs, I undressed, hanging the black suit in the wardrobe. I went into the bathroom and turned on the shower until the steam rose from it, then I stepped under, hopping in and out of water that was too hot, unwilling to turn it down. I filled the bathroom with fog until it was so thick you could see the droplets in the air. I let the water run down my face until there was no way to tell where the water stopped and the tears began. I stayed under there until I was scalded and wrinkled.

When the shower began to cool, I turned off the water. Stepping out, I scrubbed myself with the towel. In the big bathroom mirror I could see only vague reflections in the misted glass. I let my head fall forward, put my hands on the mirror and tried to breathe. I stood there while my shoulders shook and hot tears joined the drips running down my chest.

"Oh, Alex, sweetheart. What will I do?"

There was a stillness. Then a whisper of parting. Then a voice.

"Daddy?"

THREE

The voice coming from the mirror was my daughter's. Prickles crawled down the back of my neck.

"Alex?" I couldn't stop myself. Her name was out before I knew what I was saying.

"Daddy?" She sounded hollow, her voice reverberated strangely. "Where are you?"

Another voice burst into the conversation. A man's voice. "We have an intruder. Bring her down. I want her down now!"

Wherever she was, there were other people there.

"Alex, honey, where are you?" I strengthened my connection through the mirror. It glowed milky white beneath the condensation. Small sounds emerged, a persistent buzzing, distant footfalls running, the shuffling sound of a struggle.

"I don't know. I can hear you but I can't see you. Stop it! You're hurting me. Ow!"

"Honey, tell me what it looks like. Tell me what you see."

"It's all white. They're all wearing white. Stop it, leave me alone!"

The struggle intensified for a moment, then the sounds

of conflict diminished. My connection started to weaken.

Another voice: "Coming down in ten, nine, eight…"

The connection was fading on me. "Alex! Talk to me, sweetheart."

"S'all… white… white men." She sounded slurred and unfocused.

"Six, five, four…"

"Alex, stay with me. Tell me where you are!"

The mirror glowed brighter as I focused more power into it to sustain the link. The temperature in the room dropped, chilling my naked skin.

"S'white…"

"Three, two…"

The connection wavered. "Alex!"

I poured power into the connection. The mirror glowed with harsh brightness, floodlighting the bathroom. The temperature plunged. Still I was losing her. I reached into the focus of power within me and wrenched it open, heedless of the consequences. The dark well in the core of my being dilated and darkness flooded into me. My skin went black, then fell into nothing; a dark hole in existence. My hands were outlines against the milky glass. The light dimmed and a nimbus of pale fire flared around me. The condensation on the glass swirled into frosted fractals around my fingers.

Still I needed more. I drew it into me, pouring it into the mirror until the surface bulged under my hands. The connection was barely there, I was losing her. Power pulsed down my arms, emptying into the bottomless well that was the mirror.

"Niall, please! Stop! You're hurting me, you're hurting the baby!" It was Blackbird's voice.

I hesitated, and the connection snapped. The mirror bounced back under my hands, the whole surface oscillating as the link collapsed. I turned to her, angry for making me lose it.

She was leaning against the door, her lips blanched, her skin grey, her other hand cupping her belly. The power faded from me, faced with that vulnerability. It slipped inwards and vanished.

"What… are you all right?" I gasped.

"What happened? What are you doing?" She sounded weak and frail.

There was a blue-white flash, a simultaneous crack, and then a long low rumble that shook the foundations of the house. Blackbird looked up, then back to me, then around the room. Every surface was coated in delicate frost. The room looked like an ice palace.

"It was Alex," I tried to explain.

"What was? She's dead, Niall."

"She's not. I heard her."

"We went to her memorial service, remember?" She sounded strained.

"I'm telling you I spoke to her. She's not dead." My teeth were starting to chatter. The cold was numbing.

"Sometimes, Niall… the mind can't always accept…"

"I'm not crazy!" She flinched and I tried to cool the anger from my voice. "It was her. I know my own daughter."

She stepped hesitantly forward into the bathroom, wary that every surface was coated in ice. "Look, Niall." Treading carefully she went to the window and threw it wide. Outside, the forest had slipped back into deep midwinter. Every leaf, every tree, every blade of grass was white amid the gloom. "Look what you did."

Another flash bleached everything into outline and then rumbled over the house, echoing out over the hills.

"I… I spoke to her." I wrapped my arms around my naked chest, holding myself, trembling.

"Spoke to who, Niall? Who was it you were talking to?"

"She's not dead. There were people with her, living people." I was shivering now, with cold and shock.

59

"How do you know?" She took a towel from the rail and draped it around my shoulders.

"I heard them!"

We were interrupted by hammering on the front door. Blackbird glanced at the stairs and then at me. "Put some clothes on," she said.

She left the bathroom, leaving the door wide. I glanced back at the mirror, the traceries of frost outlining my hand prints in the glass. I put my hand in the place where it had been, letting a dribble of power leak into the glass.

"Alex?" There was nothing. I let my hand fall away.

Sharp comments were being exchanged downstairs. I thought I could hear Garvin. I pulled the towel off my shoulders and wrapped it around my waist. As I exited the bathroom he was coming upstairs.

"Get dressed." he said, without preamble. "We're leaving."

"Leaving? Where are we going?"

"Out of here. We have about twenty minutes, maybe thirty, before they arrive. Put some clothes on."

"Before who arrives?"

"Just do as you're told. I'll explain later." He pressed me towards the bedroom. "Clothes," he instructed, "and boots. Quickly." He pushed me into the room and shut the door after me.

I hunted out some underwear, a shirt and some trousers. I was just putting the trousers on when the door opened.

"Fionh, what are you doing here?"

"Same as everyone else. Clothes?" she asked.

"I'm getting dressed as fast as I can."

"Not those, your other clothes, and Blackbird's. Where are they?"

"In the wardrobe and those drawers." I pointed to the chest against the wall.

She took a black bin bag and shook it out so it filled with air. Then she opened a drawer and emptied armfuls of clothes into it.

"Are you mad? What are you doing?"

"I'm following instructions, which is what you should be doing. Garvin wants you downstairs." She continued filling bags.

I pulled on my shirt and boots and went downstairs. In my kitchen, Fellstamp was emptying things into cardboard boxes. I could hear Garvin in the lounge talking to Blackbird.

"It's too dangerous," he said.

"It's dangerous to stay," she pointed out.

"But maybe not that dangerous."

"Would somebody tell me what the hell is going on?" I interrupted them.

Garvin and Blackbird looked at each other. "I'll tell him," she said.

"No, I will. You concentrate on getting as much packed as you can. Tate and Slimgrin will start shifting things as soon as they're packed. Niall, outside, please."

Blackbird turned back to Amber who was packing books into boxes.

I caught Blackbird's hand in mine and squeezed it briefly as I passed her to follow Garvin outside. He was standing in the middle of the lawn, looking up. I joined him. There was a massive thunderhead floating down the wind above the house. Lightning flickered menacingly in the dark heart of the cloud.

"See that?"

I nodded.

"That was you. I don't know what you thought you were doing, but you pulled enough power to cool the air for a couple of miles in any direction. The cold air contracts and falls, displacing warm damp air and starting a convection current. That's the result." There was a stuttering flash, followed by an answering rumble.

"It was Alex, Garvin. She's alive."

"That's what Blackbird said. We can talk about that later. For now we have a different problem. See any other clouds?"

I looked around. "No."

"Neither do I." He nodded towards the tower of dark cloud. "That will be on tonight's news. A thunderstorm out of a clear sky. It'll be on flight control radar, meteorology radar, you name it. No way of hiding it now."

"I found Alex."

"I know. Unfortunately whoever has her now knows that too. You might as well have painted a big arrow in the sky and pointed it at the house with a sign saying *I Am Here*."

I looked at the flickering cloud. "Sorry."

"It's my fault," he said. "We've spent all this time on your physical training and no time at all on your power. Not that it would have done any good. Still, we have to get you and Blackbird and as much stuff as we can carry out of here before anyone arrives to see what caused the storm."

"There's nothing that important here. We can just leave."

"We can leave, but Blackbird can't."

I had forgotten. Blackbird had no power. She couldn't travel down the Way from the clearing in the woods like the rest of us. She had to travel by mundane means.

"Couldn't I take her down the Way?"

"That might be possible for her, since she has magic that is dormant, but the baby has no power and never had. It's connected to her and part of her, and it might be OK…" He let the sentence tail off.

"And it might not," I finished. "We can't risk that."

"I know. I have a car coming to the village in about an hour to collect her. She will walk into the village with Tate and wait for the car. They'll keep a low profile until it turns up. Until then we have to get as much down the Way as possible. I'm not leaving any clues."

He turned and walked back into the house to begin ferrying boxes out to the clearing in the wood where the node-point of the Way was. At a loss for anything else to say, I helped him.

We got into a rhythm. One of the team would hold something up and shout, "Yes?" and either Blackbird or I would yell back, "Yes" or "No". A yes meant it went into a box or a bag, a no meant it was tossed aside. Within ten minutes we had cleared everything that was important from the house. While Garvin supervised shipping of things down the Way, Blackbird and I went through each room in turn collecting anything remaining that had value for us. It was a small house and it didn't take long. As soon as that was done, Garvin ordered Tate to take Blackbird to the village.

She came to me and I held her close. "Be careful," I told her.

"I will."

She put her arms round my neck and pulled me down to her, pressing her soft lips to mine. "Try and stay out of trouble," she said, then turned and walked with Tate down the tree-covered drive to the lane. I watched her leave, looking small and vulnerable beside Tate. She was looking up at him, saying something. Garvin joined me.

"Will she be OK?" I asked him.

"She's with Tate."

It was answer enough.

"Are we leaving now?"

"Have you got everything?"

"Yes. Everything that matters." I glanced back at the lane.

"Give me your mobile phone."

"My phone?" I fished in my pocket and handed it over.

"Any other phones, devices, toys?"

"No. Blackbird has hers."

"No, she doesn't. Amber?" He turned to the slim figure who walked calmly from the wood, unhurried and cold-eyed. He passed her my phone and Blackbird's. "Burn it all."

She didn't even look at me. She walked up to the house and tossed the phones inside, then shut the front door. As it banged closed, she pressed her hand to the woodwork. There was a chilling of the air, an echo of what I had done earlier. The breeze stirred and then there was a whoosh. The windows downstairs burst outwards as flames pulsed through the glass. Long licks of flame began to curl languidly up the walls. The thatch, which should have steamed damp and slow, caught immediately and within seconds I was standing back from the waves of heat while Amber still held her hand to the door. The heat intensified until she nodded and turned her back on the burning cottage. Another cloud was forming over the house, piling smoke into a tower that slanted with the wind out over the woods, following the thunder.

Garvin spoke to Amber. "See if you can help at the other end. Niall and I will be a few minutes." She nodded and walked back into the wood. Garvin turned and followed her track.

"Are we waiting to make sure it burns?" I asked him.

"There'll be nothing left," he said, walking on.

I followed him into the trees. Amber had already gone. I noticed that even though we had all made multiple trips across the grass and down this path, there was barely a sign of our passing. Someone had removed the tracks as thoroughly as Amber had torched the cottage.

"Wait," said Garvin.

We stood in the clearing while the sliding crashes and steaming pops of the burning house filtered through the trees. The smell of burning thatch filled my nostrils and tendrils of smoke curled around between the trunks.

"Listen," he said.

There was a sound above the roar of the flames, a low buzzing that grew harsher until it opened out in a Doppler drone as a helicopter banked over the house and curved away over the trees.

"They get faster every time," he said.

The helicopter circled the wood, staying wide of the column of smoke. It slowed and then hovered out over the lane.

"They're looking for somewhere to land. Time for us to leave," said Garvin. "You first."

I stepped into the clearing where the node-point of the Way was. The presence of the node was one of the reasons this little house had been chosen for us, that and the trees Blackbird loved. I had loved the place initially, but now it was filled with too many memories. I took a last glance through the trees at the burning shell of the house. The thatch had collapsed inward and flames flickered in the column of smoke.

Then I turned and stepped on to the Way. The deep blue-black of the void answered my call as it swelled beneath me and carried me far from the smoke-tinged clearing to a room beneath a house filled with random piles of our belongings. I arrived a refugee. Our things were stacked higgledy-piggledy around the room, black sacks on boxes, pans holding plants. I noticed an empty vase that wasn't ours and had been in the house when we arrived. Never mind, it would have only been burned if it had stayed.

Garvin appeared after me in a swirl of twisting air. He looked around, surveying the debris of my life.

"I'll ask Mullbrook to find you rooms here for the moment," he said. "Most of the house isn't used very much."

He addressed Fellstamp and Amber. "Try and stack this lot in the corners, if you can. We may need access to the Way and I don't want anyone tripping over. Niall, you're with me."

I followed him upstairs, though the hall with the grand staircase and into a room which must once have been an elegant salon, a place for receiving guests. Now covers shrouded the chairs and the curtains were drawn against the daylight. Garvin pulled a curtain back slightly, letting a wedge of sunlight stripe the room.

"Sit," he said.

I flopped on to a two-person sofa, the covers inflating in a puff of air and dust. He turned an armchair around to face me and sat on the edge of it, his hands braced on his knees.

"Tell me everything you can remember. Start from when I left you."

He watched me while I told him what I had found out. He didn't interrupt, he just let me speak. When I reached the part where I could hear Alex struggling, I stopped.

"They were hurting her, Garvin. I could hear her yelling for them to stop."

"Finish the report, Dogstar. Then we'll talk about what we know."

Obediently, I finished the tale, ending with him telling me to get dressed.

"So" – he sat back in the chair – "we know they have her but we don't know where."

"Who has her, Garvin? Who would take my daughter?"

He clasped his hands together in his lap, then leaned forward again.

"The Feyre and humanity have lived alongside each other in peace for centuries. Peace is a relative term, though, and occasionally there are problems. When there are problems on our side, we deal with them. That is part of what the Warders do. On humanity's side, though, things are more complicated. Most humans aren't even aware that the Feyre exist, and that's the way they like it. Occasionally, though, things spill out. People can come into their gifts unexpectedly. If the gift is weak, it isn't usually an issue. Those people can live on the edges of society. They are the psychics, the faith healers, the fortune tellers."

"You think Alex has come into her gifts?"

"We know something happened. They said that three other girls died at the scene. As far as we know, Alex is the only survivor."

"So what happened to Alex? Where is she now?"

"They will have her safe, somewhere. She will be cared for."

"What do you mean, 'cared for'? What are you saying?"

"I'm saying that not everyone comes into their gifts cleanly. For some, the leap is too great. Their bodies know what power is, but their minds..."

"She's not mad, Garvin."

"She may be very frightened. If she can't control it, she may be a danger to herself and everyone around her."

"She's just a girl."

"A girl with a potentially lethal talent."

"They did things to her, Garvin. They were hurting her."

He took a deep breath. "You may... *may*, I said... be able to get her back. But the person you get back may not be your daughter."

"She'll always be my daughter."

"You may not like what she's become."

"I'm her father, Garvin. What do you expect me to do? I can't leave her there. What if she's hurt, or frightened, or lonely?"

"What if she's all of those things and much worse besides? Can you do what needs to be done?"

I stopped. "What are you talking about?"

"If she's not their problem, she's ours. That's what the Warders do, Niall. They clean up the mess."

"You're talking about killing her. You can't kill my daughter. She's just a child."

"If it comes to it, can you?"

I closed my eyes. I couldn't lie to him. "No."

"Then maybe she's better off where she is."

"But they're hurting her."

"They only hurt her when you spoke to her. If you leave her be, she could be fine. She might be able to have something close to a normal life."

"What kind of a life would that be, Garvin? Drugged up, half awake, frightened, wondering if it's the drugs that's making her see things? Is that the life you're talking about?" I was shouting. I hadn't meant to shout.

"Sometimes it's kinder to let things be," he said quietly.

"They took her from me. They snatched her from right under my nose. Christ! I even signed the consent forms. They had a truck waiting outside. I thought it was strange at the time. There was a tinge of cold iron about it. Cold iron, Garvin: the antithesis of power and utterly poisonous to the Feyre. Is that the kindness with which they are treating my daughter? Is that the care they're lavishing on her?"

"Do you want me to deal with her?"

"What?"

"If you ask me, I'll find her and deal with it. I would do that for you."

"No! I don't want anyone to deal with her. I want her back. I want my baby girl. Surely you can understand that?"

"And if she isn't anyone you would recognise?"

68

"Then I'll care for her. Her mother will care for her. Oh, God, what am I going to tell Katherine?"

"You're not going to tell her anything."

"But she's her mother. She thinks she's dead."

"Then let her grieve once for her daughter. Don't dangle hope in front of her and then snatch it away, Niall. Once is enough."

"You really think she's dangerous?"

"She killed three other girls. This was no accident. The biological contamination they were talking about was your daughter. She was the biological contaminant. They cleaned up after her. They dealt with the families of the dead girls the same way they dealt with you. They reassured you that nothing could have been done and they made sure she couldn't hurt anyone else. That's all they can do. The only other option is to put her out of her misery."

"Put her out..." I couldn't say it.

"It's what we would do. The Feyre don't nurse their sick."

He let that sink in.

"Think about it, Niall. She's safe for the moment. She's probably got the best care that can be provided as things are. Maybe you need to think about what's best for her."

I shook my head. I couldn't believe what he was telling me. He slowly stood and patted my shoulder. Then he left me to think. I sat until the light faded from the gap in the curtains and I was just another outline in the shrouded twilight. It wasn't until Blackbird found me that I stirred.

"Niall?"

"I'm here."

"What are you doing?"

"Thinking."

She stood over me, a vague figure in the gloom. "What are you thinking about."

"Nothing. Just something Garvin said."

She nudged my knee with hers until I shifted along the sofa, leaving room for her to slide in beside me. She sat on the edge, capturing my hand between hers, twining her fingers into mine.

"Niall, am I a burden to you?"

"What?"

"Because if I am, you don't have to stay with me."

"What are you talking about? Of course you're not a burden to me."

"Then why don't you talk to me any more? Ever since Alex died... since you were told she had died... you haven't said a word to me."

"I have. I've been busy, that's all."

"You've spoken to me, but we haven't talked. You're not telling me anything. Have I done something wrong?"

"No! It's not you. It's me."

"If I've done something, you have to tell me what it is."

"You haven't done anything, I promise. I was just so wrapped up in what happened. I'm sorry. I'll try harder."

"You're doing it again."

"What?"

"Pushing me away, closing me out, clamming up."

She tried to stand, but I had her hand and gently pulled her back down. "Stay, please?" She relented and sat back down beside me.

I took a deep breath and let it out slowly. She was right. I had insulated myself from the pain of losing Alex, and in doing so I had isolated myself from everyone, even Blackbird. I think she understood that better than I did. It was hard to admit that the closeness we had found together was so fragile; that it could be undermined so quickly.

"I'm thinking about Alex." I told her what Garvin had said.

"You're not seriously thinking of doing that, are you?"

"Garvin may be right. It may be what's best for her."

"Rubbish!"

"She may not be able to come back to us, and I can't deal with it. I just can't." I shook my head in the twilight.

"You're not thinking straight, Niall. This is your daughter. Did she sound mad?"

"She didn't say much. There wasn't time."

"Was she raving or screaming? Was there violence?"

"No, she just sounded lost and alone."

"Then find her. She's relying on you. You are the only person in the world who can help her. You have to have faith that she is your daughter and nothing–" She leaned forward and cupped my chin in her fingers so she could look straight into my eyes. "Nothing changes that. If she is truly beyond help, deal with it then, don't fail her now."

I stood and paced the floor between the shrouded furniture. "What if Garvin's right? What if she's insane, dangerous even?"

"What if this? What if that? Does it make a difference? You're her father, Niall."

"No, you're right. I have to find her."

"Of course I'm right. She's your daughter."

She got to her feet and came to me, easing into my arms. Between us, there was an answering kick from the bump in her belly.

She looked down and when she lifted her eyes back to mine there was a tiny glint of green fire in them. "I think something is coming between us."

I slumped back on to the sofa and she collapsed backwards into me and rested her head on my shoulder. "I am so fat," she said.

I stroked my hand over the bump that held my son. "It suits you."

"It does not. I look like a python that's swallowed a beach ball."

"A beach ball that kicks."

"A beach ball that's getting bigger. It's going to be touch and go. I could burst before he's cooked."

"He'll come when he's ready."

"And when will that be?"

"I don't know. It's been…" I counted in my head. "Nine months. A little more, maybe?"

Her sigh turned into a groan. "He's so heavy."

"Were you OK walking down to the village?"

"Of course. Tate's funny. He thinks I boss you around."

"You do."

"No, I don't. I make suggestions that are eminently sensible that no rational person could argue with."

"That's what I said."

She pressed her knuckle against my knee joint until I yelped. "Ow! You're mean."

"Don't argue with a pregnant woman. They can be very emotional."

"And violent, apparently."

She relaxed back into me, satisfied that she had won.

"How am I going to find her?" It was a question partly to myself.

"Maybe you'll be able to reach her again, and listen in to what's going on around her."

"No. They were panicking when I reached her the first time. They'll keep her sedated until they're sure I'm not looking for her."

"You may have to be patient."

"Not my strongest point. No, I think I need to find out who's got her. The obvious place to start is with Mr Phillips, the consultant who brought the consent forms. He must have known they were going to take her. Find him and I find a way to her."

"So find him."

"What, now?"

"Is there a better time?"

Over the fireplace there was a large mirror with a dust cloth draped partly across it. Blackbird slid sideways on to the seat and let me rise so I could draw the dust sheet down. It fell in ripples to the fireplace. Even in the gloom I could see the frame was ornate, two herons facing each other across the pool of glass. It was high above the fireplace and difficult to reach, but I didn't need contact to do this. I formed a connection with the well of darkness deep within me and reached into the depths of the mirror with my intention, connecting that focus to the core of power within me.

"Mr Phillips?"

I could feel the link with the mirror. I wondered for a moment how the mirror knew which Mr Phillips I wanted, but then realised that it was linked not to the words but to my image of him.

"Mr Phillips?"

The mirror went opaque as I intensified the connection, the surface glowing like fluorescent milk. There was a small ticking sound, increasing in pace until it was a buzz.

"Where are you, Mr Phillips?" I was beginning to like this. Once I knew where this guy was, I could use him to find my daughter.

Suddenly the sound changed. It was like bad feedback on an untuned guitar, jarring in intensity, full of wrongness. It rose to a deafening roar and the glass crazed and then flew apart in a rain of fine shards. Blackbird and I shielded ourselves and it was a moment before we both realised that the sound had gone.

The frame was empty, the mirror shattered.

FOUR

Fionh appeared in the doorway. She switched on the main light and the guilty carpet of shards glinted around me.

"What were you doing?" she asked.

"I was using the mirror," I tried to explain. "Something went wrong."

Garvin appeared at Fionh's shoulder. He surveyed the room and then entered. "So you decided to try and find her anyway?"

"Blackbird thinks she's not mad, and I agree with her."

"And if she is?"

"If she is, I'll deal with it."

"You told me earlier that you couldn't. You weren't lying."

"I'm not lying now, either."

"What changed your mind?"

"I'm her father, Garvin. I needed to remember that. I'll do what needs to be done, but she's not mad."

"You don't know that."

"Neither do you." It was stalemate.

Into the room bustled an old man. I had seen no one that old among the Feyre. Fionh moved out of his way, as did Garvin. He carried a dustpan and brush and offered his hand to lead me gently from the wreckage of the mirror.

"Mr Garvin, would you be kind enough to ask Mr Dogstar not to break any more of the furnishings if he could manage that?" he said. He went down to his knees and began carefully sweeping up glass. There was no sarcasm in the comment.

"I will make sure he gets the message, Mullbrook." He looked at me and I nodded my assent. "Are our guests' rooms ready?"

"I have put them in the east wing where I hope that Miss Blackbird will find the morning sunshine to her liking," he said. "The beds should be aired by now and there's plenty of hot water. If you wouldn't mind showing them where their rooms are, I have some clearing up to do."

"I'll show them," Garvin said.

We were ushered out ahead of Garvin while Mullbrook remained, carefully sweeping up the debris. I was about to say something to Garvin when he held his fingers to his lips. It wasn't until we had ascended the main staircase and turned through the double doors on the landing that he spoke.

"Mullbrook has ears like a bat," Garvin commented, "So just be aware that he will overhear anything you say."

"Is that a problem?"

"No. He's absolutely loyal and the soul of discretion. I just don't want you upsetting him. This place runs like clockwork and that is largely due to him. If you offend him we may end up having kidneys for breakfast for a week."

I glanced towards Blackbird, who had turned slightly green.

"Kidneys?"

"Or tripe. Tripe is a favourite when he's upset."

"For breakfast?"

"Just don't offend him, and try not to break anything else. This is his home as much as it is anyone's and you're his guest."

"Who is he?"

"He's the chief steward. He looks after the house and makes sure that everything runs as it should."

"He's not fey, is he?" said Blackbird.

"No. He's quite human, but he's served the Feyre for most of his life and even the High Council pay attention to him, so don't upset him. He'll look after you while you're here. If you need anything, just ask and it will be provided. There are other staff too. Try not to get in their way."

He stopped outside a double doorway, opened one of the doors and ushered Blackbird in before him. I followed behind. Inside was a suite of rooms: a sitting room with a fire laid ready to light, a bedroom with one of the biggest beds I've ever seen. The deep red coverlet had been drawn back and the quilt turned back on each side, exposing white cotton sheets. Through another door there was a marble-tiled bathroom with a huge double-ended bath.

"This is sumptuous, Garvin," said Blackbird.

"Thank Mullbrook. He thinks you need looking after."

I went to the tall French windows, discovering a small balcony with views out over the valley. The light had faded, leaving the landscape scattered with pinpoint lights under moonlit clouds. I turned back to Garvin.

"You can't ask me not to look for her."

"I could, but I'm not going to. I'm asking you not to look for her now, not from here. You've already compromised one location. I don't know whether that stunt you pulled downstairs was your idea or Blackbird's." He looked from me to her, then back to me. "But you swore to protect the High Council, Dogstar, and if you bring the sort of attention that you brought to your last house here, you will be breaking your vows."

"I'll go somewhere else, then. I can't leave her there. I'm her father, dammit!"

"You're not listening, and you're not thinking either. What do you think is going to happen? She called you Daddy. Do you think they won't make the connection? They'll be looking for you everywhere. They will go to Katherine, to your parents, to your friends, your old addresses, anyone who knows you. They will build up a profile of your habits, your likes and dislikes, your loves and hates, your strengths and weaknesses. They will seize your bank accounts, trace your credit cards, interview your friends, grill your enemies. They will want to know as much as they can before they come looking for you."

"Let them come. I'm ready for them."

"No, you're not. This isn't the first time that the Feyre and mankind have come into conflict and one thing you can say for humanity is that they learn. As far as they are concerned you are a threat to security. You'll be on every terrorist list, every warning screen. They will use everything at their disposal. They will monitor CCTV, intercept communications, watch your house, your friends, your family. When they find you they will come armed with guns loaded with soft iron bullets specifically designed to kill fey. You're a threat to them and they will want you dead."

I looked to Blackbird, but she just shrugged, confirming his words.

"You're crashing around like a pig at a goose fair and it'll get you nowhere. They will block you at every turn, anticipate your every move, and wait for their opportunity to eliminate the threat. Am I getting through?"

"I can't leave her there. I just can't."

"If you'd come to me, we might have been able to steal her from them before they realised what we were doing. Now you've kicked the hornet's nest there's no chance. If you want to rescue her you are going to need help. We are the Warders. We watch each other's backs. We look after our own and even though you are not a full Warder yet, that still includes you. You have taken the oath, you are sworn to protect the council. I want to help you, Niall, but I have other things on my plate and in case you haven't noticed, you and Blackbird are homeless. I would have thought that concern for your unborn son was high on your list."

"You don't need to remind me."

"Don't I? Were you thinking of Blackbird and your son when you froze an entire forest?"

"That was different. I didn't intend…"

"Whether you intended to or not, the effect was the same. You want Alex back. I understand, and I will help you. But right now you're just making it worse – worse for you, worse for Blackbird and worse for Alex."

I turned back to the view across the valley. I could feel the need to do something like a knot between my shoulder blades. He was right, though. I had messed this up badly.

I turned back. "When? When will you help me?"

Garvin looked at the ceiling. "What do you want me to do, Niall? Make you an appointment?"

"How long…" The knot was getting tighter. "How long does she have to stay there?"

"You will get one chance at this, Niall. If you do it wrong you will either end up captive yourself or you will force them to dispose of Alex."

"Dispose! What do you mean, dispose?" I was shouting.

His voice was calm in the face of my anger. "You know perfectly well what I mean. If you back them into a corner you will force them to make a decision. Eliminating the risk is an option. You getting angry won't change that, it will only make it worse. Right now she's useful to them and while she's useful they will look after her. It's not perfect but it's the best alternative for the meantime."

"You said that before. You said I should leave her there."

"I was trying to persuade you not to antagonise them any further. It's bad enough as it is."

"You're asking me to sit on my hands and wait."

"There is plenty you can do. You can complete your training, for a start. Even basic tactics should tell you that you learn everything you can about your target before you make contact. Discover their weaknesses, assess their resources, watch their tactics. Find out about them while they're finding out about you. You've been learning, Niall, but it's been slow. You haven't pushed yourself beyond what you think you're capable of. Now you have an incentive."

I took a deep breath and let it out slowly. He was talking sense. I needed to do this once and do it right.

"When can we start?"

"We can start tomorrow. Tonight you need some rest and to think about what I said."

"Very well, but we start tomorrow."

"Food will be brought up to you. The council are meeting tonight, so stay in your rooms and keep your heads down. They'll be gone by the morning and we can start extending your training. Until then, no more experiments, OK? Get some rest. You'll need a clear head tomorrow." He turned and left, closing the doors quietly behind him.

I stayed looking out at the darkened countryside while Blackbird inspected the room. Our clothes had been carefully hung up in separate wardrobes and our personal belongings sequestered in chests and drawers. Someone had done our moving in for us.

I felt Blackbird's hand on my back, stroking softly downwards. "The important thing is that you haven't lost her."

"I haven't got her back, either."

"You will."

"Yes. I will."

"Want a bath? I could do with it. We both smell of smoke."

"OK. You go ahead."

"It's big enough for two."

I turned and there was a hesitancy there. I thought about what she had said while we sat on the sofa, about pushing her away and keeping her at a distance. I wondered how much she was hurt by that.

"Is it big enough for three?" I asked.

There was just a hint of a smile as she stroked her hand down over her tummy. "He doesn't mind sharing."

We ran a deep bath with lots of bubbles and sank into the water, filling the bathroom with steam. The warmth of the water eased my tired muscles and I was able to relax a little for the first time since the news about Alex. Closing my eyes, I found myself going through what had happened again in my head, until Blackbird leaned forward and took a scoop of bubbles, clapping her hands together in front of my nose so that they exploded in my face.

I spluttered, wiping away the foam.

"You're doing it again," she said.

"Right," I said. "In that case…" I caught her foot from under the water and tickled her toes as she splashed and wriggled, persisting until she begged for mercy, claiming that I would make the baby ticklish. We called a peace and she soaped my back and then I hers. Finally she got out and sat on the stool to get dry. I washed my hair to rid myself of the last of the smoky taint then pulled the drain plug.

Once dry I took the body butter that I had bought in a moment of paternal inspiration and rubbed it into her stretched belly, smoothing it over her pale skin and easing it into the stretch marks. The baby liked this as he moved around at first and then settled, letting Blackbird relax under my hand.

I was only allowed to put the balm away after I had massaged it into her feet and hands as well and then rubbed her back and shoulders.

"I should make you do that every day. It was wonderful."

"I live to serve, Mistress," I told her.

She punched me gently in the buttock, but some of the tiredness had gone out of her and I began to wonder if I should do exactly that.

"I'll go see if I can rustle us up something to eat," I told her.

I opened the bathroom door, then closed it again as I realised that our needs had been anticipated again. There was a young woman standing in our room with a trolley. I grabbed a towelling robe from the back of the door and wrapped it quickly around me, then slipped through the gap where Blackbird was still naked behind me.

"Good evening. My name's Angela. Mullbrook sends his compliments and asks if you would like wine with your meal, or water, or something else perhaps?"

She was dressed in austere white cotton, her double-breasted top buttoned up around her neck and an apron around her waist.

"Just water, if that's OK?"

"I'll leave you both still and sparkling."

She had already set out plates, cutlery and glasses. She took bowls and dishes from the trolley and set them out in measured symmetry while I wondered whether I should be giving her a tip. She saved a metal cover until last, lifting it with a flourish, revealing a bowl of lamb chops, long bones arrayed to form a many-pointed star. My mouth watered as the smell of rosemary and garlic reached me.

"I'll leave you to enjoy your meal. Leave the trolley outside the door when you have finished, if that's convenient for you."

"Of course." I echoed her words.

She bowed and reversed to the door, shutting it almost silently behind her.

"Can I come out?" It was Blackbird, peeping from the bathroom door. "You pinched my robe."

"She's gone now. Dinner's here."

"How long was she here?"

"Long enough to hear you trying to drown me in the bath, I think. We'll be the scandal of the lower stairs." I slipped the robe from my shoulders and eased her into it so that she could sit at the table and eat. I grabbed some clean pants and a shirt and joined her at the table.

"Would Madame like sparkling or still?"

"Don't. If they hear you they might be offended and I can't bear the thought of tripe."

I poured her still water as I knew the sparkling would give her gripes. Almost everything gave her gripes. That didn't stop her tucking into the chops though. She had stripped two down to the bones by the time I sat down.

"I could get used to this lifestyle, having people wash, cook and clean for me," I told her.

"You don't get much privacy, though, do you? Everyone's sifting through your smalls."

"It's a small price to pay for this sort of comfort."

"It'll make you lazy and fat. You don't want to be a lard tub, do you?"

"I don't think Garvin will allow that to happen." I had put on weight since starting Garvin's regime, but none of it was fat.

We settled into gentle conversation, avoiding the events of the day. The food was delicious, the chops still pink in the middle and complemented by crispy roast potatoes and steamed sugar snap peas. I ate sparingly, but Blackbird was apparently famished.

"Don't you like them?" Blackbird nodded to the remaining chops.

"I'm just tired. It's been a strange day."

She reached forward for another chop.

"You'll be complaining of heartburn in the night."

She retracted her hand, settling for sucking her fingers. "You're right. I won't sleep if I eat too much. Being pregnant makes me greedy."

I smiled at her, remembering the months when she had barely eaten and the very smell of cooked food had her running for a bucket.

We re-stacked the trolley and I left it outside the door. Then we went to bed, Blackbird curled under my arm, the bump resting against my hip. We were both tired and she was quickly asleep. I lay in the dark, the sound of her restful breathing easing my heart if not my mind. Once again, I found myself going back through the events of the past days, trying to figure out what I could have done. I thought about how they had misled me without lying to me, turned aside my demands for information with platitudes. Garvin was right, they knew what they were doing. They must have realised that if Alex was part fey then there was a chance that either Katherine or I was too. They had been ready and they had planned well.

What if they thought Katherine was fey too? They knew I had tried to contact Alex and would assume that she had gained her fey heritage from me, but that didn't mean Katherine wasn't fey too. They would look for signs in both parents, and while they were hunting for me, they would be watching her. Should I warn her? If I did, I would have to explain everything, just when she was starting to trust me again. It would be my fault that Alex had inherited fey blood and all the old wounds would reopen. If I didn't warn her, she would continue to act naturally and normally and they would leave her alone. It was probably better not to bring attention to her, but my conscience still pricked me with guilt. I was shying away from the real problem, which was telling Katherine the truth. I told myself it was for the best.

I thought of my daughter and where she might be. I thought of reaching out through the mirror in the room and searching for her, but I had promised not to. I would do as Garvin said and learn what I could about my daughter's kidnappers before I tested myself against them again. With that thought I drifted finally into sleep.

I knew it was a dream immediately. I had been here before. I shouldn't be here, though. The person who had brought me to this frozen glade was dead, killed by Blackbird's hand. The crisp pine needles, stiff with frost, crunched under my bare feet. The tree branches draped, the long needles dragging across my naked skin as I brushed past them. I knew where this path led.

The glade was empty when I reached it, but then it always was at first. I hesitated. She had caught me here before, leeching the warmth from my bones to feed on my life essence. How could she be here? She was dead. Another like her? There must be others. I turned around. The path behind me had vanished, the trees clustering closely where I had walked only moments ago.

I stepped into the glade where the sky opened into a black bowl pierced with crystal pinpricks. The stars never blinked here, no matter what evil transpired.

I turned around, half expecting to see a grey figure in a long dress: Solandre, the shade who had brought me here to feed on me. Nothing stirred. No wind brushed the pines, no animal crept in the dense brush. There was a noise, a distant banging. I turned, trying to locate the source. It shifted direction, coming first from behind me, then from the sides. Then I was awake.

• • •

The banging was coming from the door to our rooms.

Blackbird groaned. "Tell them we don't want any."

I slid out of bed, my skin chill in the darkness, and pulled on the white robe that Blackbird had used earlier.

The hammering repeated itself. "OK, I'm coming." I opened the door.

Tate was poised to resume hammering. "Garvin wants you downstairs, five minutes ago, dressed for combat," he said.

"Do you know what time it is?"

"No more than two minutes. I'll wait."

"What does he want?"

"You. Now." Tate's eyebrows raised slightly as if he was surprised by the question.

"Is this some sort of drill?"

"No. One minute forty-five seconds."

I closed the door. The light clicked on behind me.

"What does he want?" asked Blackbird.

"Search me. I have to go. I'll be back later."

I pulled drawers open. Tate had said fighting clothes. That meant boots, heavy trousers, tight T-shirt. Nothing to encumber or snag. I dressed inside a minute and went back to the bed.

"Try and get some sleep. I'll tell you what this was about later." I kissed her forehead.

"I'm awake now."

"Don't worry. Snuggle down. I'll be back in a bit."

"Be careful."

"It's nothing. Go back to sleep."

I slipped through the door and found Tate leaning against the wall. He pushed himself forward and didn't break stride as he walked away.

"Will you tell me what this is about?"

"No."

"Because you can't or because you won't?"

"Both."

I followed him downstairs to the practice room. All the Warders were there. Amber lounged against the wall alone while Slimgrin stood beside the weapons rack. Fionh stood with Garvin and Fellstamp in the centre of the room. Garvin had with him the long black staff that he carried as a weapon, the silver tip catching the light. I knew that with a twist of his wrist a long blade could be drawn from it. I wondered what had prompted him to carry it.

He was speaking as I entered. "It's not my first choice, but the other options are worse. It's now or not at all."

Fionh was angry. "He isn't ready."

"No, but you know the situation. If we don't do this now, he never will be."

"Ready for what?" I asked as Tate closed the doors behind me.

"Slimgrin, weapons. Long-sword for Dogstar, broadsword for Fellstamp."

"Me?" Fellstamp said.

"Do you want me to do it?" Garvin asked.

"Wouldn't Amber be better?"

"Amber would kill him. Just don't let him kill you."

"Then give me something better than a broadsword."

"No. Trust me."

Fellstamp shrugged, "As you wish, but it's not my fault if I break something."

"He can heal later. Dogstar, come here. Clear some space."

Fionh and Garvin walked to the edge of the room. Slimgrin held out a heavy blade, point down. It hung like a leaden pendulum from his outstretched hand. Fellstamp accepted it, hefting the weight, and swung the blade in low strokes to get the feel of it. I was handed a longer, lighter blade, much more to my taste, and I suspected more to Fellstamp's too.

"What's going on, Garvin?"

"You're fighting to first blood, open rules." Open rules meant no rules.

"These are metal weapons," I pointed out. I had never been allowed to use real weapons other than for solo practice.

"Yes, and they hurt if you get hit, so don't."

"Why are we doing this?"

"I don't have time to explain. Fellstamp won't be pulling his blows, so you shouldn't either. Begin." He backed away.

I was about to protest, but Fellstamp lifted the blade in salute and then spun on the spot, using the falling momentum of the sword to sweep it in a wide open cut. I stepped back, allowing the blade to pass with a low whoosh. It wasn't a serious attack, but it got me moving. After that it got serious.

A broadsword isn't really a cutting weapon. The edge is sharp, but it's the mass that does the damage. It will snap bones like twigs if you get in the way. The weight is the problem, though. It's slow to wield unless you have the raw power of someone like Tate behind it. Fellstamp was good, but he preferred lighter weapons. He usually favoured a pair of long curved knives with which he wove intricate patterns of defence and attack. There's no intricacy in a broadsword.

It was relatively easy for me with a lighter weapon and longer reach to shift the attack on to Fellstamp and prevent him getting enough momentum to wield the bigger weapon. The trouble was that he could use it as a very effective shield with minimal movement, parrying my blows. My sword clanged off the edge of the broadsword, sparks flying but not penetrating his guard. I could drive him backwards, but I couldn't reach him.

"If you don't cut him soon, Dogstar, I'll come in there and kill you myself," shouted Garvin.

The distraction was enough for Fellstamp. He parried my blow sideways then danced around his blade, punching his elbow back into my face, aiming for my eye. I dodged, but received a painful jab to the cheek, making my eyes water. I dropped backwards, rolling into a tight ball, feeling rather than seeing the blade sweep over me, then rising in a single motion into an upward cut which rang from his blade. I used a series of whirling upward cuts to drive him backwards, steering him towards the corner where he would have no room to wield the bigger weapon. He saw the danger and veered sideways, opening up the space again. We circled each other, both breathing hard.

"You're holding back, Dogstar. You have the speed but not the killing instinct. If Fellstamp wasn't pussy-footing around with that thing you would be dead by now."

This goaded Fellstamp into a renewed attack. He swept in with bold strokes, drawing figures of eight in the air, forcing me to deflect the blows or lose my head. He whirled it around for another blow, building speed and power as he pressed forward. I dropped to my knee and parried it upwards, letting the blow carry through before thrusting my own blade up at a forty-five degree angle. There was a jolt as the blade found his shoulder, piercing it full through. His eyes widened as he slid forward on to the blade, carried by his own impetus. His heavy blade slipped from his hand and clanged on to the floor. He sagged, dragging my blade down with him, the grating slide on bone travelling down the springy metal to my hand. Blood welled around the cut and then ran down the angled blade in a red rivulet.

"Well, don't just sit there man! Pull the blade!" It was Garvin.

I drew the blade back with a soft sucking sound then whipped it out. The blood sprayed out in a long line across the floor and up the wall. I rose, ready to hold the blade in ritual victory at Fellstamp's throat, but his knees gave way.

"Yield," he coughed, and he collapsed forward on to his face.

"Idiot! You were supposed to scratch him, not try and kill him! Fionh, Amber, attend to Fellstamp." Garvin's instructions were crisp.

"Will he be OK?"

"You missed the heart, though not through any skill on your part. Sword." He held his hand out to me.

I gave him the sword.

"Kneel and bare your forearm."

I knelt carefully down, watching as Amber and Fionh lifted Fellstamp into a sitting position so that they could apply pads to the wound. His face was grey with pain and his shirt was soaked red all down the front. There was a lot of blood.

I did as I was bid and the blade flashed down, the line of red droplets staining the floor anew. I didn't feel the touch of the blade, but I knew Garvin well enough to know that it had cut. The blood welled from the line across my wrist.

"Your blood is mixed with the blood of the Warders. Do you accept it?"

I looked up into his stony calm.

"Do you?" he repeated.

"Yes."

"Taste it," said Garvin.

I put my lips around the cut, the thick sticky taste cloying my mouth.

"By your blood, will you serve the will of the council until released of your service?" he asked.

"I will." The metallic taste got stronger.

"By your heart, will you hold the life of any member of the council above your own?"

89

"I will." The blood made my tongue slow. It felt swollen.

"By your mind, will you seek to preserve and protect your fellow Warders even at risk of your own life?"

"I will." My heartbeat thumped in my chest.

"By your power, will you keep the secrets of the council, even to your own death?"

"I will." Red dripped from my wrist on to the floor.

"Stand, Warder Alshirian, also called Dogstar, and bow to the other Warders."

I stood, my knees unsteady, but bowed nevertheless. "What did we just do?"

"You passed the test. You took the blood of a full Warder. From tonight you are on active service."

"But I'm not ready." My protest echoed Fionh's.

"No, you're not, especially after that performance. Tate, uniform, please."

"You said we would accelerate the training, you didn't say anything about this."

"I changed my mind."

"Is this to keep me from Alex? Is that the reason?"

"Alex is the least of my worries. We have other problems. Get dressed." He handed me the charcoal-grey uniform of the Warders, trousers, jacket, turtleneck shirt. The shirt was silk; you could feel it in the texture.

He turned to Fellstamp. "Are you able to stand?" Fellstamp still looked grey.

Fellstamp nodded, Fionh and Amber helping him up. "Nothing that a week of rest and good sex won't cure."

Fionh assessed him. "If you have sex tonight it will kill you."

"Yeah, but I'd die smiling." His grin was infectious, at least with Fionh. Amber didn't appear to find it funny.

"Get him a clean shirt. Have you stopped the bleeding?"

Fionh lifted the pad and inspected the wound. "Mostly. The puncture's clean, so it won't scar. We'll keep a pad on it for a few days."

"Good. Help him dress. Slimgrin, clean the blade and find the scabbard for it."

He turned to me. Tate was helping me into the dark grey jacket, grinning at me all the while.

"As a Warder, you take orders, understand?"

"I understand, but you can't order me to leave her there." He knew I meant Alex.

"I said I would help you and I will, but you have to help yourself. Get yourself killed and you're no help to me or her. You have to learn to keep your feelings to yourself. You wear them like a badge of honour but your enemies will see them as a weakness and exploit them for all they're worth."

"I can't help the way I feel."

"You can hide the way you feel if you want to live long enough to help her. You need to learn quickly if you're going to survive as a Warder. We need to present you to the full council. Put your sword on." He took the scabbarded sword and belt from Slimgrin and handed it to me. "You don't draw that again tonight, whatever happens. Do you understand?"

"I think I've had enough blood for one night, don't you?" I nodded to the sweep of spatters across the floor and up the wall before buckling the belt around my waist. The weight of the unfamiliar blade rested against my thigh.

"Just do as you're told for once." He turned and addressed the Warders. "Get your weapons, people, we're on in three minutes. Dogstar, you're with me. The rest of you, stay close."

Garvin swept out of the room, me in close pursuit. I fell in beside him. The others followed so that our steps fell into time, a dull tattoo on the carpeted floor echoed by the rhythm of the sword slapping against my leg. I glanced backwards. The Warders followed, close enough to leave no exploitable space between them but each in their own space, unhampered by the others. Following their lead I let a little distance grow between Garvin and me. He reacted by catching my arm and pulling me back.

"Stay close. I mean it."

I nodded, acknowledging his order. This was getting stranger and stranger. I had seen Garvin fight four Warders at once and not look stressed. I had seen him stay calm when everyone else was anxious. I had never doubted his capability in any situation. Tonight he looked nervous. What would make Garvin nervous?

We arrived at the door to the main chamber. I knew the council were meeting tonight; Garvin had told me. I knew that beyond these doors there would be seven huge wooden thrones carved from bog oak and heavy as iron. I knew that the room would be dimly lit but for the figure in each of the chairs. On the left would be the empty chair, the chair reserved for the Seventh Court and held against the return of their lost brother, Altair, Lord of the Untainted. In the next would be pale Yonna, Lady of the Fey'ree and ruler of Blackbird's court. Next to Yonna would be Barthia, her huge bulk and ham-like forearms a complete contrast to Yonna's tiny slender frame, her upturned tusks no less strange than Yonna's pointed ears or over-wide mouth.

In the centre would be Krane, the most human-looking of the leaders of the Feyre, though the feline grace with which he moved would set him apart as much as Barthia's size. Mellion would be next, his smooth dark fur beautifully groomed as always, the heavy silver chain of office draped around his neck. Against Mellion's lithe grace, Teoth would look short and dumpy, his flat nose and square features so similar to Fellstamp's that I knew at once that he must be the leader of the Luchorpán. Finally, Kimlesh, Lady of the Nymphine court, would be on the right. Her hair, like

Fionh's, was never quite still, the blonde curls moving with a will of their own, winding around the finials on the chair as if they were tasting it.

I had been presented to them before, but not as a full Warder. Up until now I had been protected by Garvin's tutelage and, though I had been counted as a Warder since I first swore the oath I had repeated tonight, I had not been on active service, and so not at their disposal. Tonight that had changed. Now the council could send me anywhere they wished, for any reason they wanted, and I had sworn to obey with an oath that bound my heart. That oath protected me. It meant that others could not use their magic to extract the secrets of the council from me. It had allowed me to live under the council's protection. But it meant I had to obey.

Garvin turned before the door to the chamber, facing the rest of the Warders.

"School your faces, still your hearts. We are the Warders."

"We are the Warders!" The others echoed his words, putting their hands over their hearts in salute.

Garvin turned and paused for a second before using the end of his staff to rap three times on the door. He pushed the double doors open before us and we marched forward into the chamber, keeping formation. We approached the seven thrones in step and stopped where the light grew bolder and the seven-pointed star in the floor marked the space before the High Court of the Feyre.

There was a stillness in the Warders around me, a tension unreleased. Garvin didn't glance my way or give any indication that anything was out of the ordinary, but standing beside him I could feel that he was wound tight.

The reason was before us.

The seventh throne was occupied.

FIVE

The seventh throne was supposed to be unoccupied, the ruler of the Seventh Court and the rest of the Untainted banished to another world and kept out of ours by the barrier that I had helped to repair nine months ago. How could he be here? I glanced sideways at Garvin, who looked stonily ahead.

Altair spoke. I expected his voice to be deep and rough, but it wasn't. It had warmth and timbre like a finely tuned instrument, meant to sway hearts and invite confidences.

"What, no word of greeting, Garvin? No welcome home?"

"Your place has been kept for you, Lord Altair, as you would expect." said Garvin.

"Still, I had thought that you might have some welcome for me, returning after so long an absence."

"Forgive me. The circumstances of your departure make me cautious, as well you might imagine."

Kimlesh spoke. "Altair is here at our invitation, Garvin. Your duty is his protection, as with all of us."

"You do not need to remind me of my duty, Lady. I know it well."

"And yet I detect a hesitation," said Altair.

"When last we saw each other, Altair, I lost five Warders. That's not a night I'll soon forget. I have no wish to lose any more."

"An error of judgement put you between my purpose and the mongrels, Garvin. Had you not stood in my way, you would not have lost anyone."

"I do not regard it as an error."

"And yet you lost five Warders."

"Two of them were Tainted, as you would have it. The Warders protect each other. We stand together and die together. I would not abandon my people."

"Your duty should come before your people," said Altair.

"I fulfilled my duty. You were unharmed. The High Court survived intact."

"May I remind you that Altair is our brother," said Krane, leaning forward in his chair, "and that he has never offered harm to any of us. His quarrel is with the Tainted, not with the Courts or with the Feyre."

"Are you calling the half-breeds Tainted now too, my Lord?" asked Garvin.

"A slip of the tongue." He dismissed it with a wave. "We have to call them something."

"I call them people," said Garvin.

"And Mishla, it is good to see you looking well," Altair said, changing the direction of the conversation.

I wondered who he was referring to until Tate rumbled behind me, "Lord Altair." Since when was Tate called Mishla?

"Do you have no word of welcome either?"

Tate answered, "No."

"Am I safe here?" Altair appealed to the other members of the court. "Will I be protected if some renegade tries to kill me?"

"The Warders will do their job, Altair," said Barthia, her tusks gleaming in the dim light. "We can ask no more of them."

"Even though the Tainted are among their ranks?" asked Altair. "I would have thought that the conflict of interest is apparent even to Garvin."

"There is no conflict of interest, Lord Altair," said Garvin. "Lady Barthia is right. We are the Warders and we'll do our job."

"Very well," said Altair. "I see that I must trust you and your Warders as I always have. Better than that, I will make a gesture. You may assign your new Warder, the wraithkin, to me as a bodyguard while I'm here."

"He's already on assignment," said Garvin, without missing a beat.

"He's here, isn't he?"

"He leaves tonight. He already has a mission. You may have another Warder to guard you. Mishla, perhaps?"

"Do you refuse me protection from my own kind, Garvin?"

"Is that protection from your own kind, or provided by your own kind?"

"You know very well what I mean." A flavour of menace entered those mellow tones.

"The assignment of the Warders has always been at the discretion of the head Warder, Lord Altair, as you are well aware," said Barthia.

"Of course." Altair sat back and moderated his tone, acceding gracefully. "Whoever you prefer, Garvin. Make your choice." He waved his hand, negligently.

"Mishla will be happy to ensure your safety while you stay, then. He'll be at your disposal."

"Is that acceptable, Mishla? Will you guard me?"

"I will, Lord Altair," said Tate behind me. His voice was flat, without inflection.

Lady Yonna spoke before Altair could make some further remark. "Altair is here for reconciliation talks, Garvin. We are exploring the possibilities of reuniting the courts. It would not be well if those negotiations were coloured by any unfortunate incidents."

"There won't be any, Lady. May I ask if anyone accompanied you on your visit, Lord Altair? Is there anyone else who might be in danger of becoming involved in an unfortunate incident?"

"There are two others here with me," said Altair. "I have asked Mullbrook if he would provide them with quarters near to my own."

"Then I shall ensure that they are also provided with bodyguards to ensure their safety during their stay."

"I'm sure they are quite capable of defending themselves."

"With a Warder in attendance, there will be no need for anyone to defend themselves, I can assure you Lord Altair."

"Very well, Garvin. As you say."

"Thank you, Lord Altair. If that is all, Lords, Ladies, I have arrangements to make."

"Will you leave Fionh with us, please, Garvin?" said Kimlesh, "She can bring word when the discussions are concluded."

"Yes, Lady." Garvin held his fist over his heart and I copied his movement. Then he turned and nodded to Fionh before leading the rest of us back through the door. Fionh peeled off and stood beside the double doors while we filed through, closing them after us as we left the room.

We marched back the way we had come.

"What...?" I was about to ask what my assignment was, but Garvin held up his hand. We went silently until we were back in the training room and the doors closed behind us. For the first time, I noticed that there were no mirrors in the room.

Garvin turned to the Warders. "Amber, Slimgrin, find the other visitors. Mullbrook should know where they are. Don't leave their side. I want to know where they go, what they do, who they talk to. Go now."

They both clasped their hands over their hearts, turned and left.

"Fellstamp, go and get some sleep. You'll rotate in eight hours. Keep the shoulder covered. You'll relieve Slimgrin, then Slimgrin will relieve Amber. Keep it rotating, twenty-four hours."

Fellstamp clenched his fist over his heart, turned and left, leaving me with Tate and Garvin.

"Tate, you'll do twelve and then I'll relieve you for six. I'll watch out for the Lords and Ladies and rotate with Fionh. We don't know how long the wraithkin are staying, but until they leave I want everything locked down. No one in, no one out. Except Niall."

"Why me?"

"You're leaving tonight. Tate, get field kit for Niall, please. Low profile."

Tate placed his hand over his heart, turned and left.

"What about Blackbird? I can't leave her with them here."

"She's safer here than elsewhere. While Altair is on this side of the barrier they can bridge the gap. He can bring in others if he wants to. If she's elsewhere then she's isolated and they can pick her off at leisure. If she's here they'll have to go through one of us to get to her."

"I could protect her."

"If you stay, they will find a way to isolate and eliminate you. It will be an accident, or they'll say they were provoked. Frankly, your existence is enough to provoke them."

"I'll stay out of the way. They won't know I'm here."

"You're not listening. If they're here for peace negotiations then all is well and good. If there's peace, we all benefit. If they leave, even better. If they're not here for peace negotiations then why are they here? What could they want that's here? It's nearly solstice, Niall, the time of balance. Thanks to your efforts in restoring the barrier, this is one of the few times that they can cross from their world into ours. Once the solstice passes they will have to leave or be stranded here, so they have little time to achieve whatever they came for. Whatever that is, you can be sure they're not here by accident."

"What if they're here to prevent Blackbird having the baby?"

"If they touch Blackbird then they violate the truce. Blackbird is part of Yonna's court and she would demand blood price. That's a lose-lose. You, on the other hand, are a Warder. You're not part of anyone's court and you're in harm's way. You may even be the sole purpose for their visit."

"Why me?"

"You're a half-breed and a wraithkin. That's enough on its own. You restored the barrier, making it harder for them to cross into our world. You're a Warder. There hasn't been a wraithkin Warder since the night they left. All of that makes you a target. I'm just putting you out of harm's way, Niall. It's for your own good."

"I'd rather stay."

"It wasn't a request, Dogstar. You're a Warder. You'll go where you're sent."

I started to protest, but he held up his hand. "I want you out of here by dawn. There's a fishing town on the north-east coast called Ravensby. There are disturbing reports – some are saying it's a rogue fey. None of the courts are claiming it, so it's ours. Go there and find out what's going on. Use the Warder's discretion. It should be right up your street."

Warder's discretion – that meant: do whatever's necessary.

"What do I do when I find out what's going on?"

"Deal with it, but understand your limits. If you need

99

help, contact me and I'll send someone as soon as I can. Keep it low profile. I don't want any more house fires."

"That wasn't…"

He just raised an eyebrow.

I held my fist over my heart. "I'll go and tell Blackbird."

"And lead them straight to her? No, you leave now. Tate will kit you out with what you need. I'll tell Blackbird as soon as there's an opportunity to do it discreetly. I want you out of here now before they can organise something."

"I don't even have any clean underwear."

"The Warders were never prevented from their duty by a lack of underwear, Dogstar. You have your mission."

He stared at me until I clenched my fist over my heart again, accepting his orders. He nodded, sombrely. Tate returned with a plain black holdall.

"What am I supposed to do when I get there?"

"You'll know. Don't fail me. I have arrangements to make so I'll leave you in Tate's hands. Keep safe, Warder, and think before you act. No more accidents."

I nodded and he patted me on the shoulder. I watched him walk across the room and close the door quietly behind him.

"You're going to have your hands full," I said to Tate.

Tate ignored my comment. "No mission for the Warders is ever simple or without danger. Watch your back. We don't know whether Altair will bring any more of his cohort with him. We don't know what hazards are already there."

"Will you look out for Blackbird for me?"

"I'll do what I can. There'll be wards placed around her quarters. We'll know if they get close."

"I don't like leaving her like this."

"She survived for many years without you, Niall, remember that. She's no one's pushover."

"She had her magic before."

"Even so." He handed me a passport, an ID card, a wallet. "You are Neal Dawson, freelance journalist. You're looking for a story. It'll give you an excuse to poke your nose in other people's business."

"I'm not a journalist, Tate, and you know I won't be able to lie about that."

"It's just another label – like Niall, or Dogstar. Neal Dawson is a journalist. He's filed several stories in the last six months. A couple of them have made the national press. He's been paid for them. He's a member of the National Union of Journalists. He tends to write slightly off the wall, investigative pieces that dig into the facts – story behind the story, that type of thing. You're Neal Dawson. The fact that the stories were ghost-written for you is irrelevant."

"They were written for me?"

"The Warders need to be able to move around in the world, Niall. We all have our aliases, alternative identities. Yours was prepared for you months ago and it will be maintained for you as long as you serve. The stewards aren't just housekeepers, you know?"

"I didn't know, no."

"Preparation is key. Remember that."

"Great. I don't even know what I'm looking for."

"This one's been hanging around for a while, we just haven't had the opportunity to deal with it. It's right up your street."

"That's what Garvin said. What does that mean?"

"If he wanted me to tell you he'd have said so."

"Ever loyal, eh, Tate?"

"I follow orders. So should you. It'll keep you alive."

"Why did Altair call you Mishla?"

"It's my name."

"I thought your name was Tate."

"That's a nickname." He showed me the contents of the holdall: uniform, wash kit, underwear, all in my size.

I refused to be distracted. "What kind of a nickname is 'Tate'?"

"It's short for something. This is your codex. It shows the Way-points. If you're wise you'll ward it so no one else can read it."

It was a small, leatherbound book with pages like tissue but made from something stronger. He showed me how the node-points were listed. Each page had a number in the top left corner with notes of what to expect when you reached that place. Sometimes there was a little sketch or a delicately coloured drawing of the site. Below were the page references for other node-points that could be reached from that point and where you might go from there. Tate took me through the journey I was about to make, showing me how the index worked and what to expect on the way.

"There's space to add your own notes at the bottom of each entry. Take my advice, use a pencil. Things change."

"Thanks." I took it from him. "So what's Tate short for?"

He sighed. "The Decapitator."

I was taken aback and he could see it.

He opened the wallet, flicked through the money stuffed into it and handed it to me. "It was a long time ago," he said, "and I keep it as a reminder."

"A reminder of what?"

"If you're going to kill wraithkin you have to get in close. You get one chance or they have you. Tate is to remind me that I only have to get sloppy once and I'm dead."

"You killed a wraithkin?"

"More than one."

"That must make you nearly as much of a target as me."

"I'm a Warder. I do my job. Do yours." He thrust the bag into my hands.

I took it from him and we walked out together towards the basement room where the node for the Way was. As we came out into the hallway, a familiar voice behind me called to me from behind.

"Alshirian Dogstar, they tell me you are a Warder now."

I stopped at the use of my formal court name and turned, suddenly conscious of the weight of the sword swinging from my hip. Walking towards me were two men, shadowed by Amber and Slimgrin. The first was taller, his hair dark and full like my own, but styled in a way that suggested Edwardian gentleman rather than assassin. His face was long, his cheeks carved like mine. In a room of strangers I would have picked him out as a cousin or an uncle, maybe. His smile was filled with warmth, but I knew he hid his feelings well.

"Raffmir, I should have guessed that it would be you accompanying Lord Altair."

His smile widened and he opened his arms as if he might attempt a hug. I let my hand fall to the hilt of my sword and his arms paused and then dropped to his side.

"I asked it of him, as a special favour, so that we might meet again." He bowed extravagantly, allowing me to keep my distance.

I returned the bow with a discreet nod.

"Let me introduce you to Deefnir, another of our kind." The *our kind* part of the introduction rang sour to my fey hearing.

Like Raffmir's and mine, Deefnir's face was on the long side, his cheeks high and sharp. He looked younger than Raffmir, though perhaps that was his style of dress. His high-collared shirt ruffed out over a brocade jacket that shimmered with green like a scarab's carapace. His silk trousers were tight to his legs and were tucked into black suede boots. A black sash was wound around his waist and was caught with a silver clasp. He took a half step back and bowed slowly.

"I have heard about you, Dogstar." That at least

103

sounded genuine. "From what Raffmir told me, I thought you would be taller."

"Sorry to disappoint." I inclined my head to him in the same way I had to Raffmir. "Welcome, both, to the High Court." I could hear the falsehood in that echoing in my own voice, but I was giving nothing new away. "It will be a brief meeting, I am afraid. I'm not staying."

"I'm saddened by your departure, of course," said Raffmir. "I was hoping we would have time to renew our acquaintance, and speak discreetly, perhaps?" He turned and smiled at Amber, who met his smile with blank eyes.

"I'm really leaving, Raffmir, just as soon as I can gather my things together."

"A shame, truly. And how is your partner, Blackbird the witch?"

"She doesn't like that word," I told him.

"I know, but it suits her, don't you think? I understand she's had further accidents with fires getting out of control."

"Is there something you want, Raffmir?"

"When you see her, please pass on my greeting and remind her of me."

"Do I need to remind you that you are bound by fey law not to cause her harm?"

"As you are bound not to harm me, Dogstar. Are you planning to draw that sword?"

My hand dropped from the hilt. I couldn't use it against him. After the trial by ordeal, we were both bound by fey law not to harm each other. If I violated that agreement then I would be in contempt and he would be free of his obligations. It was better to have us both constrained.

"I will pass on your greeting, Raffmir."

"Tell her…" He paused as if wondering what to say, though I was sure he already knew what it was. "Tell her that I hope to bump into her soon."

Bump into her? Did that mean he knew about the baby?

"Good day, Raffmir." I refused to rise to the bait.

"Good day." He stood there waiting for me to leave.

I bowed more deeply than I had before and they both returned the gesture grandly, then turned and walked back the way they had come, their escorts falling in behind. I watched them go and then followed Tate silently through the halls.

The dream from earlier came back to me. I had been standing in the frozen glade, the place where Raffmir's dead sister had lured me to feed on my life essence. She couldn't be alive, surely? Blackbird had blown her to bits, hadn't she? I had to admit, my memory of those events was incomplete at best. I had been drowning at the time.

We came to the room where the Way-nodes were marked on the floor. The rest of our belongings had been cleared away, probably by the house staff. I was grateful. The fewer clues available for Raffmir to go snooping around, the better.

"Stay safe. You need this node to head north." Tate indicated one of the stars in the pattern on the floor "You can use the codex to find your way from there. Get in touch if you need help."

"I will."

I stood over the point he had indicated and felt beneath me into the rock, orientating myself to the north. The Way was there, vibrating with power. Wrapping myself in concealment so that I would go unnoticed when I arrived, I formed a connection with it, acknowledging its presence and letting it recognise me. I stepped forward. It swelled beneath me and swept me into the stream, taking me far from the basement room. The void, the element of the wraithkin, echoed around me as I swept across the blue-black emptiness, melting into existence in a darkened room somewhere. It smelled of dust and woodworm.

There was only one line into this node and one out, so I simply stepped again, feeling the rush of the Way as it picked me up and hurled me, like a boardless surfer, across the black.

The next node was a woodland clearing, just an anonymous rise in the middle of a wood. A few yards away, a dog-walker threw a stick out into the trees and her golden labrador romped after it through the bushes of the dawn-light. Neither of them noticed me as I consulted the codex in the growing light and stepped again on to the Way. This time it was harder. The Ways are great for covering large distances in a short time, but using them tires you quickly. I knew to be wary, so when I found my mind drifting to thoughts of Alex and where she might be, I forced myself to concentrate on the node-point, the place where I needed to be. I arrived in a cornfield; a twenty-foot-tall brown stone spike emerged from the gently swaying heads only yards away. Yards away, another finger of stone pointed upwards. The spike was scored with deep marks as if huge claws had scraped down it. Lichen coloured its surface with curly-edged stains of red and amber. I wondered whether the stones were part of the Way-node or here simply to mark its presence.

I consulted the codex and returned to the Way. This jump felt easier, as if I was guided in. When I reached the node a similar stone faced me, even taller than the last. It stood surrounded by gravestones in the middle of a churchyard, the pillars each side of the medieval church dwarfed by the monolith, which must have been there long before Christianity reached Britain. Once again, ancient sites had been adopted and adapted, each generation incorporating the old into the new.

I had one more jump to make, so I steeled myself and focused my intention on the Way, letting it swell under my feet and sweep me onward. I forced myself to focus on my destination, resolutely ignoring the echoes of sounds, like lost voices, that permeated the no-place of the Way. My feet found firm ground and I arrived.

The Way-point was on high ground, as they sometimes are. It sat back from the town in a hollow below the hilltop. There was no sign of a structure or habitation, but then some of them had no human significance. Through the scraggy brush I could see the road leading down through the terraced houses and below that, the streets curving around like giant steps, down to the harbour. It looked tight, enclosed by the hills, everything leading down to the harbour in the centre. Across from me on the opposite hilltop was a large building, its clean new bricks catching the dawn light in a ruddy reflection. The tinted glass and curved terrace design echoed the town, but in a way that emphasised the difference between old and new. I wondered who would have built such a dominating building so high above the town. I was surprised they had got planning consent for such an obvious eyesore.

It didn't look the sort of place where you would need a sword, so I unhooked the blade from my belt and stowed it in the long pocket on the side of the holdall, presumably meant for just that purpose. I hoisted my bag up on to my shoulder and set off down the muddy bank towards the road. Picking my way between gorse bushes and sheep droppings I found my way down to the hard paving. The roads at the back were unkempt, grass growing through the tarmac. Ramshackle sheds had been chiselled into the hillside, their backs bolstered against the hill while their fronts were propped up on old bricks and stepped with wooden planks.

There were abandoned petrol mowers and ruptured plastic sacks spilling grass cuttings on to the verge.

Further down, terraced houses bracketed the road, each rectangular door in a rectangular frame with squared windows reflecting the new day, the symmetry only spoiled by the nest of satellite dishes hastily screwed to the wall, trailing cables and hanging wires. An electric milk float, something I'd not seen in years, trundled down the road between the badly parked cars. Two lads distributed white bottles to doorsteps and returned with empties.

Once off the side streets, all roads led to the harbour. Morning traffic bunched at the traffic lights, horns beeping at a moment's delay. Tempers were short, and patience thin. I walked slowly, taking in the details. I noted the granite stone facing the buildings, the tiny church sat perched on its own shelf of rock, the youth centre with its graffiti and abuse.

I had already passed two lamp posts when I noticed the posters. I stopped and stared at the photocopied image taped to the metal, a thin plastic sheet stretched over to keep the rain off. The image of a girl's smiling face stared back at me. She looked happy, celebrating perhaps. The word MISSING was in bold lettering across the top, the question in large letters underneath – HAVE YOU SEEN THIS GIRL? I stared at it. Is that what I should be doing? Should I be pasting pictures of Alex on lamp posts, hoping against hope that she would be spotted somewhere?

I carried on down the hill, passing more images. Then I stopped and walked back up the hill. Examining the poster again, I carefully peeled away the tape and drew it out from behind the plastic. Then I took it down to the next lamp post and compared the images. They were different girls. One was named Gillian Mayhew, the other Debbie Vaughan. The photographs stared back at me. The posters shared the same format, the same type-face, the same words, but the girls were different.

They wouldn't be from the same family since they had different names, though that wasn't always the case in these days of divorce and separation, but these were very different girls. Gillian Mayhew had dark hair, slightly frizzy, and Mediterranean looks. She could be Italian, whereas Debbie Vaughan was blonde with a round face and full lips. The girls looked different but the posters looked the same. I carefully removed the second poster too. Tate and Garvin had both said that this mission was right up my street. Is this what they meant? Two young women missing from the same town at the same time was tragic for the families concerned, but it wouldn't justify the Warders becoming involved, surely? I tucked the posters into my bag and carried on walking. Gillian and Debbie alternately stared back at me from each successive lamp post all the way down the hill. Someone had been busy.

The main street was still opening up when I arrived. Window cleaners worked their way along the rows of shops while shutters were raised and awnings wound out. I walked all the way along and then discovered another street ran in parallel, so I completed the circuit and walked back along that. There were the usual chainstores mixed in with local traders; a butcher and a baker but no candlestick maker. There was a fishmonger advertising frozen fish, which seemed a bit pointed in a town with a fishing harbour two minutes' walk from where it stood.

I walked out to the harbour front. The walls fell sheer to oily water smelling of rotting seaweed and diesel. The harbour was full. The boats looked well used, the sea-water peeling the paint and rusting the steel. Men stood around talking. No one was interested in taking the boats out fishing, though. There wasn't even anyone mending nets. Maybe it was a holiday?

I scanned the frontage around the harbour. A couple of ramshackle hotels offered the possibility of a bed for the night, the signs advertising rooms available. Like the boats, the paint was peeling and the windows were smeared. It didn't make for an inviting prospect and I wondered who stayed there. Not a spot for tourists.

Among the bait shops and estate agents was the Harbour Café, tables placed out in the sun to attract passing business. I crossed the road and wandered past. It was clean enough and the smell of frying bacon set my mouth watering. I went in and approached the counter. A middle-aged woman with pink streaks in her hair looked up. She acknowledged my presence with a stream of words I didn't recognise and couldn't decipher. The accent was thick.

"Sorry?"

She looked me up and down then spoke slowly and precisely for the terminally stupid. "Sit down, luv, and I'll come over and take your order."

"Thanks."

The other two patrons sat together, old men with jackets buttoned against the morning chill even though it was warm inside the café. I found a table next to the window where I could watch the comings and goings along the harbour. It was a good position. Garvin would have approved.

"Tea, luv, or coffee?" Appearing beside me, she spoke more naturally but moderated her accent for the obvious visitor.

"I'd like coffee, please, and a bacon sandwich."

"It'll be five minutes."

She left me watching the traffic. I took the posters out of my bag and laid them on the table in front of me, wondering whether they were the reason I was here. The girls smiled in the photos. I wondered whether they were still smiling.

110

"Bunkers, aren't they?" The woman had returned with a large mug of steaming black coffee and a glass sugar dispenser.

"Why are they bonkers?"

"Not bonkers, bunkers. They've bunked off, hamp't they?"

"Have they?"

"Not the only ones, either." She folded her arms, confirming her deduction.

"What do you mean?"

She went back to the counter and returned with a newspaper, which she laid on the table in front of me.

The headline was plain – FIFTH GIRL MISSING. A photo of a young woman was under the headline and four others were below it, two of which I recognised.

"Five?"

"All bunked off if you ask me. There's nothing for 'em here, is there?"

"No?"

"Not if you don't want to spend your days in yon call centre. More like one of them sweatshops if you ask me."

"That would be the new building on the hill, I take it."

"Monstrosity, it is. They work for nowt up there, not that it's any better down here. I'll go and get your sandwich." She bustled away.

It was a local paper. The missing girls were the lead story, bracketed by a planning dispute about a road diversion and threatened job losses at the call centre. A sweatshop they might be but they were clearly a major local employer.

The story about the girls was rich in speculation and short on facts. It implied that there was something untoward happening without actually saying what it was. One family was quoted as saying that their daughter had disappeared suddenly and unexpectedly. Another said that their eldest daughter had been doing well at college

111

and asked why she would leave all her friends. The article called the disappearances spooky, but neglected to say why. The local police were noted as being aware of the situation but unwilling to investigate further.

My bacon sandwich turned up. The woman nodded towards the paper. "It's a lot of flannel, that. Don't believe a word." She paused as if she expected me to make some comment.

I thanked her for the sandwich. She turned and left me to eat it.

Leafing through the paper, I ate my breakfast, then read it through a second time while I sipped the scalding coffee. There were no other stories about the girls, but in the middle there was space for local advertising and promotions. There were two ads there that repeated the information from the posters I had taken down. The same two girls stared back at me.

On the events page there was an announcement from St Andrew's Church saying that a vigil was being held for the missing girls. People were invited to show their support for the families by attending the service and lighting candles. There was a contact number for the vicar, Gregory Makepeace. I copied the number down on to a napkin.

When the lady came to clear the plate, I handed back the paper. "I'm going to be in town for a few days, is there anywhere you could recommend for a place to stay?"

"Salesman, are ya? There's nobody buying round here, I can tell you that fer free."

"I'm not selling anything. Is there anywhere?"

She looked me over again, whether to discern my occupation or to discover if I was a suitable guest, I didn't know.

"You could ask at the Dolphin Guest House at the harbour end of Dorvey Street. Tell Martha that Geraldine at the café sent you. She'll sort you out."

I thanked her and paid, wondering what sorting me out meant.

It was too early to go knocking on doors and seeking rooms, so I walked back up the hill to the church, perched on its shelf of rock. Its stone was weathered and pitted and streaked with gull droppings but the sign said St Andrew's, so this was the place where the vigil would be. There was no graveyard as such, the ground being far too hard for graves, but there were memorial plaques and stone vases clustered into the walled enclosure. I was grateful to whoever had chained the iron gates back against the wall. I could no longer tolerate the touch of iron. Something in my fey nature reacted badly with it. I had been burned before and had the gates been barred I would probably have turned away.

The porch was open, but when I tried the door to the church, I found it locked. I scanned the notice board inside the porch. There were times for services, a rota for flowers, a crayoned advert for Sunday School. Nothing useful. I turned to leave and found the path blocked by a man in a dark coat outlined against the bright sunlight behind him. He looked imposing and yet I hadn't heard him approach.

"Help you?" The accent was local. There was no threat in the tone and as I squinted into the sunlight I could see the collar he wore was round and white against the black of his shirt.

"Good morning. I was just looking for details of the vigil service."

"Step out for a moment, and I'll open up the church for you. Everyone's welcome in God's house, though we try and make sure that people don't take advantage of that welcome."

"Sorry?"

"Don't like locking it up, but things get broken or stolen."

"Oh. I see. I'm not here to steal the hymn books." I stepped out of the porch so that he could enter.

"Can see that. Clergy?"

I looked down at my grey jacket and black silk turtleneck, then smiled up at him. "This? No, but I suppose it is a kind of uniform."

He unlocked the door and turned back to me. It was his turn to squint into the light. He offered his hand.

"Greg Makepeace. It's my parish."

"Neal Dawson."

He extended his hand and I took it. As we clasped I felt a sudden jolt. I snatched back my hand at the shock. He looked momentarily surprised and then apologised.

"Static." He shrugged it off. "I pick it up wherever I go. Sorry about that."

"No problem." I rubbed the heel of my hand.

What I had felt wasn't static. It was power.

SIX

Blackbird was woken by a persistent tapping at the door. She groaned as she pulled the duvet to one side so that she could roll sideways and push herself slowly upright. "All right. Just wait, I'm coming as fast as I can."

There was no sign that Niall had been back. What time had he been called out? Sometime after three, she thought.

She slipped into the cotton robe from the night before. The tapping resumed.

"Just wait, will you? I won't come any quicker because you keep on."

She turned the handle on the door and peeped through.

"I need to speak with you." Garvin stood in the corridor.

"You'd better come in then." Blackbird stepped back, allowing the door to open so that Garvin could enter, then looked out into the hallway. Usually where you found Garvin, Tate wasn't far behind. There was no sign of him in the hallway but that didn't mean he wasn't close by.

"Where's Niall?" she asked as she closed the door. There was no point in preamble.

"I've sent him on an assignment."

"I thought you didn't trust him for real work."

"He went active last night. He'll be a few days, I expect."

Blackbird went to pull a chair out to sit and then decided against it. She didn't want Garvin looming over her. She wasn't intimidated by his tactics, she just didn't like them. Instead she turned it so she could use it for support. The backache was constant now.

"Where have you sent him?"

Garvin ignored her question. "In the meantime, the High Court is convened and I need you to stay out of the way. Your meals will be brought to you and if you want anything you need only ask the stewards. Take some rest, you look like you need it."

"Thanks. You really know how to make a girl feel special."

"You're not my girl."

"Nor ever likely to be. Do you have a girl, Garvin?" She raised one eyebrow in enquiry.

Garvin didn't speak and his expression didn't change.

"I didn't think so. Telling Niall that his daughter was better off in an institution wasn't very kind, was it?"

"It may be true."

"Even you do not believe that. He will go after her, you know that. It's the kind of man he is."

"He needs to stay away from her, at least for now. We have other problems."

"Such as?"

Garvin was silent again.

She sighed. "You may as well tell me. I will find out regardless."

"With the Court in session the staff will be rushed off their feet. Try not to make too much of a pain of yourself. Once the session has finished we can look into finding you somewhere permanent to live."

"What are you not telling me, Garvin? That's unusually evasive, even for you."

"I'll have Fionh come up and place a warding on the doors and windows. You should be safe enough in here."

"Safe from what?" She waited for an answer. "Or would you rather I go and find out for myself?"

"The Seventh Court are here. They're in session tonight. Raffmir is here with Altair along with another wraithkin, Deefnir. They're in negotiations with the other courts."

Blackbird stood up straight, no longer leaning on the chair. "You weren't going to tell me that, were you?"

"I'm telling you now. Stay out of the way and there'll be no trouble. Altair's vouching for their conduct."

"Oh, well, that's all right then. If the Lord of the Untainted says they will behave themselves then that must be true, mustn't it? What did he actually say?"

"He assured me he'll take full responsibility for them while they were here."

"He's the Lord of the Seventh Court. He's responsible for them if they're on the moon. Are you serious? I killed Raffmir's sister. Do you think for a moment that he is not going to want revenge?"

"Raffmir has sworn by fey law to do you no harm. He can't hurt you without breaking his vow."

"That's such a comfort."

"They'll only be here a few days. Until they go, you need to keep a low profile. Stay in your room. I'll have the Warders patrol the halls whenever we have someone free. With wardings on your doors and windows, you should be secure enough."

"I want a weapon. Bring me a knife. Nothing too long, but sharp."

"I am not arming you, Blackbird. You're pregnant. What are you planning to do, stab them?"

"I can defend myself."

"You won't need to. The best defence is to stay away from them. We'll keep them away from you. They'll be gone soon enough."

117

"Don't leave me with nothing."

"You're more likely to harm yourself than anyone else. Stay calm. I'll have the stewards bring you some books, or a newspaper perhaps?"

"I want Niall here. Where is he?"

"Niall's on assignment. He'll be back soon. You have to get used to him being away. Warders go where they're sent."

"They go where you send them, you mean."

"Quite. Get some rest. I'll send the stewards up with some breakfast for you." Garvin turned to the door. "Do you want anything else?"

"A weapon."

"No, and don't pinch the butter knives. You'll only upset Mullbrook and then we'll all suffer."

"I don't like this, Garvin."

"I'm not delighted with it myself, but they have the right to be here. We'll make sure their visit is short and trouble-free. Trust us."

When Blackbird didn't respond to that, he nodded and left.

"Jumped-up…" She let the word hang and then pushed her hair back from her face, sighing heavily. "Well, it's no good standing here in your nightwear, girl, is it?"

She went hunting in the clothes drawers. "What are we going for today?" she said to herself. "Is it the beached-whale look or are we going all-out for the crashed blimp?"

She laid out trousers with an elastic waist, a T-shirt and a smock top – it wasn't the most elegant attire but then her choices were limited. She collected underwear and socks and set them to one side. In the bathroom, she brushed her teeth and then collected a toothbrush, toothpaste and hairbrush and wrapped them in a cotton flannel.

She looked up and saw her vague reflection in the misted mirror. She turned away, but then stopped and turned back. She breathed gently on the edge of the mirror and it misted lightly, then slowly cleared. The mist in the centre of the mirror was still there, though. It didn't clear. She wafted at it gently with her hand. It remained unchanged. She placed the back of her hand softly against the mirror, testing the temperature in the centre and at the edge.

"Why would the mirror be colder in the centre?" she asked herself. "Shit!" She pressed her hand over her mouth.

She left the bathroom and went to the other mirror over the dresser. It was clear. She breathed soft on the mirror until it misted and then watched it slowly clear. Then she breathed on the edge of the mirror. It cleared much faster there. Both of the mirrors in the room were colder than they should be.

She shook her head and whispered to herself, "Don't they tell you in the Seventh Court that it's rude to spy on a lady?"

She went and collected a shoe from the floor and hefted it in her hand. She walked over to the mirror and held the shoe up ready. A tap from the door stopped her.

"One moment."

She replaced the shoe and went to the door. "Who is it?"

"Steward. Mister Garvin said that you would take breakfast in your room."

Blackbird opened the door cautiously, finding the steward, a trolley and no one else.

"How long have you been a steward here?" she asked the girl in the white apron and double-breasted jacket.

The girl looked uncertain. "Two years, or there-abouts. Is there a problem?"

She opened the door. "Maybe not."

The steward propelled the trolley into the room, took a cloth from the bottom shelf and draped it over the table with a flourish.

"A beautiful morning, isn't it?" she said.

"Is it?" said Blackbird. "I haven't been out."

"Makes you feel alive, a morning like this." There was a trace of an Irish accent in her voice. "Would you like the balcony windows open? It'll let some of the fresh air in."

"Maybe later," said Blackbird. "When I've dressed."

The steward laid a single place, setting out pastries, toast and a small dish and then a pot which she placed on a warmer. "Mr Garvin said that you might like to try the porridge, and to bring you apple rather than orange juice as you weren't to have anything too sharp."

Blackbird raised her eyebrow, "Is that supposed to be some sort of joke?"

The girl stopped, looking genuinely puzzled. "I'm sorry, Miss, have I said the wrong thing?"

Blackbird shook her head slowly. "I think Mr Garvin is having a joke at your expense. Would you give him a message for me, word for word?"

"I'm not sure, Miss. I don't really like these sort of games." She finished setting out the table, glancing uncertainly at Blackbird.

"Tell him that apple juice is fine and that Miss Blackbird sends her compliments and hopes that one day soon he will grow up."

The girl smiled and shook her head. "I don't think I can say that, Miss."

Blackbird followed her to the door. "Oh, I insist, and if he says anything to you, tell him I said he should come and talk to me about it."

"Very well, Miss. If you insist."

"I do. Thank you…" Blackbird tipped her head to one side.

"Lesley, Miss. My name's Lesley."

"Thank you, Lesley. I'll leave the trolley outside the door when I've finished with it if that is acceptable?"

"That's fine, Miss. Please enjoy your breakfast."

"I will, Lesley. Thank you."

As soon as the door was shut, she uncovered the basket of pastries, wrapped two of them in a napkin and set them aside. She gulped down a small glass of apple juice and turned back to her clothes.

Sitting on the edge of the bed, she tried to pull on socks despite the hindrance of her swollen belly. She found that she could only reach her feet if she didn't try to breathe at the same time. She got one on, slightly twisted, and then had to wait a moment before she could attempt the other.

"Oh, for goodness sake!"

She leaned down and tugged the other sock on, struggling with it until she was pink and cross. She frowned down at her belly, but then her expression softened. She stroked her hand slowly down the bump. "Soon," she whispered.

Once dressed she took her bag and stuffed a change of clothes into it. Never intended as an overnight bag, it bulged rather, but she wanted to carry as little as possible. She collected the rolled-up flannel with the items inside it from the bathroom and tucked those down the side. Then she took the napkin containing the pastries and placed that on the top.

She broke the end off one of the remaining pastries and washed it down with apple juice. "Too sharp, indeed."

She hunted through the limited cutlery and selected a butter knife that would be no use as a weapon but might prove useful as a tool. She tucked that into the other side of the bag.

She drained the juice glass, then went into the bathroom and used the toilet. She washed and dried her hands while she looked around the bathroom.

Next to the bath was a long-handled back brush with a rope on the end.

"Right," she whispered to herself. "If you want something to listen to, we'll give you something."

Flushing the toilet again to create some ambient noise, she climbed into the bath and, taking the brush, reached up to hang the rope loop over the shower head. She climbed carefully out and drew the shower curtain across. When she turned the shower on, the brush swung around in the jet of water, making a convincing noise of someone showering. She grinned and turned it off again.

She left the bathroom, put on her shoes, collected her bag and placed it by the door. Taking the blunt knife, she went back into the bathroom, turned the water on full and pulled the shower curtain across. She watched the mist spread across the mirror. Then she quietly left the bathroom and, using the knife, turned the slotted bolt on the door from the outside, so that the door was locked. She listened to the sound of splashing water and nodded to herself.

Checking the corridor was clear, she turned away from the main hall, walked to the end of the hall and took the small stairway down to the servants quarters. It had the advantage of avoiding the main hallway and was the place she was least likely to encounter Raffmir and his crony. While she was sure they were aware that there were back stairs and servants' quarters, she doubted they'd ever deigned to visit any of them.

She pressed herself into a wood-panelled doorway when one of the stewards came past. He didn't see her, but then he wasn't looking for an absconder. She waited until he'd gone, then slipped down through the back of the house and came out through a disused pantry with piles of old boxes and the tang of ancient newspapers lining the shelves.

What used to be the stables was now a garage, but that wasn't much good to her since she couldn't drive. She did consider stowing away in the boot of one of the cars, but there was no way of telling which of them were going out and which were staying in the garage. She didn't want to end up trapped in there.

A better opportunity presented itself with the delivery van. The side was emblazoned with an array of cartoon cabbages and carrots with 'Coutler's Fresh Fruit and Vegetables' circled around it. The driver wasn't with the van, but the van wasn't locked so he couldn't have gone far. The back of the van had racks for trays of vegetables in it and nowhere to sit, so she went up front, climbed in and made herself comfortable. She kept a careful eye on the rear-view mirror, watching to see if it misted up. Once they discovered she'd flown the nest, the hunt would be on. She hoped they were enjoying listening to her in the shower.

She heard the vegetable man loading the trays back into the van and talking to one of the cooks from the kitchen. Blackbird hunkered down in the seat. She didn't want to give herself away too early. She heard the back doors slam and goodbyes exchanged. The driver's door opened.

"'Ere! Who are you?"

"Hello," she said quietly.

"What'ya doing in there? Get out of it."

"I'm called Blackbird," she said, offering her hand. "And you are?"

He didn't take it. "Never mind that, Miss, you can't just climb in someone's van like that. Out ya get!"

Blackbird withdrew her hand and placed it back in her lap, looking forwards. "I need a lift," she said, "into the village."

"I'm not insured to carry passengers. What do you think I am, a taxi service?"

123

"I thought you might be kind enough to take me as far as the village. I can make my own way from there."

"I told you. No way."

She looked resolutely through the windscreen.

"Come on, out you get," he insisted.

"Are you going to manhandle a pregnant woman?"

"Manhandle you? I don't even know what the word means."

"I'm not moving."

"I told you, I'm not insured. It's against the rules, see?"

"I won't tell anyone."

"It's not down to me. If someone sees you in the van I could get in a lot of trouble."

"Not as much trouble as I'm in. I need your help. If I don't get out of here quickly I will be in great danger. My baby will be in danger." She rested her hand on the bump for emphasis.

"Are you mad?"

She turned her head and stared him down. "No, not mad. Scared. There are some people here who want to hurt me and my baby. If you won't take me I'm going to have to walk, maybe even try and run. Do you think running is going to be good for a pregnant woman? That's how scared I am."

He sighed and ran his fingers through his greasy hair. "Oh, Jesus."

She waited, staring through the windscreen, not meeting his gaze.

He sighed, heavily. "You won't tell anyone, will you?"

"It'll be our secret, I promise. If you take me as far as the village, I can hitch a ride to the motorway from there." She added a hesitant smile.

He climbed into the cab. "Put your seat belt on. You might have to fish around for it. I'll take you to the motorway junction. There'll be less people see us that way.

I've got another delivery to make on the way. You all right with that?"

"Anywhere but here, as they say. What did you say your name was?"

"Tony. What's yours?"

"You can call me Blackbird. Everyone does."

The van started up in a grumble of diesel, then complained as the clutch wasn't depressed enough and the gears grated. Tony shook his head, but whether that was at the van or at Blackbird, she didn't know.

As they rumbled down the drive, Blackbird looked back at the house, wondering how long she had before they discovered she'd gone.

SEVEN

The echo of power still tingled in my hand as the vicar of St Andrew's opened the door into the church. With the narrow windows down each side it would have felt confining but for the huge leaded window catching the sea-light and fragmenting it into every corner. As I entered I felt as if I had walked in on something private but the church was empty.

"Catches you first time, doesn't it?"

"Hmm?"

"The window. Everyone stops there the first time they see it. The way it was meant to be seen, with the morning sun behind it. Local artist made it. Old one was dark-coloured glass – Victorian. Made the church feel like a mausoleum."

"You got rid of it?"

"Didn't need to. Germans did that for me, long before my time. Bomber got lost and thought we were Hull. The church was the only building in the town that got hit."

"Some might take that as a sign, no offence meant."

"None taken. I take it as a gift. No one was hurt and the bomb did no structural harm. There was temporary glass there for a long time. Then a sponsor approached me and asked if we would like a new window. Not often that churches are offered donations these days. Even so, we were sceptical. The sponsors own the big glass building opposite, a temple to Mammon."

"The call centre?"

"That's one of the things they do there. I was worried they would want their logo in the glass, or at least a plaque to commemorate the sponsorship. They were happy simply to donate. It was quite refreshing. They gave us a free hand with respect to the style, though of course they wanted to see the designs and were delighted when we commissioned a local artist. All done in the name of corporate responsibility and community relations."

"That's altruistic of them."

"Rare in these times, don't you think?"

"I expect you're right."

"You didn't say what you wanted."

"I was looking for details of the vigil."

He turned with his back to the window, outlining himself in light. "You said that was what you were looking for, but not what you wanted. In my job you get a feel for when people are being evasive."

I looked at him, haloed by the light, black against the fragmented flood. If he really had power then he would be able to tell whether I was lying, in the same way I could tell when anyone lied to me.

"I'm looking into the disappearance of the girls. I thought I might get a look at the families." I opened my wallet and handed him the NUJ card, letting him make the assumption that I was a journalist.

"Been done," he said. "All the details have been taken down, the background of the families combed for dirt. Offered to a national, but 'Young Women Leave Home' wasn't headline-grabbing enough."

"You're very cynical for a man of God."

"Realistic about human nature. Believe me, I get to see all sides of it."

"I didn't come to write a story about missing girls."

"Then why do you want to see the families?"

"If I can find the girls, find out what happened to them, why they left, where they went, there might be a story in it. Or there might not."

"You think the families haven't tried to find them?"

"I dare say my methods are different from theirs. Either way, it may be worth a try. What is there to lose?"

"Maybe more than you know."

He walked over to the far corner. A huge pinboard was mounted there, overlapping the window behind it. It was covered in photos, posters, letters of support, news clippings, anything that linked to the girls. Some of the girls featured more prominently than others. The two from the lamp posts were most evident.

"Campaign central. They come here on a Friday night to meet, talk, swap false hopes and share expectations. They asked me if they could use this corner and I agreed. I thought it might help. Not sure whether I did the right thing, now."

"You don't share their hopes?"

"Not that. Wonder whether it's doing them any good, to go over and over it each week. Loss is a terrible thing, but sometimes it's better to try and move on, learn to live with it."

"It's easier to live with it if you know what happened to them."

He looked up sharply, searching my face. Something in my voice had triggered his reaction. "Did you lose someone, Neal?"

I looked at the photographs. "My daughter."

"Missing?"

"There was an accident. She was stolen from me. We

weren't able to see the body. It made it unreal, as if she weren't lost at all."

"Ah. Sorry."

"I didn't come here looking for sympathy."

He stepped out into the middle of the church. "Do you believe in God, Neal?"

"I'm not sure I know what I believe in."

"I believe in Him. You may think that's obvious, given my profession, but you might be surprised at how many who follow this calling come to doubt the presence, if not the existence, of God."

"I didn't come looking for God, either."

"Don't have to. Rather the point, don't you think?"

He turned and faced the window. I watched him, facing the full light, outlined against the morning.

"It's not what it seems, you know." He spoke to the window rather than turning and facing me.

"Things rarely are."

"If I take you to one of the families and it doesn't do any good, will you let it go?"

"I can't say until I've seen them."

He stood framed against the light for a long while, thinking or praying or maybe just waiting for me to add something else. Finally he turned, went back to the photo board and pulled out a pin to release a photo, which he handed to me. "Karen Hopkins went missing almost a year ago. Eldest girl of four, seventeen when she vanished. Three younger children, youngest is two. Father works in the chandler's down the dock. On half-time at the moment, but he'll be at work this morning so there's a chance to meet the mother, if you want to."

"I shouldn't meet the father?"

"He won't talk about Karen. Won't even have her name mentioned. If you want to talk to Mrs Hopkins it has to be now while he's at work."

"Was there trouble between them?"

"No, nothing like that. Not everyone deals with the situation in the same way. For some it's easier to lock it away and carry on."

"Then yes, I'd like to speak with Mrs Hopkins."

"Leave the overnight bag here. I'll lock the church. If they do get in they'll steal the silver first. Stash it in the corner there."

I tucked my bag into the corner, conscious of the sword cached in the side pocket. Garvin wouldn't like me leaving it, but I could hardly carry it around with me. While my back was between the vicar and the bag, I pressed my hand to it, using a small amount of power to turn curious eyes away from it. Now anyone coming in while we were gone would have to be actively looking for the bag to notice it. It would do as a temporary measure.

Greg was waiting at the door. I passed through the shadowed porch and waited while he locked the church. He strode from the porch past me, and my stride lengthened to match his so I could keep up. We walked straight out into the traffic, which slowed around him to allow us across, then we turned uphill.

"It must keep you fit, all this walking."

"Have a car; don't use it much. By the time you've found a parking place you might as well have walked. It gets a ride out if I go out to one of the farms or when I go to the big supermarket in town."

I was thinking that having all that metal around him probably wasn't comfortable. I'd noticed that the railings around the church had been cut down. Perhaps it was no coincidence that although the east window had been replaced, the gates were chained back and the railings had never been put back.

"You said it was a calling."

"Did I?"

"You said not everyone who follows this calling believes in God."

"'Believes in the *presence* of God' is what I said. They believe in Him, but they're not sure whether He believes in them."

"But you do. You were called?"

"You wouldn't do it for the money. The pay is awful."

"You still do it, though. Was there a revelation, a road to Damascus?"

"Why do you ask? Am I part of your story too?"

"Perhaps. You're holding it all together, aren't you?"

He paused, considering.

"Were you called?" I asked.

"Not sure you'd call it that. I was born here. Maybe I just came home."

I could tell by his voice that there was more to it than that, but I didn't press him. After a few moments he continued.

"When I was a lad, I had an Auntie here." The word "Auntie" came out as "anti", as if it were a protest against something. "We were living away by then, but we used to come and stay. Fishing off the dock, ice cream for tea; that sort of thing. It was only summers, like. In the winter it's a different place."

He continued striding up the steep hill, breathing easily but momentarily reflective.

"Grew up in Rotherham. Back-to-back terraces, no work, no jobs. The men used to play dice on the corner, out of sight of the wives." The accent had slipped, giving way to flatter vowels, harsher consonants. "School were a boring place, most of the time we were out of it unless you were caught. If you were caught, you were caned."

He grinned, without humour.

"I had a dicky leg, though. Couldn't run. Couldn't keep up. Too easily caught. They'd leave me behind."

The pace he set showed no sign of the bad leg now.

"So I would be in school while they ran the streets. I did exams. Got into grammar school. Used to come

131

home every night in the uniform and they'd throw sticks and bottles at me."

"You must have hated them."

"No, I wanted to be with them. Out. Free. The posh kids at school called me Makeshit, the kids at home Gimpy Greg. I know which I preferred." He turned into a side street, keeping the same long stride. "Coming up for school board exams I got a fever. It was touch and go for a while. The doctors didn't like it. Didn't know what to make of it. It was there and then gone. I was delirious then lucid. Sick then better. They said it was a virus, fighting my immune system. Long before HIV, this was."

He set off down the street again.

"I was sent here to recover. Never did the exams. I was here for months. The vicar, Georgeson, my predecessor, came every day. He would lay his hand on my forehead and tell me that He was looking out for me and He wasn't going to let me go. He said He had big plans for me. At the end of it I was changed."

"Changed?"

"No gimpy leg. No pain. I could run along the tops, jump over the heather. I would race on the bike down the hill, no fear, pedalling like a madman. I crashed twice. Wasn't hurt. Not a scratch. Wrecked the bike the second time. Then Georgeson came to see me. He said there was a place at the seminary if I wanted it. They would get me my exams, teach me what I needed, show me my path. It meant going away, but I knew I would return. Been here ever since."

He stopped where steps led down to the street below, opening out the skyline, showing the moving shadows of cloud across the sea beyond the rooftops.

"You feel blessed." It was obvious when you looked at him.

"It was a gift."

132

"Have you ever been back? To Rotherham, I mean?"

"It's all gone. The old bomb sites are supermarkets and the kids don't play in the streets any more. Too scared of child molesters and drug dealers." He set off down the street again.

The temptation to ask him about the fever, the moment when his leg recovered and he began to change, was intense. Had he felt the same opening inside? Was he conscious of the power within him? To ask, though, would beg too many questions I didn't want to answer.

We arrived at a doorway, mid-terrace. The sound of a child squealing indignantly percolated through the window beside the door. Without preamble, Greg pressed the bell button. A distorted electronic chime sounded inside. There was a pause, then more shouting – an older voice with harsher edges. "Shelley! Shelley! See who's at the door, will ya?"

There was another pause and then the rhythmic thump as stairs were descended at speed. The door was pulled open, revealing a sullen girl in a sparkly T-shirt and jeans.

"It's Shelley, isn't it?" said Greg, giving no hint that we'd heard the yelling.

"S'right."

"Would like a word with your mother, please, Shelley? If she has a moment?"

She grimaced, but turned and shouted down the passage towards a back room. "Mam! It's the vicar. He wants a word."

The sound of a baby crying erupted from the kitchen.

"Isn't it a school day, Shelley?" Greg enquired.

The girl lifted her chin. "I'm poorly, aren't I?" Her expression dared him to contradict the obvious lie.

A middle-aged woman emerged from the kitchen wiping down the front of her top with a tea towel. "Well, don't just stand there like a ninny. Invite him in."

Shelley opened the door a little more, revealing me.

"He's got someone with 'im, hasn't he?"

Shelley retreated into the hall, allowing us into the house.

"You bringin' round the bailiff now, vicar?" the woman asked.

"Like a quiet word, please, Mrs Hopkins. About Karen."

"Nothin' left to say, is there?" she said.

"Neal here's a journalist. Wants to try and find the girls."

"Does he now?" She paused, looking me straight up and down, not disguising that her frank assessment left me wanting.

"A quiet word? Five minutes?"

A wail started up from the kitchen behind her.

"Shelley. See to the tiddler, will ya? I need to talk to the vicar."

"Oh, mum!"

"Now! Or you can put your uniform on and go to school. One or t'other."

She sighed, shrugged and pushed past her mother to the back of the house. Mrs Hopkins opened a side door and ushered us into a sitting room. It was tight with furniture, dominated by a big-screen TV over the fireplace where a mirror or a picture would once have been. The screen was off and reflected the room darkly.

"I'd offer you tea, but we're off out as soon as tiddler's fed." The lie was obvious to me and must have been to Greg.

"Don't want to put you to any trouble, Mrs Hopkins. Neal here just wanted to ask a few questions about Karen."

"Nothing to say. She's gone." She shrugged but glanced towards the fireplace. There was a family photo crammed in among the ornaments. Karen was smiling out of it, tucked under her mother's arm. Her father

134

held a baby, and Shelley and a younger boy sat in front. I wondered if it was significant that Mrs Hopkins had placed herself between her daughter and her husband.

I cleared my throat. "Was there any indication that she was going to leave, before she disappeared?"

"The police asked all this. We've been over it a hundred times."

"It'll help me form a picture of her. I might be able to find her."

"She's gone and there's no bringing her back. It doesn't help to keep going over it, you know."

"So you've given up hope?" I asked.

She sighed and looked at her hands. " No. I still hope she'll come home. I don't think she will, but I hope."

"I'd like to try and help you, Mrs Hopkins."

"That's kind, Mr… Neal, is it?"

"Neal Dawson," I said.

"But I think everything that could be done has been done. If she wanted to come back to us by now, she would have done."

"What if she can't? She may not have any money. She may be lost, or alone."

"I think if she meant to come back, she'd find a way, don't you? All she'd have to do is pick up the phone. She could even reverse the charges."

She stood and went to the door and opened it. "I think we'll have to go out shortly, if you don't mind. Thanks for calling round, vicar."

Greg and I stood and eased our way out of the cramped sitting room and into the hallway. We said goodbye at the door.

"Thanks for seeing us, Mrs Hopkins," said Greg.

"You were very good to us when Karen disappeared, vicar. We've not forgotten that."

"Least I could do."

"Come any time. You're always welcome."

"God bless."

"You too." She closed the door quietly.

Greg paused for a second before the blank doorway and then turned and strode away, his long stride making it hard to keep up. He didn't speak and I mulled over what we'd heard before I started asking questions.

We retraced our steps and came to the road leading down to the hillside church. He paused before the busy traffic, waiting for a lull between cars.

"What is she not saying?" I asked him.

"What makes you think there's something she's not saying?"

"I offer to help find her missing daughter and she turns me down. She says everything's been done. I tell her that her daughter may need help and she dismisses it. All she has to do is pick up the phone? What happened to leaving no stone unturned? If it were my daughter…"

"Not though, is it? It's not your daughter. It's hers."

He strode out into the traffic, the cars braking to let him through. No one beeped at him or shouted. Maybe they were used to this tall dark man walking straight into the road, his eyes ahead, heedless of the danger.

I had to wait for a gap in the cars to follow. He was unlocking the church doors when I caught up.

"Like you, in my profession there's a feel for when people aren't telling you the whole story." I carefully didn't mention what that profession was. "Call it a hunch."

"As you say, a hunch." He walked over to the pinboard and unpinned a picture. He took a parish news-sheet, ripped the back page from the staples and wrote out a name and two addresses, one a college, one a café. He gave them to me.

"What's this?"

"Want to find the lost girls? This is what they call a clue – better than a hunch. Be outside here –" he pointed to the address "– it's part of Hull College. Be there at four

136

o'clock this afternoon. Ask for Zaina. Find Zaina, you'll find Karen. If she's not there, go to the café. The address is there underneath."

"You know where she is?"

"I know where she'll be."

"Why didn't you tell her mother?"

"Before you help people, Neal, you have to find out what they need. Otherwise you end up making things worse."

"You could at least ease her mind; tell her that she's OK."

"Go and find Karen, Neal. Then come back and tell me what I should do." He found my holdall in the corner easily, regardless of the warding I had placed upon it, and pushed it into my arms

"Tomorrow," he said, "when you've had time to sleep on it."

He patted my shoulder and then walked slowly up the central aisle of the church, halted before the altar and slowly knelt. I left him to his prayers.

Hull was a good few miles away. If I was to be there by four, I would need to use the Ways. Before that I needed somewhere to stay. I walked back down the hill to the harbour and then along to Dorvey Street. The Dolphin Guest House was the third in a terraced row. It looked clean and cared for, but the sign said 'No Vacancy'. I almost turned away, but then remembered that Geraldine at the café had said that Martha would 'sort me out'. Maybe she had somewhere else I could stay. I rapped with the polished door knocker and waited until the door was opened, revealing a small woman wearing a plum satin blouse with huge flowers on it.

"Can I help you?" she asked.

"Hi. I'm Neal Dawson. Geraldine at the Harbour Café said you might be able to recommend somewhere to stay for a few days, just while I'm in town."

"Selling something?"

"No, I just wanted to ask about rooms. Geraldine at the café said…"

"I meant, are you a travelling salesman?"

"No, a journalist."

"What kind of journalism? None of that smutty stuff, celebrity muckraking and sensationalist claptrap?"

"It's mostly human interest stories. I've had my name in some of the quality papers."

She looked me over. "Better come in then." She stepped back and opened the door wide so that I could bring the bag inside.

"It said 'No Vacancies' outside."

"I only take recommended guests; a certain type of gentleman. You get such riff-raff otherwise. It drags the whole tone of the place down. The sign discourages passers-by."

"Trade must be good if you can afford to turn away business."

"We get by without taking in waifs and strays."

Waifs and strays. I had once been described as a waif and stray. I looked around the well-appointed hall, white-painted and clean. The waxed wooden floorboards could be seen at the side of the patterned carpet runner. A dark wood mirrored sideboard had a number of daily papers on it, including those of the scurrilous press.

She caught me eyeing the papers. "We keep those for guests – a selection of daily papers."

"Very convenient," I said.

"It's strictly no visitors, I'm afraid."

"I'm not expecting any."

"No women, or men."

"So you do have a room for me?"

She named a daily rate. "Breakfast is between seven and eight-thirty. If you're going to be out after ten, let me know and I'll let you have a key."

"May I see the room?"

I followed her up two flights of stairs to a short corridor with two numbered doors. "Number 21. No smoking in the rooms, I'm afraid. If you want to light up you'll have to do it outside on the fire escape."

"That's OK, I don't."

The room was small, but had its own toilet and shower, a small wardrobe and a matching chest of drawers. The single bed was tucked under the sloping ceiling.

"How long will you be staying?"

"A few nights, three or four, maybe a little longer. Is that OK?"

"If you book for a week, the seventh night is free."

"I think I'll be gone by then, thanks all the same." How long were the Seventh Court likely to stay? Until after the solstice, Garvin said.

"If you come downstairs I'll take your credit card details."

"I'd rather pay cash, if that's OK?"

"Cash?" She looked wary at that. "If it's cash it has to be in advance. We've had problems before with gentlemen being called away urgently and forgetting to settle their bill."

"I'd say that they weren't gentlemen, then, were they?" I paid her for the next three days from my wallet. "Obviously I'll settle up in advance if I intend to stay on."

I half expected her to tuck the money into her bra where the VAT man wouldn't find it, but she simply smiled. "That's fine, Mr Dawson. We always welcome customers who pay promptly. I'll bring a receipt up for you."

After she'd gone I went through the room carefully, finding only a Gideon bible in the bedside drawer and empty coat hangers in the wardrobe. I left my gear in my bag, not really wanting to move in. It was only temporary.

I placed my hand on the mirror screwed to the wall over the chest.

"Blackbird?"

The curtains billowed in the draft from the window as the air in the room chilled slightly. A sound entered the room, thrumming an uneven rhythm.

"Blackbird?"

"Not now."

"What's not now, darlin'?" Another voice, coarse and unschooled. It sounded enclosed; raised to be heard over the rumbling background noise. Where was she?

"I was just thinking, there isn't so much traffic on the motorway now."

"It's gonna get a lot busier as we get closer to London, you can be sure of that. You all right like that, darlin?"

"I'm fine, thanks. My boyfriend's going to be so surprised when I get there, isn't he?"

"He is if he don't know you're in that state." He laughed, but the humour leached out of it. "He does know, doesn't he?"

"Yes, he knows. I'll be fine, don't worry."

"Only you look like you're gonna drop it any minute."

"There's weeks to go yet. Don't worry."

"Is it your first?"

"Yes. Why?"

"First ones are always late. You talk to my missus. Our first was three weeks late. I was beginin' to think he weren't coming."

There was a knock on the door to my room and I dropped the connection with the mirror, the sound dying suddenly.

"Yes, who is it?"

"It's me, Mr Dawson. I brought up your receipt for you."

I opened the door to find the landlady. She offered the receipt.

"Strange," she said. "I thought I heard voices."

"I like to have the radio on," I told her, avoiding the fact that I didn't have a radio with me. "It's company."

"I like the radio myself. Is there a play on?"

"I'm not sure what it was." I stayed with the truth. "I didn't hear enough to work out what was going on."

"Oh, well. You mustn't let me interrupt then. I'll see you at breakfast tomorrow. Seven till eight-thirty."

"Thanks for the receipt."

"My pleasure, Mr Dawson. Enjoy your day."

I closed the door, but had the feeling she lingered in the corridor. To make the point, I went into the tiny bathroom, quietly filled the small plastic cup there and used it to pour a long trickle of water into the toilet before flushing it noisily. The fire door down the hall thumped gently as she made her way back downstairs.

In any case I wasn't about to contact Blackbird again. *Not now*, she said. I would try again later. Where was she? Garvin had said he would tell her that I'd gone, but he'd been insistent she would be safe at the courts where she could be guarded. Had something happened? Wherever she was, it clearly wasn't the courts. What had caused her to leave?

The urge to return to the courts and find out what had happened was strong, but that would mean disobeying orders. Also, I assumed that once I had left they had closed the access to the Ways, sealing off the High Court while the negotiations with the Seventh Court were in progress. I comforted myself with the reassurance that Blackbird had looked after herself for many years before I knew her.

Instead, I would try and find Karen. If I was going to Hull, I could hardly take all my things with me. I'd have to leave my bag but my instinct told me that as soon as I was safely gone the landlady would be back and my belongings would be gently searched, if only to confirm my identity. I slid out the sword and laid it on the chest. If I took the sword and the codex with me, there was nothing else incriminating in the bag. Still, I resented the intrusion.

I placed all my belongings back inside my bag and used a warding to seal the zip, so that it would jam if anyone tried to open it. I left it in plain sight on the bed. The warding was simple but effective. Now if she wanted to look inside it she would have to risk damaging the zip trying to wrench it open. I didn't think her nosiness extended to damaging her guests' luggage. If anyone seriously wanted to look inside they could slit the bag, in which case they would find the clothing and other personal items, but the damage would be obvious. I didn't think anyone would steal my change of clothes.

I would take the sword with me, partly to prevent it being discovered and partly because Garvin would expect me to. His words echoed in my head. "The Warders come armed, Dogstar. Always." I felt momentarily guilty about having left the weapon in the church earlier. No one knew and there was no harm done, but somehow Garvin's disappointment didn't need a witness.

Walking around with a sword, though, wasn't exactly in the spirit of the discretion he had advised. Of course, I could turn all eyes away from me so that no one would notice me or the sword, but that would mean no one would see me, not even anyone whose attention I wanted. What I needed was a way to carry the sword without anyone noticing it.

As long as it was with me I could use my glamour to make it appear to be whatever I wanted: a violin case, a pool cue, a baseball bat. Things that were the same size and shape would be easier, but I could make it appear as anything. None of that would blend in easily for a journalist, though, and the idea was not to raise suspicion.

I settled on an umbrella. The day might be fine, but this was England and even at midsummer the weather could change radically at any time. An umbrella was about the right size and would not cause comment. It also meant I could carry it rather than having it swinging from my hip. I could even shelter under it, if it rained.

Blackbird had done her best to explain that while glamour could not change the nature of a thing, it affected more than the appearance. She had changed a beaker of water into brandy and invited me to drink it. It smelled and tasted like brandy and I had felt the burn in my throat as I swallowed it. The alcohol found its way into my bloodstream and I could feel it warming my blood. Within moments, though, the effect was gone.

"As long as it's brandy, it's the same, but as your body absorbs it, it loses its form and returns to being water again. Your body absorbs the water and you become sober."

Holding the sword, I focused my power until I held a long black umbrella. Was it an umbrella or a sword? Did it matter as long as I stayed dry? I shook my head, still not understanding the difference.

I locked the door behind me and went to find the landlady to ask for a front door key, explaining that I didn't know what time I would be back. She wished me a good day and I left, climbing the long hill from the harbour to the backstreets where the gardens blended back into the hillside. I wrapped myself in misdirection, using my glamour to turn curious eyes away and allowing me to leave the town unnoticed. I found the Way-point and consulted my codex.

From here there was only one place I could go: the step out to the churchyard where the monolith stood among the gravestones would take me in the right direction and after that I would have to turn south. The codex showed a little sketch of the monolith with the church behind it, making me wonder who had drawn it. I followed the references through the codex until I had a plan of how to reach Hull. It was a circuitous route, but there didn't seem to be a better way and it was only four short hops.

I stepped on to the node and felt beneath me for the Way. In a second, I was somewhere else. The churchyard was silent and empty, the rising sun striping the shadow of the standing stone across the graves like an ancient sundial. I felt down into the rock below me and found the branch in the node, leading away in the direction I wanted. The next node found me unexpectedly in a room full of people. There were brooms sweeping and sounds of banging. My arrival swirled dust up into people's eyes, my misdirection turning them away as I barely registered the clamour, stepping again, using my momentum to skip across the node, heading in vaguely the same direction.

I arrived in pitch darkness and stayed quiet in case there were anyone in the dark with me. I listened for a few moments but the only breathing I could hear was my own. I cursed myself for leaving behind the torch I had been given. Garvin's words about preparation echoed in my head. Then a memory surfaced: I had once seen Raffmir conjure a cold light like foxfire from thin air, but after several unsuccessful tries I came to the conclusion that there must be a trick to it. The room stayed resolutely black.

I called the only light I knew how to make. Gallowfyre spilled out of me, rippling and shifting around me like moonlight through treetops. This was the gift of the wraithkin, a dappled light that illuminated only dimly but would allow me to absorb the life essence of other beings, which was its true purpose. Using it as illumination was like using a finely crafted sword to chop wood. It confirmed that I was alone, though. This was underground, as many of the Way-points were. Blackbird had told me that they were often found closer to the earth. The space was arrayed in long arched compartments, like a wine cellar, each identical to the next. Walking around, I saw no remnant of occupation and no sign of wine. Whoever used this space had cleared it bare. Something about the arrangement felt claustrophobic, even though it was empty.

I pulled out my codex but the shifting light was tricky to read by. Following the links, I found the description of the cellar and was relieved to discover I was in the right place. The next step would take me into the edges of Hull. Returning to the spot where I had arrived, I let the Way carry me from that bare utility to a more familiar musty smell of damp stone and old books. Thin shafts of light sliced through the dust created by my arrival, allowing me to find the external doorway.

I could hear the city noises before I unbolted the door. Beyond, there was a small set of stone steps leading up to daylight. I closed the door behind me and climbed into the sound of traffic and seagulls. I had arrived.

A newsagent was the first call, for a street map. After that it was easy enough to make my way through the streets down towards the river and find the college. It took me longer than I'd thought and I began to wonder if I should have used the Way to travel further in towards the centre. Then I had to find the bit of the college where I needed to wait for Zaina. Looking around, it all seemed very modern. There were few old buildings and much new development.

At ten past four I arrived at the main college entrance. I waited by the glass doors, leaning against the wall, watching the young people leaving, clothed in every style. Greg had said that Zaina would know where Karen would be, but if she had left early and I had missed her then I would have to go to the café named on the slip of paper Greg had given me. The trouble was that I had no idea what Zaina looked like. The name sounded Middle Eastern, maybe? Lebanese would fit with the name of the place – the Cedars Café.

Two Asian girls turned my way.

"Excuse me, I'm looking for Zaina. Do you know if she's left yet?"

"Zaina who?" they asked in unison.

I shrugged. "I don't have a second name."

They shook their heads as they wandered away.

I tried again with a girl who might have been Middle Eastern. "Do you know where I can find Zaina?" She shook her head and continued walking.

The crowds were starting to thin and I was asking everyone as they left. No one knew Zaina, and there was no sign of Karen. I asked a tall guy with long shaggy hair in a leather jacket. He didn't recognise the name or the café. "Sorry, mate."

I was getting nowhere at the college. I wasn't even sure I had the right door or the right building. The flow of people had thinned considerably and I was running out of people to ask. I switched instead to asking for directions to the café, and after a couple of blank looks I got a set of directions. It was about a mile away and I had already walked a fair distance, but maybe I could get a drink and a sit-down when I got there.

When I reached it, the café was on a side street not far from the main road and had a sign over the door with a stylised black and green cedar tree. It didn't look like much from the outside but when you got close you could tell it went back quite a way. The window advertised Lebanese delicacies like kibbeh and falafels in pitta. My mouth watered at the thought of food. The bacon sandwich had been a while ago.

Inside, the café smelled of spices and coffee. We were long past lunchtime but the lingering aroma had my stomach rumbling. There were tables all down one side and a counter at the back. I had not come here to eat, though. A tall man with dark eyes and residual stubble watched me as he busied himself behind the counter.

"Hi. I'm looking for Zaina. Is she around?"

He glanced up at me but continued cleaning out the remains of lunchtime sandwich fillings. "You a friend of hers?"

"Not really. I'm trying to find someone, a friend of a friend, you might say. I thought she might be able to help."

"She's not here." The lie was clear and plain in his voice.

"OK," I said. "She's not here for me, or she's just not here?"

He wiped his hands on the cloth he'd been using. "Who are you? What do you want with Zaina?"

"I'm only looking to talk with her for a few moments. It won't take long."

The man spoke in a rapid guttural tongue to two men at a nearby table. They stood up, pushing their chairs back noisily. One of the other men further down the café stood up as well. Suddenly the space seemed narrow and claustrophobic.

"I'm not looking for any trouble," I said, shifting my grip on the umbrella. "I just want to speak to her."

"Why can't you people leave her alone?" said the man.

He dropped the cloth and moved around the counter. I retreated, placing my back to the wall and trying to watch both sides at once. The umbrella stayed an umbrella. None of them were armed. There were four of them and one of me. It would be better if we could avoid conflict, but if there was a fight, the big guy from behind the counter would be the one who would start it.

"I don't want anyone to get hurt," I said, trying to calm everyone.

One of the two young men spoke. "You're the only one who's gonna get hurt. If I were you, I would leave while you still can."

"What is this? What's going on? Ahmed, who is that man?" The voice came from the doorway to the kitchen at the back of the café. It should have been

Arabic-sounding, but the accent was pure Ravensby. I peeked past the big guy to see who spoke. The head-scarf and the long dress did not look out of place, but the face was too pale for the Lebanon. Besides, I recognised her from the photo.

"Hello, Karen," I said.

EIGHT

Karen Hopkins bustled forward. "What are you doing? Ahmed? Who is this man?"

"He's just leaving," said Ahmed, meeting my eyes and nodding towards the door.

"How do you know my name?" she asked me.

"I saw your mother this morning," I told her. "I was looking for Zaina, but now I've found you."

"Well, as you can see, I'm not lost. What do you want?"

"Look," I said, "I don't want any trouble. I just want to talk to you for a few minutes."

The young man looked angrily at me. He shook his head. "He was asking about you, poking his nose in."

"And so you threatened him." She walked up to him and straightened his clothes, her distaste for violence plain.

"I didn't threaten anyone. I just wanted him to leave us alone."

"Us"? This was an interesting development.

She turned to the men standing in the narrow aisle. "Please, sit. You're not helping."

They looked at Ahmed and he nodded. They slowly sat down again, watching me all the while as if I might suddenly sprout horns. I tried to look as relaxed and unthreatening as possible.

"I won't keep you long," I said. "I just wanted to ask you a few questions."

"Did my mother put you up to this?"

"No, but I did talk to her. She wants you to call her."

"She said that? Really?"

"She said you'd only have to pick up the phone. You could even reverse the charge."

"Right. That sounds more like her."

"Don't you want to talk with her? You could just let her know you're OK. She's bound to be worried about you."

"She said that as well, did she?" She watched my expression. "I thought not."

I was missing something here. I looked at her again. The headscarf and the long skirt were almost ethnic dress, not so much a fashion statement as a cultural statement.

"I'm sorry, I was only asking about Zaina and your boyfriend here got heavy with me."

"He's not my boyfriend."

Her voice was like her mother's but she had picked up some of his accent. "Whatever you say."

"He's my husband."

It suddenly came into focus. "Of course, you're Zaina. Greg Makepeace told me, 'If you find Zaina, you'll find Karen.'" I mentally kicked myself for being so dim.

"Mum's vicar?" she said. "He came to the café one day. We talked for a while. He brought me some things from home, personal things. What's he got to do with this?"

"So your mother knows you're here too?" I said.

"Who *are* you?" Ahmed said. "Why is this any of your business?"

"I'm sorry," I said. "My name's Neal Dawson. I'm looking into the disappearance of a number of young

150

women from Ravensby. I thought Karen was one of them."

"Do I look like I'm missing?" she asked.

"No, I guess not."

"Then you can cross me off your list." She guided her husband gently towards the counter, turning her back to me.

"Does your father know where you are?"

"I do not discuss my personal affairs in public like a soap opera." She moved towards the door into the back of the café.

"Your sister?"

She stopped and turned back.

"Why can't you let it alone?" she said.

"I have my reasons."

She looked up at her husband and he looked back at me. Then she came forward again and pointed at the table next to the window, away from the other customers. "Sit there." She instructed.

I moved slowly past the men who had stood to help Ahmed. They watched me with cold disapproval. Karen spoke with Ahmed behind the counter in low tones until he turned away and picked up his cloth, sulkily continuing to clean out the counter. Then she disappeared into the back for a moment, reappearing with a white cotton apron tied around her waist to serve the men who sat near the counter with hot tea and sweet sticky pastries. When she had spoken to them for a moment she came and placed a glass cup with steaming liquid with a spoon in it on my table.

"Mint tea," she said. "It makes you look more like a customer and less like a bouncer."

I thanked her and she turned back to the older gentleman. She addressed him in a mixture of English and what must have been Arabic. After talking with him for a moment she went back behind the counter, removed the apron and brought her own mint tea to sit opposite me.

"It's normally busier than this," she said, sliding into the seat.

"That must be good for business," I replied.

"We get by." She glanced towards her husband.

"Was that Arabic you were speaking?"

"I'm not very fluent," she said modestly, "but our customers appreciate the attempt."

"It must be hard for someone with your background."

"I need to learn it anyway, in order to study the Qur'an."

"Is that what you're studying at college?"

"No. I converted. It's part of the faith to understand the words of the prophet."

"To Islam?"

"No, Buddhist. Of course to Islam. I converted so that we could get married."

I looked over at the man behind the counter. He was trying to talk to one of the young men and watch us at the same time.

"Jealous type, is he?"

"Jealous? Ahmed? Don't be daft." The way she said Ahmed was soft, like a sigh.

"He hasn't taken his eyes off you since you sat down."

"He thinks you're going to steal me away, take me back to my family." She looked up. "Are you?"

Her eyes were grey, at odds with the Muslim dress and Arab café, but they held my gaze, waiting for an answer.

"No. I'm not here to take you back."

"Did Mum hire you?"

"Hire me?"

"You're a private detective, aren't you? That's what people like you do, isn't it? Dig around in other people's business."

It was my turn to laugh. "A detective, me?"

"What then? You're not church and you're not a copper either. They've been and gone. The police won't interfere now that I'm eighteen and the vicar only came to check up on me for Mum. You're not a fisherman and you move like a fighter. Ex-military? Private security?" It was her turn to watch me.

"I have done some security work," I admitted. I liked this girl. She had spirit and intelligence. She knew what she wanted and it sounded as if she was working hard to get it. The contrast between her and the soft resignation of her mother was stark.

"I saw your mother this morning."

"What did she say?"

"Very little. I asked her whether she'd given up hope and she told me she hadn't."

Karen looked back towards the counter.

"She said if you wanted to come back then all you had to do was pick up the phone."

She stirred the mint tea slowly. "Was my sister there?"

"Shelley? Yes."

"She should be at school. What was she doing at home?"

"She said she was ill."

Karen looked up from her tea.

"She didn't look ill," I said. "She looked like she'd blagged a day off."

"She should be at school," she repeated. "But maybe my parents think education is not such a good thing any more, when you can have ideas, friends of your own, people from outside." She looked again at Ahmed. "What did my dad say?"

"Your dad wasn't there."

"Did he call Ahmed a wog again?"

"He wasn't there, Karen. I only met your mother."

"Pity."

"I didn't come to persuade you to come back either. Only to find out what happened to you."

153

"Did Mum ask you to do this?"

"No. Your mum said that if you meant to come home then you'd find a way."

"Then who?"

"I came on my own. Greg Makepeace told me where I might find you."

"The vicar? What for? What does he get out of this?"

"He wants me to leave it alone, to stop looking for missing girls. I think you were meant to persuade me to let sleeping dogs lie."

"That still doesn't give me a reason."

"Sorry?"

"You still haven't told me why you came looking for me. If it wasn't for anyone else then why?"

"I'm writing a story, if I can find enough material. It might sell to the Sundays, or a magazine."

"A journalist?"

"Perhaps – when I'm not doing private security."

She looked again at Ahmed. "It's not much of a story. I met my husband at college. Everyone else wanted to get in my knickers but Ahmed saw me as a person. We talked and spent time together, we got to know each other. We were friends long before anything else. Last year his father died, suddenly. An aneurysm, they said, leaving him and his mum to run the café. I started helping out and we got to know each other better."

"You helped in the café, and he asked you to marry him?"

"You make it sound mercenary. It wasn't. He told me that if he could, he would ask me to marry him, but that it could never be. He had the café, his mother, his religion. There were too many barriers. I didn't hesitate. I said yes, even though he hadn't asked. We had to wait until I was eighteen and I'd converted, but the answer was always yes." She hadn't taken her eyes off him the whole time. I didn't need to ask whether she loved him.

"And your family don't approve."

"You're joking, aren't you? Little brown grandchildren?"

"You're pregnant?"

"No. We'll wait a while; not too long, but a little." She smiled wistfully. "So that's my story. Not exactly Anna Karenina, is it?"

"It might make part of a larger piece, if I can get your parents' view."

"I wish you luck. They won't even talk to me. My father won't have my name spoken in the house." She retied the knot on her headscarf. "It doesn't matter now. I have a new name, Zaina, and a new life. Ahmed said it means beauty. Will you change the names for your story?"

"I can if you want me to. I thought you didn't care what your parents think."

"Ravensby's a small place. Everyone knows everyone else. I don't see why I should be a source of amusement for them."

"I thought you were proud to be where you are? Shouldn't they be allowed to know that there is happiness in the outside world, beyond the harbour and the call centre?"

"As in Christianity, pride is a sin for Muslims. And I don't want to be held up as an example for anyone else. I love my husband, but I still miss my family. Even my dad."

"Do you want me to carry a message to them?"

She stared at her tea for a long time. Then she lifted her eyes to mine. "No."

I drank down the remaining tea and stood, collecting my umbrella from beside the chair.

"Sure?"

"Too much has been said already."

"As you wish. Thanks for the tea. Please give my apologies to your husband. I didn't intend to provoke him."

155

I turned and nodded to Ahmed, who watched me to the door. She stood to clear the glass teacups and crossed back to the counter.

As I was closing the door, she called back to me, "Please?"

I put my head back around the door.

"Tell my sister I miss her." There was a pensive tension in her expression. I think she would have said more if she could.

I nodded and left.

As I walked back through the centre to the bus station, my mind circled around Karen and her family. I could see why Greg wanted me to leave this alone. If the disappearances were all this messy then they were better left as they were. I couldn't help feeling, though, that there was more to it, that Karen was only part of a larger picture. When Garvin had given me the mission and said it was up my street, he must have meant more than elopement, surely?

Having used the Ways twice already that day, I did not trust myself to use them again without becoming distracted and lost. Instead, the nearby bus station offered me a ride that would eventually carry me back to Ravensby. I would arrive late, but despite the interrupted sleep of the previous night I felt restless, not tired. A daughter I couldn't find, a pregnant girlfriend somewhere on the road, an enemy returned and a puzzle I couldn't fathom. I let my mind chew on all those as the bus rumbled over the Yorkshire wolds and down to the coast, the twilight creeping up the hillsides as shadows slid into the valleys. When it finally hissed to a stop in Ravensby, it was dark.

The pubs along the seafront spilled drinkers out on to the pavement. The wind died leaving the evening cool but not chilly. The chip shop was open so I bought cod fried in batter, fresh cooked, so I had to wait. I asked if the fish were locally caught. The answer was terse: not likely. Was there so little support for local industry?

I took my paper-wrapped parcel down to the bench at the end of the harbour wall where the green and red lights gleamed to guide returning boats and the scents of diesel and seaweed were replaced by salt and ozone. I watched the waves trying to undercut the steep bank on the other side of the harbour and ate until my fingers were greasy with chip fat and my lips gritty and sore with salt. I dropped the paper in the bin and walked slowly back along the harbour wall, counting the boats and noting that there were too many to moor at the wall. Some were tethered to others, in places three deep. Was this the consequence of fishing quotas: no reason to work the boats any more? Or did the call centre have its attractions compared to the waves, the weather and the dark?

The dock wall ran in a long seashell spiral, punctuated with iron rings every few yards. I followed it round, watching the lights reflect off the water. I had caught fish from such a harbour, years before, using a line weighted with lead, hooks hanging off the side, baited with bread. I thought Alex would be delighted to catch the wriggling slivers of silver, but she was only concerned that they be released unhurt. When one swallowed the hook and I had to kill it to get it loose, she cried and would not look at me for the rest of the day. I didn't catch any more.

At the end of the harbour the road kinked around the headland, leaving it without pavement and rising to look over the harbour at one side and a shingle beach at the other. Below, massive blocks of concrete tumbled out into the water at the promontory, breaking up the waves, but you could already see that the water was winning. Sooner or later the road would crumble into the sea.

The road curved around and followed the line of the hill above the beach, each house perched above the next to get a better view. The lights dwindled until there were only the pale ghosts of gulls riding the updraft from the cliff. A path dropped away from the road on to the beach and I crunched my way down, my boots sliding on stones until it levelled out into shingle, shifting with the sea.

The waves were luminous in the dark, rising sharply to foam on the shore then sift back into the swell. The breeze buffeted me, tugging at either end of the umbrella, twisting and testing my grip. Each wave was a rush, then a sigh. It had a rhythm of its own, irregular and slow, a leviathan snore.

My thoughts drifted to Blackbird and I was thinking that I would retrace my steps before the tide turned and cut me off from the road, when I encountered something strange. I would have noticed it earlier if I'd been concentrating, but the slow thrum of power beneath me echoed the crump and slide of the waves in a way that felt so natural, it was almost invisible. A Way-point? There was nothing in my codex about a node on the beach.

I felt downwards beneath me, testing the power. Not a Way-point, but something else. I walked slowly up and down the shingle, using the feeling to follow the line. It tracked the line of a stream that ran from tumbled rocks below the cliff down to the sea, staining the shingle dark. I followed it upstream. As I came to the rocks I felt another sensation, a dark prickling across my skin, an urge to turn away. There was a warding. I pushed into it, curious now as to who would place a warding here, and why. What was there to protect?

The warding changed. I found myself looking up at the rock face, wondering how safe it was, imagining rocks crumbling, falling in an avalanche of tumbling stone and dust, crushing bones. Even more curious. The simple warding I had placed on my bag was for the zip to jam, but it was just that. If someone tried to force it, it would not change into something else since I was not there to drive it. There was no intelligence in it.

This was different. I pressed forward again and had the immediate sense that the tide had changed. If I didn't leave right now, I would be trapped. I looked behind me. Was the water closer? Were the waves coming higher up the beach? I looked back at the rocks. The cliff face leaned over me, hanging unsupported. A strong wave would bring the whole cliff down, sliding and crashing into the surf, burying anything in its path under tons of soil and stones.

The last time I encountered a warding this strong had been in the Royal Courts of Justice. The Shade Solandre had left a foreboding, a sense that there was danger waiting for whoever entered. It had been left to keep away the security guards and as a distraction from the real peril that awaited there. She had not remained to guide it, so I was able to overcome it by embracing the creeping unease, holding it up to examination and recognising it for what it was – a baseless fear.

The way this warding shifted and altered, seeking to exploit my fears and find the cracks in my confidence, meant that there was someone giving it intention, someone with power. As I pressed against it, recognising it for what it was, the reaction would warn them that I was here. They would feel me pushing the boundary, testing their strength. The umbrella in my hand became a sword.

I pressed in, clambering over the rocks, following the stream of power. Great slabs of stone lent each other support, tumbled and tilted after some great collapse. The gaps between were deeper darkness, slimy with seaweed and treacherous underfoot. My mind conjured sharp-clawed crabs and poison-barbed spiny urchins. I rejected those too, easing under the arch of rock into the space beyond, finding a smooth cleft in the rock-face, softly luminous with algae where the stream emptied out under the rocks. The warding was intense now, leaving me sweating and claustrophobic as I squeezed through a shallow dip into the gap. The narrow gash of stone clenched around me so that with only a minuscule shrug the earth would grind me up and spit me out. I felt the beginnings of that shrug, the initial trembling in the earth before the quake that would grind one face against the other, chewing me between granite teeth, and then it was gone.

The cave was a tall arch, smooth-sided and worn to the touch, buttressed by pillars of striated stone. The rock floor was gently dished with the stream running through a net of intricate grooves cut deep, so that the water babbled and tinkled beneath my feet. A soft glow filled the space, lit from hollow niches scooped from the wall. In each niche was a skull, human size, bare teeth glinting in the light from the rock behind, eye sockets bearing empty witness. The skulls looked old, the bone yellow and waxy in the diffuse light, the pate parchment-thin. I drew the sword from the scabbard, slowly, silently.

I started counting the grisly trophies as I followed the meandering stream back into the cave. At twenty-something I had to slide between two pillars. I squeezed through, holding the sword unsheathed in one hand, the scabbard in the other behind me, ready to fend off any ambush, but found only more eyeless masks to mark my progress. Ahead, the rock overhead dipped, the roof running into stalactite dribbles between long teeth of stone, open like a maw. The atmosphere felt damp here, and there was a slow dripping. Through the maw, a night-black pool opened out under an upturned bowl of swirled stone. Drips from the roof created expanding circles in the mirror surface, reflecting the ring of glowing grins from the niches spaced around the pool. The skulls looked newer here, the brow-bones white and gleaming.

"You are unwanted here." The voice came from beyond the pool – the dark, the water and the rock making it difficult to pinpoint the source.

"The warding gives that impression."

"You bring bare steel and expect a welcome?"

I slid the sword slowly back into the sheath, holding it ready. I could draw it if I needed to. "Is that better?"

"Improved. Now it is only marred by your presence. Remove that and my equanimity will return."

"Do you make all your guests so welcome?"

"You are not my guest, Warder."

"Or do you let them stay only as long as they light your domain?" I swung my arm out, following the ring of lights from empty eye-sockets.

"Do the Warders involve themselves with trifles now? Is the business of the High Court so dull that the Lords and Ladies must concern themselves with me? What have I done to draw such attention?"

"That's a good question. What have you done?"

"Me? I have kept my promise, that's what I've done. I kept my word. It is for others to keep theirs."

"And what promise is it that you keep?"

"Four times score, times score again. Where are their promises now? Where are they? Faithless, feckless, feeble scum, worth naught but the ground they grub in. A few toys, a few trinkets and they're lost. Well, they're reaping a just harvest now, aren't they?"

"Are they?"

"Leave, Warder. Leave and do not return. There is nothing for you here. Just hollow bones and hollow promises. An empty harvest."

"Where are the girls? What have you done with them?"

"The girls? Ah, yes, the girls. Maids, mothers and daughters. See them arrayed around you, proof of a bargain sealed and kept. But there must be another, and soon! It is time!"

"No more. That's enough." I drew the sword, letting the blade ring. "You may not have another."

"Fool! Let's see you sharpen your steel with water and stone. Then see how keen you become."

There was a slithering sucking sound and the water bulged momentarily, ripples spreading from the opposite side of the pool out towards me. I braced my feet, readying my stance, expecting a lunge from the water. The ripples bounced from the edge and reflected. Then a low rumbling shivered through the rock. The grinding of great stones vibrated through the floor. The pool shivered and bulged, then exploded in a great fount of white water. My feet were swept out from under me and I was skimming backwards, slithering in the wild water. I slammed against the twin pillars and the water pressed against me until I was squeezed through the gap. I struggled to hold my sword as I was bounced between the smooth walls, feeling it score down the rock. The water crashed into the crevice and I was thrown up and out, popped like a cork, to thump heavily into the shingle under a stream of spray, my scabbard and sword still in hand.

Garvin would have been proud.

A low chuckle greeted me as I slowly sheathed the sword and rolled over, testing for breaks and bruises.

"Dogstar, you look a little flushed." It was Raffmir.

"Very funny." Nothing was broken and I was used to the bruises.

"I see that you are enhancing the reputation of the Warders, even as we speak."

"What are you doing here?" I looked around but he was alone. "Weren't you supposed to have an escort?"

"My diplomatic liaison appears to be unable to follow where I lead, but I'm sure someone will arrive in due course. However, I thought I would take the opportunity to speak discreetly. I must apologise. I hadn't expected to find you bathing, and fully dressed too." He smiled and offered me his hand.

I waved him away and stood, pushing myself unsteadily to my feet on the shifting shingle. "What do you want, Raffmir?"

"If it's a bad time, I can come back later. Perhaps you hadn't finished your ablutions?"

"Just... say what you came to say. You didn't come here to give me marks on style and presentation."

"Hmm, presentation. Is that weed in your hair?"

I brushed sand into my hair, trying to remove the weed, before realising that there was no weed. "Very funny. Am I keeping you? Is there someone else who would appreciate your banter, someone with a more childish sense of humour, perhaps?"

"I can think of no one for whom it would be more appropriate, but I didn't come to comment on the weakness of your tactics, I came to offer my help."

"Your help? Doing what? Are you volunteering for the Warders?"

"Not as a Warder, no. I wanted to offer my personal assistance with the difficulties you're having."

"Difficulties?"

"Your daughter. I believe you may have misplaced her."

"Why would you think that?" I didn't want Raffmir anywhere near my daughter, even though he was sworn not to harm her.

"Is she not lost, then? Do you have her secreted safely somewhere?"

"I'm not sure where she is," I told him, being careful to speak only the truth, "but that's not unusual. She has her own life."

"All's well, then." The sardonic smile appeared on his lips. "But if you do happen to lose track of her, then my offer of assistance still stands." He made to leave, walking back along the beach.

"Why would I come to you for assistance, Raffmir? I told you before, you don't have anything I want."

He paused in his walk across the shingle, and spoke without turning back, his voice almost drowned out by the sibilant crash of the waves.

"Dear boy, because I am the only one who can show you how to reach her."

He walked away into the dark. I stumbled after him, my feet sliding on the loose stones underfoot. "You know where she is. Where is she, Raffmir? Where have they taken her?"

I ran after him, following the track just above the tide where the ground was more solid. It was no use. He'd gone. My words found an empty beach. I willed the sword to be an umbrella again and scrambled my way back up the incline, covered in grit and sand, still soaked to the skin. The wind chilled me quickly and by the time I reached the road I was shivering, despite the warm night. All the way back to the guest house I watched the shadows, wondering if he was lurking there, amusing himself with my misfortune. When I arrived at The Dolphin, I had to use my key. Nevertheless, Martha was waiting for me.

"Oh, Mr Dawson, it looks like you've been in the water. What on earth happened?"

"I went for a walk on the beach. I slipped."

"Oh dearie me, we can't have you walking round like that, the carpets will get wet."

"Well, I can hardly strip here in the hall, can I?"

"Come through to the kitchen. I'll find you one of Gerald's robes. What were you thinking of?"

"As I said, I slipped."

I followed her through a door at the back of the hall to a kitchen with a vinyl-tiled floor. She made me stand on newspaper until she'd found a towel and brought a towelling robe from the back rooms.

"There's a toilet through that door behind you. You can get out of your wet clothes in there. I'll have to dry your shoes out in front of the range. I must say, I never expected anything like this." She handed me the robe.

"I'm quite all right. I can manage."

"Nonsense. You're shivering and you'll get sand everywhere. Get out of those clothes and I'll get them washed tomorrow. There'll be an extra charge for a service wash, especially with the state they're in. You do realise that, don't you?"

"That's fine." I was beginning to think she was enjoying herself.

"That's one of Gerrald's old ones. It doesn't matter if it gets wet. Just get yourself dry. Here's a towel." She passed me a hand towel that had also seen better days.

There was barely room to turn around, with just a hand basin and a toilet. I squirmed out of my clothes, dropping them in a soggy pile on the floor, then dried myself with the towel. The harsh cotton combined with the remnants of grit and sand to chafe my skin. I dabbed off the worst and shrugged into the robe, belting it tightly with the tie, then picked up the pile of sodden clothes and edged out of the toilet.

She held a plastic bag out and I dropped them in.

"Gloria at the laundry will take care of those for you. She does all the linen for us, a proper job. You won't know them."

"Thank you. If it's OK, I'll take my key and go to bed."

"Do you want me to dry your umbrella out in front of the range with your shoes?"

"No, it's OK. That's the one thing that's waterproof. I'll take it upstairs."

"Mind you don't get sand and grit everywhere," she said as I made my way back into the hall and upstairs.

"I'll be careful. See you in the morning."

"Good night, Mr Dawson." She closed the kitchen door behind me.

Back in my room, I locked the door and went straight to the bathroom. Standing in the bath, I unsheathed the sword, washed the blade and wiped it with my hand towel. Then I rinsed out the scabbard, removing any grains of sand, wiped it down and left it over the sink to drain any remaining water. Weapons first, that's what I had been taught. You never knew when you'd need them next and it wouldn't do to have the sword jam in the scabbard from sand or rust.

Discarding my robe, I showered off the remaining sand, setting the shower hot enough to ease the aches and bruises. I wiped the mirror with the towel and inspected my scrapes and scratches. None of it was worthy of attention.

I put on my own robe and left the bathroom light on to keep the fan running, then released the ward on my bag and brought out clean clothes. Whoever had packed had put two full changes in the bag. I wondered whether shopping was also a service the stewards provided. I dried my feet and put on clean socks, pulled on a shirt and trousers and laced my spare boots, feeling immediately better.

The alarm clock at the bedside said it was close to midnight. I was dog-tired. Woken before dawn, using the Ways twice in one day, the walk into Hull, the disaster on the beach – it was all taking its toll and I wanted nothing more than to crawl into bed.

Garvin said that Warders didn't get tired and I wondered if there were a trick to that or if it was just sheer force of will.

Either way, I still had things to do. I tightened the laces of my boots.

NINE

Blackbird or Garvin: who to speak to first? I needed to update both of them, but if I spoke to Blackbird first, I would have to tell Garvin what I knew. I didn't think Blackbird would want me telling him more than she wanted him to know. I sat on the single bed and reached with my intention beneath the surface of the mirror, connecting it to the core of power within me.

"Garvin?" The glass clouded.

"Dogstar? One minute. Stay with me." His voice was loud in the small room. I heard sounds of movement from the mirror, a door closing. "What's the situation?"

"Raffmir was here. I was down on the beach and he was waiting for me." I recounted what had happened.

"Is he there now?"

"No, I went after him, but he vanished."

"The wraithkin delegation were ordered to stay with their escorts. I've lodged a protest with Altair and he says they'll be disciplined as soon as they can be found."

"They've both gone?"

"Yes. They were in their accommodation. The windows and doors were warded. When no one came out we sent in the stewards to see if they wanted anything and they were gone."

"How did they get out without anyone noticing?"

"They're wraithkin. They have their ways."

I was wraithkin too, but I didn't know how to get past a warding without triggering it. "We know where Raffmir went. Any idea about Deefnir?"

"Nothing confirmed. Blackbird's gone too. He may have gone after her."

"I know. I tried to speak to her earlier. She was in a car or a truck. I don't know where she was headed – London maybe?"

"We can't protect her if she's not here, Niall."

"It sounds like she's looking after herself."

"I've sent Amber after Raffmir, Slimgrin to find Deefnir. If they find them they'll bring them back here. Fionh is acting as liaison for the negotiations. Tate, Fellstamp and I are rotating shifts, keeping things tight, though Fellstamp is only managing six-hour stints. So far Altair is happy to sit and talk while we run round after him."

"You want me to come back in?"

"No. I told Altair you were on assignment. It doesn't sound like it's going too well."

"I have to figure out what the assignment is first."

"That's often the way, Dogstar. Keep your head up and your eyes open."

"What did Raffmir mean, when he said he was the only one who could show me how to reach Alex? How did he even know she'd been taken?"

"You already know the wraithkin can listen in on other people without them knowing. If you're his target, Niall, you have to assume that he's overheard every conversation you've had since he got here, maybe even before that. He may have been watching you for months."

"He can't harm me, or cause me to come to harm, without breaking his oath."

"I said before, Niall. They're not here by accident. The negotiations have hit deadlock. Neither side is willing to concede on the major issue – what happens to Blackbird, you and the rest of the half-breeds. Altair's treading water. He's waiting for something. We have to find out what."

"Maybe if Raffmir appears again, I'll ask him."

"Watch out for Deefnir. Raffmir's sworn not to harm you, but there's no restriction on Deefnir. If he gets close, use Warder's discretion."

"If he comes for me, I'll defend myself."

"Try not to kill him. If you do you've made a worse enemy. Deefnir is Altair's grandchild."

"His grandson? I thought Fey weren't fertile?"

"They have problems conceiving, but it's not unknown. Deefnir was born in exile. This is the first time he's been to our world. Try not to make it his last. If it comes to it, though, don't hold back. We can sort out the diplomatic ramifications afterwards. Besides, maybe he's gone sightseeing?" The doubt in that last sentence came clear through the mirror.

"I'll be careful."

"I want to know if you see either of them again. Let me know."

"I will. Thanks, Garvin."

"Stay tight."

I released my connection with the mirror and the cloudiness diminished to a spot in the middle, then vanished.

I reached out again. "Blackbird?" The mirror clouded again, then lightened to a misty grey.

"Blackbird? Can you hear me?"

There was a hissing sound that deepened to a low buzz. I rose and placed my hand on the mirror, strengthening the connection with touch. The mirror chilled under my hand, outlining my fingers in condensation.

Snatches of her voice stuttered through the mirror, fragments of words, jumbled together.

"Blackbird? Where are you?"

I let the connection build gently under my hand, conscious of how the mirror had shattered when I tried to contact Mr Phillips. Where was she?

Suddenly the connection cleared and I could hear her. "Niall? Is that you?"

"Yes, can you hear me?"

"Yes, I'm out on the fire escape. Where are you?"

"I'm in Yorkshire, a fishing town..."

"You disappeared. I had no idea where you'd gone."

"Garvin was supposed to tell you."

"Garvin told me to sit tight and twiddle my thumbs. Why didn't you tell me the Untainted were here?"

"I didn't know until I was summoned before the High Court. Then Garvin told Altair I was on assignment and Tate bundled me out of the building before they could start anything. Garvin was supposed to warn you."

"He wouldn't say where you were or what you were doing. He told me that Altair had turned up and to stay in the apartment and not to come out for any reason."

"He was trying to protect you."

"Well, he failed. I checked the mirrors in the apartment. They were cold, much colder than the room. They were listening to everything. It wasn't safe. They were just waiting for an opportunity."

"So where are you now? Wait! Don't tell me. They could be listening to us now."

"Let them. I'm with Claire Raddison, the Remembrancer's clerk. No one thought to tell her the Untainted were in town, did they? She's not protected by the Warders or the Courts. We have all the protection we need now. We have all six horseshoes here and if they come for us they're going to get a beating they'll never forget."

"Iron horseshoes? Isn't that difficult for you?"

"You forget. I don't have any magic. There's nothing to react with the iron. I can pick them up and hold them."

The connection suddenly wavered, a strange whining sound coming from the mirror like distorted static. "I'm losing you. Are you there?"

"Sorry, I've put it down again now. They're heavy enough to slug a troll with. We had to carry them between us to get them back to Claire's flat."

"Not exactly a handy weapon."

"It'll do the job, if it comes to it. They won't be able to cross the doorways and if they get inside they'll get a surprise they won't believe. We have more than horseshoes to defend ourselves."

I told Blackbird about Raffmir's visit and Deefnir being Altair's grandson.

"I don't care if he's the Prince of Persia, if he comes near my baby I'll nail him to a doorpost."

I smiled. I should have known she'd find a way to protect herself. "Just be careful. We don't know where they've gone or what they're doing. You'd better warn the Highsmiths at the farm in Shropshire as well, just to be on the safe side."

"It's already done. I spoke to Meg earlier. She said they would take suitable precautions, and they still have the broken Quick Knife. That alone should discourage visitors."

"I'm sorry. I should have warned you myself."

"I will admit, it was a shock. Why are they here?'

"Negotiating a peace settlement. At least that's what Altair says they're doing. Garvin thinks they're here for some other reason."

"Does he know what?"

"No, but Altair asked to have me as his personal Warder. That's why Garvin assigned me here with this mess."

"How is it going?"

I explained about my success in finding the missing girls and my encounter in the cave.

"You went in blind. That was… bold."

"Garvin was good enough not to point that out."

"It's your life you're risking, Niall. A visit from the Warders isn't generally a social call. What were you expecting, a welcome mat?"

"I'll be better prepared next time."

"You're lucky there is a next time. You need to find out what you're dealing with before you go poking about in someone's cave."

"Yeah, I think I got that. I guess I was thinking it was all nothing. The girls weren't missing, they were just somewhere else, doing something else."

"And there were many skulls?"

"Thirty or so, maybe more. Some of them looked really old. This isn't new. It's been going on for a while."

"Then why doesn't anyone know about it?"

"They do. It's in the papers. There are missing posters all over town."

"No, that's for the five or six missing now. Where are the others? If this has been going on all this time, why aren't there records of missing women going back fifty, a hundred, two hundred years? Those skulls could be anyone's. They could be missing sailors, washed up on the beach, for all you know."

"No. Maids, mothers and daughters, he said. They were all women."

"Then they came from somewhere, Niall. Find them."

Another thought occurred to me, sparked by the memory of my stay at Claire's apartment the previous year.

"Do you think Claire would do me a favour?"

"She might. Hang on, I'll get her."

There was a rustling sound and then receding footfalls. Then voices returned.

"And I just talk to the mirror, do I?" It was Claire's voice.

172

"Just like a phone," Blackbird confirmed.

"Hello?"

"Claire, this is Niall."

"Yes, I remember. How are you?" The polite greeting was typical.

I smiled. "I'm a little bruised at the moment, but well, thanks, and you?"

"We're a little jumpy." That was understandable.

"I wanted to ask you a favour."

"Yes, Veronica said." She used the name Blackbird had given herself when they first met.

"You have a friend who works for the government, in the area covered by the Official Secrets Act, by the name of Sam?"

"Sam? I haven't spoken to Sam since that night in the hospital. I think I made it clear that it was over between us."

"I know, I remember. It's just that I need someone who knows that world. It's about my daughter. Black... Veronica will explain. I've lost her and I think the government have taken her. There must be records. Maybe he would be able to find out where they've taken her?"

"I don't even know if he would have access to that information. It's probably not his department."

"It's certainly not mine. I need all the help I can get and I need someone who can make discreet enquiries without setting off alarm bells."

"I don't know, Niall. He probably won't even speak to me."

"Or someone else in that line of work. Is there someone else you know who might be able to find out where they've taken her?"

"No, I don't know any of Sam's colleagues. He never talked about work. Then again, I didn't tell him anything either – not really. We're both quite secretive people."

"Could you ask him for me?"

"It's not that I don't want to, Niall. Without you… well, I don't know where we'd be. But I can't promise anything. He can be really stubborn."

"I really appreciate that, Claire. Thanks."

"I'll see what I can do."

"I'd better go. I have more to do before I can rest."

"I'll let you say goodbye to Veronica, then." Her footsteps receded.

"What makes you think that Sam can help you, Niall?" said Blackbird.

"Maybe he can't, but at least he will know how to find things without drawing attention to me. They don't know there's any connection between us, so even if they find out he's been asking questions, they won't tie it back to me."

"He has no reason to help us, you know that."

"I know, but it's worth a try. The only other option is Raffmir."

"Raffmir?"

I described our encounter on the beach. "He said he was the only one who could show me how to reach her."

"Was he telling the truth?"

"So far as he believes it, yes, though he didn't precisely say he knew where she was, either. It could all be one of his games. He's sworn not to harm me, but there's nothing to prevent him from twisting the knife on my misfortunes to make them as painful as possible. That would count as amusement as far as he's concerned."

"Even bound by his vow, he's dangerous."

"I know, but if Raffmir wanted to harm me he could have sent Deefnir instead. I was vulnerable enough, lying on my back in the shingle. No, he's up to something."

"Like what?"

"I've no idea, but whatever he's offering me, he is going to want something at least equivalent in return."

"A favour in return for the life of your daughter would be a big one, I think. Be careful, Niall. It would please Raffmir greatly to make you choose between your duty as a Warder and your daughter."

"That crossed my mind, too. Then there's the baby. He swore an oath not to cause harm to you or to Alex, but he didn't know about our son. That may be the entire reason they're here."

"We're ready for them. We have some surprises laid on for them if they come."

"I'll tell Garvin where you are, next time I check in. Maybe he can release someone to keep an eye out for you."

"Just make sure they don't walk in on us unexpectedly or they might get a welcome they'll never forget."

"I'll tell him. Look after yourselves. Try and get some sleep."

"We're taking turns. It could be a long night."

"For me too. Take care."

"Bye."

The mirror cleared as the connection faded, leaving condensation dribbling down the glass. Wiping it with my hand only spread the water around. I went into the bathroom and returned with a hand towel to polish the water away. Even afterwards my handprint still showed faintly as the glass slowly warmed.

I wished now I'd said more than "take care". What if something happened to her? What if those were the last words I ever spoke to her? We had been living together since October and I still hadn't figured her out. Sometimes we were so close you couldn't get a sheet of paper between us, while at other times she was distant. I had been trying to puzzle out where I stood for nine months, with little progress.

She'd told me first off that the Feyre didn't marry and that it was up to the females to choose a partner. I had no fundamental objection to that but it left me wondering what there was between us and why she needed me. She was fiercely protective of her independence, to the point where it seemed as if there wasn't room for me in her life at all, but then she could be so possessive that it left me feeling claustrophobic.

Of course, the baby had number one place in her heart, and given how long she had waited for a child, that was no surprise. I knew what that felt like, having a daughter of my own, and there was no resentment. It was just that sometimes I wondered whether second place was really where I was. I caught myself in a sigh and turned it into a shrug.

Maybe I would never understand her.

I slipped into my charcoal jacket. I could conceal myself with glamour, but the dark grey would stand out less in the dark, providing less contrast than a hard black and leaving me free to concentrate my power on other things. I gathered my wallet and keys and left the loose change on the side table so that it wouldn't chink in my pocket. I picked up the small black torch from my bag and sheathed and belted my sword. I jumped up and down twice, testing for rattles. The soft shuffle as my clothes settled and the gentle thump of the sword against my thigh were the only sounds that might give me away. It would do.

Nevertheless, I wrapped a strong concealment around me as I left the room. The fire escape would allow me to leave without using the front door. I nudged it open gently and then let it close quietly behind me. If Raffmir was watching my comings and goings then he couldn't watch the front and the back at once. By using the rear stairway, I could make it harder for him to observe me, assuming I wasn't just being paranoid.

The fire escape led down to a concrete backyard arrayed with wheelie bins and an old stove. This backed on to the yard of another guest house on the next road along. It was easy enough to clamber the wall and exit from there, keeping to the shadows and not showing myself till I was well away from the guest house. I made my way up the hill to St Andrew's church. There were no cars at this time of night, just the faint echoes of the sea on the hush of the breeze. A gull's call broke noisily into the night in a squabble for roosting space and then subsided.

The east window was dark and the door was locked. Greg had said he kept the church locked to prevent theft and vandalism. He hadn't said whether the church was alarmed or not. I scouted round the building. There were two other doors, one tucked behind the church at the west tower and another vestry door on the far side from the main door, but no sign of an external alarm box. Those windows that could be opened looked as if they hadn't been touched in years and were too far off the ground to access without a ladder. I circled back to the main door. If any of the doors were alarmed then the likelihood was that they all were, and at least I knew that this one gave me access to the photos and personal items of the girls who were missing. With those, I could use my power to discover whether the girls were really missing or had simply chosen not to stay in Ravensby.

Merging with the shadows in the porch, I surveyed the black oak door. I had seen Blackbird open locked doors like this a number of times but I had never done it myself. While I knew it could be done, I had never had call for such skills over the past months. I had been immersed in the regime of Garvin's training. I had once asked Garvin when he would start training me to use my power.

"Do you feel confident and competent with a sword?" he had asked.

I had shaken my head while he smiled his quiet smile.

"Knowing your limits is part of your training. I'll teach you the subtlety and flexibility of power when you can handle something simple, like a sword."

I had accepted his answer with good grace, seeing the sense in his words, but I wished now that I had made better progress so I would have some idea what I was doing. I guess I would just have to improvise.

I felt inside and connected to the core of power within me. A dark tendril wormed its way out of the cold bright core at the centre of my being. Not for the first time, I wondered what it was that I connected with. Was it a creature? When Blackbird called me back to life on the London Underground last year, had she conjured some creature to live within me like a parasite? Was I simply its host? If I summoned gallowfyre it was like releasing a tentacled creature of dark shadows. Was that what lived inside me? It would suck the life energy of anything within reach unless I constrained it, and feed me with the life energy of others. Did that make it some sort of symbiotic life-form? Blackbird said not. She said that gallowfyre was an expression of my link with the void, the element associated with the wraithkin. She laughed when I asked whether it was alive.

"Only as much as your arm or your leg is alive." She laughed. "It's you, Niall."

I wasn't sure that explanation made me any more comfortable.

I placed my hand on the dark oak of the door and allowed the tendril of power to worm its way into the wood. In my mind's eye, it explored the crevices and cracks, tasting the bitter wood. Though there was no physical taste, my mouth still ran with saliva in reaction to the sensation. It wound around the knots, following the grain.

Suddenly there was a hard jolt. I almost jerked my hand away. It felt sharp and hot. The tendril had discovered something embedded in the wood. It felt sour, a spike of harsh metal embedded in the door. I realised we must have encountered an old nail or a bolt, embedded in the wood. The essence of it had seeped into the surrounding wood, tainting the oak. The tendril curled around it, avoiding where it pierced the door.

My power threaded slowly through the wood, searching for weaknesses and flaws, exploiting cracks. It was slow and difficult, worming through, looking for a way to release the lock, and it took all my attention. I realised that if anyone came looking in the small porch while I was there I would be discovered. I didn't have the concentration to hold my glamour, investigate the door and keep a lookout at the same time.

Momentarily distracted, my attention came back to the tendril. While my mind was elsewhere, it had done something strange. It had branched. Where there had been one exploring tendril before, now there were two – no, three, four, it was branching quicker than I could count. The whole door was soon threaded through like ivy on a wall, woven through every crack and crevice. I could feel every nail, each knot and curve in the grain. It was still locked, though. How did Blackbird get doors to pop open?

I could feel where the lock was screwed into the door. I tried extending the tendrils into the lock, but it was as sour and bitter as the nail had been. I could force my way into it, but all I could discern was the bitterness of the steel with no sense of the lock. Anyway, what was I intending to do, try and pick it? I had no idea how to pick a lock, even if I had tools and could do it where I could see it. There had to be another way.

Using the power threaded through it, I felt the door and willed it to open. The wood groaned under my

179

hand, flexing at my will. It pinged and creaked until I thought it would crack. Breaking the door wouldn't help: it would be obvious that someone had broken in. I wanted to be inside, but I didn't want anyone to know I had been there.

I withdrew the tendrils of power from the door and dropped my hand away. Dispirited by my failed attempt I walked around the church again, looking for a way in. I could break in, but that would be vandalism. I didn't think Greg deserved that. I could wait until the morning and ask for his help, but I didn't want to explain what I was intending to do. He was far too good at seeing the truth in things. I could contact Blackbird and ask her how she did it, but I was hoping she would be asleep by now, tucked up with horseshoes for comfort, and if I asked Garvin he would likely tell me that I shouldn't be there in the first place.

I returned to the porch and sat on the bench that lined one side. It was ridiculous to be defeated by a simple locked door. I had watched Blackbird do this a number of times. What would she say if she were here?

You're trying too hard. Relax, let it come.

That was all very well, but it wasn't happening.

You don't catch a pigeon by chasing it.

That wasn't much use, either, was it?

A cake is a cake, a mouse is a mouse, a door is a door.

What had she been talking about when she said that? She had been baking, something I never expected of her, but which made her happy even when she was throwing up from morning sickness. The smell of cooking had woken me and I had come down to find her in full production. While her back was turned I stole a small bun dotted with currants, still warm from the oven. She had smiled when the crumbs on my cheek had given me away, but then frowned when I asked what it was made of.

180

"Cake," she said.

"I meant, what were the ingredients."

She picked up a bun and examined it critically. "Cooking is like magic. A cake is more than butter and sugar and flour. When you bake them they become something else. A cake is a cake, as a mouse is a mouse and a door is a door. You can't unmake it and get sugar, butter and flour back. It's made of cake."

How did that help me open a door? A cake is a cake, a door is a door.

I had once sealed a door in my flat by imagining the door nailed shut. That had worked fine, so why didn't it work when I wanted a door open?

You're trying too hard.

I placed my hand on the door. It was a locked door. I wanted an open door.

It *was* an open door.

There was an answering clunk. I tested the handle and the door swung open. Success! I had been trying to unravel the door into a lock, wood, nails, handle and everything else that went into it, instead of treating it like a door that was either locked or open. Chalk up one to me. I closed the door behind me and stood in the darkened transept. Inside, the church had a silence only buildings made of solid stone can muster. Placing my hand back on the door, I re-locked it. I didn't want to be disturbed.

I clicked on the torch, being careful to keep the beam low so it wouldn't show through the windows and attract unwanted attention. The photo board in the corner was what I wanted. I already knew that Karen wasn't dead, so maybe the others weren't either. That would still leave the mystery of where the skulls had come from, but maybe that was a different question.

I needed a link with the girls to find them and the photos from the board might provide that link. Asking Greg

181

if I could borrow them might prompt questions I didn't want to answer. Besides, they weren't really his photos.

Maybe with them I could discover whether the girls really had bunked off, as Geraldine in the café had said, or if, instead, they were lining the walls of a cave by the shore. I selected photos that were good clear pictures of the girls and removed them, taking care to note their positions and leaving the pins in place.

I looked around for a mirror. I couldn't see one in the body of the church, but then weren't mirrors symbols in themselves? I recalled that I had been told once that mirrors were the domain of the father of lies, Satan himself. An image of a Baptist minister who had visited my school when I was a young child popped into my head. He had talked of brimstone and fire and everlasting damnation until the teacher had thanked him coldly for his time and ushered him out. He wasn't invited back. I wondered what he would think of me now, with my affinity for mirrors and ability to change my appearance at will. It would have been enough to give him apoplexy then, but he would be an old man now, if he was still alive. Maybe he had mellowed, though somehow I doubted it.

Wandering around slowly, I deduced that even if mirrors were the symbol of the devil, you still wouldn't want to stand up in front of a congregation without combing your hair first. A door marked 'Vestry' provided the answer. I entered and found a room with a rack of vestments hanging on one side and on the other a mirror at head height. On a night-stand under the mirror was a small bowl containing pot-pourri, adding a homely touch.

I set the bowl aside and, taking the photos, laid them out on the night-stand below the mirror. The smiling faces of Debbie Vaughan, Gillian Mayhew, Trudy Bilbardie and Helen Franks looked out at me. I set Debbie's picture on top and looked at it, trying to get a feel for the girl from the photo. In the dim light of my torch the face was bleached out, but maybe the photo had been overexposed. Her eyes were bright and she seemed excited about something. Maybe it was a birthday celebration, or a party.

I set my hand on the mirror and focused on the photo. "Debbie? Debbie Vaughan?"

The mirror chilled under my hand and the glass clouded. A soft glow crept into the vestry. Whereas before it had felt enclosed and small, it now felt as if it had expanded. I had opened a window to somewhere else and the sounds from that place were drifting through. There was a breeze, and a clock chimed distantly. Then it veered, the clock chime dimming as if we were moving away fast. There was a motorbike sound, but we passed it as if we were speeding in the opposite direction. It hovered, the sound of cars somewhere below.

"Debbie? Where are you?" My voice was like a whisper on the breeze.

The sound suddenly focused and burst into the room. The heavy beat of dance music, driving bass over a thumping electronic drum beat. I released the mirror, suddenly conscious of the cacophony and worried I would attract attention, but not before I had heard voices. A female voice shouted over the music.

"Yeah, a'right?" The accent was unmistakable. I had found Debbie.

I listened intently, expecting any moment for thumping to sound on the outer door with demands to come out and show myself. The church stayed silent. Wherever Debbie was, she sounded as if she was having a good time. I was beginning to think the whole missing-girl scenario was a wild goose chase to keep me busy while they dealt with Altair and his entourage back at the courts.

I swapped the pictures over, replacing Debbie's face with Gillian's. She looked relaxed and comfortable. Her frizzy hair framed her face as she leaned forward to speak to someone. The picture looked as if it had been taken without her knowledge and I could imagine her being shy and not wanting to be photographed.

My hand returned to the mirror. "Gillian? Gillian Mayhew?"

The sense of opening repeated, shifting the ambience. It sounded close: the wash of waves and the distant screech of gulls echoed around. Was she here in Ravensby?

The sound expanded as if we were rising, the waves receding and the breeze stiffening. It diffused until we were far above the landscape. Was she up in the hills? The sound continued to expand, until everything was faint and diffuse.

"Gillian?"

Under my hand, the sound dissipated and faded to nothing. The mirror dimmed, then cleared.

I tried again. "Gillian? Are you there?"

The mirror clouded under my hand momentarily, then cleared. No sound emerged.

My mind sifted through the possibilities. Maybe she was asleep. Maybe she was unconscious, or in a coma in a hospital somewhere. Maybe she just couldn't be reached.

Or maybe her eyeless gaze flickered in candlelight over a darkened pool in a cave by the beach.

TEN

I took my hand from the mirror. I'd thought this would give me some certainty, not leave me with a gnawing doubt. Surely I would be able to tell if someone was alive? I slid the picture of Gillian towards me and looked down at her. If I couldn't find her through the mirror, where was she?

I swapped her photo for the one of Trudy Bilbardie. Trudy was pressed between two other girls, all in long dresses, bright smiles for the camera, flowers in their hair and dressed up in finery, perhaps for a party or a summer ball. I knew which girl was Trudy because she was in the other photos pinned to the board in the church, but this had been the clearest and the best. I wondered whether the two other girls missed their friend and what they thought had become of her.

I placed my hand on the mirror and murmured to the glass.

"Trudy. Trudy Bilbardie. Where are you?"

The result was the same as for Gillian. The soundscape of Ravensby opened up and expanded until it dissipated into nothing. After that, no amount of trying would persuade it to focus. Was it the pictures? If they had changed their appearance, dyed their hair, changed their look, would that prevent me from finding them through the mirror? While part of me hoped that might be the explanation, another part came to a simpler conclusion.

I swapped pictures again. This time, Helen Franks had simply posed for the shot. She was smiling, but with that slightly forced look that people have when the photographer waits a little too long.

"Where are you, Helen Franks? Are you there?"

The mirror around my hand misted and then went milky white, spilling moonlight on to the photos. Background sounds shifted and wavered. Then the sound suddenly focused. It became muted and soft as if it were close or contained, matching the ambience of the vestry. Then came a whine, some way off, like a small animal. It grizzled then paused, then grizzled again. Suddenly it developed into a full-blown wail, a baby's insistent cry, a repetitive insistent yell that would not be denied.

Soft rustling followed, then another voice emerged. "All right, I'm coming, I'm coming. Mummy's coming. I can hear you."

There was a shuffling, shifting noise and the wail was briefly muffled, then came again, even louder.

"There, I've got you. I've got you. There, there. Shh-hhhh. There's no need for that, is there? It's all here for you."

There was a snuffling, mumbling noise and then a soft rhythmic slurping.

"There, then. That's better. You were just hungry, weren't you? All better now. All better."

Feeling as if I was spying on something deeply personal, I gently removed my hand, not wanting to disturb that moment of quiet intimacy, even slightly. Wherever Helen Franks was, she was probably sleep-deprived, irritable and wondering whether she could cope, but that was motherhood. I had found her and she was well. I didn't want to intrude any further.

I placed the photographs of Helen and Debbie on one side and returned to the pictures of Trudy and Gillian. I'd started with five young women who were missing. I had Karen, who was living in Hull with her husband, Helen, who was a nursing mother, and Debbie, the party girl. Even if no one knew where they were, they were OK, and that was all that was important. As Greg had said, you had to figure out what people needed before you tried to help them. If Helen and Debbie didn't want their families to know where they were, then maybe they had their reasons. They were young women, not children.

That left me with two who were still missing. I looked up into the mirror. The bags under my eyes spoke of too many late nights and early mornings, but there was one more thing I could try. I placed my hand gently on the mirror and whispered softly into it.

"Alex?"

The glass cooled and clouded again, bringing a stillness into the room. No sound emerged, no hint of space or location, just deep silence. The glass under my hand chilled and moonlight crept into it, until it glowed from within. Still no clue emerged, but I knew she was there somewhere. With Gillian there had been a sense of dissipation, of dilution beyond any ability to hold the link. This was different. I couldn't reach my daughter, but I knew she was there. I dropped my hand again before my unconscious desire to find her intensified the connection and set off alarms as it had before. I would find her. It was just a matter of time.

It meant something, though. It meant that the two missing women were not unconscious, or somewhere in a coma, or protected from me. I couldn't find them because they weren't there to be found.

That thought stayed with me while I collected the pictures, replaced the bowl of pot-pourri and went back out into the church. I carefully placed the photos back in the positions they had occupied and, checking I was leaving everything as I'd found it, I locked the door behind me and returned through the darkened streets to my room at the Dolphin. The night was quiet. As far as I could tell, no one saw me leave or return, if indeed anyone cared.

Finally done for the day, I undressed and brushed my teeth and crawled into bed. With the light out, the glow from the window reflected a rectangle of orange on to the wall opposite. I thought of Blackbird, sharing watches throughout the night, surrounded by iron horseshoes, listening for any noise that might be an unwanted visitor, knowing that, by the time they heard it, it might already be too late.

My mind drifted to thoughts of Karen, tucked up with Ahmed above the café. Was she happy? It wasn't fair to have to choose between your family and your husband, but then life wasn't fair. I had found myself liking Karen, perhaps because she'd made her choice and was determined to be happy with it. A glimpse into Debbie's life and the contrast couldn't be more vivid. The quiet contemplation and study of the Qur'an were a long way from the pounding music and adrenalin rush of the dancefloor. What time would it be before Debbie made it home? Maybe after first light? If that was her choice, did it make it any less valid?

Was Helen happy? Had anyone known she was pregnant? Is that why she'd disappeared so suddenly, faced with a situation she felt unable to share with anyone? Did she wonder whether she could ever come home? If it were me, it wouldn't matter. An unwanted pregnancy was a serious matter and would affect the lives of more than just the mother and the baby, but it could be accommodated. It was nothing like the hopeless empty loss of a daughter that wouldn't or couldn't be found. Then again, I knew from past experience that not everyone felt the way I did. For some people the public disgrace of an unexpectedly pregnant daughter meant more to them than their child's safety and happiness, an attitude I found incomprehensible. Still, I knew it happened, the parents whose attitude and actions harmed the girl, the baby and ultimately themselves. Was that what Helen feared?

The fey were more pragmatic about such things. They had so few children now that every babe was treasured beyond sense or reason, except by the Untainted. Fey like Raffmir believed that children who were half-breeds, mixtures of fey and human heritage, were an abomination, an affront to nature and a pollution of their racial purity. They thought that humans with fey ancestry would be the downfall of their race, their bloodlines diluted until it made no difference who was fey and who was human. They had tried to prevent the mixing of the races through diplomacy, failed, and then tried to kill all the half-breeds in one fateful night. They failed, and as a result Altair had taken them into exile to another world, an exile he was now trying to end though negotiation.

But how could he? In order to return, the Untainted would have to accept the existence of the gifted, those humans who had, directly or indirectly, inherited the genes of the Feyre. Either that or the rest of the courts would have to abandon their children to a massacre, something I could never see happening. It was a stalemate, so why were they here? What could they possibly hope to achieve? The Untainted would no more accept the sharing of bloodlines with humans than humanity could accept the sharing of their bloodlines with animals.

That thought brought back the mewling, whining cry that had roused Helen from sleep. It was an animal noise. It was a noise I would have to get used to again, once my own baby was born. Feed one end and wipe the other; that was the way it went. I remembered the sleep-broken nights when Alex was tiny. At the time it seemed as if it went on forever but, looking back, it had flashed past. Before I knew it she was walking, talking, running and playing, from teddy bears and ponies to boy bands in the blink of an eye. I was beginning to think she didn't need me any more. Then she was snatched from me.

I would find her. I would.

I lay in the dark, staring at the ceiling. Bruised and exhausted, sleep should have claimed me, but the images of the young women were there every time I closed my eyes. Each time it ended with Gillian. The way she leaned across just as the camera flashed, capturing that moment of unconscious grace, preserving a tableau in two dimensions. In the morning I would have to find a way to tell Greg what I had discovered, but I would leave that problem for later. Maybe he would know how to tell Gillian's and Trudy's families what they needed to know?

But even if Greg told them, how would they know it was true? I knew what it was to be told of a death without the evidence of my own eyes – without proof. Even if he told them, would they believe him? The anger at what had happened to Gillian, to Trudy and to Alex, welled up in me, making my heart pound in my ears and banishing sleep. My thoughts returned to Blackbird and my unborn son, and I started again.

How many times my thoughts travelled that circle, I couldn't say, but sleep must have come eventually because I knew I was dreaming.

• • • •

It was always cold here, yet I didn't feel cold; certainly it was nothing like the bone-chilling ache that Solandre had induced in me to feed from my life force when she trapped me here. Naked, I walked along the path, brushing fingers of pine branches that only moved as I stirred them, the faint scent of resin hanging in the air as I passed. No breeze ever stirred this place.

Looking up, I saw the black sky freckled with stars. They hung there without blinking, like pinpricks in the veil of night, silent watchers of all that transpired here. Beneath my feet, layers of hushed pine needles muffled my tread as I walked between the trees. The path was outlined in moon-shadow where no moon ever shone. All was dark, yet I could see away from the path that the trunks clustered together until there was no space to squeeze between them.

The path widened, as it always did, opening out into a glade surrounded by tangled briars as thick as ropes, spiked with thorns an inch long and wickedly barbed. I hesitated at the boundary, but it was already too late. By the time I looked behind me the path had vanished. The thorns had closed around me and I was trapped.

In the centre of the glade were clothes – a shirt of black silk, trousers of peach-soft black cotton. There were soft leather boots for my feet and silver rings for my fingers. I dressed, but slipped the rings into my pocket. I was wary of accepting gifts if I didn't know who the giver was.

I walked to the centre. It was bigger than I remembered and the ground rose so that all I could see about me was thorns and trees. The sky formed a bowl above me, echoing the ground beneath it.

"Where?" The voice was behind me and I spun around.

A figure was standing at the edge of the thorns. Her hair was short and spiky and she was slightly overweight. I could see this because she was naked. Her skin was pale in the starlight and it made her breasts look full and heavy. She was wearing dark eye make-up and her lips were stained purple, contrasting oddly with her naked state, as if she'd just got undressed and had yet to clean off her make-up. Suddenly conscious of her nakedness, she cupped her arms around her breasts, failing to conceal the bush of pubic hair between her legs.

"Where am I?

I walked slowly towards her, not wanting to cause alarm.

She watched me. "Who are you?" she asked.

I already knew who she was. I had been looking at her photograph, but the accent confirmed it.

"My name is Niall, and you are Debbie."

She looked around and then back at me.

"Niall," she said, as if testing the name on her tongue. "I like your shirt."

"Don't you want to know how I know your name?" I asked her.

She shook her head, "No, don't be daft. You're in my dream. Of course you know my name."

"This isn't your dream. It's mine."

She looked around. "Where is this?"

"I don't know," I admitted.

"If it's your dream, how come you don't know where it is?"

"That's a good point," I said. "Maybe it isn't my dream either."

"Are you going to do me?"

"Am I what?"

She shrugged, then let her arms fall away and cupped her breasts in her hands, holding her nipples up as if for inspection. "You know, here on the ground. It'll be good. All the guys say I'm good."

"All the guys?"

"Are you trying to make out I'm a tart? I'm very choosy, me. I like the strong ones. Do you work up a sweat?"

"A sweat?"

"In the gym. You're pretty toned for an old guy. You are old, though. I would have liked you younger." She started walking around the edge of the glade. "Isn't there a bed, or at least a mattress? I don't wanna get grass stains, even in a dream."

"Debbie. We are not having sex."

She turned back to me. "You're shy." She smiled sweetly. "I like the shy ones. Do you want me on top or underneath?"

"Neither. I mean it. We're not having sex and you have to go now."

"Why?" She turned away. When she turned back, her eyes had filled. "What's the matter with me? Why are all men such bastards?" A wet tear trickled down her cheek. "Now even my dreams don't fancy me."

I stepped forward. "It's not like that. I'm sure you're very…"

She stepped in towards me, sliding her arms round my waist, pressing her breasts into my chest. She lifted her face. "Kiss me," she whispered.

"Debbie!"

I tried to gently ease her away, but she only used the opportunity to rub her breasts on the silk of my shirt, gripping me round my waist and grinding her hips into mine.

"You want me. I know you do. I can feel you."

"This isn't what you think it is."

"You're not small either, are you, baby?" She grinned. "Maybe there's somethin' to older men after all."

"I'm old enough to be your father." I was trying to disengage her, but she clung to me, pressing in.

"You could actually be my father for all I know. Would that make it better? Do you want to be my daddy?"

I grabbed her arms and unwound them from my waist, holding her wrists up between us. I was trying not to hurt her, but she was very determined. She tried to pull her hands away, but I held her tight. She was breathing hard, but it wasn't from struggling. Her pupils were dilated and her tongue licked across her purple lips wetly.

She tested my hold on her wrists. "You're in control, baby."

"Stop it. Stop it now."

She tried to twist out of my grip, forcing me to tighten my grasp. She wriggled under her arms, turning under them so that she could twist into me, her rear pressing roundly into my groin. I released her arms and gave her rump a firm shove, not wanting to hurt her, but making space between us. She stumbled forward, unbalanced, and fell forward on to the nest of thorns.

She screamed as the spikes bit into her flesh, thrashing on the barbs, making it worse. I tried to grasp her arm, to help her back, but she struggled and shrieked, jerking out of my hand. I stepped away, giving her some space. Gradually she stopped struggling and gently and painfully extracted herself from the tangle, unable to contain the gasps of pain as the thorns withdrew. Turning, she opened her arms.

"Look. Look at me."

The blood was running in tiny dribbles from the scratches and punctures all down her arms, legs, breasts and body.

"Look what you've done!"

She wiped her hand over her breast, striping it across the skin so that her hand came away smeared with red. That wasn't what was disturbing me, though. Where the drops fell to the ground or rolled off her skin they vanished. No spot marked the grass. Every one was absorbed by the ground where it fell.

"You're all such bastards," she wailed. "All the same."

She cried, real tears this time, running black mascara down her cheek. Wrapping herself in her arms, she sobbed, and as she held herself, she faded, until there was only the echo of her. The echo died, leaving me alone in the glade under the silent stars.

I jerked awake, sweating. The sheets had clung to my skin where I was wrapped tight into them. It took me a moment to disentangle myself, wondering whether the briars in my dream had been created by getting tangled in the sheet in my sleep. I wrestled free and then stopped. I looked at my arms.

Where I had tried to pull her from the thorns, my arms were criss-crossed with livid weals and deep scratches. My dream had left its mark.

Going back to sleep was out of the question. The thought filled me with a chill that had nothing to do with the temperature. Besides, it was getting light and I had things to do.

I went into the shower and washed the scratches on my arms, drying myself with a towel still soggy from the previous night, dabbing gently at the cuts. The day had dawned wet, heavy clouds hanging low with driving rain coming in off the sea, making the windows rattle and leaving the room in semi-darkness. I left the lights off and opened the curtains, allowing in the minimal daylight through the condensation-clouded window. By the time I'd got clean and dressed, only the worst of the weals remained. One of the advantages of my fey heritage was that I healed pretty quickly, and these were only surface scratches. Even allowing for that, though, they healed with extraordinary speed, as if they weren't really there.

I looked up at the mirror and hesitated. If Blackbird was sleeping then I didn't want to rouse her. They would have swapped watches during the night and she had started out with a sleep deficit. The last thing I wanted to do was wake her when she was getting what little sleep she could. On the other hand, I needed to talk to her and I had no idea whether she would be sleeping now or later. I would have to take my chance.

I placed my hand gently on the mirror and reached within to connect it to the core of power within me.

"Blackbird?"

ELEVEN

Blackbird wasn't happy to be woken by being prodded. "What?" It had taken her forever to get to sleep and now she was awake again.

"There's something wrong with the mirror," said Claire.

"What time is it?"

"Just after six."

"Six? I thought it was my turn at four?"

"I didn't wake you. I'm not going to be able to sleep with all this going on and you looked like you needed it."

"You're the second person to say that to me," Blackbird grunted as she struggled upright.

Claire stood by the bed, wringing her hands. "It's doing that thing again, where it makes noises."

"Someone is trying to talk to us. It's probably Niall. Give me a moment."

Claire bustled away while Blackbird struggled back into the smock-top and pulled on clean socks and shoes. She pushed her hair back from her face and scrubbed her eyes with her knuckles. It would have to suffice.

"Listen," said Claire, returning from the kitchen, nodding towards the big mirror over the fireplace.

There was a random ticking sound coming from the mirror, like an insect compulsively scratching.

"Have you got the portable mirror we used last night?"

Claire fished around in her handbag while Blackbird retrieved the horseshoe she had secreted under the pillow. Blackbird took both items to the fire door at the back of the kitchen. She tugged back the curtain and surveyed the grey morning. There was no sign of anyone on the fire escape, but then she knew she would be unlikely to see them until it was too late. Holding the horseshoe up like a talisman she prodded the fire door open and edged out on to the metal balcony. Checking carefully around, making sure that nothing had been tampered with and that the balcony would still hold her weight, she surveyed the back of the flats. Then she jammed the door open with the horseshoe and opened the mirror compact.

"Blackbird?" Niall's voice came clear through the mirror, making her smile.

"I'm here," she said. "Can you hear me?"

"I was beginning to wonder if you were OK," said Niall. His voice sounded tinny and distant.

Claire made hand signals through the doorway.

"Not coffee," said Blackbird. "Tea would be nice, though."

"What?" said Niall.

"It's just Claire. She woke me when she heard you trying to contact us through the mirror. She's getting me a drink."

"Sorry, I didn't mean to wake you. I had no way of knowing whose turn it was."

"Never mind. Claire was supposed to wake me hours ago, but she didn't feel like sleeping, so she left me. My back aches like a coal miner's. That sofa should have a warning sign on it."

"It did have a label," said Claire. "I peeled it off." She handed a steaming mug to Blackbird.

"What was that?" asked Niall.

"Only Claire. Stop fretting."

"You sound as if you're getting on OK," said Niall.

"Well, there's nothing like shared adversity to bring people together, is there?"

"Any sign of visitors?"

"Not as far as we can tell. If they came, they went away again. Maybe they didn't like the welcome reception."

"How are you feeling?"

"Apart from the chronic backache? Tired. I'm always tired at the moment. It comes with the territory. How are you?"

"I'm OK. Tired too, but for different reasons. I need your help."

"My help?

"Yes. I need your advice."

"Niall Petersen, Warder of the Seven Courts, protector of the weak, vanquisher of the enemy, scion of the wraithkin, needs the help of the beach-ball once known as Blackbird."

"Are you going to help me or not? What's a scion, anyway?"

"A descendent of a noble family. Has Raffmir been back?"

"No, it's something else." Niall described how he'd been trying to find the girls through the mirror and how that had somehow led to the encounter with the girl. He recounted the dream and told her about the scratches it had left behind.

"Are the scratches still there?"

"Faintly. They're healing fast, but they're definitely real. It can't be Solandre, can it? She's dead. You killed her."

"The wraithkin can be very hard to kill. Maybe she was just scattered. Did you feel her presence in the dream?" Blackbird sipped at the steaming mug.

"Not directly, but I've had the dream more than once. When Tate woke me the other night, I was dreaming I was in the glade then as well. I thought it was because Altair and Raffmir had turned up. Maybe I could somehow feel their presence and the dream was my subconscious, warning me."

"Are you sure you didn't scratch yourself in your sleep?"

"My nails aren't that sharp. Anyway, it's more than that. At first it was just me, but now other people are being drawn into the dream too."

"Are you sure you weren't just dreaming? You were looking at pictures of young girls and one of them turns up in your dream, all naked and willing. I'm a big girl. I know what men are like. It's not a completely unnatural thought."

"Blackbird, she's young enough to be my daughter."

"And I'm old enough to be your great-great-grandmother. It didn't stop you having sex with me."

"That's different. You're not old. You've just been around for a long time."

"Thanks. Now I feel ancient. I know where to come when I want to fish for compliments."

"Don't be like that. I don't know what I'd do without you." Suddenly he sounded hesitant, unnerved.

"I expect you'd get into worse scrapes than you already have." She changed the subject. "I want you to try something."

"What?"

"Try and find Solandre through the mirror."

"What! Are you nuts?"

"Old and nuts as well. You are doing well this morning."

"I just meant…"

"Try and find her in the mirror. You don't have to speak to her. Just find out whether she's alive."

"What if she knows I'm trying to find her?"

"Well then, she's already found you, so you're not giving much away. If you know she's hunting you, maybe you can do something about it?"

"OK. Give me a few minutes."

"I'll wait."

The mirror went silent, leaving Blackbird surveying the fire escapes and sipping her mug of tea. It was a few minutes before Niall's voice returned.

"Nothing," he said. "I can't find her."

"Well, that's a relief. For a moment I thought she was coming back for a rematch."

"It doesn't explain the dream, though, does it?"

"There is another explanation."

"Which is?"

"Some of the Feyre are very old."

"I know that. I've met some of them."

"They tend to get cranky and become difficult to live with. Some of them withdraw and become more and more reclusive."

"You think Solandre might be hiding away somewhere?"

"No, I think Solandre's dead. Your dream, though, may not be a dream."

"How do you mean?"

"Some of the very old ones don't really die. They fade into the landscape, and become part of the scenery. No one even knows they're there. They don't harm anyone or do very much, so they get left. Over time, they drift, and become detached from the world. They're not dead, they're just... disconnected."

"Like hibernating. What's this got to do with my dream?"

"All creatures need to feed, Niall, even if it's only once in a while. The ones that fade, they survive on the life that passes, taking only what they need to keep going. A fallen tear here, a drop of blood there. If you're really not doing anything, you don't need very much."

"This is a dream, Blackbird. It's not a place." Niall sounded worried.

She tried to explain. "You know yourself that there is more than the world we live in. There are other worlds, and spaces between those worlds."

"Dreaming isn't a place. Is it?"

"You have scratches all down your arm, Niall. What makes you think you were dreaming?"

"I was asleep."

"Your body was asleep, but your mind was awake. You drifted, and ended up somewhere else."

"But Solandre summoned me there to feed on me."

"Solandre may have discovered the glade, and then used it to feed on unwary sleepers. By taking people there she could feed on them with minimal risk of exposure, while supplying her host with a steady stream of unwilling victims for itself. It would work for both of them."

"But Solandre is dead."

"And now there is no food coming to the glade."

"So you think it's bringing me there to feed from me?"

"Not from you, Niall. It honoured you. It clothed you in silk and made you welcome. It plucked Debbie from your mind and brought her to you, all willing and naked. Sex is as much food to such a creature as blood is. I don't suppose it would mind either way."

"That's horrible."

"It's no better or worse than any other creature. It wants to survive and it's offering you the chance to benefit from the arrangement. It's offering you a symbiosis."

"Why me? I don't want anything to do with it."

"You were the last person there, apart from Solandre."

"No, I wasn't. She had Jerry Crossland, the Queen's Remembrancer, trapped there. He was there after I was."

"But he's not fey, Niall, and you are. You're wraithkin, as Solandre was. Maybe it was wraithkin too? Maybe as long as you provide some nourishment for it while you're there, it will let you do whatever you want."

"I'm not providing it with nourishment. It's gross."

"Then you're condemning it to death."

"No, I'm not. I don't want anything to do with it."

"It doesn't know anyone else, Niall. Solandre was its link with the world and now she's dead. We have no idea how long she'd been feeding it or how often. She wasn't exactly a spring chicken herself. They could have been living off each other for centuries."

"How do I tell it I don't want it? How do I tell it to find someone else?"

"I'm not sure you can. It may hear you if you speak to it, but such a creature is beyond conversation. In some ways it's more a place, now, than a person. How will you tell a place to find somewhere else to be?"

"Can I ward my dreams against it?"

"Yes. I suppose you could, but it will die without someone."

"I'll introduce it to someone else, then?"

"Who, Niall? Would you want Raffmir to have it? Or Garvin, even? Who would you trust to look after unguarded sleepers? You know what Solandre was doing with it."

"This is awful. I can't feed people to it."

"Then kill it, but don't just let it starve to death."

"How?"

"You're wraithkin. You already know how."

"You want me to use gallowfyre?"

"It's not my choice, Niall. It's attached itself to you and for better or worse you have to deal with it. You're a Warder now. If you can't deal with one ancient fey then you're going to have real problems when they start giving you executions to carry out."

"If I brought you there, could you deal with it?"

"No! If I end up there, it will feed on me and your unborn child. Don't even think about it."

"No, you're right. I have to kill it. It's the only way. What's that racket in the background?"

203

The sound of sirens echoed around the backs of the flats, one of the unwanted consequences of city living.

"It's a fire engine, or a police car maybe. I think we're OK. They do seem to be slowing down, though." The noise became deafening. A police car drove into the alley below, filling the narrow space with a cacophony.

"What's happening?" Niall's voice was almost drowned out.

The sirens were joined with another noise. A piercing alarm sounded from the flat. "Claire? What's that? What's going on?" She could hear Niall asking the same questions.

Claire appeared in the doorway. She was holding a short piece of black pipe, wrapped with a bunch of red roses, gathered together with a black ribbon with a gift tag dangling from it.

"Where did you get that?" asked Blackbird, taking it from her. The tag had the single letter D.

"It was left by the front door. I went to get the milk in," said Claire.

"I told you not to open the door!"

"I had my horseshoe with me. This was outside on the doormat."

The sound of distorted speech reverberated up between the buildings.

"Blackbird? What's going on?" Niall's voice was barely audible.

"Someone left a piece of pipe outside our door with some flowers. There's a label. It just has the letter D. Niall, I think it's written in blood."

The loudhailer came clearer the second time. *"Exit the building as quickly as you can. Extinguish all smoking material. Do not touch any light switches or show any naked flame. Move quietly and quickly. Do not panic. Do not delay to collect personal possessions. Leave now."*

"Go? Go where?" asked Claire.

"There is a mains gas leak in the building. Please leave immediately. Do not touch any electrical equipment. Do not use matches or smoking equipment. Extinguish all cigarettes immediately. Leave immediately!"

"Niall? I've got to go!"

"Where to? Deefnir's probably waiting for you!"

"If he is," said Blackbird, "he's going to find out how unreasonable a pregnant woman can truly be."

She snapped the compact shut.

"Get your horseshoe," she said to Claire. "We have to leave."

TWELVE

"Blackbird, what's happening..."

The sound vanished and I lost the connection. I slammed the top of the chest with my fist. I looked up into the mirror; the face there seemed distorted. Slowly, I let the anger fade. A lot of good that would do me, miles away and helpless. I pressed my hand to the mirror.

"Garvin?" The mirror glowed brightly under my hand. "Garvin, dammit! Where are you?"

His voice came through clear after the din from the flat. "Niall. You're not due until tonight. Can you wait two minutes?"

"Not really. Deefnir is trying to blow Blackbird up."

"Say again?"

"You heard me."

"Ten seconds, stay there."

I waited, counting slowly to ten. I had reached thirteen by the time his voice came again.

"He's doing what?"

I told Garvin about Blackbird and Claire and about the gas leak. "I'm sure he's caused it deliberately to flush them out of the building. They need help, and fast."

"I'm thin on the ground here, Niall. I'll send someone as soon as I can, but Fellstamp's laid up, Fionh is preparing for the day's negotiations, Tate's asleep and I'm holding the watch. Amber has gone after Raffmir and Slimgrin is chasing Deefnir. I'll get a message to Slimgrin as soon as I can."

"That won't help if he's waiting to ambush them."

"If she'd stayed here, where we could keep an eye on her…"

"She'd likely be dead by now."

"You don't know that."

"Nor do you."

"I'm trying to help, Niall, but you don't make it easy."

"I'm going to London."

"No! Stay there."

"And do what? This missing-girl thing? It's a shambles."

"Then unshamble it. You're not going to London."

"Why not?"

"Because you'll walk straight into a trap. This is exactly what Deefnir wants. You go running in there to defend Blackbird, and he'll have every excuse to kill you."

"He may find that harder than he thinks."

"He may find it easier than you imagine. He's prepared and you're not. He's laid the bait and now he's dangling it in front of you."

"She's pregnant, Garvin. Any moment now my son could be born. It could be the baby that Deefnir's after, not me."

"Slimgrin is on it. He'll find Deefnir and bring him back here."

"Slimgrin isn't even there."

"You don't know that either."

"If he's there he should be protecting them."

"With the amount of iron they have around them, I don't suppose he can get any nearer than Deefnir can. He's a Warder, Niall. You have to learn to trust the team."

"He's watching them?"

"We each play our part, Niall. Play yours, and let Slimgrin do his job."

"And I'm supposed to sit here and wait for news."

"No. You're supposed to do your job, as I'm doing mine. Altair is complaining that his retinue's deserted him. He's talking about bringing more of his court across."

"More? But they're following his orders. He's the one that told Deefnir to go after Blackbird."

"We both know that. Everyone knows that, but we can't openly acknowledge it."

"So we let him bring over anyone he wants? We're already beyond our limits. If he brings more people across I'll have to come in."

"No. You're playing into his hands again. Stay where you are. The Lords and Ladies can handle Altair. He's one where they are six."

"He's three, likely to be four or five soon by the sound of it."

"Krane asked him if he had anyone he could bring across that could be relied upon to follow protocol, and not just wander off sightseeing. He suggested that perhaps his grandson's inexperience in these matters hadn't made him the best choice for his retinue."

"What did Altair say?"

"He had to admit that Deefnir wasn't as experienced as others. He could hardly admit that he had given Deefnir orders to pursue Blackbird, could he?"

"That sounds like an excuse to bring more with him, though."

"Yes, until Yonna suggested that they each bring in two or three people from their own courts to help the visiting wraithkin become accustomed to courtly ways again. She said they couldn't help it if being exiled meant that they lost touch with fey customs and that they might make new friends."

"Right. I see what you mean."

"Altair thanked them for their consideration, of course, but the subject of his retinue hasn't been raised again."

"But no one knows where they are."

"Altair knows. The pressure will be on Raffmir and Deefnir to do what they came here for. He can't keep stalling for ever."

"Can't they push it to a conclusion?"

"Not without cutting short the negotiations. The Feyre want to see the courts reunited. They expect their leaders to negotiate in good faith. If the negotiations break down prematurely then it could be disastrous for the High Court and for the Lords and Ladies. They have to at least give the appearance of wanting to negotiate, even if that's not why Altair is really here."

"So we play along."

"It's the oldest game: wait and see. It'll come out eventually. The courts will never agree to culling the gifted, so if that's his stance it'll look as if he's being intransigent and we return to the status quo. The courts continue to support the Lords and Ladies and the Untainted return to exile. It's the best outcome."

"Unless he's here for some other reason."

"Then it's our job to find out what that reason is. You're in a good position. You're forcing Raffmir to come to you. He wants something too, maybe for Altair, maybe for himself. Make him come to you. When you find out what he's after, I want to know."

"What about Blackbird?"

"I'll put any help I can in, but it's hard to protect a moving target."

"It's harder to hit one too."

"That depends what you're hitting it with. Try and persuade her to come back here."

"She's not going to want to do that, Garvin."

"Talk to her. If she comes back to court I can protect her, and Deefnir will have to come back here to get to her. She'll see the sense in that."

"Maybe. It didn't stop them last time."

"I'll ask Amber to sleep with Deefnir if necessary. Just get her back here."

"I'll do what I can."

"Report later. Meanwhile get on with the assignment. Don't worry about Deefnir, Slimgrin will handle it. And if Raffmir comes to you, find out what he wants."

"OK, but warn Slimgrin."

"I will. Be careful, Niall. Whatever they're up to, they've been planning this for some time. They've got us on the back foot. Now they think they're in the driving seat and we'll see where they're going."

"I'll report later."

"Do."

I lifted my hand from the misted glass. Part of me still wanted to go to London, though by the time I reached Claire's flat, whatever was going on would have already happened. I felt helpless and frustrated. Maybe Raffmir's plan was simply to make me feel as miserable and impotent as possible. If so, it was working.

I thought about Garvin's instruction to do my job. Then I thought about Blackbird and what she was doing now. Deefnir had been unable to breach their defences, so he had simply undermined them. Once outside the flat, they would be vulnerable. With glamour, Deefnir could be anywhere. He could be the fireman offering blankets or the kindly neighbour offering sweet tea and sympathy. It wouldn't be hard to get close.

The image of Blackbird wrapped in a blanket and clinging resolutely to a horseshoe came into my head. If Deefnir went for her, I could see her beating him to death with the damn thing. Would there be headlines tomorrow – Pregnant Woman Arrested in Horseshoe Assault?

Despite my worries, I smiled. I could just see that happening.

I knew Blackbird was resourceful, intelligent and very determined. I also knew she was heavily pregnant and without any power. I could disobey Garvin and go to London, but would I be making the situation better or worse? If Deefnir was using Blackbird to draw me in, then he needed her as bait. He wouldn't move against her until I was there. By riding in unprepared, I could trigger the trap that would fall on both of us. On the other hand, if he was really after the baby then I should be there to protect my unborn son, shouldn't I?

I was torn between helping Blackbird, trying to find my daughter and dealing with Raffmir and his friends. The suspicion that Raffmir was leading me on with speculation and half-truth was probably well founded but, as Garvin had said, they were here for a reason. Could that reason have anything to do with Alex? Did he really have a way of finding her?

Eventually I came to the conclusion that if Blackbird needed me, she would have said. It wouldn't matter what Garvin wanted, or anyone else for that matter; if she needed my protection she would let me know. She had surrounded herself with iron, which I could no more abide than Deefnir could. Ironically, her protection against the wraithkin would work just as well against me. I had to trust that she knew what she was doing. I knew she would protect our baby whatever happened.

I was sure Raffmir would appear as and when it suited him, and be as cryptic as ever, but he was the best lead I had on Alex so far. There must be a better way of finding Alex, surely? Perhaps the truck that was parked outside the hospital would provide a lead? Not for the first time I wished I had noted the registration number, but at the time my head had been full of Alex and the accident, not tracking rogue trucks.

It was a clue, though, and I would have to find a way of linking it to other clues. With enough information, maybe I could piece it together and get a lead on her location. If I could find her I was sure I could help her. In the meantime Garvin had given me an assignment. Perhaps I should get on with it.

The church wouldn't be open yet, nor would the library. Breakfast was served after seven, so I made myself go down and eat plastic sausages and limp bacon and drink cups of thin coffee. Martha asked me if I wanted seconds, but I patted my stomach and shook my head.

"Thanks, but I'd better get going."

I went back upstairs and cleaned my teeth. The grease sat heavy in my stomach and I made a mental note to ask her for cereal the next day, or toast. The rain threw itself against the window, driven by the blustery wind. The taste of summer in yesterday's sunshine was a fond memory.

Emptying out the black holdall revealed a dark grey coat at the bottom, light but silk-lined and waterproof. It would serve to keep the worst of the rain off. I shrugged it on to my shoulders, pocketed my keys and collected my sword. It slid into the shape of an umbrella in my hand, though it was too windy to be useful in that capacity. Still, no one would question my carrying it on a day like this.

The harbour was deserted. The spray from incoming waves kicked up against the outer wall of the harbour, only to be hurled at the town by the wind. I walked down the front, turning up my collar and putting my back to the worst of the weather. I could see the clouds sliding into the hills above us. It made the town look cut off, as if reality stopped where the mist began.

Walking up the hill I debated how to approach the subject of the missing young women with Greg. Maybe

I needed a new approach. So far he'd helped me find Karen, if only to persuade me from getting further involved. He'd said we would talk again this morning after I'd slept on it. Well, I had slept, but it hadn't made things easier. For a moment I thought about Debbie. If my dream wasn't a dream, did that mean that she'd woken to find her sheets covered in blood, her body marked with punctures and arms covered in scratches? What would she make of that? Would finding that her dreams had leaked into her life change her? Would it make her less willing, less wilful? Whatever choices she'd made, she was still someone's daughter. There were parents who missed her terribly or there wouldn't be the posters and the appeals for information, would there? How would news of their daughter's new lifestyle be received?

The church of St Andrew stood against the wind, and not even a window rattled. The rain ran down the roof and into the gutters, but it did no more than stain the stone a darker shade of brown. I hurried under the porch out of the rain. No one had been to open the church yet, but now that I knew what I was doing it was a simple matter to get inside. I closed the door behind me but didn't relock it. I wanted Greg to know there was someone waiting.

The board pinned with photos looked more colourful in daylight. Anything from hair ribbons to teddy bear keyrings had been pinned to it, filling in the gaps left by lack of news. I picked out an early photo of Debbie astride a new blue bike. Her hair was longer and she was leaner than she was now, but I thought I could see a girl who would pedal to see what was around the next bend, over the next hill, or maybe that was just my knowledge of her colouring my perceptions. In the photos, though, her evolution was revealed. In later ones her hair was blonde, not brown, and shorter. As she got older, she wore more make-up and her choice of clothes drifted into darker fashions. The girl with the bike had become a girl with few limits and a determination to wring every last drop from life. I pinned it back.

Yesterday these girls had been blank faces. Now they were people. Helen's uncomfortable smile revealed a shyness and a hesitancy. Other photos revealed a plain simplicity to her. She looked straightforward and honest, with none of the artifice that Debbie had adopted. I wondered how that had translated into becoming a mother. Had she planned it or had things simply got out of hand? It was hard to imagine her getting carried away with some boy and ending up pregnant. Maybe the baby wasn't hers? Maybe she was looking after it for someone else? With that thought came the memory of that quiet reassurance and rhythmic suckling. "Mummy's coming…" No, the baby was hers. The photo, though, revealed nothing of that.

There were pictures of Karen there, though they tended to be at the back, covered by newer postings. As a girl, Karen had looked a lot like her sister, Shelley, reminding me to find a way to pass on Karen's message to her sister. I would do it discreetly, away from her parents. Karen smiled out of the picture at me, reminding me of the way she had looked across at Ahmed. I couldn't help wishing that one day she would find a way to be close to her family once again.

In every picture, Trudy Bilbardie was with someone else. I had looked for a good picture of her by torchlight the previous night and settled for the one with her standing between friends because it was a clear image of her. It wouldn't have mattered, though. Trudy was always the centre of attention, hugging those about her close, a big smile for the camera. She looked bright, sparkly and full of life.

For the first time I wondered whether there were other photos of these women. How much had the choice of pictures been governed by the people searching for them? Were there pictures in a drawer somewhere of Trudy on her own looking nervous? Were there photos of Helen in glamorous dresses and Debbie in jeans and no make-up? If there were, the people searching for them had not chosen to show them.

That left me with Gillian, her hair framing her face like a halo as she leant forward. It must have been a recent picture, or perhaps she was older than the others, since there were drinks on the table behind her and the photo had been taken with flash so that the shot faded out into a vignette of darkness – a nightclub, perhaps?

What had she been leaning forward to do? Was someone offering her something, or repeating something not quite heard? Of all the pictures, this one was the least posed. It captured an unconscious moment. There were a couple of other photos, but they looked like mobile phone pictures or shots taken of someone else that Gillian had happened to be with. I could imagine her holding up a hand when the camera was raised, or stepping aside, but for this one shot she'd just been Gillian.

Replacing the photo, I stepped back. Greg had been right. It wasn't just about finding the girls. It was about knowing what became of them, where they went and why they'd made whatever choice they'd made. And for two of them it was about closure. I would never know if Gillian and Trudy were like their photographs. It was too late for that question. I knew that now.

Greg said that you had to find out what people needed before you tried to help them. I knew what it was like to lose a daughter. I knew the emptiness and the nagging thought that there was something more I could have done. The parents of these girls needed to know, good news or bad. This wasn't news I could carry, though. I needed Greg.

When he arrived I was sitting in a pew at the back of the church, listening to the rain and the wind and thinking about the girls, about what to say, and how to say it.

"Was the door open when you got here?" he asked me.

"No."

"You borrowed a key?"

"Not that either. I let myself in. I hope you don't mind. I'm not here to steal the silver or make off with the collection."

He closed the heavy door behind him, shutting out the weather, and walked into the centre of the church and genuflected towards the altar. He was silent for a moment.

"You saw Karen?"

"Yes."

"How is she?" He came and sat beside me in the pew, looking down the church towards the big east window.

"She's well. Ahmed is very protective of her. He looks after her."

"A good man."

"A protective man. He took exception to me asking around for her."

"There was a fight?"

I shook my head. "It didn't come to that. Karen intervened. We had mint tea together."

"Quite refreshing, isn't it? Not with sugar, though. That spoils it."

"She asked about her family. She misses them."

"It's difficult. Tony, Karen's father, isn't a racist. He just can't deal with the fact that his daughter loves a man whose culture, upbringing, religion and way of life are so very different from his own. He doesn't know how to speak to Ahmed; doesn't know what to say. It comes out as aggression. He doesn't mean it."

"Karen thinks he does."

"And that's why they live apart. It's better. At least for now."

"But why the photos? They know where she is. They could ring her up if they wanted to. Why make a show of it?"

"When Karen first vanished, they thought Ahmed had kidnapped her. They made a huge fuss. The police were involved, everything. Then they found out where she was and what she was doing. They'd already joined the group, posted photos, made a public statement. I think they thought she'd realise what a mistake she'd made and come back. They could say she'd run away and then decided to come home."

I shook my head. "She's not coming home."

"I know. So do they. The fiction remains, though."

"I spoke to Debbie, too."

"Debbie? You found her?"

"Not exactly. I spoke to her. I don't know where she is, but she's alive and well, mostly."

"How did you find her?"

"She found me. I don't think she's coming home either."

"Can you get in touch with her?"

"Maybe, I'm not sure. It's not easy to talk to her."

Greg steepled his hands in front of him. He thought for a long moment before speaking. "Debbie's mum isn't part of the church community. Comes to the meetings on a Friday. Makes tea when its her turn. Talks about her daughter, mostly. Never met the dad. Not even sure there is one. A series of boyfriends, maybe. What we used to call uncles."

"Stepfather?"

"Not that involved, or that reliable. They come and go. I don't know, but it's possible that one of them took a shine to Debbie."

"You think that's why she left?"

217

"Maybe. You'd have to ask her that question. Her mother doesn't know, I can tell you that. She'd kill them if they touched Debbie."

"She might not know, though."

"D'you think you could get her to phone home? It doesn't have to be from her own number. A call box would do it."

"I don't know whether I'll speak to her again."

"If you do. She'll know the number, I'm sure. Just a call. It would mean a lot."

"I found the others too, Greg. Some of them."

He looked directly at me for the first time. "What do you mean, some of them?"

I stared resolutely at the east window, avoiding his gaze. I was reminded of a technique I'd learned professionally, on a course on presentations. It's called a shit sandwich. If you have bad news then you wrap it between two pieces of good news. It helps to make it more palatable. There was no way of making this any easier.

"Gillian and Trudy... they're not coming back."

I sat under his unwavering stare. It was a little while before he looked away.

He cleared his throat. "You only started looking yesterday. You could give it a little more time."

"When people say things to you, Greg, you can hear whether they're lying, can't you?"

He became still beside me.

"And when they tell the truth, you can hear that too."

He might as well have been carved from the same stone as the church.

"So you'll be able to hear in my voice whether I'm telling the truth. Trudy and Gillian can't be found. I think they're dead."

"How do you know?" His voice was close to a whisper.

"I told you yesterday. I have different ways of finding people. If they're alive, I can find them."

218

"What if they've moved away? They could have gone abroad, taken a plane, maybe."

"Let's call it a talent, like knowing whether someone's telling the truth. If they're out there I can tell they're there. I can't find any trace of Gillian or Trudy."

"What about Helen?"

"Helen I found. She's OK. She has her hands full."

"She's had the baby? Thank God. I thought she'd gone for a termination."

I saw the news of the baby's safe arrival spread relief on his face and I felt like I'd cheated. There should be no good news after that. Once again, though, it meant he knew more than he was saying.

"You knew she was pregnant." It was a statement, not a question.

"No. Young man came to call. Wanted to know whether her parents had found her. Whether she'd been in touch. I had to tell him, no. Sat him down, made him tea. Asked him why he didn't go to her parents, if he was so worried. It was like pulling teeth."

"He's the father?"

"Thinks he is. She was underage. He said it wasn't supposed to happen. They were holding hands, kissing, that sort of thing. All very sweet. Then one afternoon after school she takes her clothes off in front of him. He's a good lad, but he's not made of stone."

"Just bad luck, she got pregnant first time?"

"Hardly. It became a regular thing. He was scarlet by the time he told me this."

"Why didn't they take precautions?"

"He wanted to. She wouldn't hear of it. Her family are churchgoing, strict with it. She said it would be up to God."

"You believe that?"

"He moves in mysterious ways, but usually within the sanctity of marriage. By then it was too late. She'd

219

gone and I dreaded the worst. It's a relief to hear she'd had it. Boy or a girl?"

"I don't know. I didn't get to ask."

He studied the glass in the big window. "Quite a gift, that."

"What?"

"Finding people. These girls have been missing for months, more than a year, some of 'em. You walk in one morning and by the next day you know where they are."

"I know they're there. Where they are, I can't tell."

"Still, quite a gift."

"As you say."

"Ever been wrong?"

"You know I'm telling the truth. You can hear it."

"I know you believe it. I just don't know whether I believe it."

"Even if they were in a coma, down a mine, gone to Australia, I think I would know."

"A gift and a burden."

"Pardon?"

"It isn't easy, always knowing the truth. When people say, 'I'll see you on Sunday', and you hear the lie on their tongue, it isn't easy."

"I don't suppose it is."

"Worse when they say things like 'thank you' or 'hope to see you soon'."

"Yes. It must be."

"This daughter you lost. Must be a burden knowing for sure that she's dead, but being unable to see the body."

"I didn't say she was dead."

"No, you didn't, did you?"

There was another long silence while the rain lashed against the windows. It was Greg that eventually broke that silence.

"We live in hope."

"I'm not a religious man. I said that before."

"You don't have to believe in Him," he said. "The important thing is that He believes in you. If you have a gift, then it's for a purpose. Maybe you were brought to us to give us certainty. I think you know what that means."

"Closure."

"Perhaps. I will need to think about this, Neal. I believe you are sincere and that you know what you know. That doesn't mean I'm going to tell the parents. That might mean explaining how I know."

"I understand."

"If you could tell me where, it would be easier."

"Debbie? A city. Somewhere with nightclubs and loud music. Helen? Could be anywhere."

"Gillian? Trudy?"

"There's nothing, Greg. If I knew, I'd tell you."

"You would. Let's leave it there, then, for now. Try again for me, if you would? Not that I don't believe you, but it can't hurt. People have been mistaken before. If you get the chance to speak to Debbie or Helen, tell them their parents are worried sick about them. A phone call would make all the difference."

"I don't know if I'll be able to speak with them."

"You could also tell Helen that there's a young man who's desperate to hear from her and wants to do the right thing, and not just because it's the right thing to do."

"I'm not sure I should be the one to bear such news. It's too important."

"When you have my job, you get to deal with the shitty end of the stick too often. You see people at their worst, at their lowest, at the end. When, from time to time, you get the chance to share the joy in people's hearts, you grasp it, not for yourself, but because next time you're dealing with the shit you can look back and think, it isn't all like this."

"I'll remember that."

We sat in the church for a good few minutes after that, listening to the wind and the rain.

"I should go," I told him.

"Don't feel bad about this, Neal. The convention is not to shoot the messenger. Not your burden to carry."

"That doesn't stop me feeling responsible."

"Then be responsible for the good you are doing. Maybe we can put some families in touch again. You of all people know what it's like to deal with unexplained loss, I think."

I picked up my umbrella and buttoned my coat.

"Since you appear able to let yourself in, feel welcome here. If you need time to contemplate, it isn't a bad place to think. God doesn't mind. Just make sure you lock up when you leave."

"I will. Thanks."

I left him in the pew, and went back out into the rain. It showed no sign of slackening off and by the time I had crossed the road it had found its way under my coat and soaked through my shirt and trousers. There was no point in raising my umbrella as the wind would blow it inside out and I had no idea what would happen when it became a sword again. Would it too be broken?

I strode down the hill with the wind tugging at my coat and the rain running down my face. The main road was busy with cars and the shops had opened.

I needed to do something more than bring bad news. Time for some research.

Thirteen

Blackbird grabbed her bag, "Come on, Claire, we'll use the fire escape."

"I'm not sure if I locked the front door."

"Leave it. If they really want to get in they'll just break the door down and then you'll have a broken door to deal with."

"But someone might steal my things."

"There may not be anything left to steal if the building goes up, and even less to worry about if you go up with it. Move, woman!" She bustled Claire out on to the fire escape.

"I don't even have shoes on," complained Claire. "All my shoes are in the apartment. I'm wearing slippers, for goodness sake. People will see."

"It could be worse. You could have been naked in the shower. At least you're dry, clothed and alive."

As they reached the bottom of the metal staircase, fire officers came to meet them bearing blankets. Blackbird eyed them warily, grasping the horseshoe in her left hand.

"This way, Madam. Everything's under control." A tall man in a fluorescent jacket looked warily at Blackbird and ushered them away from the stairway.

Blackbird shrugged his offer of a blanket away. "If everything was under control, young man, we would not be standing out here."

He raised his eyebrows at the "young man" comment. "Feeling our age this morning, are we?" he said with a grin.

Claire came to her rescue. "Don't you even think about patronising us, just because you think you're in charge."

His attitude shifted. "No, Madam. My boss is in charge and that's him over there by the appliance, so you can write to him with any complaints. In the meantime we'd like to prevent you from being incinerated. Please come this way."

They were guided out of the alley and across the road. The police were stopping traffic and there were a number of people gathered, looking back across to their flats and homes.

Blackbird caught Claire's arm. "I'm going."

"Going? Where?"

"Never mind where. Deefnir will follow me, not you, so you should be safe. Keep the horseshoes with you just in case. Place them like I showed you, and don't open the door to strangers, even to get the milk, understand?"

"But where will you go?"

The police were shepherding them towards the crowd and Blackbird didn't like crowds. It was too hard to see what was going on.

"Don't worry. I'll get in touch when this is over. Watch out for yourself."

Blackbird veered sideways.

"This way, Miss," said a short policeman with a padded anti-stab vest over his uniform. He indicated the gathering across the road.

"I'm just passing through," she reassured him. "What a kerfuffle, eh? Is it a bomb scare?"

"Just a gas leak, Miss. No cause for alarm. Keep to the right there, please, let the emergency services do their job."

Walking down the pavement, away from the flashing lights and the milling people, she glanced behind frequently to see if someone separated from the crowd, coming after her, knowing she probably wouldn't see them until it was too late.

Rule one of survival, don't go where you're expected to be.

That gave her a problem. She did have places she could go, but many of them would be places she was known. She didn't want to take trouble where it wasn't welcome, but her choices were few.

She pulled the bag up on to her shoulder, letting her hand dip down where the reassuring weight of the horseshoe was cold against her fingers. If anyone using magic got close, it should disrupt their power momentarily, giving her a split second to decide between fight and run. She shifted her hand to the hard black handle of the kitchen knife she had borrowed from Claire. She would return it, of course, when she had no more need of it, but for now it would give her a chance to even the odds, should the answer be fight rather than flee.

Making herself slow down, she crossed the road between the traffic. The drivers stopped for her, something she had never known happen in London, but then there had to be some advantages to being obviously pregnant, apart from the obvious one, of course. Almost unconsciously, she stroked her hand down her belly.

Her best option was a taxi, but her funds were low and getting a taxi in rush hour on a morning promising rain was going to be difficult, even if she did play the mother-to-be. Second choice was the Tube. That had other advantages in terms of where she could go.

She crossed another street, watching to see if anyone else crossed after her, then turned down a side road past a school where mothers were shepherding rowdy youngsters between iron gates – not the sort of school her child would be welcome at. She veered away from the iron even though it wouldn't affect her in her present state.

"Force of habit," she muttered to herself, earning a strange look from a young black woman who pulled a small boy close to her as an older girl prodded him, then danced out of reach into Blackbird's path.

"Mind what'cha doing, Helena. You nearly had that lady over."

Blackbird turned back to say that it was no problem, and it was then that she noticed the pale foreign man in the black suit. He didn't quite fit somehow, or maybe he wasn't used to wearing a suit and tie. He carried on walking towards her, not breaking step and studiously ignoring her gaze, but Blackbird couldn't help looking up at the heavy grey clouds and thinking that on a day like today most people would at least have worn a coat over an expensive suit like that.

She waved away the apology and hurried along the pavement. There were people around, walking to work or on their way to see friends, but that wouldn't matter. If it came to a fight it would be a private conflict. No one would see. No one would intervene.

When she looked back, the man had gone. Was she barking at the moon, seeing phantoms, making something out of nothing? She wasn't sure, but her pace increased and she kept glancing back whenever she had an opportunity.

She reached the tube station at Pimlico and took the ramp down to the ticket hall. She was at the barrier before she realised she would need a ticket and had to turn back. She dug in her purse for money and fed the machine coins while she tried to watch all the entrances. There was no sign of the man in the suit by the time she reached the barrier again. Slotting her day-ticket through the machine, she went through and took the escalator down.

She chose the platform for the southbound line headed for Brixton. A single youth sat on a bench, eyes closed, nodding his head to the sound of the music pumping from his headphones. Blackbird could hear it clearly from yards away. She could not imagine any member of the Seventh Court tolerating such a racket, and therefore judged the youth harmless. Ignoring him, she moved quickly along the platform until she found the passageway through to the northbound side. She stood in the gap between platforms, breathing hard.

It was a few minutes before the train arrived and she used the time to catch her breath. The humid air in the station didn't make her any cooler and she could feel where the sweat was soaking through the smock-top under her arms. She considered peeling off the top, but then she would have a moment when she could neither see anything nor fend off any attack.

She fanned herself with her hand instead.

The train rattled on to the platform a moment later, but she didn't move immediately. She waited until the alarm for the train doors closing was beeping and then stepped out on to the platform. At the far end she saw a tall man lingering where the departing passengers left the platform. As she jumped between the closing doors, she saw him move quickly through the remains of the crowd and jump for the door. She watched carefully as the train departed, hoping to see him stranded on the platform, but he wasn't there. That meant he was on the train.

She looked around in the carriage. The seats were all occupied and no one offered to give up their place to the obviously pregnant woman. She moved down the car, stepping between the feet to get one door further away from the far end of the train. At the end of the car there was a group of six young men, hair cropped tight to their heads, tattoos on their arms. The nearest one wore a baseball cap while they all wore hoodies. The surly way they viewed other passengers meant that they went unchallenged for their end of the car, even through there were a number of spare seats between them.

"Wanna sit down, darlin'?" The nearest one leered at her.

To some men pregnancy was not a barrier. For some it was an attraction. She was about to tell them to get lost when an idea occurred to her.

"Are you boys patriotic?" she asked, noting the wavy Union Jack tattooed on the arm of the lad sprawled in the far corner.

"What's 'at about?" asked the one in the baseball cap.

"She wants to know whever you lav your country," said the one in the white hoodie across from him, grinning.

The pronunciation of the word "love" as "lav" almost made Blackbird smile.

"I lav my country as much as the next bloke, dun I?" said baseball cap.

"It's just…" she said. "Never mind."

"What?" he said. "You don't fink I do? I do, dun I?" He challenged his mate to deny it.

"It's just… there's a man, clearly a foreign gentleman, following me. He was walking behind me down the street and then he jumped on the train as soon as he saw me boarding."

"Where?" said hoodie. He stood up in the carriage, making Blackbird stand back.

"He's in one of the carriages towards the front of the train, a tall, dark-haired man in a black suit. Do you think he might be following me?"

228

"Sounds like a bit of a perv to me," said baseball cap.

Hoodie agreed. "I don't care if he's foreign or not, he shun't be following you about, should 'e? That's pervy, that is."

Hoodie squinted up the carriages, failing to see beyond the next car. "'Ere, we're coming into Victoria. Let us off first, and we'll walk down the train and 'ave a look." He spoke quickly to the rest of the bunch and they gathered around Blackbird protectively.

"This is really very good of you," she said. "I'm just a bit nervous, what with being in my condition."

"That's all right, darlin'," said the one with the tattoos. "Never let it be said that chivalry is dead in England."

Blackbird smiled her thanks while recalling that chivalry was introduced into England by the French and realising that this probably wasn't the time to mention that to them.

They rumbled into the platform at Victoria and rolled to a halt. As the doors opened, the group tumbled out on to the platform, jostling each other and laughing loudly. They moved up the train, making a complete pantomime of acting natural. Blackbird waited a moment and then followed them.

As soon as she stepped on to the platform, the suited man stepped off at the front and began walking towards her, merging into the group of people at his end of the platform heading towards the exit. When he reached the exit he paused, as if remembering something, so that the group dissipated around him.

The lads took this as a sign.

"'Ere, what's your game?" shouted Hoodie. They picked up speed as they got closer, urging each other on, the testosterone levels rising like a flash flood.

"Get out of it, pervert!" shouted baseball cap. They gathered round him, penning him in, shoving and pushing him towards the exit.

The alarm for the closing doors sounded and Blackbird reversed her direction and jumped back on the train. As the doors whirred closed behind her she heard an outcry as the conflict suddenly escalated. The train lurched and started accelerating. As she passed the exit door she saw Hoodie hurtle through the air and land sprawled across the platform. There was a blur of tangled bodies as she passed and trundled into the tunnel and they were out of sight.

She fanned herself with her hand again. "Hooray for chivalry," she murmured to herself.

At the next stop she changed for the Piccadilly Line. She didn't know how long it would take for the suited man to follow, but she was counting on London Underground to intervene. With any luck the Railway Police would be involved. If the man in the suit was fey that wouldn't slow him down much, but now she was at least one train and one connection ahead of him. She knew where she was going. She hoped that he didn't, otherwise the distraction wouldn't work and she would have to try something else.

She got off the Piccadilly Line train at Covent Garden and waited near the lifts until the coast was clear. The door down was a problem. She couldn't unlock it with magic and the CCTV cameras were everywhere. When she tried the door, though, it was open. Was she expected?

She slipped through into the dully lit platform beyond and waited on the stairs for her eyes to adjust. Then she made her way down the spiral stairs until she reached the tunnel near the bottom. The arch of the tunnel extended into the gloom beyond the light until the green and white of the walls merged with the darkness. She stepped forward confidently and then paused, returning to the steps.

"No good arriving with this, is it?" She dipped into her bag, extracted the horseshoe and laid it gently under the bottom step where it would function as a warding but not be noticed by anyone coming down the stairs.

As she turned back to the corridor, a huge shaggy shape materialised out of the dark.

"Gramawl!"

She ran forward and nearly tripped, but giant hands snapped out and caught her. She was swept off her feet, gathered up into huge shaggy arms.

There was a thrumming sound, low enough to vibrate the marrow in her bones. She grabbed handfuls of fur and hugged him close.

"Gramawl, I've been so scared."

The mountain of fur shifted, settled down cross-legged on the cold tiles and cradled her in its lap, stroking her hair from her face with one massive gnarled finger. She pressed her face into the fur, breathing easy at last.

There was a rumbling sound. Blackbird looked up.

"You want to feel?"

Golden eyes the size of saucers gazed down on her. She grabbed hold of two of his fingers in her hand and moved the hand around until it rested against her belly. The hand curled around the curve of the bump. She sighed, relaxing under his hand.

There was a low "Humph!" from Gramawl.

"Oh! Did you feel him? He kicked."

A sound like grating granite filled the tunnel. It resolved slowly into a gentle huffing that was Gramawl's laughter. She laughed too, like a descant over heavy bass.

"There! He did it again. He can hear you."

Gramawl removed his hand and took Blackbird's hand in his. He held her hand open and then tapped rhythmically on her palm with the pad of one finger: pat-pat, pat-pat, pat-pat, pat-pat.

She looked up. "Is that his heart? You can hear it?'

He held out his hand as if he was dangling a sweet or holding a mouse by the tail, then folded in his thumb and closed his fist. Finally he wrapped one hand around another.

"Small but strong, safe inside," she said. She took his hand and opened it again, pressing it to her belly, folding her own hands over the top. She relaxed into him. A low purring sound reverberated within the tunnel, soft and deep, and for a while she rested against him.

Eventually she stirred, shifting in his lap. He turned his face down to her and she stroked her hand down the side of his face. "Is she awake?"

Gramawl nodded slowly and allowed Blackbird to climb from his lap before rising easily, filling the tunnel again with his bulk. He turned and led the way into the darkness. Blackbird followed, her footsteps sure despite the lack of light. He would not lead her astray.

The tunnel curved then straightened, and she could see the dim light from the steps spilling down from the side tunnel. He stopped on the far side of the tunnel, eyes gleaming in the dark. She reached up to pat his cheek, then mounted the steps carefully, holding the handrail so she would not falter, up to the half-landing, turning back on herself. She could see the opening above, the lamps in their metal shuttered cowls, the smell of cloves mixed with new turned earth.

"Who is it?" The voice was crackly, but clear. Blackbird smiled in the dimness.

"It's me. I've come to see you."

"Girl? Is it you?"

As she mounted the remaining steps, she could see dark rich hangings in heavy Persian designs draped across the opening,

"Yes, Kareesh. I'm here." She put her hand into the gap to part them.

"One in two. Two in one." The voice had changed.

"Isn't one and isn't two. Two and one. Knit together, entwined and entangled, made together, pulled asunder."

Blackbird hesitated, caught between going to help and making it worse. Kareesh's high delicate voice cracked as she spat out the words.

"All together, all apart. Two made one, made three, now two, make two, make one. One to shine, one to rise, one to live, one to die…"

Blackbird could hear the stress rising, the words tumbling like stones in a stream. She was shouting now, punching words out so that Blackbird could hardly separate them.

"…One is two, and two is one, then one is none, all is gone, so many gone and all is won and lost and gone for all that none can be alone…"

Blackbird hurried down the stairs, away from the shouting. As she descended it slowed and quietened a little.

"One and one and two by two. One is son and sundered son. Two is son and one shall rise. Sun shall rise and shine for all. Then all shall fall…"

When she reached the bottom, Gramawl was waiting. He moved her gently to one side, gesturing for her to wait down the tunnel, then stooped into the stairway and quickly mounted the stairs. Using her hand against the wall to guide her, Blackbird slowly made her way back along the tunnel to the light.

She was sitting on the stairway when Gramawl returned some time later.

"Is she all right?" she whispered.

The question hung in the air between them.

Gramawl lowered himself down again and sat in the corridor. She stood and went to him.

He made a stirring gesture, then patted his palm, then touched his forehead, his eyes and his lips. For once he looked tired and sad.

"I know she's old, and it's not her fault. She sees

233

what she sees. I know that."

He repeated the gesture with his lips.

"It doesn't matter whether she means it or not. It's not her saying it, really, is it? It spills out of her and there's nothing any of us can do."

He reached out and touched her belly gently with a finger then rocked his head between his hands.

"You think so? You may be right. Having two lives so close together, the new one with so many futures, it could send her crazy like that."

They were silent for a moment.

"She said, 'One to live, one to die,'" Blackbird said quietly.

Gramawl touched his nose, his head and his ears in quick succession, then opened his hands.

"No, I suppose you're right. It may mean something else entirely. There's no way of knowing."

He rose to his feet and she stepped in, burying her hands up to her elbows in fur as she hugged herself close to him, breathing in the scent of new-turned earth, resting against the solidity of him.

"I have to go."

A giant hand stroked her hair, holding her for a little longer.

She disentangled herself and drew her hair back from her face. She collected the horseshoe from below the step and stowed it carefully in her bag.

"When she wakes?"

Gramawl cocked his head.

"Tell her… tell her I wanted to see her. Tell her I'll bring the baby, after it's born. Tell her I'll try."

Gramawl bowed low, a low rumble filling the space and echoing down the tunnel.

"You too. Take care."

She mounted the stairs, climbing back to the world of men.

FOURTEEN

I'd thought they would have records in the library: archives of town newspapers and local history. I was disappointed. A fair-haired young man who looked as if he needed a good meal told me that the rest of the records were kept in the County Record Office in Northallerton. If I wanted more, I would have to go there. He glanced meaningfully at the rain running down the windows, suggesting that I might stay a while out of the rain.

I settled for scanning through three or four books on the history of the area. They were better than I had expected. They followed the town from its beginnings as a Bronze Age settlement, showing monochrome photographs of Victorian men in bowler hats with shovels and picks posing as archaeologists over the trenched-out remains of an Iron Age long barrow. Having met one or two modern-day archaeologists, I knew exactly what they would think of this particular brand of institutionalised vandalism. These were fortune-hunters at best, and kept no record of the placing, distribution or arrangement of their finds, being only interested in their value as antiquarian treasure.

The books followed the community through mediae-val times under the priory at Bridlington into the inevitable conflict of civil war and the Industrial Revo-lution. The coming of steam meant larger vessels with deeper draught, and the shallow harbour fell from use as a shipping port into fishing and light trade. Nowhere was there any mention of dark deeds or missing women. Rather, the community supported itself through the best and worst of times, rising to each new challenge and meeting each change with determination and vigour. If there had been women going missing on a regular basis, I would have thought some sort of mention would be made, even if only as a passing reference.

Since it was still raining hard, I made use of the free internet access to Google a search for Ravensby. It threw up the usual discount offers and, with some persever-ance, I found the reports of the five missing girls. If there was a long list of missing women from Ravensby, though, it wasn't on the internet. I also used the image search to look for the symbol I'd seen on the truck wait-ing near the hospital where Alex had been taken. The nearest I could find was a hazardous load symbol for a biohazard, but that symbol was subtly different. A fur-ther hour of browsing brought me no closer. I found companies that could provide transport for hazardous material and there were lots of theories as to how certain diseases had found their way into the population, but nothing that would lead me to Alex.

Just out of interest, I googled 'Feyre'. The list of hits that emerged mainly led to Sainte-Feyre in central France, mak-ing me wonder whether the place had any fey significance. There were no references to creatures by that name.

"Are you all right with that?"

The young man appeared by my side, making me can-cel the search quickly before he noticed what I'd been searching for.

"I'm fine, thanks."

He smiled thinly and moved away. He probably thought I was using it to look at pictures of naked women. Putting my wet coat back on, I thanked the librarian for his time and asked him where I might find further local history to fill out my picture of the town. He directed me to the local newspaper, saying that he thought they kept their own archive. I picked up my umbrella and left.

The woman in the newspaper office was far less helpful. As soon as she realised that I didn't want to buy advertising space, she lost interest. Yes, they probably did have back copies of the newspapers in an archive but no, I couldn't look through them. Had I tried the public library? When I said I had, her expression didn't change. Two words were on the tip of her tongue and one of them was "off".

That left me with one more avenue to try before a trip to the record office became necessary. The local museum was a small affair and survived from a combination of local authority support and donations from tourists who must have got lost to end up there. The sign outside proclaimed that the Maritime Museum was open, though the windows were dark and there was no obvious sign of life.

When I pushed the door open, a small bell jangled, the sort that graced shop doorways and announced customers to men behind counters wearing brown overalls. It took a moment for my eyes to adjust. Inside was a small hallway, the wall festooned in trawl netting and blown-glass floats.

"Put wood in t'hole."

I hadn't noticed the gentleman sitting behind the desk in the room off to my left, not because I didn't see him, but because he looked like an exhibit.

"Sorry?"

"The door, lad. Shut it, before t'weather comes in."

I closed the door behind me. The bell jangled again.

"Is the museum open?"

"Y're in aren't ya?"

"I suppose so."

"We're open then."

I looked around. The museum appeared to be two terraced houses knocked into one, with an arch between them to access one house from the other. Almost every surface was covered in items of differing size and in various states of disrepair or assembly. Museums I'd been in before had display cases with carefully controlled temperature and humidity. This one had shelves and tables, desks and chairs, all covered in what could only be described as... stuff.

"It's three quid," said the man.

A sign on the desk said that all donations were purely voluntary and gratefully accepted.

I looked meaningfully at the sign.

"You get naught for nowt round 'ere," he said. "I've got change."

I delved in a pocket and came out with the money. He accepted the coins with a nod and carefully wrote me a receipt. It was unreadable.

"You pay tax?" His look said that I probably didn't. "We can claim the tax back if you do."

"No," I said. Since I'd lost my job, I didn't get paid a salary any more, so I didn't pay tax either. If I needed money, I was given some, though I had little enough to spend it on.

"Thought so."

"Is there a guidebook?" I asked.

"It's another pound," he said.

I handed over a further coin. He passed me a bundle of photocopied sheets that had obviously been read before.

"These aren't new," I pointed out.

"We'd like 'em back when you've finished. Recycling."

I took the sheets and wandered on into the house, looking at all the objects strewn randomly around. The guide was interesting enough and talked about the history of the town and the people that lived there. It provided no clue as to the origins and purpose of most of the things in the museum. I figured you probably had to be born here to know that.

Amid the collection there were farm implements, examples of lace, ancient comic annuals and discarded toys. Nothing was in any order or sequence. A rusty lobster pot provided a resting place for a child's doll with no indication that there was any relationship between the two.

On the first floor I came into a room full of photographs and pictures. There were engravings showing ships ploughing through mountainous seas in great storms, and shadowy photographs of grim-faced men hauling a lifeboat on a trailer. Sepia-tinted portraits showed families tricked out in Sunday best, hats on and children scrubbed. In amongst these pictures were photographs of men and women, a mayor and a schoolteacher, a town clerk and a governess. None were smiling.

"All dead now."

The man from downstairs was standing in the doorway. I hadn't heard him approach, which was surprising given how the wooden floors in the houses creaked as you walked.

"Some fine people," I commented, gesturing to the wall.

"They worked hard, 'n' built this town from nowt. Better than it is now. It's a shadow of what it was."

I scanned the pictures. "They don't look too happy about it."

"Don't believe it. Sitting for a portrait in them days was just that. Took forever to take a photo. Imagine standing in a starched collar, buttoned up. You wouldn't be smiling, neither."

"I expect you're right."

He walked over to stand beside me. Surveying the pictures, he pointed to an oval portrait of a rather stoic, round-faced young woman dressed in black with white lace at her collar and cuffs.

"Only time I ever saw her without a smile. She were a grand old lady."

"You knew her?"

"I should do. She were my great-grandmother."

"She must have lived to a good age, if you knew her."

"Aye. Right until after the war."

"The First World War?"

"No, second one. She died in nineteen forty-eight. Six children, and seventeen great-grandchildren. Related to half the town, one way and another."

"Quite a woman."

"You didn't mess, that was for sure. She never raised a hand, though. Didn't have to."

"How old was she when she died?"

"Into her nineties, I should think. Not the sort of question you could ask."

"That's old for those times, especially after six children."

"Aye. Never complained. Always smiling, except for that photo. Never liked a fuss made, Sea Queen or not."

"Sea Queen?"

"Aye. Used to be a big event. Parade round the harbour, a band, mayor's speech and that. Used to make a big thing of it. My sister had it one year. She were a bonny lass too."

"Runs in the family."

"Aye, well. None of 'em interested now. No call for herring or mackerel. No call for Sea Queens neither, though there's some that would like to start it up again."

"Really?"

"Always some mad bugger wants to go back to the old way."

"Not you, though? No grandchildren, wanting to follow in great-great-grandmother's footsteps?"

"They're all telly watchers now. Wouldn't know one end of a gutting knife from another. Last thing they want is to smell of fish. It's all changed."

"I suppose it has. Still, she's a grand old lady."

"She is that."

"There's something I wanted to ask," I said.

"Oh, aye?"

"These young women that have gone missing; there are posters all over town."

"I've seen 'em," he said, nodding.

"Is that a new thing, or has that always gone on?"

"What d'ya mean, gone on?"

"I was wondering. Has it always been like that? It's a small community. You could understand if people needed to get away, find a new place for themselves. Would anyone care?"

"You've never lived anywhere like this, have you?"

"I grew up in the country. This is a bit like a village, isn't it? Everyone knows everyone else's business?"

"It's a small community, I'll give you that, and people do know what each other are about, but it's not like a village. Come through here."

He took me through an archway into the adjoining house. There was one room at the back that was different from all the other rooms in the museum. It had a small table with a book open upon it. On the walls were more pictures. Some were photographs, some paintings, some black and white and some colour. One or two looked quite recent.

"Ravensby's not a village, it's a town. More important, it's a harbour town. If you've never lived in a place like this, then you wouldn't know."

"These are all boats from the town?"

"Some are, some are from other harbours. They're all still here, though, in a way."

"Still here?"

241

"Every one of these went down off this coast. These boats are out there somewhere, or were smashed to pieces against the rocks, or were driven up on to the beach. If they were lucky, the men will have been rescued. Often as not, they were never found."

I looked around the room. There were boats of every size: trawlers, steamships, cargo ships, even lifeboats.

"The ninth of February, 1871 was a nice day. Boats put out in a fair north-westerly. With the dawn on the tenth, though, the wind veered."

The old man's eyes were open, but it wasn't the pictures he was seeing.

"By seven o'clock next morning it had turned one hundred and eighty, south-easterly and building hurricane force. The waves came up and the sleet and snow were driven flat. Some boats tried to run before it, but the waves overpowered them, the wind stripped the rigging and they were driven on to the rocks, the bottoms ripped out. One tried to make port; it was crushed by the swell against the harbour wall, the men pulled from the sea on ropes thrown from the harbour by rescuers who lashed themselves to the mooring rings so as not to get swept away theirselves."

His voice was soft, but somewhere in it was the force of the storm.

"Others went for the beach. They grounded the boats on the shingle and the men jumped into the waves, only to be dragged back by the undertow. Men from the town were standing chest-deep in the waves, trying to haul them out, their hands numb with cold, their faces frozen with shock.

"The lifeboat went out time after time, dragging men from the waves, but it was only one boat. There were ships swamped by the waves, men hanging from the rigging, calling out for aid. It was piteous. No one could

242

reach them. The lifeboat went out for a collier brig. It was foundering and the men were clinging to the stern. The lifeboat tried to reach them, but a wave picked it up and smashed it into the fully laden brig. The lifeboat crew and the men from the brig were all lost."

"It sounds horrific."

"It was. Forty-four men were lost that day from this town alone. Up and down this coast, Scarborough, Bridlington, Filey, many more, 'twere the same. Women stood on the harbour within sight of their menfolk and watched them drown."

"That's awful."

"Not quite like village life, is it?"

"No."

"That was a bad one. There were other bad ones too. Happens about every twenty-plus years. The weather forecasting's got better now, and there's more warning, but even a warning's no good if you're two or three days away from port. You just have to sit it out."

"You still lose boats?"

"Aye. Even with the new lifeboat down the coast. All the technology, navigation equipment, radios; it's all naught if the sea takes against you. There's no fighting nature."

"It must be harsh."

"It is. It is harsh, but it's a way of life. The women are strong. They know what can happen. Many of 'em have seen it. It's a small community and a close one. There's always help, always someone to catch you when you fall. We look after our own."

I wasn't sure what to say to that.

"Not these lasses, though. Gone to the big city, lure of the bright lights. I can't blame them. It's a hard life when you don't know whether your man's coming home or not. The day was, they didn't know owt else. It's what they were brought up to. Now, though, it's all

243

internet and mobile phones. They've seen a different life. That's why they've gone. I can't blame them."

"So it's not happened before?"

"Oh, there's always been those that didn't stay. They married out, or moved inland. The ties are still there, though. They never went far. It's in the blood, see?"

"So what changed?"

"These girls are part of it, going off, God knows where. What are they thinking? Who'll keep things together, if they've left? Who'll keep the lights on, make it worth coming back to port?"

"Maybe they don't see themselves that way?"

"The boats sit tied up in t'harbour. They say there's no fish, that the sea's turned its back on them."

"Has it?"

"There's fish, but you have to work for 'em. They don't jump into your hold on their own. It's hard, I know, but you don't catch fish in port."

"Maybe they're only allowed to catch so many. Aren't there quotas for fishing these days?"

"Aye, there are. None of our boats are close to reaching 'em. If they go out they come back wi' nowt. Empty nets, empty holds. It happens. The sea has lean years like everything else. It's happened before, it'll happen again. You don't stop. You keep at it until the nets are full again and things come right."

"Maybe they've over-fished it. Maybe it needs time to recover."

"Aye, well, it's time they don't have. No fish means no money. If they can't pay the loans on the boats then the banks'll pull the plug. By the time it comes back we'll be buying fish frozen from Norway. The town'll die and that'll be that."

"There are other things. The call centre looks pretty impressive. Won't that keep things going?"

"The council's golden goose? Don't be daft. It's only

there cos of grants and incentives. As soon as the money dries up they'll move the jobs out to India or somewhere."

"What about tourism?"

"Look outside. It's not Scarborough, is it? That beach is so steep that if you get in t'sea you can't get out again. No, this town lives and breathes fish, and at the moment it's mightily short of breath."

"That's a very pessimistic view."

"It's a realistic view. The women of this town are the lifeblood. When you never know if the men are coming back, they've had to be. Once the women start leaving, it's the beginning of the end."

"Maybe they didn't leave. Maybe something happened to them?"

"Something did happen to them. They lost faith." He turned to the book on the desk. "Every man that ever went missing, lost, drowned, is in there. There's no book for missing women, and I'm not intending to start one."

He turned away and stomped down the stairs, leaving me with the book of names and the pictures of lost vessels. It was a sobering experience. I leafed through the pages, seeing the same names crop up again and again. By the time I'd reached the present day, I was wondering why they ever left port at all. To me it was inconceivable, after suffering such personal loss, to send another family member out on to the waves. But then, as he'd pointed out, I wasn't born here. I wasn't part of this community and I would probably never understand what kept it going.

After a while I went back down and passed the printed guide back to him. There was no word of thanks or invitation to return. He didn't speak, just took the sheets from me and replaced them where he'd found them. As I turned to leave, the street door opened and a middle-aged man stepped inside.

"It's bucketing out there. Fit for neither man nor beast." He shook the water from his sleeves.

"Back again, Ted?" said the man behind the desk.

He looked sceptically at my umbrella as I approached the door, knowing it would be useless in the wind, but then held the door open for me so I could leave. The water dripped from his orange waterproofs leaving a puddle inside the door. I stepped through quickly, not wanting to keep the door open longer than necessary and then found myself struggling to fasten buttons and turn up my collar in the blustery wind.

Within moments, I was wet again. The rain found every gap, every crease. I made my way back to the harbour front, shoulders hunched against the wind, the halyards on the moored sailing boats tinging like manic vespers bells against the aluminium spars. Rather than make my way back to my room, I headed for the Harbour Café. The door was so swollen with damp that I had to push hard to get inside. I wedged the door closed again, shutting out the weather.

I took my jacket off and shook it over the doormat, earning a disapproving look from Geraldine. I hung it over the back of a chair at a table by the window and took the other seat.

Geraldine bustled up. "What'll it be?"

"Coffee, please. Filter will do."

She looked expectant, so I disappointed her further. "That's it, thanks."

Her walk as she returned to the kitchen said just what she thought of men who ordered only coffee when it was still officially lunchtime. A scalding mug of coffee was delivered moments later, making me wonder whether she had simply put a mug of this morning's dregs into the microwave. It was far too hot to drink, but I was in no hurry and the café was all but empty.

The windows of the café were steamy with condensation inside and running with rain outside, offering little in the way of a view. It left me to my thoughts: of the men and boats lost in storms like this one, of the girls and their different reasons for leaving the town, and of Blackbird. Where was she now? Where could she go that would be safe with Deefnir stalking her? The desire to follow her down to London was strong, but what would I do when I got there?

I was lost in thought and took no notice when the door juddered open again and slammed against the stop before being shunted carefully back into place.

Geraldine came forward and then hesitated.

"I'll have whatever he's having." The voice brought me out of my reverie.

"Raffmir."

"May I join you? I find the weather here quite inclement, even for this forsaken backwater."

I remembered Garvin's instruction to find out what he wanted. Then I remembered who it was I was talking to. "There are plenty of other tables."

"True, but I thought we might talk."

"About what?"

He sat opposite me, unconcerned by my rudeness.

"I was wondering whether you'd had an opportunity to consider my offer to assist you in the matter of your daughter's whereabouts," he said.

"Her whereabouts?"

"Oh, come. You're not still pretending you know where she is? Surely we're past that, aren't we?"

"I'm not sure what it is that we're supposed to be past. Why don't you tell me what you want and then you can go and find somewhere where the weather suits you better. I think Mars is supposed to be dry."

"You don't trust me. I understand that. I sympathise."

"Fuck off, Raffmir."

"No need to be abusive. I'm trying to help you."

"I neither want nor need your help."

"That's where you're wrong. You need my help more than anyone's. I'm the only one who can bring you to your daughter."

"You don't know where she is." It was a statement. I was calling his bluff.

"I know where she will be."

Geraldine appeared with another mug of coffee. This one was freshly made and smelled considerably better then the one I was drinking. He smiled at her as she leaned down to place it at the table for him and she hesitated, then blushed, and hurried back to the counter.

"Are you flirting with the staff?"

"Flirting? Good grief, no." He shook his head, then sampled his coffee and grinned at me.

Mine was still too hot to drink.

"How will you know where she is, Raffmir? You don't have any more idea than I do."

"Ah, then you admit you have lost her."

"Now who's playing games?"

"You are a hard man to help, Niall Petersen."

I sighed. "You're not helping me. Whatever it is you're doing, you have your own reasons for doing it and they do not involve helping me."

"That's where you're wrong. Hear me. Without me, your daughter will be lost to you. Without me, you will never reach her in time. Time is running out, Dogstar. Soon, you will have to make your choice."

"What choice?"

"The choice between obedience and duty, between honour and love."

"What are you talking about?"

"That time is fast approaching, but you need to trust me."

"Why should I trust you? What possible reason would I have?"

"Because I have sworn to see you unharmed. Because, despite your rudeness and your arrogance, I know you will do what's best. We are cousins, you and I. We are alike."

"I am not like you."

"We are more alike than you know."

"We killed your sister, Blackbird and I." It was a remark meant to taunt, and for a fraction of a second there was something in his eyes that looked like hate. It vanished as quickly as it appeared.

"It was the witch's hand that did the deed," he growled.

"It was her hand, but raised in my protection. Your sister would have killed me otherwise, trial or no trial, rules or no rules. You know it's true."

"I will not gainsay it." He drank carefully from his mug.

"So why would you help me? You owe me nothing, Raffmir, nor I you."

He stared out of the rain-smeared glass for a moment. "I cannot tell you why. You are right. There is more to this than can be seen, but hear me when I say this: your daughter's life hangs by a fragile thread. Her fate is intimately bound in with mine, I know this now. When I tell you that I am the only one who can help you recover your daughter, you know it's true. The lie would be obvious to you, were it otherwise."

"OK. But nothing is free, is it? What do you want in return?"

"For now? I need your silence. I am aware that Garvin and the other Warders will want to know what we have discussed. It is only natural that they will try and come between us. But if you want your daughter back, you must keep the subject of our discourse to yourself."

"What? No way…"

"Then you seal her fate. Will you do that, Niall Petersen?" He looked straight into my eyes and spoke levelly and calmly. "For as sure as you can hear the truth in my words, if you tell them, your daughter will die."

FIFTEEN

"Are you threatening her, Raffmir? Because if you are—"

Raffmir shook his head. "As always, Dogstar, you interpret my actions in their least favourable light, and quite unfairly, I might add. I have taken an oath that I will not harm your daughter and I intend to keep it. If you will only let me help you, I will see to it that you are reunited. How can I say fairer than that?"

"You could tell me what you're doing here."

"I did tell you. I'm trying to help you. There are things here that I am not at liberty to discuss, but I am not the only one who is holding things back."

"What does that mean?"

"Has Garvin told you how the negotiations are progressing?"

"In summary, yes."

"He's not mentioned any of the detail, then?"

"He doesn't normally discuss the inner workings of the High Court with me. I'm not his confidante."

"Even when those discussions concern you and yours?"

"What does that mean?"

"I am merely saying that while you are ostracised here in outer obscurity, negotiations are taking place that affect you and all the other mongrel fey. Did you never wonder why neither you nor any of the other half-breeds are part of those negotiations?"

"That's clever, Raffmir. Without directly saying anything you attempt to drive a wedge between me and the other Warders."

"Then why are you here?" He gestured through the rain-streaked window at the blurry harbour.

"I'm here because of you. Garvin's well aware that if I stayed at Court, you would create some sort of incident. It's just the sort of thing you would do."

"I am offended. Have I not sworn to see you unharmed?"

"Then call Deefnir off. He's out there somewhere, harassing Blackbird."

"Deefnir is not mine to command."

"How convenient."

"That still does not explain why you were sent all the way out here. If the purpose was to keep you away from me, we can both agree that it isn't working. Perhaps there is another reason."

"Garvin wouldn't lie to me."

"Neither would I. There would be no point. Can I suggest that the reason you are not in Court is because your very presence would prejudice the negotiations. With you there, it would be awkward to place certain options on the table."

"Suggestion and innuendo – it's your usual trade, isn't it Raffmir?"

"You are letting your prejudice blind you to the truth."

"And what truth would that be?"

"That if it is to the High Court's advantage, they will sacrifice you and all the other half-breeds without a moment's thought. You are pawns, and this is a game with very high stakes."

"That may be true, Raffmir, but we've had this conversation before. You're not offering any better, are you?

Whatever the outcome for the half-breeds, it will always be better than anything you and your friends have to offer."

"You're assuming that loyalty works both ways, Niall."

"And you're assuming I'll follow your convoluted logic. I have sworn loyalty to the council and they have sworn not to harm me or mine. I trust them more than I trust you."

"Then your trust may be misplaced, for they will always choose the path that benefits them most, regardless of who stands upon it. It has ever been thus."

"That's irrelevant. I still don't trust you."

"And I have given you no reason to, a mistake that I will remedy. Come." He stood in one easy movement."

"I haven't finished my coffee."

"It is bitter and spoiled."

"I could say the same of you."

He sighed with exaggerated impatience. "Accompany me now and I will share with you a secret of the wraithkin, something that none of your Warder companions can do for you. I do this as a gesture of good faith against some future need, so that you may better care for you and yours. There, is that good enough, or will you sit and sulk for no other reason than that you are too cynical to do otherwise?"

I watched him, considering. He had carefully avoided mentioning anything I didn't already know, while attempting to undermine the relationships I already had. He was being evasive and deceitful. None of that was any surprise. Still, I would not find out what he wanted sitting in the café.

I rose and put on my coat, making a show of straightening it where Raffmir had leaned on it, then collected my umbrella. He ignored me and went to the counter to pay. I stood and watched him while Geraldine smiled and then laughed at some comment he made.

When he came back, I held the door open. The worst of the wind had died down, but it was still raining steadily.

"You two are getting on well. Will you be returning later?"

"Politeness costs nothing, Dogstar. You would be well advised to remember that." He stepped out into the rain and I followed him.

"Nah," I said. "She fancies you something rotten."

"I do not fraternise with her like."

"You're fraternising with me. It's just one big slippery slope, when you think about it."

"Do you make a habit of goading me?"

"Everyone should have a hobby."

We walked up the hill in silence. It was quite rewarding to realise that I could get under his skin. It was also an interesting development; after all, he didn't have to be here. It left me even more convinced that he wanted something from me. I had only to find out what it was.

He walked uphill into the layer of wet clouds shrouding the upper parts of the town, and navigated directly to the Way-point, stepping easily up on to the spongy grass and making no attempt to conceal our presence. As we climbed the grassy bank, the billowing mist blurred the houses below and then obscured them completely. It felt as if we were alone. A prickle of tension crept up the back of my neck. Had he brought me here so that we would not be seen? He had sworn not to do me harm, but if no one saw what had happened, who would accuse him?

"You know how to use the Ways?" he asked.

"Of course."

"Do you think you can follow where I lead?"

"Where are we going?"

"Somewhere dry. You do not need to be concerned."

"I'm always concerned when you're involved."

"This is where you have to decide to trust me. Once I've gone, you'll need to follow quickly or you'll lose the trail. Try and keep up."

"Is this where I choose between, what is it…. honour or love?"

"That comes later." He stepped on to the node and the mist swirled in around him. The vortex turned and collapsed and he was gone.

At that moment, part of me wanted to set off back down the hill and forget him. Part of me knew that whatever he wanted, it was in his interests, not mine. All of me knew that whatever it was, it would lead nowhere good. The vague insinuations about my daughter, the innuendo about Court politics; they were a smokescreen for something, but I couldn't help feeling that not knowing would only make it worse.

I stepped on to the node and felt the Way rise beneath me. The sense of a passage in the Way was there, a trail left by another traveller. Unlike Blackbird's warm trail this felt cold, but it was distinct. I let the Way pick me up and hurl me after him, sensing the warp of space as I swept through the emptiness, echoing his passing. The Way contracted around the next Way-node and then veered at the last second, bypassing the node and flinging us back into the black. We sped through a night-black veil streaked with hanging clouds of luminescent frost until we reached another node and slingshotted around that, not touching, but whipping tight around it, accelerating outwards and away. I found myself spinning, legs and arms outstretched, unable to orientate myself while my eyes watered without blinking, unable to focus. Space contracted and blurred and then shot me out, bouncing and rolling on to the hillside, my umbrella flying out of my hand. Instinct and training broke my fall, slowing me down until I could roll to a stop and rise to my knees.

Raffmir stood, watching me. "You have no style," he said.

"That," I said as I picked myself up from the grass and collected the umbrella, "was interesting. Where are we?"

"I promised you better weather, did I not?"

I looked around. We were on the rise of a high hill-top, with other hills arrayed around us and deep valleys in between. The overcast sky lent a sourceless light, but even so the shade deepened in the valleys. The grass was dry, and it was obvious it hadn't rained here today.

"Wales?" I asked.

"It's really not important. We are not here for sightseeing."

"Then why are we here?"

"You have not yet promised me that you will keep our conversation from Garvin."

"Nor will I. I have no reason to keep this from him."

"Your daughter's life is insufficient reason?"

"Your threat is not sufficient reason. You still haven't told me precisely what peril she is in and what you have to do with it. For all I know it could be you that's threatening her."

"I have sworn not to harm her. I can do no more."

"We've had this conversation. I will tell Garvin what I need to tell him."

"Very well, I see that in order for you to trust me, I must first trust you. It is good that one of us has some faith in his heart,"

"Oh, I have plenty of faith in other people."

He gave me a sour look, but then straightened his coat. "You already know the Ways, though I think you did not know them as well as you thought."

"It was an enlightening experience, I'll admit that much."

"Now I will show you something of the wraithkin, something your Warder brethren cannot show you."

"If it's card tricks, I've seen them before."

"You test my patience, Dogstar. You would scorn the magic you inherited. Your sarcasm reflects badly on you. You have respect for no one. It is no wonder my brothers and sisters will not harbour you."

"That's not the reason, and we both know it."

He stared at me. I did not look away. It was he who finally looked to the next hill across the valley. "See the copse atop the hill there."

"I see it."

"How long would it take you to get there?"

"Walking?"

"By whatever means."

"Half an hour or an hour on foot, maybe. Less in a car, assuming you can get a car up there." The only road in sight wound along the bottom of the valley, but there might be side roads up the hillside, hidden in the shadow of the hill. "If there's a Way-point it would be quicker."

"There is no Way-point nearby other than the one we arrived on. It is a closed end. That's why we are here. The only path from here is back where we came."

"So what do you want me to do?"

"Learn, Dogstar. Watch and learn."

He stood, gazing across the valley. I sensed a creeping spread of power, enveloping and concealing, hiding us from view.

"I can do that myself," I commented.

A sudden chill fell on the hilltop, so sudden and distinct that it made me focus my attention on him. He was drawing in power, building a store of energy. The tips of my ears were suddenly cold and I wrapped my arms about me against the hard edge in the breeze.

Around Raffmir flickering fingers of light formed a nimbus. It built until he was outlined in white fire. He glanced sideways at me, grinned, and then stepped forward.

The light flashed and blinked out and it was a moment before I could see again. I was alone on the sunset hilltop.

I looked about me, searching for where he had hidden himself and then realised the point of the demonstration. Shielding my eyes, I searched the treeline opposite. Against the dark woodland, there was a darker patch in the distance. The figure raised an arm and waved slowly. Even from there, I could tell he was grinning back at me.

It was a grin that said, "I know something you don't."

· After a moment, I began to see a glow around him. He made no attempt to hide it this time, and even from a distance I could see the white fire dancing across his shoulders. There was a bright flash, and he was walking back across the grass towards me.

"You will not allow it, but you are impressed."

"It's a fine trick."

"Do you always disparage that which you do not have? I find it tires me."

"It helps me keep things in perspective."

"I will give you free advice, cousin. If you stay that sour, the wind will change and you will stay that way. Learn to appreciate the things you are given and you will have a better time of it."

"Never look a gift horse in the mouth."

"Exactly so."

"And yet, gift horses do have a knack of dropping dead at inconvenient moments, don't they?"

"That cynical streak will give you ulcers. Now I want you to try. You may find it more difficult. The ground has cooled and it will be some time until it recovers. It will be possible, nevertheless."

"You want me to do that."

"You are wraithkin born, and gifted with power. Will you disappoint me?"

"I'm not here to please you, Raffmir."

"Nevertheless, it is a useful skill, is it not?"

I had to admit, the ability to travel a distance in an instant might come in useful. "Show me."

"Stand here. You need to see where you are going. Memory is not enough, you need to see your destination. If you can't see it, you can't go there."

I felt his magic creep out around us, concealing us once more.

"Focus on the distant point. Bring it closer with your eyes, if you can. What do you see between here and there?"

"Nothing."

"Yet there remains a distance between you. There is something. There is air, and space, and the distance between."

"Of course."

"But you are wraithkin. The space between is your space. The gaps between the gaps belong to you. If you concentrate, you can step around the distance. You can get from here to there without travelling in between."

"How? I don't see…"

"Don't see! Your sight is not to be trusted. It tells you lies. It says there is distance between here and there when there is merely a flimsy curtain with the world depicted upon it. Step behind that curtain and out again, do you see?"

"I'm not seeing it."

"More power; draw what you need. Use more than your eyes. Find the gaps, the cracks and crevices between the walls of the universe. Your sight tells you the world is solid. Your touch confirms the weight and texture of reality. But you are wraithkin. You have other senses. You can sense that the world is nowhere near as solid as it wants you to believe. It is thin and insubstantial. Push through."

"Into what?"

"Never mind what. Feel. Your element calls you as it calls all the wraithkin. Answer it and you will see."

259

And I did see. As I gathered power into me, the world began to dim. The sense of a solid reality fell away and I began to perceive it as a construct layered on top of something else. It lost its density and its stiffness and became more flexible, more permeable.

"Now. Focus on the hillside. Focus and step through."

I looked across at the copse of trees. I saw through the space between, not across the valley, but through space itself. And I stepped.

A blinding light flashed into my eyes. I raised my hand, but the light had already vanished. I was facing trees. The distant copse was in front of me, the leaves fluttering in the evening breeze. I turned and the valley stretched out beneath my feet. On the far side, a lone figure stood. There was no wave or acknowledgment. He simply watched.

He was right, it was impressive. I stared across the valley. As the man in the museum had said earlier, you get naught for nowt round 'ere. The Feyre were like that. They understood the basic economics of favour and return, and Raffmir had just shown me something quite spectacular. There was real value in it, so what did he want in return? Across the valley, he did not move.

I wrapped myself in misdirection, unwilling to be as open and obvious as he had been. Opening the well inside myself, I drew energy into me, letting it pull power from the surroundings. The light breeze acquired bite as the temperature fell. I lifted my hand to see filaments of white light drifting up my fingers, creating a tingling sensation and forming a corona around my hand. I let the power build, feeling a tension as the air and ground around me cooled.

The world dimmed before me, the hill becoming a shadow hill, the valley obscured in the dusk-light. It made me feel that I would fall through the delicate membrane on which I stood. In that veiled light, I could see other shadows, a wrinkle in the substance of the hill, flimsy curtains in the air, shifting layers in the air. I wondered what they meant, and whether I was seeing distortions in the fabric of reality or if it was simply the way things were formed.

Lifting my eyes, I saw that the sky had dimmed, taking on a twilight quality. The overcast clouds had faded, leaving a blue-grey mantle, prickled with faint stars. A sickly green-tinged moon lay close on the horizon. It was a world beneath the world, a level below or alongside, matched but subtly different.

I reminded myself why I was here and focused upon the far hilltop. This time it was easier to slip behind the curtain of reality and re-emerge on the far side. There was no rush. I didn't feel flung across space as I did on the Way. It was only a step. Raffmir waited patiently, his gaze focused far out where the purple hills merged with the grey cloud.

"You're right. It is impressive."

"What? No word of thanks? No gratitude?"

"Tell me first what you would have in return. There is something, isn't there?"

"I offer you my assurances. I would ask nothing from you that you would not give, and gladly. There, that is generous, is it not?"

I smiled wryly and shook my head. "I have no idea, Raffmir. But I will wait to offer my thanks until I know what it is you want in return."

"I desire only your trust, and your silence. The time will come soon enough when you will have to choose and it is never an easy choice between love and honour. I do not envy you."

"Tell me why I must choose, then."

"I offer you gifts and your first response is to ask for more. Your gratitude knows its bounds, cousin. But it must wait in turn, like all else. We cannot reach the end without passing through the middle."

"I thought that's what we just did," I said, looking back across this valley.

"A bad analogy. I have shown good faith and more besides. It is enough for one day. Come, I will return you to your seaside banishment."

I followed him across the ragged grass to the Way-node.

"Follow closely, and this time, try to exhibit some style."

He stepped on to the Way-node and swirled away without pausing. I followed close behind. We slingshotted around the first node and away towards the second, but instead of following him onward, I entered the node and arrived, wrapping myself in concealment. It was another high hilltop, somewhere in the Welsh borders, maybe.

Reorienting myself, I stepped quickly away, taking a side route away from his path. I had other plans and they did not include having Raffmir shadow me wherever I went. The next node-point was a barrow mound in a meadow, open to the sky, the smell of wet grass rich in the summer air. I diverted again. He would wait a little while for me to follow and then, perhaps, retrace our journey. If he tried to follow me, I wanted to make it as difficult as possible.

This time, I used his technique of skipping across the nodes and using their momentum to accelerate out again, making the most of the momentum and maximising the distance. There was no time to consult the codex, but I had a vague idea of direction and I used the node-points to guess my route. Nevertheless, I took a couple of unintentional wild detours, unable to quite control the helter-skelter freefall. I hoped that would only make me harder to follow.

I ended up in a woodland clearing, the steady drone of cars indicating some main route close by. I moved out of the clearing quickly, using a fallen branch to brush across my footprints, heading towards the road. It was afternoon, but I was counting on the midsummer daylight lasting late into the evening. It would be bright enough to be seen on the road for a while yet.

I'd hitched rides as a student. Before I'd learned to drive or had the money for a car, I'd stood on motorway junctions with a cardboard sign hoping for lifts. I knew the roads around Kent and the south-east fairly well. Sometimes my patience was rewarded, but often lifts were a short distance only or not quite in the right direction. I had been marooned on deserted junctions in appalling weather, so the sound of the busy road was encouraging. I tramped out of the woods on to a four-lane road with fast-moving cars.

The traffic was moving too quickly where I emerged, so I walked along the grass verge, keeping the traffic on my right so that I would head vaguely southwards. The cars and trucks rushed past, buffeting me as they passed. I knew that drivers were unlikely to stop unless they could get a good look at you as they went by and there was somewhere safe to stop. If I was lucky, one of them would decide I wasn't a drunk or a weirdo and pick me up.

After fifteen minutes' walking I came to a large roundabout. I had done better than I thought and had come out on the A5 somewhere south-east of Ashbourne. There was no sign of anyone following me, but I guessed that if Raffmir wanted to follow me without being seen then he could manage that. I stood on the hard shoulder, close enough to be seen by cars coming off the roundabout but not so close that they would be unable to stop without the car behind rear-ending them.

I took the first lift offered, which may not have been a good idea. The truck driver was Polish and grinned insanely the whole time. His truck cabin looked and

smelled as if he lived in it. After twenty minutes of trying to get me to talk about football, which I neither
knew nor cared about, he put the stereo on and filled
the cab with thrash metal. We stopped at a set of lights
just outside Derby and he passed over a pack of tablets.
The writing on the foil was obscure, presumably Polish;
it certainly wasn't English.

"You like, yes?" he asked me.

"I don't think so, no."

"Is caffeine, with spike for the head." He tapped the
side of his temple and nodded knowingly.

I couldn't decide whether they were pep-pills or
drugs. "I think I'll be OK without, thanks." I passed
them back to him.

"Better," he said, "not sleep and drive."

I agreed that would be bad. He turned up the music
to a point where it would have been impossible to sleep
even without the pills. When he reached the M69 near
Leicester, he was turning off, so I asked him to drop me
at the roundabout. Climbing out of the cab, I thanked
him for the lift.

"Good journey, my friend." He offered his hand and
I shook it.

He rumbled away, merging with the moving traffic. I
stood on the slipway back on to the M1 and waited for
another lift south. I could have made my way to a Way-
node and travelled much quicker from there, but this
way it would be much harder for Raffmir to follow me.
I had carefully not discussed my journey in the cab, so
even if he used the rear-view mirror to eavesdrop he
would not be able to find where I was or in which direction I was headed. Part of me liked the idea of him
cringing to the sound of thrash metal while trying to
eavesdrop on our conversation.

My next lift was a blue BMW and the guy driving it
was wearing sunglasses, even though it was overcast.

He drove fast, staying in the outside lane and rarely dropping below eighty. He talked incessantly about the car, how much fuel it used, where he bought it from, how much he paid for it, what torque it produced, on and on.

"I'm gonna have it chipped," he said.

"Chipped? Is that so they can track it if it gets stolen?"

"Nah, it's already got that. That was the first thing I had done. You have to with a car like this, don't you? Nah, I'm talking performance chipped."

"You've lost me." It wasn't the first time, either.

"You can have the engine management chip upgraded. The standard chip cuts out at six thousand RPM and limits the fuel intake. By upping the chip you can get another thirty brake horse at four K and wind it up to six eight hundred."

"Won't that damage the engine?" It was fairly powerful as it was. What was he going to do with even more?

"Not if you're careful."

He flashed his lights at a car that didn't get out of his way quickly enough, and then roared past when there was barely room to pass.

"Best be careful, then, eh?" I suggested, gently.

"Oh, I'm always careful." He grinned as the car accelerated past ninety again.

I spent the entire trip on the edge of my seat, wondering whether the next close shave would turn into a multi-car pile-up. He dropped me in North London. It was a relief to stand on solid ground. He roared away, ramming the car up through the gears.

From there it was a half-mile walk through the humid evening air to the bus stop. I felt bad slipping on to the bus unnoticed. It wasn't expensive and I would happily pay, but that would mean explaining where I wanted to go to the driver and I did not want to give any clue about that. Instead I sat alone near the back where I could watch who came and went. It took a rambling route, so that I didn't arrive near my destination until mid-evening. If anything, by then the air was heavier with moisture. That felt right, somehow. The last time I had been here had been for a memorial service.

I wanted to see for myself where Alex's accident was supposed to have happened. I knew the area had been sealed, pending an investigation, and that I would not be allowed access. At this time of day, though, there would be no one around and I could see what I wanted to see without needing permission.

The Alice Steadman Comprehensive School was in the middle of a large housing estate in North London. It served all the houses around and was a good enough school to attract children from outside the catchment area. It was difficult to get into, which was one of the reasons that Katherine and I had originally moved here. It was close enough to a Tube line to commute and had the amenities to make a decent area. It had a reputation for looking after its kids, even the difficult ones, and for getting results. It didn't have a reputation for drugs, knives, bullying or gang violence, which was more than you could say for some of the schools in the area.

The original Victorian buildings had been demolished when we first moved there and replaced with 1980s brick. There had been a protest, but the cost of bringing the old buildings up to standard had settled the matter. The new buildings were spacious with large windows and much improved facilities. The frontage was not imposing but looked efficient and functional, with the administrative offices facing the road to act as a barrier between visitors and the children. The teaching facilities formed a big E behind the admin block so that all classrooms had windows. The playground was behind that, which was where the gymnasium stood visible over the top of the other buildings.

I knew the school well enough to be aware that a foot-path diverted around the edge of the playing field where a high fence protected the play area and sports fields. The access gate would be locked to prevent dog walkers fouling the pitch, but a locked gate wouldn't slow me down.

To reach the fence I had to walk around the estate, passing houses with upstairs windows open for the evening air and music spilling out over the neighbourhood. It wasn't a dangerous area, but I used my power to turn away curious eyes. I reached the side gate unnoticed by the kids playing football on the green space with piles of jerseys for goalposts, or mothers out wheeling buggies, older children trailing behind.

My experience with the church door had the padlock on the gate loose in my hand in seconds and allowed me to lock it again behind me. I strode across the field in full view of all the houses around, knowing that no one would see me. The door into the PE block was also locked but that was no harder than opening the gate. I crossed the sprung wooden floor, my footsteps echoing around the empty basketball courts. The door to the changing rooms was at the rear. Beyond was a small corridor leading to changing rooms marked "Boys" and "Girls". On the girls' changing room was a sign in large bold letters saying "Out Of Order", and underneath that, as if to emphasise the point, "DO NOT ENTER". The door to the girls' changing room was not locked. It swung closed behind me with a prolonged screech, making me wonder whether it had always done that.

I had been expecting some sign of what had happened here: not taped outlines on the floor or a sign saying "This is the Place", but some indication of what had occurred. Instead it looked like a building project.

The room smelled strongly of disinfectant and there was a power washer parked behind the door. Where the toilets had been there were bare holes in the floor, each stuffed with polythene bags. There were no sinks on the wall, just pipes and screw-holes in the walls where mirrors had been mounted above them. There was a blank screen wall where once showers had been fitted, and space for rows of benches where the children could get changed. All of that had been stripped back to the bare tiles.

In the centre of the floor near the sinks was a hole. I knelt down to examine it and drew my finger around the edge. The screw-holes were enlarged where the screws had been torn out and the tiles were cracked and jagged-edged. The drain was spotlessly clean and smelled of bleach.

I stood again and turned slowly around. There were small rectangular windows high along one side wall, high enough to stop the boys peeking in while the girls were changing. I could see the window catches had limiters, allowing the windows to be tilted for ventilation but not opened enough for anyone to escape through.

I closed my eyes and tried to sense what had happened here. All I could feel was the chill of a room scoured clean and left long empty.

"Hello? Anyone there?" The voice came from the corridor to the main hall. I moved around behind the wall for the showers. There were footsteps on the tiles outside. I drew concealment around me, feeling the air chill in response.

The door squealed open. "Hello?" It was a question hoping not to be answered. "Is there someone there?"

I concentrated on being unseen.

"I coulda sworn I locked that door."

There was the scrape of a footstep as he entered the room. "This place gives me the creeps," said the voice. "Shoulda knocked the bloody thing down."

The door hinges protested and the footsteps receded. I waited until the spring closure pressed the door closed with a final thunk. I heard him entering the boys' changing room, his voice reverberating through the adjoining wall. He moved around for a while and then retreated.

What light there was in the changing room was fading, so I went back to the door. Trying to open it quietly just made it worse, so I opened it as little as I could and slipped through to the corridor. The owner of the voice had departed, so I could slip out of the fire door on the far side of the gym, shouldering it closed behind me as quietly as I could. I strode back across the field as the light from the overcast clouds faded and the evening deepened into twilight.

Once through the gate in the fence, I was back in the estate and as unremarkable as anyone else. I let the concealment slip away and made my way along the streets, past smells of cooking and noises of TV: family life in the suburbs.

Originally, I hadn't intended to go and see Katherine, but my mind was pondering the clean-up after the accident at the school and whether that meant anything. Were the school paying for the refurbishment or had they got funding from somewhere else? Would the source of the money provide any clue to where Alex was? How could I get access to that information? My feet were on automatic and followed the route from Alex's school through the streets, across the park and back to the street where we had made our home.

I nearly stumbled when I noticed where I was. It brought me suddenly to a halt when I realised that if I saw Katherine she would ask me how I was and what I was doing there. I moved so there was a tree between me and the house. I couldn't just turn up unannounced on her doorstep, could I?

Lying to her would be extremely difficult and the subject of Alex was bound to come up. Garvin was right about one thing: I could not explain to Katherine that

Alex wasn't dead. It wasn't that I wanted to lie to her or that I didn't want her to know, but what could I say to her? I could hardly tell her that Alex was alive but I didn't know where she was. If I accused the authorities of kidnapping her then I was going to look as if I had lost my grip on reality. Grief was one thing, delusion quite another.

If I managed to convince her, she was likely to turn up on the local MP's doorstep within the hour and demand the return of her daughter, and then she would have to explain how she knew Alex was alive, making it look as if neither of us was sane. Besides, Garvin had said the authorities would be looking for me, in which case wandering into an MP's office or a police station probably wasn't a good idea.

Maybe it was the thought that people were searching for me that made me peek around the tree to see if anyone had noticed me arrive. That's when I noticed the car. It was parked across the road from the house and would not have been remarkable but for the two men sat inside it. They didn't get out and they didn't drive away.

Instead, they sat waiting, watching Katherine's house.

SIXTEEN

The two men could just be parked, listening to the radio, or waiting for a friend in one of the other houses, but the way they glanced towards the house periodically and talked without looking at each other made me suspicious. Katherine was my ex-wife and one of the people I'd had recent contact with. If the authorities really were trying to find me then this is one of the places I might turn up.

Using glamour, I could walk right past the car and they would not recognise me, but Garvin had told me they were prepared and that they learned from past encounters. They'd already had the better of me twice, once at the hospital and once at the cottage. That made me cautious.

I moved back along the pavement and walked away. I wanted to get a closer look at them, but walking straight up to the car was not the way. I had the advantage. I knew where they were and as far as I could tell they didn't know I was here. I also knew the ground. I had lived here for a number of years and I was betting I knew things they didn't.

Along the road was a concrete drive that went behind the row of houses opposite Katherine's house, leading

271

to a block of garages. I knew this because we'd had problems with vandals breaking into the garages and setting fire to them. The neighbours had called the police and fire service out on more than one occasion.

I strode between the houses and through into the parking area. A couple of kids were passing a ball between them, kicking it against the side wall of the end garage. They looked a bit young to be out in the late dusk but I ignored them and they did not see me. At the end of the row of garages was a path that crossed between the streets, allowing pedestrians from either side to access the garages. It was used as a cut-through for bikes and an escape route for vandals until the gates had been padlocked and only the garage owners given keys. The gate was almost opposite Katherine's house.

I peered around the end of the last garage, noting that the gate was shut, and then walked quickly between the houses. There were hedges either side but the gate itself was metal with a chain-link mesh and so I would be able to see through to where the car was parked only yards away.

I wanted to see them without being seen myself, so I intensified the misdirection around me. The air chilled and, as it did, a persistent beeping started. The car doors opened and the beeping got louder. I pressed myself closer to the hedge.

A low voice spoke. "See anything?"

"Nope."

"Could be a false alarm?" The voice sounded hopeful, but also excited.

There was a pause.

"Could it?"

"Watch the house. Tell me if there's any movement. Have any lights come on?" The other voice was calm, low and level.

"No."

There was another long pause.

"It's a false alarm, right?"

"The alarm went off," said the calm voice.

"Yeah, but that could just be natural, right?"

"Didn't you feel it get colder?"

"Sure, but the sun's just gone down."

"It suddenly gets colder in a car with all the doors and windows shut."

"Right." There was another pause. "Hear anything?"

"Only you."

"Right."

We all kept silent, not ten yards apart. I waited to see what they would do.

"Shall I call for backup?"

"No. It'll be over by the time they get here."

"We should report it."

"We will. See anything?"

"No, it's getting dark."

"Yeah, that's how it goes."

Keeping a reassuring grip on my umbrella, I moved quietly back down the alley to the garages. I had been right to be cautious. While I had seen no sign of weapons, I had the distinct impression that these people were armed, or at least one of them was. What were they going to do, shoot me? For what? What about human rights? Then I realised that human rights probably didn't apply to people who weren't entirely human.

I had disappeared off the radar as far as the authorities were concerned. I no longer paid tax, owned a flat, had a job that could be called a job or even had a bank account. My life had been cleaned up and cleared away. It made me feel suddenly vulnerable. They could kill me and no one would ever know. The way fey magic worked, if I was killed, my own power would be released and it would consume my remains, leaving only dust. There wouldn't even be a body to explain.

I was used to a world with rights and obligations. As long as I lived peacefully and paid my taxes I expected to be left alone. But I no longer paid taxes, the umbrella I carried was really a sword and my loyalty was not to any human authority.

I walked through the garages and cut back to the street, turning away from the house and feeling isolated and exposed. Wrapping the dark around me like a shadow, turning away glances and avoiding notice. Part of me wanted to go back. Part of me wanted to return to the car and show them what being fey really meant. I knew if I used my training and my power, two men with guns would be no match for me. I could kill them both before they even saw me.

The anger boiled up in me, making me squeeze my fists together. They took my daughter and now they were denying me access to my ex-wife. Even though Katherine and I were no longer married, even though she had Barry to care for her, I still felt protective about her. How dare they camp outside her house, waiting to see if I would appear. What did they think they were doing, protecting her?

It was that thought that killed the anger for me. What were they protecting her from? Where was the monster?

That would be me.

I stopped. I was walking around the streets blindly, just as likely to walk into trouble as away from it. I needed to get my head together and start behaving like a Warder. What had Garvin said? I needed to find out about them while they were looking for me. Well, I had learned something – several things.

I knew they were watching places I was known to frequent. I knew they had a way of detecting fey magic, probably using some sort of heat sensor. They had mentioned the fall in temperature and that would make sense. Any strong use of power triggered a cooling in the general area, indicating that fey magic might be close by. I had the strong impression they were armed and that they were prepared to use their weapons.

I wondered how much of this Katherine knew. Did she even realise she was being watched? She had no reason to be suspicious and if she wasn't looking for it, she probably wouldn't notice.

I'd been making my way through the estate until I reached a particular cul-de-sac. Recent experience made me cautious. I stepped into the shade of an over-hanging tree and merged with the shadows there. Glamour used very little power and would not cool the air around me. I shifted appearance and became an old man out for an evening stroll, my umbrella now a walking stick. I stepped out from under the tree, moving slowly and gently, as an old man might.

The kerbs here were crowded with cars and vans. Most of the houses had been extended at some point, leaving no room for a garage. With two or three cars to each family, parking was at a premium. I did a full circuit of the cul-de-sac, stopping to look at an interesting shrub outside one house. There were lights on and in the upstairs room at the front the window was ajar and I could hear a radio playing. I knew this house. I had dropped Alex off here many times for sleepovers and homework sessions. It was Kayleigh's upstairs window that faced the front and it sounded as if she was in her room.

I continued my walk, finding all the cars unoccupied.

"You all right, Grandad?"

Two large lads walked towards me, just as I reached the road.

"What's that?" I growled, preparing myself for an assault.

"I said, are you OK, Grandad? You were looking a bit lost. A bit deaf, are ya?"

"I'm quite well. thank you, young man, and I can hear perfectly well."

"All right, keep yer 'air on and mind your step. It's getting dark."

They walked past, and I watched them cross the end of the road and walk on into the evening. They were just lads out for a walk, or on their way to the pub, maybe. They still made me jittery. Being ultra-careful, I walked back around the cul-de-sac the other way. Every few yards I stopped, as if for a rest, and used a little power to create a concealment around me, cooling the surroundings. Each time I listened carefully for an alarm, seeing no one and nothing.

A lady came out of one of the houses with a dog and bid me a good evening. The dog growled at me in an uncertain way until the owner yanked the lead and told it to stop being silly. Even so, it watched me as it was led away out of the Close. I followed it slowly until I reached the end of the Close again. Opposite was a small park with a few swings, a seesaw and a round-about. There were some seats where parents could sit and watch the children play in the daytime, only now one seat was occupied by a pair of teenage lovers who were focused entirely on each other. On the swings nearby a small group of lads were trying to impress two teenage girls by engaging in the sort of antics that consistently failed to impress while simultaneously providing an opportunity to lose several teeth. One was standing on the swing with one leg while hanging from the chain by one arm, jerkily swinging back and forth.

I walked slowly across to the park and sat on one of the vacant benches as the twilight slipped into night-time. Carefully and slowly I drew a stronger and stronger concealment around me. Gradually the temperature in the park fell. The lovers cuddled together while the teenage girls zipped up fleeces and said they were cold. The gang coalesced, leaving the swings oscillating wildly, and called to the couple to follow. They lingered a moment more, pressed to each other, and then moved off, the girl wrapped in under the boy's arm, soft murmurings between them.

I needed to talk to Kayleigh. She was the only living witness to Alex's accident, and I needed to know what happened. I could call at the door, but then it would be Kayleigh and her parents. Although I knew her parents, we were acquaintances rather than friends. They had probably been told to look out for me.

This was a conversation I needed to have with Kayleigh alone. I was making some wild guesses and I needed to know whether they were correct.

I let the night gather around me and watched the dog lady return down the road. The dog kept looking nervously towards the park, though to my relief it did not howl. When it was fully dark I walked back across the park to where a van was parked against the kerb. It said 'No Tools Left Overnight' on the back and the windows were silvered to prevent anyone from seeing inside. The mirrored glass was what I needed.

Focusing, I placed my hand upon the glass. This would be more complicated than I had attempted before. To make it easier, I tried to break it into stages. The concealment was first, then came the glamour.

I knew my daughter well. I had held her as a babe and carried her on my shoulders. I had comforted her while she cried and hugged her when she laughed. I had never looked like her before, though, and it felt very strange. The difference in size was difficult. It took more power to change size as well as shape, but for this it would be necessary. I needed to be convincing.

I felt my body shifting around me, more than an image, less than a shape. I held the image of my girl in my head until her hair tickled about my neck and my frame felt lithe and light. I opened my eyes and stared at the reflection of my lost daughter.

I reached out with my fingertips to touch the reflection. It blurred and when I blinked my eyes clear I was looking at my own face again. Damn, this was difficult. It ought to be easy. There was no one in the world I knew better. I knew every curl, every inch of her, yet every time I tried to build her image it slipped from me. I could hold it for a second, but then it would unravel. It was as if I could not accept so profound a change.

All I really needed was her voice. Perhaps that would be easier.

"Hello?" It sounded odd, hearing it from inside myself when I had only ever heard it from her.

I tried again.

"Can you hear me?" This time it sounded like her, though not like her. Voices sound different when it's you that's speaking.

I looked into my face reflected in the glass and heard my words echoed in her voice. "My poor lost girl. I will find you. Trust me."

I looked around, checking again that there was no one nearby. I put my hand on the mirrored van window and whispered into the glass.

"Kayleigh?"

The glass clouded under my hand and cooled. The sound of a radio emerged, with the gentle scraping and shuffling of writing. I listened for a few moments, and could hear no other presence.

"Kayleigh, can you hear me?"

There was a sudden sharp breath, the sound of a glass being knocked over, liquid spilling out, a chair scraped back.

"Who is it? Who's there?"

I waited a moment. It wouldn't help me to scare her witless.

"Kayleigh, it's me. Are you alone?"

"Alex...? Is that you? Alex, you're dead."

"I'm not dead. I need you to do something for me. Are you alone?"

"Who is this? This isn't funny."

I had to take a gamble. I had to convince her. The last thing I wanted was her tearing down the stairs, shouting that her room was haunted. I had a hunch that Kayleigh knew more than she had told anyone. Alex had shared everything with Kayleigh. If anyone knew the truth it would be her. It was just a matter of teasing it out of her.

"You have to trust me. You know my special secret – it's about that. You remember, don't you?" It was like dangling a line, waiting for a bite.

There was a pause. "I promised. You made me promise I wouldn't say anything. I haven't told anyone."

So there was a secret. I was right.

"I know. I trust you. But I need you to do something."

A voice came from downstairs. "Kayleigh? Who are you talking to? Is that the phone?"

There was a scuffling sound.

"It's OK. It's the radio."

"It sounded like you were talking to someone." There was concern in the tone.

"It's OK. I'm fine, really."

"Are you coming down?"

"In a bit. I'll come down in a while."

"OK. Have you finished your homework?"

"Not yet. I'm nearly done. I won't be long."

"Don't work too late, honey."

"I won't."

I heard the door slide gently closed.

"Alex?"

"I'm here."

"Where are you? Everyone says you're dead."

279

"I know. It's hard to explain. I need you to trust me. My dad's waiting down in the park at the end of your road. I need you to explain what happened at school to him."

"Why can't you tell him?"

"I don't have much time. He's trying to help me. Can you do it?"

"You made me promise."

"I know, but he needs your help so he can help me. I don't have much time," I repeated.

"I'm not allowed out this late."

"I don't know how long he can stay."

"OK, OK. I'll try. Tell him to wait."

"Kayleigh?"

"Yes?"

"I know it's been hard. You did the right thing not telling anyone. I have to go."

"Alex, where are you?"

"I have to go. Bye."

I took my hand from the glass. I felt like a complete bastard for deceiving her, but she was the only one who knew what had really happened and she had resisted all attempts to get her to tell the real story. Neither the school nor the police had been able to make her break her promise. She and Alex had been buddies since primary school and the bonds were far stronger than mere authority.

I walked back across to the park and sat on the bench, allowing my voice to fall back to how it sounded naturally, then letting my glamour fall away completely, becoming Niall Petersen, Alex's dad. Having not worn that shape for months it felt strange. Blackbird was right, using glamour did become a habit.

I let the concealment around me fade and waited for Kayleigh, watching cars drive by and occasional pedestrians pass. I was beginning to think she had either been caught by her parents or chickened out, when I saw her small figure cross the road.

She hurried across the park, wrapping her cardigan tight around her.

"Mr Petersen?"

"It's me. Is that you, Kayleigh?"

She hurried across to where the bench seat was, but then stopped short.

"I'm supposed to tell the police if I see you," she told me.

"You must do what you think best, Kayleigh."

"Are you really a terrorist?"

"Me? No, of course not. Whatever made you think that?"

"They said you got involved with some bad people last year. They said you might be being forced to co-operate with them. They wanted to know if I saw you, so they could help you."

"Do I look like I need help?"

"You went missing, after the memorial service. Is Alex alive?" The change in subject was abrupt.

"Yes. I think she is."

"She… she spoke to me. A moment ago in my bedroom. She was in my mirror."

"That wasn't her, Kayleigh. That was me."

"You? But…"

"I know. It's difficult to explain and I can't tell you too much without dragging you into it. You know how serious this all is, don't you? If you tell them, they may want to know what else you know. They will want to know why you didn't tell them before. You're a bright girl, Kayleigh. I've always thought that. You work it out."

I waited in the dark, deliberately staying seated so that I didn't spook her. I could see the tension in the set of her shoulders, the way she kept wrapping her cardigan around her more tightly. She wanted badly to run for home, but she stayed.

She looked back to the house and then at me.

"You're the same as her, aren't you? That's why they're looking for you."

"Actually, she's like me, but yes."

"That's how you… got into my mirror. That's how you made it sound like her. You tricked me."

"I did deceive you, but only so we could speak alone. You wouldn't have come out here just for me."

"I gotta go." She turned away towards the Close.

"It went badly wrong that day, didn't it?"

She stopped.

"But you knew about Alex before then, before the accident."

"I can't talk about that. She made me swear."

"I'm her father, Kayleigh. And what I said to you about her not being dead was true. She is in trouble. She needs my help. And I need yours."

She spurred herself back into motion, crossing the road and vanishing between the hedges and the row of cars parked at the pavement.

The urge to chase her and try to pull her back was strong, but that would only make her run and clam up even more. Instead I tried to look as calm and patient as possible. I stayed on the seat, doing my best to look as if I would still be there in the morning when she went to school. I couldn't see whether she was watching me, so I concentrated on waiting. If she had gone inside, I had lost her, at least for now. If not…

It was a full five minutes before she reappeared. She crossed the road again, walked across the grass and plonked herself down beside me, folding her arms.

"It's colder here."

"Would you like my coat? It'll keep your shoulders warm."

"No. I'll be OK."

I waited for her to speak, but she didn't. If it was a

contest, I broke first. "Are you going to tell me what happened?"

"I promised I wouldn't tell."

"Kayleigh, it's dangerous to know any more. If you let something slip they will assume you know much more than you do. They may think you're involved."

"I am involved. I was there!"

"I need to know what happened so I can help her."

"I thought she was dead. We had a service at school. You were there. Everyone was."

I sighed. "I didn't know she was still alive then. I only found out later, by accident. Even I'm not supposed to know. I swear that's the truth."

"How do you know she's alive?"

I debated how much to say. I didn't like telling Kayleigh any more than I had to, but she had already proved that she could keep a secret. If I wanted her to trust me then I had to trust her.

"I need you to swear the same to me as you did to Alex. You tell no one about this conversation, OK?"

"Who will I tell? My best friend is, like, dead."

"I need your promise, Kayleigh. This is serious."

"OK, I promise. Hope to die."

"Is that what you promised her?"

"Mostly. Sort of."

I put my hands in my lap. It was cold here, but I wanted to keep people away.

"When I spoke to you through your mirror, a little while ago, that was how I found Alex. I could hear her, but I didn't know where she was. I think she was taken, somewhere safe but away, because of the accident. That's why I need to know what happened. I need to know what she did."

"She didn't do it on purpose! She wasn't like that."

"I know that. I'm her dad. I know what she's like, but I need to know what happened."

"They were there. Tracy Welham and her lot. They were in the changing room."

"Before that. You knew about it before that, didn't you?"

"She made me promise."

"Kayleigh?"

There was a long pause. This time I won.

"She came into school one day, really excited. She wouldn't tell me what it was about. We tell each other, like, everything. Everything about everything. Boys, even." She stopped.

"Go on," I prodded gently.

"She was really cagey. I kept asking her whether it was a boy, but she kept... evading me."

"OK."

"It wasn't like her to be so cagey, but when school finished we went back to mine. We shut the bedroom door and put the stereo on, and I made her tell me. She swore me to secrecy, but I made her."

"What, Kayleigh? What did she say?"

"She didn't say anything. She got my water glass and emptied it on to my table. I was like, hey, pack that in, but she just carried on. The water stayed on the table, though. It shoulda run on to the floor, but it didn't. It all gathered in the middle, in a circle, like mercury, waiting for her."

"Waiting?"

"She goes, watch this. She puts a finger out and draws a K for Kayleigh, and the water does it too. It made a K, right there, I swear. Then she drew an A and it made an A, just like that. It was spooky."

"Did she say how she did it?"

"And then, like, she draws her finger in a circle and wobbles it towards the edge and all the water rolls to the edge, off the side and back into the glass, just like that. I swear."

"How did she explain it?"

"She said she had cramps in the night, you know, like… girl cramps?"

"I know what periods are, Kayleigh."

"Yeah, well. When she woke up, she was different. She said the water obeyed her. It wanted to do what she wanted. She said she thought she was a witch."

"A witch?" The irony of that remark wasn't lost on me.

"Yeah, we thought she might be able to do spells and stuff, but it was just water. She could do some cool things, though. Dry her hair by making all the water drop out, stir her tea without a spoon. It was pretty neat."

"And she could control it?"

"Yeah, mostly. It was getting stronger, though. She said… it was like it was calling to her and she didn't know what it wanted."

"But she had it under control."

"She wouldn't go near the river, and the swimming pool was right out. She said it was too strong. There was too much of it. She was frightened about what it would do."

"Was that when she had the accident?"

Kayleigh went quiet. She sat, pulling her cardie around her.

"I need to know, Kayleigh. I can't help her until I know."

The silence persisted. Then there was a snuffle.

"You could just tell me. I'm her dad. I'll understand."

"Yeah, but…" she snuffled.

"Yes, but what?"

"The accident." She sniffed.

"What about it? What happened?"

"It wasn't an accident, was it? She did it. She killed them." The tears overflowed and I found myself holding her as she wailed into my shoulder. I drew concealment closer around us, so as not to attract attention. Kayleigh shook, convulsing with great heaving

285

sobs as it all spilled out. Between heaving gulps of air she told me.

"She didn't mean it. She never meant it. It was too strong. It got loose. They were trying to hurt her. Trying to dunk her – in the toilets. They hurt her – they were shoving her – into the water. They put her – in the water – don't you see? They put her in it!"

I hugged her to me. "It's OK. I think I do see."

She gulped and hiccoughed in my armpit and I held her until the sobbing subsided. I passed her my hanky and she dabbed her eyes and then blew her nose. The mascara around her eyes had run and stained it. She offered me back the hanky.

"No, keep it."

She stuffed it into the sleeve of her cardie.

"She wouldn't have done it on purpose, would she?" she asked.

"No. If they were putting her into water and hurting her then they probably brought it on themselves. I don't think she meant it to happen." The truth of that statement rankled with me. I wasn't a hundred per cent sure it was true, but speculation was not what Kayleigh needed to hear.

"I tried to get them to stop. They wouldn't listen. She knew it was bad." She sniffed. "We were supposed to meet. She wasn't there. I knew something was wrong."

"How did you find her?"

"You can't get out the front. There are the offices and they watch the gates like hawks. I went out the back, where the playing fields are. I thought she might be there. I heard her. She was in the toilets in the changing block. I think she was hiding. Welham and her mates went in there, smoking."

"So you followed her."

"I tried to warn them, but they wouldn't believe me. They were gonna get me too. I ran out into the corridor and closed the door so they couldn't get me. It was me. I trapped them in there with her." She took out that hanky again and mopped at her nose.

"No, you didn't."

"I did. If I had been with her she might not have lost it. They wouldn't have done much. I've had worse. They're all mouth, that lot. They were. They're all dead now. All of them." She started crying again and I hugged her close.

"It was an accident, Kayleigh. You didn't know what would happen. You did the best you could. You ran for help, didn't you?"

She calmed a little and snuffled into the hanky. "It was too late. The water was filthy. It went everywhere. It was streaming out the windows. Where? Where did it all come from?"

"She called it, I think. She panicked when they tried to drown her. She lost control. Someone once told me that magic responds to need. They must have been hurting her pretty badly."

"Not that badly. Not to deserve to drown. Not in that. There was stuff in it, ugh, it was horrible. The smell was awful. It's taken them weeks just to clean it up."

"Who cleaned it up?"

"Workmen. They all came in suits with plastic masks on. The smell was atrocious. You weren't there."

"Was there a big truck? Really new, like an American one. All white and shiny?"

"No. I don't remember a truck. Why?"

"Just something I saw somewhere. I thought it might be a clue."

"No. They had a van, but it was a beaten-up old thing."

"Did they say anything?"

"To me? We weren't allowed anywhere near it. The whole area has been off limits for weeks. It still is. You can understand why."

"Is there anything else, Kayleigh? Anything you remember? Anything that might help me find her?"

"No, I don't remember. It all happened so fast. I wake up nights. Mum says I'm dreaming. I can hear them in there, screaming, clawing at the door to get out." She shuddered.

"OK. Thank you. I think you've been very brave. I'm sorry I had to trick you to get you out here."

"It's OK. I feel better. I couldn't, like, tell anyone. Not even Mum. I daren't."

"You'd better get back before you're missed."

"I left my radio on. They think I'm doing my homework."

"Best go and do some, then."

She handed me the hanky back. "You better have that, otherwise I'll have to say where I got it."

I took it from her.

She turned and walked three paces and then stopped and turned around.

"Remembered something?"

"No," she said. "No, but I need to know. What is it? What is it with you and her? How is it possible? I mean, I've seen it and I don't believe it. I'm sure it was a trick." She watched me. "Is it? Is it a trick?"

"No. It isn't a trick. You mustn't tell, though. They will be watching you."

"Who's they? Who is it that's watching?"

"That's the question I'm trying to answer. I'm just a man looking for answers. You should go."

She sighed and nodded, acknowledging that it was true and walked back towards the road. I watched her check for cars before crossing and then I stood and walked across the park to the swings, so that when she turned back the bench was bare and she could not see me in the gloom. She scanned the area from the far side of the road, then shook her head, wrapped her cardie tighter and headed for home. I followed discreetly until she went inside, and then waited until she appeared at her bedroom window. She looked out on the empty street and I think she knew I was there somewhere, even though she couldn't pick me out. She drew her curtains closed against the dark, but couldn't resist a last peek through the crack.

I found myself hoping that she would sleep better from now on, now that she had been able to share her burden.

I left the cul-de-sac and turned away from Katherine's house, heading for the Tube station. I set a strong pace, knowing that the walk would take me half an hour and that if I lingered I would miss the last tube and end up waiting for a night bus.

The walk gave me chance to think. If Kayleigh was right and Alex had drowned the other girls, then it would make sense that the authorities had acted to take her out of circulation. She was a danger to others, but where would be safe? Blackbird had once told me that there were places for people like Alex, who couldn't control their gifts. She'd never said where any of them were, though. I made a mental note to ask her later.

The reality was that my daughter had killed three girls, however unintentionally. Garvin had said that was likely and Kayleigh's story confirmed it. They had tried to hurt her and she had drowned them in sewage. I thought I should feel bad about that, but my honest reaction was that they deserved it. They had been intent on hurting her when they should have left her alone. It was harsh, and sad that they had been caught up in it, but they weren't my daughters.

I was beginning to understand why they had taken her, though. If she couldn't control her gifts then she was dangerous. They would act to protect other people and to prevent her harming herself. That didn't mean that I would leave her there, though. I was her father and I had got her into this mess. If anyone could look after her, it was me.

I found the Tube station in time to get a ride into central London. The long ride lulled me, but I had too much still to do to allow myself to sleep. I used the Tube to get into the West End and then used one of the Warders' houses as a gateway to the Way. Using Raffmir's slingshot technique I was back in Yorkshire within two hours of meeting Kayleigh. When I stumbled out of the Way-node, it had mercifully stopped raining. The ground was sodden, and the grass squelched as I tramped down the bank into town.

The lights were on in the church as I passed, but I ignored that and went straight down to the guest house. I still had my key, so I let myself in.

"You're very late again, Mr Dobson." Martha was in the kitchen with the door open, sewing.

"And it's late to be still sewing. It's bad for your eyes, you know."

"I'm just doing some buttons, then I'll be retiring. You look like you should do the same, Mr Dobson."

"I won't be up long, I assure you."

"I'll wish you good night then."

"Good night."

I took the stairs up to my room and locked the door behind me, stowed my gear and sword and hung up my jacket. Then I sat on the end of the bed and collapsed backwards. What with the cumulative effect of the Ways, lack of sleep and a long, long day, I fought to keep my eyes open. I sat up. I needed a shower before bed anyway, so it was pointless getting comfortable.

I stood in front of the chest and rested my hand on the face of the mirror.

"Garvin?"

The mirror misted gently and there was a muted thumping sound.

"Niall, you're late. I was about to send out a search party." There was humour in his tone. He was obviously in a better mood than last time.

"How are things at Court?"

"They are progressing. Fellstamp is recovering from that scratch you gave him and between us we have been able to keep track of Altair. He hasn't brought any more over, so we are coping. Have you seen anything of Raffmir?"

It was pointless lying to him as he would hear it immediately. "He came to the café. We talked. He said that you'd sent me here to keep me away from the negotiations."

"He's right. I did."

"He said it was because the High Court were negotiating for the fate of the half-breeds. He said you were keeping me away from it so I wouldn't prejudice the negotiations."

"He's right about that too. If you cause an incident, the High Court might be less able to defend their position on the half-breeds. It would look as if you were undermining them."

"I don't think that's what he meant."

"I know exactly what he meant. He means to sow discord among us. You need to stay tight and not let him get under your skin."

"He's already under my skin. I just want to tell him to get lost."

"As long as he's with you, he's not somewhere else, Niall. Speaking of which, we've lost Blackbird again."

"What do you mean lost?"

"As in: we don't know where she is. She's hard to protect if we can't find her."

"She's hard to hurt if Deefnir can't find her."

"As long as they don't know where she is either, that's true. If they've followed her, then that could be trouble."

291

"I don't know where she went either, if that's what you're asking."

"Would you tell me if you found out?"

"That would depend on her. I think I'd let her make that choice. It's her life."

"That's a dangerous game, Niall."

"They're all dangerous games until the Untainted take themselves back home and leave us in peace."

"True. Talk to her, please. Try and persuade her to come back in."

"I'll pass on your request, Garvin. She'll make her own mind up, you know that."

"So I do. Very well."

"Anything else to report?"

This was the moment. I should tell Garvin about Raffmir's secret conversations. I should explain about the ability to make small jumps using magic. I should tell him Raffmir knew where my daughter was. But if I did, Raffmir said she would die. He had been straight about that, at least.

"No, there's nothing else I want to tell you."

"How are the missing girls?"

"Some of them, fine. The others are still missing though, as in missing from the records. They don't appear as missing women anywhere in the archives, as far as I can tell. There's no local knowledge of lost women. I have thirty or forty skulls and no owners. I'll have to go to the Records Office at Northallerton to confirm it, but that's the story here. If there were a string of murders, even over a timescale of hundreds of years, there would be something. Instead, it's a blank wall."

"So what's your conclusion?"

"I don't have a conclusion yet. I'm following the evidence."

"Good. Let me know when you get somewhere."

"I will."

"And get some sleep. You sound like death warmed up."

"I'm just tired. Long day."

"Report tomorrow evening, earlier than this, if you can?"

"Will do."

"Sleep well, Niall."

"I'll try." That came out ringing with untruth, but Garvin said nothing and I took my hand from the mirror.

The night wasn't over yet.

SEVENTEEN

Having spoken to Garvin, I could try Blackbird. I placed my hand back on the mirror.

"Blackbird?"

It misted under my hand.

"Blackbird, are you there?"

A strange whistling sound came from the mirror, followed by a buzz and crackle that made it sound like a badly tuned old-fashioned radio set. The buzz grew into a whine until the mirror vibrated with it and I was forced to remove my hand or risk the mirror. The condensation on the surface slowly contracted around my vacant handprint until it vanished. Wherever she had gone, it was secure against eavesdropping, by me or anyone else. Was that good news or bad? I tried to look on the positive side. If I couldn't find her, then maybe Deefnir wouldn't be able to either.

I had exhausted my enquiries, though I would dearly like to have talked to Blackbird before I slept. I suspected that I would find myself dreaming of the glade again. This time I was going to have to deal with it properly. If I didn't, I was never going to have a restful night's sleep again.

With a sense of mounting trepidation, I showered and prepared for bed. It felt more like girding my loins than readying myself for sleep. I slid in under the covers and lay in the near dark. I was so tired that my eyes felt gritty and heavy, but sleep would not come. Part of me knew what would happen when it did, and so I rolled on one side and then the other, delaying the moment.

I thought about all the things I'd learned: about the boats and the harbour, the men who never made it back to port, the way the town was changing, the feeble attempt to become a tourist resort with a disorganised museum and an unsuitable café. I puzzled about Raffmir and the reason for his unsolicited generosity. I questioned whether Garvin's reasons for keeping me away from the courts were really as straightforward as they appeared, and I wondered whether Kayleigh was sleeping any easier.

There must have been a moment when I wasn't thinking about any of these before I found myself on the path in the forest, but if there was, I do not remember it.

The transition was seamless. It was as if I was expected. I was clothed again, in fine black silk. My fingers were adorned with silver rings and an intricate silver clasp belted my waist. My feet were bare, and I could feel the crush and prickle of the pine needles beneath me. The air was heavy with resin, though frosty cold. Undisturbed in the dry, freezing air, the pine scent clung to my clothes and swirled around me as I moved slowly forward.

Looking behind me, I saw that the path vanished into pine-boughs where the rough trunks pressed together. The only sound was the brush of the soft needles against my arms and the prickling tread of my feet.

The clearing was unoccupied yet the sense of expectation, of invitation, was palpable. There was no doubt in my mind that I was recognised and welcome here. It made what I was about to do feel like treachery. I walked forward, knowing without looking that where the path had been there would be only snags and thorns.

"You've brought me here again." The emptiness ate my words. There was no echo, no reverberation. It was soft and smothering, like an unwanted aunt's embrace. "I can't keep coming here. You can't make me. You'll have to find some other way."

The temperature fell, deepening the chill.

"You again?"

I recognised Debbie's voice immediately. When I turned she was behind me, naked.

"Stay away from me." She hugged her arms around her, hiding her breasts. "I know about your sort. You're crazy. You need help."

I turned my back and ignored her. "Send her back. I will not touch her."

"You're completely barking. Mental, that's what you are."

Even as she spoke, her voice faded. I was alone again.

Then a new voice. "I must be asleep."

I turned, recognising the tone, the memory of an insistent cry and a weary voice roused from sleep, giving me a name.

"Helen?"

"Do I know you?"

She held the baby in the crook of her arm as it nuzzled into her armpit, making little whimpers. The naked child was cold in the exposed air, though Helen herself was dressed in a cotton shift. She had a practical, straightforward look to her that I had not seen in the photo. She gathered the baby to her and looked about, a sense of growing panic in her eyes. She was searching for somewhere to run, and there was nowhere.

"What is this?"

I didn't answer her. Instead I spoke to the pinpricked sky. "You can send her back too. I will not touch her, or the babe."

"Who are you talking to?" she asked. "There's no one there."

The babe began to mewl as the cold seeped into them both.

"Send them back, now. I do not want them here."

"I said, there's no one there." She was starting to sound angry.

I stripped off the silk shirt, undoing the buttons and then pulling it over my head.

"What are you doing?" Her voice held the edge of panic.

I approached her slowly, offering the black cloth bundle. "Here, wrap the babe in this."

She took it from me, hesitantly, understanding dawning on her face. As she lifted the child on to her shoulder it started to wail, but then quieted as she wrapped the shirt around it and cuddled it close, using her warmth for comfort.

"Thanks," she murmured, but the disquiet was still in her eyes.

"I have a message for you."

"For me? How? I mean... do you?"

"And a question."

She shook her head. "This is strange..."

"Let me get this right. The message is that there's a young man who's desperate to hear from you and wants to do the right thing, not just because it's the right thing to do. He's waiting for you."

"How do you know this?" Hope had lifted her voice.

"And Greg, the vicar, would like to know whether it's a boy or a girl, though I think I already know the answer to that question."

She smiled for the first time. "He's called–"

"Shhhh! Do not name him here. He's too young and far too vulnerable." I turned to the glade. "Let her go now. She has what she came for. Release her."

"Release me from what?"

I ignored her. "Let them go."

"It's only a dream," she said. "It'll finish when I wake up."

"Release them. You'll get nothing else from me."

When I looked back, they'd gone.

"It doesn't matter who you bring. I'm not feeding from them and neither are you. Now send me back."

The only answer was the deepening silence.

"You can't force me to stay. Send me back where I came from."

A new voice. "Where *did* you come from? Kent, wasn't it?"

The voice from behind me startled me, partly because it was male. I turned and found a man, dressed in shirt, tie and trousers, watching me.

"Who are you?"

"You don't recognise me? That's weird, because I recognise you. How is it that my dreams don't know who I am?"

"Your dreams?"

He started walking slowly around the ring of thorns, speaking as he went. "Yeah. I'm dreaming. I must be. It's the only way I'd come up with this weird shit."

I turned, following his movement. I was beginning to think I did recognise him.

"We did meet, didn't we?"

"Course we did. You were with that weird woman at the hospital, the fake witch."

I remembered then. This was Claire's friend who had been at the hospital last year when the Queen's Remembrancer had been taken ill. He was the friend who'd been in charge of security, the one with connections.

"You still think she's a fake?" I asked.

"You're not trying to tell me you think she's for real? I mean, I know you're a dream, but try and stay a bit believable."

"Claire's friend. The secret squirrel. Sam Veldon." I had the name at last.

"Friend no longer. Your witchy woman saw to that. Claire rang me the other day, you know?"

"I know."

"Course you do." He continued walking.

"How did you know I come from Kent?" I asked. I was sure it hadn't been mentioned in our original encounter.

"It's in the file. When she mentioned your name, I looked you up. She said you needed my help. Bloody cheek if you ask me. Personally I wouldn't piss on you if you were on fire, but I wanted to know why she was asking."

"And what did you discover?"

"Red flags. You're quite the celebrity these days, you know. Apprehend with caution, may be armed, possibly dangerous. You don't look dangerous."

"It says armed?"

"That's what it says on the file. I didn't write it." He completed his circuit around the glade, and continued without breaking step. "You were tagged amber after that policeman died last year. I didn't know you killed a policeman."

"I didn't. They didn't even charge me."

"Not what it says now. You've been hiked to red, possible murder, possible terrorist. Notify if seen."

"Will you tell them?"

"What, that you were in my dream? You think I'm nuts?"

"You're talking to me now," I pointed out.

"Got nothin' better to do. I'm asleep en't I?"

"Are you?"

"Course I am. Coulda done with prettier company than you, though. No offence, like."

"None taken. What else did the file say?"

"Who wants to know?"

"Well, me, since it's about me."

"Can't say. I've signed the official secrets." He tapped the side of his nose knowingly.

"Not even in your dream? I could be an extension of your subconscious, here to help you reach some hidden insight."

"You could be full of bollocks, sounds like." He laughed.

"Why do you think you're here then?"

"To puzzle it out, I s'pose."

"Puzzle what out?"

"The file references. They don't make sense."

"Which file references?"

"The one on your file and the one on hers."

"Who?"

"Alexandra, this daughter of yours. The one who's missing."

"She has a file too?"

"Course she does. Major incident, three dead at the scene. Sewer explosion. Biological contamination. It's all in there."

"Did it say where she is?"

"That's the thing. It's a B reference. So's yours."

"What's a B reference?"

"A reference starting with B. Other than that, no idea. Never come across one before. I asked one of the archive bunnies."

"You have bunnies?"

"The girls in Archives, or Knowledge Management, I think they call it now. Pity you're not like one of them. This could be a very different kinda dream."

"Think you're in with a chance, do you?"

"Nah, they're all married. Makes things difficult, doesn't it?"

"I wouldn't know."

"Yeah, right. Her indoors might look in her tea leaves and put the eye on you."

"Tell me about the archive bunnies."

"What, the blonde or the redhead?"

"No, about what they said."

"You're not much fun, are you?"

"You said they were B references."

"Yeah, I thought they were messing me about, y'know? B references? Load of bollocks, like a long stand, or a left-handed screwdriver."

"They like to wind you up, do they? I can see why."

"Turns out it's kosher. The file references are all centrally allocated. They usually go with who owns the case, or the suspect. I know the ones for criminal investigation, terror suspects, organised crime, military, drugs, counter-intelligence – all of that, but I'd never seen a B reference before"

"So what did they say?"

"They have this whole Mulder and Scully routine, you know? Alien spacecraft, ghost stories, spooky houses, telepathy? They reckon it's all in the files if you know where to look."

"And that's what's in Alex's file."

"They reckon all the B files are weird shit. They all have some *unexplained* thing, going way back."

"Way back where?"

"Into the stacks. Into the paper archives before they computerised everything. They have B files going back so far you have to go into a special room to see them. It's all temperature-controlled and humidified."

"So what's a B file?"

"Oh, they're into the full act now, aren't they? Rolling their eyes and telling me I don't have clearance, they'll have to kill me if they tell me."

"They wouldn't tell you, would they?"

"No. But I found out anyway."

"You did?"

"Sure. What do I look like? Cabbage?"

"So go on then, tell me."

"Why? I don't owe you anything. You've never given me anything but shit."

"I'm just a dream, though, aren't I?"

"Yeah, well, I don't owe a dream much either. Go screw yourself."

"No, Sam. It's you who's screwed."

"Yeah? You and whose army?"

"I don't need an army. You've forgotten where you are."

I moved to intercept him. He stopped, stepped back, balanced on the balls of his feet. I knew enough to know that he was ready to fight, even if it was a dream.

"You've got the wrong idea, Sam. I'm not going to punch you. I don't have to."

Standing facing him, out of range of fists or feet, I reached inwards and connected with the core of magic within me. It flared into life, dark shadows spilling outward. My skin went black and lightless, reflecting not even the dim light of the pinprick stars. Dappled moonlight swirled across the grass where no moon shone. Sam backed away, an expression of disbelief and distaste on his face. It was the wrong thing to do.

The briars behind him wound out and coiled around his legs, tugging at him. He tried to fend off the barbed strands with one hand, only to find it tangled and snagged. He yanked at the hand and it came away streaked and bloody.

"I'm not your dream, Sam. I'm your nightmare."

With an inhuman grunt, he fell sideways and dragged himself away from the briar, across the frozen grass, while the thorns tore his trousers and bit into the flesh of his legs.

"You're a freak!" he shouted. "A fucking freak!" With a wrench he freed himself and rolled away across the grass. He pushed himself up to his knees.

302

"There's nowhere to run, Sam, not here. And you're not leaving till I say you are."

He pushed himself up to his feet and dropped into a fighting stance, fists bunched and held tight against him. He dodged in, jabbing out fast.

I was in no mood to play games. I swatted the first punch away, stepped sideways and stamped my booted foot hard on the back of his calf. He collapsed and I hit him hard, once, with my elbow on the side of the head, making sure he went down. I hadn't trained for nine months to be sucker-punched by an amateur, and I wasn't fighting for style, I was fighting for effect.

He rolled on to the grass, curled up, groaning. I wasn't even out of breath. The violence felt good, a kind of release for the anger I had bottled up inside. He lay rubbing his temple with his hand. I could see he was watching me, though, waiting for an opportunity to lash out.

"You think that's grass you're lying on, do you?"

Taking its cue from my words, the grass began to lengthen into strands, weaving its way around him, knotting together and tying him down. Panicked into action, he tried to rise, only to find himself caught by the tangle. He fell back as the grass lengthened and wove around him.

"Agh, get it off, get it off!" He thrashed and struggled, but couldn't free himself.

It knotted around his throat and dragged him down into the fresh green sward.

"It's strangling me," he choked out.

I recalled the gallowfyre, feeling it withdraw back into the core of magic within me. The glade returned to pinpricked starlit grey. The sound of Sam's struggles faded as the shoots knotted together.

I looked down at him. "No. Once again, Sam Veldon, you do not understand. It doesn't want to kill you. It

303

wants you alive so that you can be slowly absorbed into the ground and every ounce of you can be digested. You will be fertiliser, every last drop of you."

I walked away, hearing the struggles behind me diminish as he was wound tighter into the grass. Ahead of me the path opened up so I could leave.

"Wait. For God's sake, help me!" he croaked.

"Help you, Sam Veldon? Why should I do that? Wasn't that your phrase – you wouldn't piss on me if I was on fire?"

"It's getting in my skin! You can't leave me here. It's inhuman!"

I paused. For the first time since the moment I first discovered my fey heritage, I looked at myself and what I'd become. "What makes you think," I asked him, "that I regard that as a problem?"

There was a gargled, choking cough and then a spitting, strangled cry. "It's in my mouth. You have to help me. Please?" His voice tailed off.

Standing there, with my back turned, I could not walk away and leave him, not and live with myself. No matter how I tried to deny my own humanity – however I might like to be fey-hearted, I was not. I could not abandon him.

I walked slowly back across the glade. There was a mound of new grass, strangely like the fairy rings you sometimes see. As I got closer I found his form almost completely subsumed into the strands. They knotted and twisted, pinning him down like a grass-tied Gulliver tangled into a verdant Lilliput. His eyes darted sideways, wide with panic, but he was unable to move even his head.

"Are you beginning to understand now, Sam Veldon? I asked for your help and you told me where to go. Would you now ask for mine?"

His eyes widened, imploring me. A low mumbling sound came from beneath the grass.

304

"Very well. Perhaps you will consider my requests more seriously in future."

I stood back and addressed the glade. "Release him."

The briar tangles around me rustled and quivered, but Sam was not released. I had thrown it a lifeline, and granted a reprieve. With him tangled there it could survive for a very long time indeed. It would not release him easily.

"Release him and I will see to it that you are rewarded."

The words died in the still air. I could still hear Sam fruitlessly trying to struggle against the fibrous bonds.

I reached inside and released the power within me once again. Gallowfyre spilled out, dappling the glade in the moonlight. In the still air, the shifting, sliding glimmer was incongruous, as if made by the wrong kind of tree in the wrong place.

"I said, release him."

There was only further rustling. Sam remained trapped under the grass. The glade had refused the carrot. Now we would try the stick.

Blackbird told me that gallowfyre is an expression of my inner self, the core of magic that makes me fey. To me it was more like a creature that lived inside me, a creature with appetites. I opened myself to the power and my call was answered. Into the dappled light, wriggling tendrils of darkness emerged, sparking with deep violet at their unseen edges, hinting at writhing tentacles unseen.

They were shadows in shadow, barely visible. They threaded into the grass, seeking downwards into cracks in frost-hardened soil. Each was an exploring thread of power, a questing tongue. Whether as an extension of self or by some inner communication, I knew where they licked and what they tasted. I found Sam, cold and sweaty, streaked with green juices, red from weals and oozing from cuts. Beneath him was the ice-cold ground, and beneath that was a darker presence, hugging close to the warmth leaching into the soil. I drew back a tendril and then launched it, stinging the hidden presence, biting into it with cold, energy-leaching darkness of gallowfyre.

It recoiled from the touch, squirming downwards into the frozen loam, vanishing into the soil. The grass around Sam relaxed and parted. An arm came free and he tugged at the strands until he could push himself up with an elbow. He pulled grass from his hair and from across his face, then yanked at it where it tangled his legs until he was in a frenzy of wrenching and tugging, throwing shreds of grass in all directions. He rolled over on one side and then crawled away from the spot. He did not collapse back on to it, though, but knelt up, brushing the remnant shreds from the tatters of his clothes.

"Fucking grassy shit!" he spluttered.

I recalled the gallowfyre, returning the glade to its normal pallid grey, while I watched him pull every last strand away until there was not a scrap of it left. Finally he stood.

"I suppose I should thank you," he said.

"Don't put yourself out."

"Yeah. Well, thanks. I thought…" He shook his head, clearing it. "Fucking grass. I'm getting a lawn mower, a fucking big one. Better still, I'm getting me some gravel. Can't go wrong with gravel."

"You'd better leave. I'll be in touch, Sam Veldon. I want to know where my daughter is."

He stared at me for a moment, meeting my eyes. Then he looked away, and nodded.

"Go. Leave this place."

At my dismissal, he faded. I was alone in the glade.

I looked around me. The still air held no hint of presence. The frozen ground was undisturbed but for the one patch of new growth, now torn and trampled.

"It's time for me to leave." My words were thin in the cold air. "You cannot fight me. I am finished here. We're done."

There was no echo. My voice sounded flat and empty.

I walked around the glade. The thorns remained still where I passed and all was quiet. My feet on the crisp-cold grass made the only sound.

"If you try and hold me here, it will be worse for you." The threat sounded hollow with no one to witness it.

For the third time, I reached within me, releasing the gallowfyre and dappling the glade with shifting moonlight. The glade responded immediately. The thorns retracted, winding back down into the ground; the grass shrank until it was the barest hint of a sward. Within moments I was standing in an empty field, bordered by distant trees. Where there had been the barest minimum of presence before, now there was none.

I looked around. Everywhere was the same. The ground rose slightly so that I was on the crown of a low rise. At the edges, scraggy firs edged the forest, backed by larger trees fading into the dark beneath the evergreens.

"Hiding will not help you," I shouted. There was no reply.

I set off towards the trees. I walked smartly, showing my determination, making it clear that I would brook no dissent. After a few minutes, I stopped. The trees were no nearer. Nor were the ones behind me any further away. I broke into a jog and then into a full run. I pushed myself, racing for the trees. Eventually I staggered to a hoarse halt.

The trees remained at a distance.

I put my hands on my knees, breathing hard. It was time to stop messing about. I straightened myself and opened the core of magic within me. I released the tendrils of gallowfyre, sending them questing through the bald grass, into the cracks, exploring the crevices, searching for the taste of life, the sense of a presence. They found only dead soil. There was nothing living in it. Even the grass was dead.

"Show yourself! Come out and face me!" I shouted. My words evaporated in the thin cold air.

I resolved to wait, then. I sat down on the cold grass, feeling the chill from the ground through the thin silk of my trousers. I missed the shirt I had given Helen to wrap the baby in. I shook my head. No, poor scrap, he could have it.

In the stillness I found myself listening to the sound of my own breathing, the light draw and relax. I rubbed my hands together and heard the soft rasp of skin on skin. There was no other sound.

I shook myself. There was a wriggling, scurrying sound. I looked down. Where my hand pressed to the ground, the grass had grown around it, sending little shoots up between my fingers. As I watched, they withdrew, retreating back into the soil.

I jolted myself awake. What was I doing? I had let myself be lulled by the peace. I was tired and hungry. I had let my head fall forward and fallen asleep where I sat. I shot to my feet, suddenly realising the danger I was in.

If I fell asleep here, I would never wake up. The grass would pull me down and strangle me until I was immobile and unconscious, but not dead. No, it wouldn't want me dead. With Sam it could survive for a long time. If it kept him and hoarded him, he would feed the glade for as long as he lived, maybe for another forty years.

But me? I was fey.

If it could overcome me, it would have my full fey lifespan to feed on me. I could keep it alive for hundreds of years. I would be the meal that never ran out, the well that never ran dry.

All it had to do was wait, and it was very good at waiting.

EIGHTEEN

I made myself walk up and down. If I fell asleep I was worse than dead, but that only made the exhaustion more acute. My throat felt dry and my bones ached from the cold. I needed to get back, but where was the exit?

I thought about bringing others. Maybe if I summoned Debbie? She had a strange idea of what constituted fun – maybe she would like it here. Ultimately, though, that would be fruitless. Whoever I brought here, when they had gone, I would still be left. Unless I could think of a way to escape, I was going to be the meal on tap for as long as I lived.

I tried delving into the ground, sending fingers of gallowfyre questing deep into the soil. There was nothing. It was as if the fey had developed the glade as armour. The glade was the fey, but only in the sense that my hair or my nails were me. I could cut them off and it would neither hurt nor harm me, but they were still me. The fey was like that. Somewhere under the layers of soil and the fringe of forest was a creature, but I was damned if I could find it.

I tried tempting it, sitting on the grass looking as if I was asleep. It ignored me. I tried hurting it, pulling out little tufts of grass until I had a bare patch several feet across. As soon as my back was turned the grass grew again. I walked steadily towards the trees, testing whether there was a limit to how far I could go before I would make some progress. If there was a limit, I didn't reach it.

The cold was creeping into my bones and the exhausting day and lack of food were starting to get to me. Eventually I would fall asleep, and then I would be in real trouble. I sat back on the grass, determined to think, and not under any circumstances to fall asleep.

I tried to think of some way to summon help. I shouted for Garvin, and then Blackbird, to no effect. There was no surface in the glade that would reflect, nothing I could use as a mirror. My imagination conjured the fey that was the glade watching this from a distance, realising with smug satisfaction how increasingly desperate I was becoming.

Would Garvin come and investigate if I didn't report that evening? If he found my sleeping self back in my room, was there anything he could do? In any case, might it be too late by then? The seductive thought of my sleeping body, resting in my bed, crept into my awareness and I began to feel warm. I shook myself awake again, momentarily toying with the idea of summoning Sam back. Maybe if I fed him to it, it would let me get some sleep?

I stood up again and began pacing in a circle. There had to be a way. I was a Warder, for goodness sake! Garvin would be wetting himself at this performance. I had to think, but I was so tired.

There was no Way-node here, so I couldn't use that. I wasn't even sure this was a place, never mind whether it had Way-points. Maybe if I could get to the trees I could find a way out? I had tried walking and running, but I had another possibility. Raffmir had shown me how to reach places I could see.

I found a spot and focused on the distant tree-line. I opened myself to my surroundings and gathered energy to me. My skin fell into unreflective blackness and the cold deepened. I needed more to be able to jump across. The cold black core of magic within me dilated and the air around me chilled to bone-numbing intensity. The energy built slowly; it had started out cold. I held out my arms, extending my reach, increasing the area from which I drew, feeling downwards into the soil, upwards into the starlit sky. I drew it into me until the pale nimbus started flickering across my skin with tiny fingers of light. As the energy mounted I began to see.

This was not the real world. I already knew that in my mind, but now I could see it. I had discovered earlier how the fabric of the real world lay draped across the frame of reality. It was possible to step beyond that curtain and pass through, but the curtain and the frame remained.

What I found in the glade was a shimmering skin of a world with a liquid underbelly, formless and yet shaped. I peered beneath the skin of it and found within the liquid depths a beating heart.

"Got you."

Gallowfyre spilled from my hands, and in my heightened state I could see the tendrils of power reaching through the fabric of the skin and pricking that heart.

I awoke in my bed and sat bolt upright. The scream of anguish echoed in my ears still, though the glade had gone. Little normal noises, the bark of a dog, cars moving outside, the distant call of a mournful gull, all told me I had come home.

The mirror in my room was misted over. The whole room was deathly cold. Patterns of frost traced the inside of the window glass. It was midsummer and I had frost. Even as I watched, the frost blurred and clouded

312

as the warmth transmitted through the glass turned frost to mist and then cleared.

The day was brighter than the four o'clock my watch showed. I held the watch to my ears and it ticked lightly. I looked at it again, making sure I wasn't holding it upside down. Ten o'clock would make more sense. Four o'clock was what it showed. I turned back the duvet, went to the window and peered through the misty glass. The sun was over the hill at the back of the town. It was four in the afternoon. not four in the morning. I had more than slept the clock around and I still felt exhausted.

I opened the window to let in some of the warm air from outside to heat the room, then went into the bathroom and spent a good ten minutes under the shower with the temperature wound round as hot as I could bear it. I never wanted to be cold again. I emerged, pink and steaming, and put on clothes from the previous day.

Once dressed I looked at myself in the mirror. There were dark rings under my eyes and my cheeks looked sunken. No wonder: I was starving. My stomach grumbled at the first thought of food. Before I could feed myself, though, I needed to follow up on the night's work.

Pressing my hand to the mirror, I told it what I wanted.

"Sam Veldon – his mobile phone."

I had discovered the ability to tap into the phone network from something Raffmir and Solandre had done when I had first encountered them. I had then discovered it was also possible to contact mobile phones, even if they were turned off. How the connection worked I had no idea, but it would enable me to cash in a favour I was owed.

Sam's phone was difficult to reach. I lowered the temperature of the room again as I drew in more power for the connection. "Sam Veldon, speak to me."

The line squeaked and chirped, making stuttering chattering noises. Then a broken ring, distorted by poor line quality. It rang eight or nine times before it answered.

"Is someone there?"

It was a strange question from someone who had just answered a phone.

"Sam, you know who this is, right?"

"I can't hear you." The lie in Sam's voice was blatant.

"I know perfectly well you can hear me, Sam Veldon. Now listen…"

"Stupid thing shouldn't work at all." He was addressing someone else. "This whole building is shielded. Here, let me take it outside. When will they get these things right?"

I could hear him moving around. Then his voice came back on. "Give me your number. I'll ring you in five."

"I don't have a number, Sam. I'll call you in three." I released the mirror.

Why were the phones I wanted to call always so difficult?

Having said I would call him in three, I waited four minutes before trying again. This time the call went straight through without problem. It rang once.

"How the hell did you get this number?"

"Good afternoon, Sam. I'm well, thanks. How are you?"

"Scratched to high heaven and sore to boot. What the fuck happened last night?"

"Not quite what you were expecting, was it, Sam?"

"Let's get back to where you got this number from. It's supposed to be unlisted."

"You only think I'm phoning you. This isn't real. The scratches on your arms and the weals around your throat aren't real either. You owe me a favour, Sam Veldon, and I intend to collect."

"This isn't happening."

"I told *you* that. Do you have the information on my daughter?"

314

"What am I, fucking Wikipedia?"

"Either you have it or you don't, Sam."

"Stop saying my name. Bloody GCHQ will be monitoring this. I'll lose my job and then no one will have anything."

"Then tell me what I need."

"Tate Britain. One hour. Can you do it?"

"Yes. Why there?"

"Because it's not far and there's something I want to bloody show you, all right?"

"If you're setting me up, Sam, I'm going to leave you up to your neck in grass."

"There's no set-up. Meet me. I'll show you." I could hear the truth in his voice. He was not setting me up, but I would still be cautious.

"One hour. Wait for me." I took my hand from the mirror and dropped the call.

I put on my jacket and checked the pockets, making sure I had the codex, a torch, my wallet and anything else I might need. I unsheathed, wiped and resheathed the sword and then held it until it was a black umbrella. I left the window ajar to air the room; if Raffmir wanted to get in, a window wouldn't stop him, and there was nothing valuable in the room to steal.

Leaving quietly, I found the downstairs rooms silent and empty. Making myself unremarkable, I exited the guest house and turned towards the harbour. Yesterday's rain had been swept away, leaving the sky looking scrubbed. I looked out beyond the harbour where the gulls perched on the bastion watching the tide ebb from the walls to the horizon where the sea melted into the sky. It was a beautiful day, and I had slept through most of it.

I marched across the harbour front and up the hill, past the church and into the narrow streets. Mounting the bank, I climbed up through the tussocks to where

315

the Way-point nestled in the dip near the hill-top. Turning around I saw the town laid out below me, the roofs washed clean and shining in the afternoon light, the distant sound of children playing mixing with the mewling cry of the gulls. In this light, on this day, you could see why people stayed here.

I stepped on to the Way-point and felt it rise beneath me. I launched myself into the flow, letting it sweep me away inland. As I approached the next node, I twisted slightly, letting it slingshot me around to the next point. My heartbeat accelerated as I came to the next node and veered around it south, using the nodes to slalom southwards, reversing the route I had used the previous night to traverse the darkness with the minimum of effort. It was still draining, but it was less tiring than traversing the nodes point by point, one by one. I had Raffmir to thank for that, at least.

As I approached the Way-points around London I began taking them wide, shedding momentum and letting them slow me. Aiming to show some style after Raffmir's remarks the day before. I was shedding momentum as I shimmered into being in the crypt of the Church of St Clement Danes on the Strand in London, and I only stumbled forward slightly. I glanced around, finding no one there to witness my attempt at a graceful landing and grateful at least for that. I gently eased the misdirection around myself, leaving just enough to make me unremarkable so that I could climb the curving stairway to the entry hall and slip out into the evening air. London was noticeably warmer than Yorkshire and I found the jacket suddenly heavy across my shoulders. It held too much to carry it, though.

As I walked past Australia House, I noticed the iron gates barring the door, and found myself rubbing my palm where I had touched them the previous year. Simply touching them had thrown me backwards, leaving a livid burn mark on my hand that had faded slowly, teaching me a valuable lesson about iron and the Feyre. I steered around them, setting a steady pace along the Strand to Trafalgar Square.

Checking my watch, I realised I had enough time for a small diversion, so I strode up the rise past the white portico of St Martin-in-the-Fields and stopped at the coffee shop where Blackbird had taken me and where she first told me about the Feyre and my magical heritage. Thinking about it, somehow it felt like two lives, one ordinary, punctuated by dull commutes and arguments, and one unreal, where at any moment I might lose my home, my daughter or my life. I shook my head and then had to apologise to the young man who served me coffee, while I paid for the drink and for a sandwich I had picked up.

"Are you sure you're OK, Sir?" The young man looked concerned.

"It's fine, thanks. I was just thinking of someone I was with the last time I was in this coffee shop."

He took my money. "I hope it worked out well for you," he said with a smile.

"I'm not sure," I said. "I'll have to let you know."

I took my coffee outside to the seats overlooking the square, choosing the same seat I had taken when Blackbird was there. Things had seemed simpler then. It had been run or die, fight or flee. Blackbird had been open and inviting. The memory of her suggesting an afternoon of sex and seduction made me smile, until I remembered that she also thought I wouldn't last the night. Now I knew her better, I realised that she had her own reasons for everything, even that.

The coffee was very hot, so I ate the sandwich, realising only as I licked mayonnaise and crumbs from my fingers how hungry I had been. Then I had to wait until the coffee cooled to drink it.

Last year when I was in the same spot I had been hunted. Blackbird told me that I would have to fight to survive the dawn. Well, I had fought and mostly I'd won. The victory, though, had its bitterness, and its losses. I wondered where Blackbird was. I was aware that she was smart and quick and knew things that I had yet to learn, but I also knew she was alone, pregnant and had no magic to protect her. I wondered where my daughter was and what had been done to her to make her turn on the three girls in the changing room. I wondered how that had changed her. It made me consider again whether this life was truly worth the price.

I blew on my coffee to cool it, having dawdled long enough, and drank as much as I could before dropping my cup and sandwich wrapper into the bin. Then I walked across the road, down across Trafalgar Square, past the bronze lions and over into Whitehall.

The walk took me down past Downing Street, where I wondered if the iron gates at either end of the Prime Minister's and the Chancellor's residence were entirely coincidental. I walked on past Big Ben and the grand East window of Westminster Abbey. The pedestrians thinned and changed from tourists to civil servants as I passed beyond the Palace of Westminster and into Pimlico.

The grand facade of the Tate Gallery was in front of me. I had fifteen minutes to spare. I diverted for a few moments into Victoria Gardens and used the shelter there to re-establish the concealment I would need and adjust my glamour so that no one would recognise me, even if they saw me. Then I crossed the road and climbed the steps to the entrance, slipping inside to the cool interior, passing the helpful gentleman directing visitors and avoiding the gaze of the security guards. I worked my way around the gallery, moving from room to room, checking the location of cameras, watching for additional security guards, looking for people who had ear-pieces or seemed out of place. If there were people there watching, they were doing it remotely. My glamour would deal with that.

When I saw Sam had arrived early too, I should not have been surprised. He was walking around the gallery much as I was, watching the people, not the pictures. He passed within a couple of feet of me and even glanced at me as he passed. He did not recognise me, though he did look twice. Something about my demeanour made him do so. I let him take a good look, and then move on.

Moving slowly after him, I made my way around until I was sitting on the benches behind him where he waited. I watched him as the meeting time came and went, looking for any sign that he was communicating with anyone. He looked impatient and edgy, but he made no sign and gave no signal that I could discern.

Slowly I increased the concealment around me, allowing it to seep into the room. Gradually people turned away, glanced into the room and decided to turn back. They wandered slowly into other rooms. Eventually we were alone. The camera in the corner was still active, but it would record nothing useful. The warder standing at the doorway watched with decreasing interest until her head nodded and she fell asleep. I watched Sam become aware that almost everyone had gone.

"You wanted to meet me, Sam Veldon. Did you tell anyone else we were meeting?"

He glanced at the warder and then at me. "Do you always creep around like this?"

"I am not creeping. I am sitting. Did you tell anyone, Sam? Is there anyone listening to our conversation?"

He came across and sat on the bench beside me. "I could lose more than my job for this."

"You didn't answer my question."

"No." He shook his head and smiled, wryly. "Who am I gonna tell? Oh. I'm just going out to meet a guy from my dreams." He looked at me, carefully. "It is you, isn't it?"

"Have you managed to get the taste of grass out of your mouth?"

He looked away. Then he wiped the back of his hand across his lips. "Not really. Kinda sticks with you, doesn't it?"

"You would do well to remember that."

"If I'm being followed, I don't know about it, but it's a risk in my business. We all know that we could be subject to surveillance at any time."

"What did you bring me here for, Sam? What did you want to tell me that couldn't be said over the phone?"

"Yeah, you need to watch that. They're coming in tomorrow to check the electromagnetic shielding. You're not supposed to be able to phone in or out of that building. Only the desk phones, that's how it is."

"You will have to make an excuse."

"Just don't call me there again. It's not supposed to work, right?"

"Don't tell me what to do, Sam. You owe me."

"I don't owe you anything!" His voice was raised and the warder at the door startled slightly, but then nodded again. "This is crazy, I shouldn't even be here."

"Just tell me what I need to know and I'll go. You can get back to whatever it is that you do."

He stood up and for a second I though he was leaving, but then he walked over to the wall opposite, where two small paintings hung.

"Take a look at this. What do you think."

I followed him over. "I'm not here for art appreciation, Sam. I want to know where my daughter is."

He continued as if I hadn't spoken. "The picture is called The Fairy Feller's Master-Stroke. Ring any bells?"

The mention of "fairy" made me look afresh at the painting. It was a small dark square painted in exquisite detail. It depicted a small man in a long coat, not unlike Raffmir's. His back was turned and he held a hatchet high, ready to strike down at a cob nut. The scale was all wrong, with tiny figures peering between the strands of grass, watching. When you looked closer you could see that some of the figures had wings, but they weren't butterfly wings. They were somewhere between a leaf and a bat. Each time you looked closer it showed even more detail. In places the faces looked distorted, as if seen through a crooked glass or under water.

I looked up at Sam. "No bells with me, Sam. Should it?"

"It was painted by Richard Dadd. Name mean anything?"

"Not really. I didn't do art school."

"How about this one?"

The painting next to it was of two faces, but they weren't human faces. Something about them reminded me of people I had met in the High Court of the Feyre. The eyes were intense and watchful and they had an aura about them that somehow reminded me of fey glamour.

"This isn't familiar either, though it is striking. What's the relevance of this?"

"When you were at the hospital last year, there was a grey woman in the room. I thought it was an illusion, but she was there, wasn't she?"

"She was."

"And then she'd gone. She just faded away. And last night, I woke up covered in scratches. I had red marks all over me where the grass bit into my skin."

"Dreams can sometimes spill over into your life, Sam. It depends whose dreams they are."

He looked at me and then back at the painting. "One of the files is on him, the guy who painted these."

"One of what files?"

"The B files. He's one of them."

"An artist? Why would an artist have a government file on him?"

"Did you know he was mad? He claimed to see things that weren't there? Yet he painted these incredible pictures. Look at the detail. Look at the way it's almost three-dimensional. What do you think he saw?"

"Who knows? You said he was mad?"

"He spent a good deal of his life in mental hospitals, and one hospital in particular. St Mary's Bethlehem."

"I don't know it."

"Oh, but you do. At least you know of it. It's infamous. St Mary's Bethlehem, also called Bethlem Hospital... also called Bedlam."

"The Victorian freak show?"

"So you do know it?"

"I've heard of it.

"That's where the B files lead. That's where they all went, eventually. They all ended up in Bedlam."

"Didn't the Victorians used to run tours round it, so you could go and laugh at the mad people?"

"That's one way of funding the health service. I told you, the files go way back. I talked to Cruella."

"Who's Cruella?"

"Camilla de Veirs. She's the posh totty in the archives. Loves to bang on about the value of contextual knowledge. Those who cannot remember the past are condemned to repeat it – that kind of thing. She told me some of them are thirteenth-century. They go back to the Stone House; used to be out near Charing Cross when it was still fields and farms. Then it moved up to Bishopsgate where it became St Mary's Bethlehem, or just plain Bethlem. That's where they put all the oddballs, the bag ladies and the tramps, until it got bad. Disease, overcrowding – they had it all. When it got worse, they moved it to St George's Fields, where the

Imperial War Museum is now. This poor bugger painted these pictures while he was there."

"So where is it now?"

"Bromley."

"You're joking."

"Straight up. It's part of South London and Maudsley Health Trust. They don't do tours any more though."

"Is that where Alex is?"

"No. I checked. She's not in Broadmoor either, which is where this poor bugger ended up. Twenty years in a hospital for the criminally insane. What a way to treat an artist."

"Then where is she?"

He turned away, walked back to the bench and sat down. "I don't know."

I followed him and stood over him, looking down into his grizzled face.

"I need to find her, Sam. I need to know where they've taken her."

"I told you, I don't know. When they abandoned St George's Fields they broke it up. The easy cases went to Monk's Orchard at Maudsley. The dangerously psychotic ones ended up in Broadmoor, or at Rampton up in Nottinghamshire. Some went to other institutions where they could be nearer family or just where they had room. She's not in any of those, I can tell you that much. When St George's Fields closed, the references for the B files changed. They have a suffix. B/BWPD."

"What does it mean?"

"I don't know. The archive bunnies only know it as a reference and the ownership of the files shifted to military. We only get summary data now, unless we request it." He looked up at me. "No, I won't request it. This is bad enough already. Do your damnedest."

"You don't know how bad my damnedest really is, Sam."

"I'm not much use to you if I'm inside for offences relating to the Official Secrets Act, am I?"

"You're not much use to me now."

"Oh, come on. You'd never have known any of this stuff if I hadn't told you. If I request access to a military file I'm going to be asked why I want it. I have no plausible reason to be in there. Military don't take kindly to people poking around in their stuff."

"I need to find her, Sam."

"Then find her. I've given you all I have."

"There's more."

"Not from me. If I ask for the file, I will have to explain why I want it. Before you know it I'll be on leave for stress pending an investigation. No." He looked up at me. "No. They wouldn't give it to me anyway. Not without a valid reason."

"Create one."

"You're joking, aren't you? This isn't my field. I'm out on a limb as it is."

I went back to the paintings. "Monk's Orchard, Broadmoor, Rampton. Where else?"

He shook his head. "Somewhere else. Somewhere military. Scotland, maybe. They have stuff up there no one talks about."

I turned back to him. "How do I find her, Sam? How?"

"Maybe there are records at Maudsley? No, they only got the ones that were no danger to anyone else. Broadmoor and Rampton got the psychotics. The military reference may be a mothballed facility, an old camp or a disused barracks. It could be a nuclear bunker for all I know."

"How do you find out?"

"I don't. I've gone as far as I can."

"I could make you."

"You could try, but I have nothing else for you." He stood up. "Don't call me again. I don't want to hear from you."

"I saved you, Sam. I could have left you there."

"If anyone else finds out we've had this conversation, what you'll do to me is pigeon shit compared to what they'll do to me."

He walked towards the arch leading to the exit, then paused and looked back. "And they'll leave me there."

When he'd gone, I went back to the paintings. Strange angular faces looked out at me through knowing eyes. The more I looked at The Fairy Feller's Master-Stroke, the more faces I saw. Tiny figures peered through the long strands and around stones, but like the Feyre they were only there if you looked for them. It was a perspective on a world I knew, but I could see why they questioned his sanity.

Sometimes I wondered about my own.

NINETEEN

The afternoon sunlight was bright after the muted light of the gallery, but the day's sunny disposition did not match my mood. Sam was right, he had given me something, but not enough. I knew that there were government files on my daughter and on me. I knew that files like that had existed since the thirteenth century. It tied into what I already knew about the Feyre.

When I was first presented to the High Court, Kimlesh had told me that the Feyre had taken a risk and mixed their bloodlines with those of humanity. She hadn't said when that happened, but I knew that the Quit Rents Ceremony, which was part of the barrier that kept the Seventh Court from visiting our world whenever they wanted, was almost eight hundred years old. That meant the barrier against Raffmir and his kindred dated from the late twelfth or early thirteenth century, shortly before the Stone House, which Sam had mentioned, was moved to Bishopsgate and renamed Bethlem.

That humanity would treat its mad and vulnerable as freaks was not news to me. I had lived and worked in London for years and the sight of homeless, helpless individuals living in cardboard boxes and begging was so much part of the wallpaper that most of the time I just didn't see it. When occasionally something or someone got past the social blindness, the best I could offer was the price of a meal or a hot drink. Even then, I was never quite sure whether I was actually supporting a drug habit or an alcoholic binge. Some people were hard to help, but that had always been the case.

Blackbird had once told me that the genes of the Feyre were mixed with humanity and could manifest unpredictably in the population. She'd told me that some of those people were like her and became part of fey society, and some managed the way they were, rationalising their abilities as an uncanny talent or a psychic ability. I was reminded of Greg, who lived and worked in the community, using his fey sense to follow his vocation, knowing he was different but not knowing why. If he chose to regard that as a gift from God, who was I to argue with him?

Others, though, did not cope with the discovery of their fey nature. Fey gifts could be very strange, and if you woke one day to find your reflection was no longer a face you recognised, or that items in your possession took on odd and perverse properties, then I could see how that might tip the balance of your mind. It was hard enough to accept it for yourself, but then to try and tell friends and loved ones that weird things were happening to you, that your perception of the world had shifted radically, that inanimate objects held strange messages or that you could see the fragmented futures of other people? It was no surprise that people like that ended up in institutions for the delusional.

What happened, though, when it turned out that you *could* see the future? What happened when the mad people turned out to be right? There had been witch-trials in the seventeenth century. Were those women simply people who had inherited an ability they could neither understand nor control? Wasn't it better to treat those people as mad rather than hang them or burn them at the stake? Or was the treatment worse than the cure?

Mankind knew about the Feyre. The helicopter over our burning cottage, the strange markings on the truck outside the hospital where Alex was being treated, the men waiting outside my ex-wife's house – all these pointed to an organised response. Somewhere, someone knew what was going on and had for a long while. As Garvin said, they were prepared and every time they encountered the Feyre they learned a little more. Now they had my daughter and they were looking for me.

As I walked slowly back up through Whitehall it occurred to me that somewhere behind the blank exterior were civil servants making decisions about people's lives. Somewhere buried in a department – Health, maybe, or perhaps Defence – was a small office that dealt with the incarceration and treatment of people for whom there was no place in society: not criminals, not enemies, just people that didn't fit.

In a democratic country it should be impossible for people simply to disappear. That method of dealing with dissent ought to be confined to banana republics and despots, but I knew it happened, either through choice or through intervention, as in my daughter's case. They had tried to do it to me. A passing thought occurred to me that I could give myself up and thereby discover what happened to people like me, but I did not think I would enjoy their concept of care.

They must know that she had not intended to harm anyone. They must know that she was innocent, mustn't they? How could they blame a fifteen year-old girl who had been bullied – tortured even? The girls that had persecuted her had used methods that would be illegal in most decent countries – water-boarding, they called it, didn't they? A form of torture banned under international law. How could they blame someone for retaliating, if they had the opportunity?

Yet three girls had died. It might not be murder, but they were still dead. The state would treat her as a murderer. It brought home to me that even if I managed to find her, Alex would not be able to go back to her life. It made me regret telling Kayleigh, since they would never be able to resume their friendship. Their lives would diverge rapidly. Alex couldn't go back to school. She would not be able to live a normal life. The moment she appeared in normal society, she would be arrested, the same as me. More final than that, Kayleigh would grow up and get older. Alex would grow up, but once she reached her adult size, she was going to age far more slowly. Kayleigh would be dead before Alex looked middle-aged.

It meant she would no longer be able to live with her mother either. It left the issue of whether to tell Katherine that her daughter was alive unresolved. If it was me, I would want to know. I would need to know. If I had found out that she was alive and that someone close to me knew that, I would be incredibly angry. It made withholding the information from Katherine feel like treachery. I would hold back, though, until I had Alex back. I would not tell her now, only to have myself proved wrong later. We weren't out of the woods yet. Instead, I promised myself that as soon as I knew that Alex was safe, I would find a way to tell Katherine. She was her mother. It was not in me to let her continue what was left of her life believing that her daughter was dead, when she was alive.

I had turned across the lower end of Trafalgar Square down the Strand to the church of St Clement Danes, where I knew I could get access to the Way through the crypt, but then I stopped. I had become used to being fey, following their ways, adopting their methods, but there were other ways to find things.

I went north towards Drury Lane and the theatre district, looking for something that always popped up in the tourist areas: an Internet café.

The one I found can't have been there long, but even so it had the odour of stale sweat and the yellow stain of nicotine on the keyboards. A couple of youths were smoking outside as I entered and one of them followed me in to relieve me of the money for an hour's worth of Internet. I sat down and opened the screen on Google, typing in the letters B/BWPD. The full reference came up with nothing, but BWPD apparently stood for a number of things: Barrels of Water Per Day, a Boston PC support company, Black and White Polka Dot – none of it made any sense in the context of mental asylums. I branched out, trawling through the official websites for South London and Maudsley Health Trust, the sites for Broadmoor and Rampton secure hospitals, the Wikipedia pages for St Mary's Bethlehem and numerous sites on Bedlam at St George's Fields, where the Imperial War Museum was now housed.

I knew something had changed. When St George's Fields was handed over to the Imperial War Museum, the file references had altered. Sam said it was military and restricted access, but that in itself marked a shift in approach.

Perhaps originally the mongrel fey were treated as undesirables and misfits, then later as freaks and even as entertainment. Why then a change in 1930? I tried to remember from documentaries and the distant memory of school what had been significant about 1930. Further searching brought up information about the Great Depression, the slide into Fascism and numerous other events, but not about what had happened to trigger a change in policy with regard to the Feyre. The Feyre themselves weren't mentioned at all and I wondered whether that was by design.

What had prompted someone in authority to say that these files were no longer a civil matter and would thereafter be a military concern?

The initials, BWPD, appended to the B file reference marked the change, but did not explain it, while the initials themselves were obscure.

My hour had expired some time ago, but no one seemed to care. I stood, stretching my neck and easing knotted muscles in my shoulders, then made my way out, nodding to the youth, and headed back to the crypt of St Clement Danes.

Avoiding the door to the main body of the church, I took the spiral stairway to the side and made my way down. The whitewashed walls with the commemorative plaques and the rows of simple seating gave this place a dignity and simplicity that the larger church above didn't have. The traffic rumbled past outside but did not disturb the peace that existed there.

I stood for a moment, trying to borrow some of that peace, then I stepped forward and whirled away, veering around Way-nodes so that I was thrown far from London. Within moments I was standing on the hill looking down on Ravensby. The graded streets were ranked bands of shadow, but the harbour still looked bright and colourful, at least until you got close enough to see the grime.

Slipping back into the town, I headed for the guest house. The room was as depressingly bare as I had left it. I stowed my sword and hung my jacket on the back of the door. Sitting on the end of the bed, I tried to clear my head. I felt as if I had the fragments of a picture but no clear idea of what I was looking at.

Sam had failed to find Alex for me. I could push him harder, but I didn't think that would get me anywhere.

Sam had helped me, not because I had threatened him, but because I turned back and saved him when I could have left him in the glade. He had gone as far as he was prepared to go and pushing him further would only result in him digging in his heels. I consoled myself that I knew more than I did before.

Blackbird was a different problem. I stood and went to the mirror. Laying my hand upon it, I whispered her name into the glass.

"Blackbird?"

The mirror clouded, a sickly glow coming from within. There was a growing buzz, then a stuttering clatter erupted from it and I snatched my hand away before the mirror broke. The glow faded slowly. I could not find her that way.

A different idea occurred to me and I replaced my hand. "Claire?" The mirror glowed with a more hopeful milky white. "Claire Raddison?" I could hear vague snatches of words, cut off and jumbled, like a conversation that had been taped, shredded and reassembled in random order. She also had protection against eavesdropping, though not as aggressive as Blackbird's. Were they together? If they were, wouldn't the same protection apply to both of them?

Who else could she be with? Would she return to the forest where she grew up? I could see her wanting to have her baby among the trees, to let him be part of the forest from the very beginning, but the tenuous safety there had failed her before. I could not see her relying solely on that.

Maybe I was looking at this from the wrong angle. I was searching for Blackbird, or a place she would go, or a friend she would turn to. Maybe I needed to come at this from an entirely different direction.

I placed my hand back on the mirror.

"Deefnir?"

I had only seen him once, hanging back as Raffmir came forward to greet me, but I remembered the sardonic curve of that lip, the foppish mop of black hair that fell over his eyes, the way his smile never reached his eyes.

"Deefnir, where are you?"

The mirror clouded then cleared. Into the room came a subtle shuffle and soft hush, the sound of outdoors. I was getting somewhere. I focused on the mirror, slowly increasing the connection, not wanting him to realise that I was listening in or trigger his defences, keeping it low profile.

Wherever he was, it sounded remote. There was no buzz of cars or rumble of diesel engines, so if it was London then it was a park or a common. No, even then there would be the bark of distant motorbikes, the distant cry of sirens or the rumble of the jets turning for Heathrow. No, this was somewhere altogether more remote.

If Deefnir wasn't in London then Blackbird wasn't either. Should I break off to pass this information to Garvin? The first question he would ask would be: "Where is he?"

I concentrated, trying to decipher the layers of sound coming through the mirror. A breeze gusted, the grass rustling in response. Where there other rustlings behind that? The distant caw of crows echoed for a moment, but not nearby. A forest, maybe, but where was the sibilant hush of the breeze in the trees? No, this was in the open.

There was a droning, a distant airplane maybe, except it didn't pass. Was it an air-conditioner? It didn't sound right for that. Maybe a car, but then why didn't it drive away? Wherever Deefnir was, he wasn't moving. Then a shout, tantalisingly short. Not near enough to recognise a voice or a word, but a sign that people were close by. He was watching someone, or something, but what?

Now came the sound of movement, a sliding shuffle. Was he moving closer? What was he trying to do? Wherever he was, he was being cautious. What would make Deefnir cautious? What was there that he would be afraid of? He was wraithkin and pure-bred at that. There was little that would stand against him. What was causing him to hang back?

The rumbling sound in the background rose in volume, a diesel rumble, but constant, not like a bus or a taxi. Was it a generator, or maybe a stationary vehicle? Then it came. The memory snapped into place. It was a tractor. Then came a sound I recognised, and I knew straightaway where he was. I could see it in my head. A baying bark, deep and full, followed by another. Two dogs, heckles up, legs braced: I could see them in my imagination, coats the colour of burnt honey bristling down their backs as they picked up the scent of the intruder. He was in Shropshire, at the farm owned by the Highsmith family, where Blackbird and I had gone last year to get the Quick Knife reforged for the Ceremony of the Quit Rents.

I heard Deefnir turn and retreat, moving cautiously away from the unwanted attention, then accelerating as the sound of the barking increased. His pace increased until there was a steady padding and the sounds of the farm diminished, but I dropped my hand from the mirror. Now I knew where he was.

The farm should have given it away, and with my rural upbringing I should have recognised the sound of a tractor, but what sealed it was the sound of the dogs, the two mastiffs that Jeff and Meg Highsmith kept on their farm in Shropshire. Their distinctive baying brought the memory back immediately, and if Deefnir was there, then so was Blackbird. It made sense. The place was steeped in iron. The Highsmiths knew about the Feyre and had their own ways of protecting themselves. I was surprised, though, that Meg Highsmith would take Blackbird in. As far as Meg was concerned, Blackbird was trouble that Meg didn't need. She was there, though. Why else would Deefnir be there?

I needed to let Garvin know. I replaced my hand on the mirror.

"Garvin? It's Niall."

The sound from the mirror was of traffic, somewhere busy, maybe London or somewhere equally urban. "Garvin, can you hear me? It's Niall. I've found Deefnir." There was no response.

I removed my hand, then placed it again. "Tate?"

The sound of traffic re-emerged. Where you found one you found the other. What were they doing? I took my hand away again, letting the milky light fade from the mirror. Who to try next?

"Fionh?" This time the mirror filled with milky light, but then quickly cleared leaving no sound at all. The mirror was completely silent. I wondered whether she was with the High Court, in which case it was no surprise to learn that it was not possible to eavesdrop on that conversation.

I was running out of options. "Fellstamp?" This time a sound emerged immediately, the harsh drone of someone snoring. "Fellstamp? Wake up, it's Niall. I need to speak with you."

The snoring continued its rasping rhythm. "Fellstamp! Wake up! I need your help!"

There was no change. He seemed to be making more noise than I was.

"Amber?" This time the mirror filled with a sour sickly green, the light pulsing in strange ways as it made strange clicks and ticks. Where on earth was she? The connection faltered and I let it drop.

That left one more to try. "Slimgrin?" The mirror filled with light once more.

This time the sound was outdoors. There was a hush of trees, the sound of leaves in the breeze. The raucous cry of rooks disturbed the quiet, their harsh accusing voices crying out of the sky. It felt open and wild; I could almost picture them circling around the trees, returning to roost in the evening light, cawing and calling to each other as they spiralled down.

"Slimgrin, can you hear me? I need you to get a message to Garvin. Tell him Blackbird is in Shropshire with the Highsmiths. Deefnir's there too. Did you get that?"

The only sounds were the call of the rooks over a muted shuffling, a sense of shifting weight or changing position. Where was he? Had he heard me?

"Slimgrin, are you there? I know where Blackbird is. She's at the farm near Bridgenorth. Can you hear me?"

There was a loud thumping, not from the mirror, but from outside my room. Someone was banging on my door.

"Slimgrin? She's in Shropshire. I found her. Deefnir's there. Can you hear me?" I was shouting now, making myself heard over the thumping. It rose to an insistent hammering.

"I'm going to have to go."

I released my hand and the sound dissipated, making the thumping on my door sound as if someone was trying to break in, rather than simply get my attention.

"Mr Dawson." Martha's voice came through the door. "Are you in there?"

I went to the door, unlocked it and opened it just enough to see who was there. "Sorry, I was talking to one of my…"

Martha was standing in the hallway with a look of sour disapproval on her face. Behind her was the larger bulk of Greg, the vicar. "Never mind that," he said over her head. "She's gone."

"Who's gone?" I asked.

"Shelley, Karen's sister. She's vanished."

TWENTY

"What do you mean, Shelley's vanished?" I asked Greg.

It crossed my mind for a moment that she was the same age as my daughter. If she had fey ancestry then maybe she truly had vanished from sight. Is that what was going on? Were these girls disappearing because they were fey?

Greg looked at Martha and then at me. "I need a word."

"What kind of a word?" I glanced from one to the other. Martha's scowl did not improve.

Greg eased around Martha, steering her towards the stairs. "Thank you, Mrs Humphries, you've been most helpful. Neal will be able to help me out now. Done all you can do in the circumstances. Thanks very much for your help."

"There's something going on here. I can smell it," she protested.

Greg wasn't to be distracted. "I'll handle it, don't you worry."

He escorted her to the fire door and waited until it swung closed behind her. I could hear her disgruntled tread on the staircase, all the way down. I left the door ajar and picked up my sword, keeping my body between the doorway and the weapon until it was an umbrella that I held in my hand.

Greg appeared in the doorway.

"Don't know how long we've got."

"Until what?"

"She was meant to come straight home from school. She's not home and she's not at friends'. Her mum's worried sick. She's already called the police. Her dad's going spare, saying it's all Karen's fault."

"You're worrying too much. She'll be behind the bus shelter with a boy or down the chip shop with her friends. I have to go."

"Where?"

"London, Shropshire… I'm not sure yet. I have a message to deliver."

"Can't leave now. We need you."

"I'm needed elsewhere."

I moved towards the door, but Greg filled the doorway. I halted in front of him. "She's probably fine. What makes you think she's not?"

He dug into his coat pocket and pulled out a small bundle of plastic. He placed it in my open hand. It was pink and crushed. "Her mobile phone."

"Where was it?" I turned it over in my hand. The screen was cracked and the innards hung out, dangling on little ribbons of wire. It looked as if it had been comprehensively stamped on.

"Small park between school and home. More of a play area. Her mum followed the route back to school. No sign of her. Then she spotted this. Kicked under a hedge at the edge of the park, next to the road."

"This should go to the police. It's evidence."

"You've never seen it before?"

"No, why should I… you think I had something to do with this?"

Greg sagged and shook his head. "I'm sorry, Neal. I had

to ask. You knew so much about them. You knew about Helen's pregnancy, Debbie's clubbing… when I found out you knew Gillian and Trudy were dead, I realised there could be more than one way of knowing."

"Not because I had anything to do with their disappearance! I'm not some sick…"

"I know that now. You do understand, don't you? Had to ask." His eyes held a sadness from hearing lies too often, seeing what people truly meant and knowing too much.

"I really have to go." I needed to get a message to Garvin.

"No, don't you see? It means something. You were sent to us. You were meant to be here."

"I'm really meant to be somewhere else."

"Shelley needs you. You may be the only one who can find her. Would you put her family through what you've been through? Not after losing your own daughter, surely?"

That stopped me. "That's not fair, Greg."

"No, it isn't. But who else will find her? At least tell us if she's still alive."

The need to be on my way burned in me, but I could not just abandon him. "Come inside. Shut the door."

He came in and closed the door behind him.

"I want your word, Greg. On whatever you hold most sacred. You tell no one about this. Are we agreed?"

"I swear on the Holy Cross, on Him who died there and on the Father who raised him up to heaven." It rang as true as anything I've ever heard.

Tossing the umbrella on to the bed, I turned to the mirror. I placed my hand flat upon it, watching Greg as I did so.

"Shelley Hopkins?"

The mirror clouded under my hand and Greg's face held a mixture of hope and uncertainty.

As the mirror started to glow from within he said, "That looks like…" He faltered before the word he was going to say.

"Shhh! You wanted to know. Now we find out."

The mirror cleared slowly and through it came the sound of the town. It wavered above the harbour and I thought it would rise and dissipate. My heart fell at explaining what that meant to Greg, and he must have seen it in my face, but then it focused, suddenly and vividly. There was a clunking scraping and a low murmuring, indistinct and fuzzy. Then a whimpering, a lost sound, more like a wounded animal than a girl.

"Shelley? Shelley, is that you?" My voice echoed strangely.

The whimpering sound continued. Then the clunking came again. It sounded metallic.

"Where is she?" Greg asked.

I shook my head, straining to hear. He came closer, trying to decode the sounds.

"It's indoors. She's not outside. Can she hear us?"

"Only if there's a mirror close to her. Wait, listen."

The distinctive call of a gull, *keeeya, keeya, keya, kya, kya kya,* came from outside and echoed through the mirror into the room in a double image of sound.

Greg said it first. "She's here! By God, she's right here!"

"No, listen," I said. "The sound is delayed, further away from the gull than we are. Wherever she is, she can hear it."

"A warehouse? There are some around the harbour. Or maybe another guest house?"

"Outside," I said. "We need to be outside. I'll bring the mirror."

I unhooked the mirror from the wall. Greg held the door open as I went through and we barged open the

340

fire door and ran down the stairs. Martha came out of the kitchen and waited at the bottom of the stairs as we barrelled down.

She pointed at the mirror. "You can't take that. That's private property, that is!"

Greg intercepted her. "Don't worry, we'll bring it back."

I slipped past them out into the street. Holding the mirror pressed to one ear I turned slowly. The sounds were confusing, on one side muffled and indistinct, overlaid with scrapes and shuffles, and on the other, clear but wide open. I closed my eyes, turning slowly. There was an abrupt blare of a car horn as a car swerved around me.

"Watch where you're going, ya prick!" The voice was female, but the car had gone before I could see the face.

The gull call came again, and I turned towards the harbour, but then another joined in, and another. The rooftops echoed to the call of the gulls and I couldn't get a fix on it.

Greg appeared. "Where?"

I shook my head, waving my hand at the gulls, then gestured towards the harbour. We walked together slowly, me listening to the mirror, him watching out for me. He stepped out in the road, gesturing the traffic to a halt as we came out on to the harbour front. No one questioned the stern-faced vicar. He stood in the road, holding the traffic while I scanned the rows of shops and houses, the chandlers, the fishing shop. There were windows above the shops, facing on to the harbour. She could be behind any one of them. I stepped back on to the pavement, following the line of the shops.

A truck rumbled past, changing gear, and the echo of the sound reverberated through the mirror. Close – I could hear she was close. I trotted down the front of the shops, scanning side alleys, looking for dumpsters and bins, anything that might be metallic and big enough for a person. I saw a skip and raced for it. Greg followed and started pulling off tangles of polythene, slabs of plaster-board, pitching them on to the floor. There was just rubble. Nowhere big enough for a girl.

We went back to the front.

"We need more people." I pointed to the row of windows facing out over the harbour. "We need to be in these shops. Every one of them has an upstairs. The police can go house to house. Two of us simply isn't enough."

A gull call came again, and I pressed the cold of the glass to my cheek. There was almost no difference. I could hear the muted call coming through, but it was muffled, as if it were under blankets or filtered through something.

"Here. Somewhere here."

I threw my arm out and turned slowly, looking for some sign, some indication of where she was.

Greg stared about, his eyes feverish. "The light's going. The sun's already down. We lose the light and we'll lose her."

"Look for a light in the windows. There might be one that's occupied."

We scanned the front, looking for signs of occupation. In the upstairs room of a junk shop a single bulb hung bare behind the glass. I rushed to the door, repeatedly pushing the bell-button and rattling the door until a shadow appeared and pulled the door ajar.

I shoved my way inside, followed by Greg. The bell rattled maniacally on its spring. A bearded man, piggy eyes behind round glasses, looked confused at Greg and offended at me. I barely broke pace, pushing through to the back of the shop. Greg stayed with him.

"Dave? What's upstairs?"

He made to follow, but Greg's giant hand landed on his shoulder and held him back.

"Upstairs – what's up there?"

"My stockroom…"

I took the stairs upwards two at a time and burst into the room.

The single bulb presided over stacks of old rubbish in an array that made the Maritime Museum look tidy. I snatched an old blanket from a pile in the corner to find only a badly stuffed armchair, piled with broken toys. It was just rubbish.

A sound rumbled through the mirror, an engine, gravel-ground and diesel-driven. It had started up. I barrelled back down the stairs, heading for the street.

"Wrong idea. A truck. I can hear the diesel. It's just started. He's moving. We've got minutes at most."

Greg piled out of the shop behind me and we scanned the road. I raced down the front. A white van was manoeuvring back and forth in a parking space. I raced for it and went for the back. It reversed towards me then stuttered to a halt.

A big guy, blue-dyed tattoos down his arms, jumped out.

"What'ya think you're doing? I nearly ran into you, idiot!"

I yanked at the back doors of the van. They were locked.

"Open this. Open it now!"

"There's nothing in there. I'm picking up, not dropping off."

Greg appeared at my shoulder. "Do what he said."

I don't know whether it was the dog-collar or the set of Greg's shoulders, but the big guy fiddled with his keys and inserted it into the lock. He yanked the doors wide.

"See?"

The van was bare. I stepped back, scanning the line of traffic. We needed more time. It could be any one of them. I held the mirror up to my ear. Big truck, little truck, van, car?

The noise was much louder in the mirror, a dull thrumming that reverberated through the glass. A constant rumble that you felt rather than heard. I stepped back, turning slowly through a full circle, trying to hear a sound that matched that deep growl. I found myself facing out.

Across the road, on the far side of the harbour, one of the boats was moving. A couple of men walked up and down the sides of the boat as they disentangled it from the ones around it, slipping tethers and untying mooring ropes. I watched it in fascination. The boat pulled around and skewed sideways, drifting into the one next to it. From the mirror there was a deep thunk as they gently collided.

I started walking towards the harbour, Greg following me, eyes on the traffic, not seeing the boat.

"Can you hear it? Is she still there?" he asked.

I concentrated on the boat. Lights came on, white, red and green. A spout of diesel smoke erupted from the rear with an answering roar from the engine in the mirror. I quickened into a trot, following the line of the harbour wall where it circled around.

Greg shouted behind me. "Is she there?'

The boat rumbled loudly and pulled back into clear water. It drifted out into the centre of the harbour, turn-ing slowly. I could see lights on in the cabin and men scurrying around on the deck. I could hear the engine idling again, not across the harbour, but through the glass of the mirror. I tucked the mirror under my arm, moving into a run, wrapping concealment around me so they wouldn't see me racing around the harbour wall, tracking the boat.

Three men, all fishermen, one in the cabin steering, the other two on the deck. The engine grumbled and the water foamed behind it. The boat pushed forward, heading for the harbour entrance.

A moment for decision. If I was wrong – if it wasn't that boat – then I would lose her. If she was on shore I would lose her. I dropped the mirror; it bounced once,

344

twice behind me, then smashed as I ran on around the curve of the harbour wall. Seven years' bad luck. I'd better be right.

The boat pulled around and headed towards the harbour mouth. I increased my pace, wrenching open the well of power within me, intensifying the concealment and misdirection. I wanted to be invisible. The boat turned into the opening, heading for open water. I raced for the end of the harbour wall, timing my run.

The boat accelerated and the well within me dilated, flooding my muscles with power. My body sang with it and I sped forward, heading for the end of the sea wall. As the boat crossed into open water, I leapt up off the harbour wall, sailing out into space, my legs still pumping, the boat coming up fast beneath me so that I landed with a *whump!*, crashing on to the cabin roof, rolling forward, carried by my own momentum. I tipped over the side, momentarily airborne again. *Thump!* I hit the side of the boat as it rose on the swell, grabbed the rope mesh draped over the side, my body hanging over so that my feet dangled in the frothing water.

"What were that!" a voice called out of the cabin.

"What were what?"

The answering voice came towards me and I tightened my grip on the mesh and deepened the concealment that hid me.

"That thump. Sounded like we hit something."

There was a pause. "Driftwood maybe? Somethin' in t' water, most like."

"Any damage?"

A figure passed by above me and headed for the bow. While they were busy, I hauled myself up on to the rail. The boat started oscillating as it met the swell from the open sea. It ducked and tipped, the bow sending up a shot of spray into the last light of the day. My lips tasted

345

salt where I licked them and my jacket clung to me. I hauled myself over the rail and limped towards the stern, still wrapped in concealing power. My side hurt where I had hit the rail and the nerves on my left side still jangled from the impact.

Now that I was aboard I could see that this was more of a work-boat than a trawler. It didn't have the spars and the drapery of nets ready to haul over and drag through the sea on the end of booms, but rather piles of wire pots and smaller nets that could be cast overboard by hand. It still had the tall prow and deep stern of a deep-water boat, and there was a small nest of radio aerials rising from a mounting bar above the cabin. It would be seaworthy for days at a time, and as I watched the harbour dimming behind me, I wondered how far they planned to go.

The wind was cold now, chilling the water that had soaked into my trousers and sleeves, and I pressed my hand to my side. I didn't think I'd broken anything but I would have bruises to match anything I'd acquired in training. The three men gathered ahead of me under the electric lights in the cabin. The occasional red-point glow of a cigarette glowed through the dirty glass. They ignored me, intent on the water ahead, but even so I kept my concealment close.

The diesel engine thrummed in a slow rhythm as I looked back over the stern, watching the harbour wall recede and the town lights come on behind us. Above the hills, the last light flared under the wispy clouds, turning them pink, then purple. I turned my back on the town.

If Shelley was on board, it wasn't obvious where. I crept forward, using my magic to hide me, and climbed on to the raised half-deck behind the cabin to peek inside. Lights on the instrument panel illuminated the faces of the men, staring forward. There was no banter or chat. Each stood apart, unable or unwilling to break the mood. To one side were steps leading down into the bow of the boat. If I wanted to get to them I would need to go through the men and even if I were invisible they would notice me. Treading carefully and avoiding the line of sight from the cabin, I crept forward up on to the bow area. There were hatch coverings opening down into the bows, but no obvious catches to release them. I slid forward on my belly, pressing my ear to the nearest hatch while I watched the men to make sure they stayed in the cabin. All I could hear was the thrum of the engine and the hiss and hush as the bow thrust into the waves. I slid backwards, retreating to the stern while the light died over the hilltops behind us and the foam merged back into the dark water.

I didn't have long to wait. The boat began turning, drawing a slow arc with the luminous foam of the wake. It steered a half circle until it faced back towards the town. The engine died, and the wind died with it, the boat drifting on the rocking swell.

The men were active now, busy in the cabin and under the foredeck. I watched two of them carry out a long bundle between them, guided by the third. It kicked and struggled, and the two men swore that they would drop her over the side if she wasn't still. That was when I knew I had not been wrong.

She struggled again and one of them dropped an end, uttering a profanity.

"Keep hold of her, Freddy."

Freddy tried to catch her legs, but each time she kicked and thrashed.

The other shoved him aside, picked her up bodily and threw her over his shoulder. He kept one arm wrapped round her legs while she grunted and wriggled. She wasn't making it easy; good for her.

The lights on the gantry above the cabin blazed into life, illuminating the bow of the boat. Another man emerged from the cabin, dressed in orange waterproofs, flicking a cigarette butt into the water with a practised gesture. His hair was grey and his face lined. He looked vaguely familiar.

They had brought this girl – and she was a girl, younger than any of the other missing young women, barely more than a child – out on to the open sea. For what? Even after long days of searching, of investigation, of rebuffed enquiries and cold shoulders, I still had no idea what they were doing. Was this some dark perversion shared between these three? Were they planning to rape her and then toss her over the side? I crept up on to the half deck, up behind the aerials and the lights where the shadows would hide me. From there, the boat rocked like a giant cradle beneath me. I watched them take the girl to the bow and lower her carefully to the deck. If they meant to harm her, why were they treating her so gently?

The older man came forward and bid the others stand back. I recognised the voice. I knew this man. I had met him in the past few days. The hard tone, low and rough, was distinctive. He took a bright blade from his belt and slashed into the silver-grey tape wrapping the bundle. The bundle kicked out, but he was careful. In moments she was struggling free from the coarse blankets in which she'd been rolled, pulling away sticky strands of tape. She tugged at the tape over her mouth and ripped it away in a single swipe.

"You BASTARDS!"

The man with the rough voice stepped forward. "Now then. No need for a foul tongue."

"You fucking bastards. My dad's gonna have you, I'm tellin' ya. He's gonna do you proper!"

She struggled to her feet. I admired her spirit. These were big men, used to rough work. They could pick her up in one hand, easy, but she was undaunted. She

348

shook out her hair and wrapped her cardigan close around her.

"You bedda take me back, right now! You're all in deep shit."

The leader stepped up to her and casually back-handed her across the face. There was a yelp as her head snapped back and she went down, curled into the bow against further blows. I would have intervened then, but he stepped back again, leaving her.

"I told you to keep a civil tongue," he growled.

Shelley was crying softly, a snuffling noise that showed just how thin the bravado was. She pushed herself up with one arm, pressing her hand to the side of her face where he'd hit her.

"My dad... my dad... he'll..."

"He won't do nothin'. You just wait. When he sees how we turn things round he'll do precisely nothing."

"He'll fuck you up good," she muttered into her hand.

He stepped forward again and my hand slipped down to my belt, and my sword. My fingers found nothing. My sword was lying on my bed, back in the guest house, disguised as an umbrella.

She shrank back, but he didn't hit her, though the warning was clear.

"He won't, because his girl's going to be a star. She's going to save the town. She's gonna be at front of all the parades and in all the papers. She'll be headline news."

Shelley snuffled to herself, then said, "What?"

"You're going to be a heroine, just like in the stories. You, Shelley Hopkins, your name will go down in history. It'll be recorded in the museums and the archives and passed down from generation to generation."

It came to me then, where I had seen him. He was the rain-soaked figure in the museum. He had come in as I left, and held the door open for me. What had the museum curator said? "Back again, Ted?"

He stepped forward and she cowered back, but he grabbed the front of her clothes and almost dragged her to her feet. He stood her up and then straightened her clothes while she stood and shivered in the night air.

"It's all in the archives, if you've a mind to look. This isn't the first time we've had it tough and it won't be the last. Ravensby's special. We all know it that lives here. We feel it in our bones, we know it when we breathe the air. The town has survived far worse."

"Can I go back now?" Shelley's voice sounded very small.

"Back? Of course you can go back. This is why we brought you here, so that you can see the town, so you know why it's important."

He stepped up to her and turned her shoulders to face the shore.

"There, lass. That's what you've come for." He pointed towards the thin strip of lights dancing and winking at the horizon's edge.

"I want to go home," she said with a sniff.

"Then go. We won't stop you."

She looked back at him. "You have to take me back."

"Me? No, lass. You don't need me. You are the sea's chosen, the bride of the deep, the Sea Queen of Ravensby. You could walk back if you had a mind to."

"Walk?" The word hung in the air. She flicked her eyes to the shore and back to his face. "We're a mile out. It's deep water."

"Not for you. You're pure. You are the maiden of the deep."

"Yeah," said one of the two younger men. "That's where the others went wrong."

There was a pause. She said in a small voice, "What others?"

He took her by the shoulders and turned her so that no matter how she twisted she was facing the shore. "Look, girl. Look!"

"The others weren't worthy, were they, Jake?" said the other younger man.

Jake shook his head. "Tonight is special. Ted, Freddy and me have waited all year for this. It's the solstice – the longest day, shortest night. If it can be done, it'll be done now."

"Of course it can be done." said Ted. "This is what the records tell us. When the town is at the nadir, when all is lost, the sun will find the zenith and the dark of the moon will shine upon the chosen. Do you see a moon, girl? Do ya?"

Shelley wasn't looking for the moon. She was shaking her head and saying, "No, no, no," over and over again.

"The dark of the moon. You hear? The spirit of the sea shall rise and claim his bride, taking her to him for life and love, so that the town may thrive once more. A maiden shall walk among them, a queen, crowned of the deep, and she shall live long and happy and have many children to follow in his line. Thus the town is reborn. There, d'ya see? You can't fail."

Shelley shook her head. "You're mad. You're fucking mental, all of you."

Ted answered her. "No lass. We're sane. We're the only ones with the guts to do it. The rest of them are spineless, gutless, feckless. They'd rather stand and watch the town die than do something about it. Well, we're doing something. We found the cure. It's not far. You'll be home in time for supper. All you have to do is step over." He steered her by the shoulders to a gap in the rail opened up by Jake in front of her.

It was time to intervene. I knew what had happened to Gillian and Trudy. I knew what they'd done to them. I knew why I would never find them. I was unarmed but for what I had to do I didn't need weapons. I thought of Gillian's photo, her hair framing her head like a halo. I thought about what they had made her do and it was all

I could do to control the anger that boiled up inside of me. I wanted revenge, and I wanted Gillian to share it.

It's not that hard, once you have the knack of it. Glamour is like a comfortable skin. Gillian was not as tall as me, nor as well built, but my anger fuelled the change and I did not find it hard. I only had the one photo, but after weeks in the water it didn't have to be accurate.

I visualised the unconscious grace. I took the image captured by the flash of a camera. I held that image close and embraced it, drawing it to me. To that I added the sallow pallor of death and the blue-lipped pout of a bloated corpse. I tangled sea-weed in her hair and made her clothes ripped and ragged. I left the water dripping from her, fresh from the deep. The Gillian I made was beyond life, beyond hope.

The men were intent on the girl, backs to me so that my climbing down to the deck would have gone unnoticed even had I not been cloaked in magic. Only when I stood behind them did I drop the concealment and reveal myself. The voice I imagined was soft, cracked by salt, hoarse from the water.

"Leave her alone."

The words were softly spoken, but they came from where no one should be standing. They all turned, snapping around at the sound.

The closest made the connection first.

"You. It can't be. We drowned you." He pointed, but his finger shook.

"I came back. Let her be." The voice was a hushed whisper, a sibilant accusation.

Shelley's face was frozen in a rictus of absolute horror. She put her hand up to her mouth and bit into her finger to stifle the scream.

"You did wrong," I whispered to the men. "Let her go."

Shelley did the one thing I did not expect.

She pulled away and jumped into the water.

TWENTY-ONE

They must have seen the change in expression as surprise and shock crossed my face when Shelley jumped. It changed the mood in an instant. Freddy, the one who'd said the others weren't worthy, pulled at his belt. A wickedly long blade emerged. "'Bout time you went back where you came from," he said.

He leapt forward, driving the blade upwards into my stomach in a gutting stroke. My training kicked in, and I swivelled sideways from the blade and caught the wrist, twisting it so that he gasped with pain. There was no time for finesse. In the water, even in the middle of summer, Shelley would not last long. The well of power within me opened and I felt my muscles flood with heat. I flicked my wrist and felt the bones torsion, then snap.

"Aieeee!"

The knife rattled to the floor.

Using his broken forearm to turn him to me, I pivoted and hit him hard with the flat of my hand under the chin. His head snapped up and he catapulted backwards. Catching the rail with the back of his legs, he tumbled over into the water. There was a splash and his scream was silenced as he went under.

As fast as he vanished, Jake and Ted moved either side of me, Ted wielding a heavy crowbar and Jake holding a long wooden-handled pole with a steel hook at one end. Jake moved first, making the mistake of trying to swing the pole at me rather then using it to thrust. I stepped inside the swing, twisting around and turning him so it put him between me and Ted's crowbar. I punched the shaft of the pole back into his throat. There was a crunching noise and he gagged and coughed. His hands went slack on the pole and I used his momentum to swing him around so that he crashed sideways into the rail. A shove with my shoulder and he joined Freddy in the water.

I half saw the blur as the crowbar swung down at my head. Twisting sideways, I felt the air shiver against my cheek as it flew past my face, slamming with a loud clang into the rail where I had been a moment before. Ted was so close his spittle spattered my face as he roared in animal rage. He dropped the crowbar and grasped at my throat, forcing me back on to the rail. I grabbed his wrists, his arm muscles bunching under my hands as he tried to close his grip on my windpipe and thrust me over the rail.

There was no time to wrestle. I summoned gallow-fyre, the dark power of the wraithkin.

My skin fell into blackness and the air suddenly chilled, all semblance with Gillian falling away. Flickering moonlight covered the deck where there was no moon, swimming and swaying, exaggerating the movement of the boat.

His face registered shock as a hungry tide swelled within me and coursed down my arms into the skin of his wrist. He shrieked as the cold bit into him, jerking in spasms as he tried to wrench his hands away. My hands clamped on to his wrists, leaching dark power into his skin. He tried vainly to headbutt me but suddenly his strength failed him. The grip faded as black threads of power found his veins and followed them to his heart. His skin sank inwards upon his frame and he fell to his knees, all colour blanched from his skin as it withered on his skeletal frame. I released him and he fell backwards, all life sucked out of him. I kicked what was left through the gap in the rail and it fell with a light splash and sank.

The deck was clear. Three men, less than thirty seconds. My heart pounded in my chest, but I was not breathless. It wasn't a fight. It was a massacre.

I pulled myself back from contemplating what I had just done. My body felt fuelled, burning with energy, but I had just killed three men. They might have deserved it, what they'd done might justify it, but I had killed them. There was no time to think about what that made me.

Turning back to the rail, I searched the water. I could hear splashing away to my left as the boat rocked on the swell, the grunts and shouts identifying them as the men who had gone over. I could not see Shelley. The moonless night cast flickering starlight on to the water, made worse by the glimmering gallowfyre. I recalled the power and it slid back within me like an ocean creature sliding back beneath the waves. The worst of the shifting glimmering vanished, but I still could not see Shelley. She had jumped straight in, but surely she hadn't swum far?

I ran back to the cabin. They had all this radar and technology, surely that would show me where she was? There were banks of switches and battered console screens arrayed behind the wheel, but I had no idea how any of it worked. It looked as if it was all switched off and I could not see an obvious way to activate it. Even if I turned it on, would I understand what it was telling me?

I ran back to the rail and worked my way along it, looking for signs of something in the dark water.

"Shelley? Can you hear me?"

There was no response.

I knew she would not last long in the cold water. All the crap about her being the maiden of the deep, saving the town, had been just that – crap. Shelley was just a girl and she would drown like any other if I didn't find her soon. I needed some way of finding her in the water. I had all this power, I must be able to do something.

Then I knew what I needed to do. I moved to the bow of the boat, standing where she'd stood looking out over the water to the town. I reached within and opened myself to the well within me. I felt it dilate and an answering pulse that thrummed through my veins. I began drawing in power.

In using gallowfyre against Ted, I had stolen his energy, robbing him of that which made him vital and alive. I took that energy and drew more. The air around me chilled, the breeze whipping suddenly about the boat. I reached further, drawing power from the water on which we rode, gathering it into me, building a great well of energy. As I did so, the world began to fade, overlaid with another view. The boat appeared most solid, the metal of the hull standing stark against the fluid insubstantiality of the water. The sea beneath us was vast, but it was also flimsy, a gauzy veil that didn't appear strong enough to support the hard metal of the boat that perched upon the surface while the currents shifted and swirled beneath us. The men in the water were flotsam, threads of life, floundering in the water, and there, beyond the light, was another thread. Pale and weak, it lay in the water, pulling vainly towards the land in sporadic bursts of effort while the life within it cooled and faded. She had got surprisingly far, but now she was fading fast.

I ran back to the cabin, trying to reconcile the dual images of the boat and its mechanisms and the shadow world overlaid upon it. I found a panel of buttons and switches and started pressing all of them. The lights flashed off and then on again, screens flickered into green phosphorescent life, then I found what I sought. A low groan thrummed through the boat as the engine caught and rumbled into life.

There were shouts from the water as the men heard the engine spark. I heard the sudden fear in their voices as they realised that their only hope of rescue was leaving them behind. For a moment I felt their fear, my stomach sinking in response, but then I thought of Gillian, and of Trudy, and I pushed the throttle forward, slowly easing the boat into motion.

Using my shadow-sight, I steered the boat to where the pale figure in the water struggled. It took only a moment or two, but already I could see the life fading from her, her strokes weakening. Whether she heard the boat coming from behind or she simply found the strength for one last effort, I saw her kick out again, once, twice, then a pause, then another stroke.

Easing the throttle into idle, I ran to the bow. I grabbed a length of rope, tied the loose end to a metal ring, pulled the other end around my waist. My fingers felt numb as I fumbled to secure the knot. Then I climbed up to the rail and leaped into the water after Shelley.

The water took my breath with cold, salt filling my mouth and flooding my nose. I surfaced and spat seawater, a wave washing over me and making me splutter again. Shelley was yards away. I thrashed forward, vowing to myself that one day I would learn to swim properly. My ungainly half-crawl made achingly slow progress. As the gap closed I could see her fading, the strokes becoming languid and ineffectual, her body lying low in the water. Then she slipped under.

I flailed my arms, thrashing though the water, then gulped air and dived. My legs kicked out, my fingers stretching out to catch her as she sank beneath my grasp. I kicked again, propelling myself down. My out-stretched hand brushed something, fingers grasping, floundering for contact. A flaccid touch of drifting frond, no, a handful of limp-loose sleeve. I wound my hand into it and turned for the surface, punching, reaching for air. I felt the anchor-tug of her weight be-neath me as she hindered my rise, resisting the return to life. She weighed me down as I kicked and pulled myself upwards with the rope. My lungs burned for air, my heart pounded, my muscles screamed in protest. Suddenly there was air.

I heaved huge gulps of it down, not caring when salt washed into my mouth, making me cough and retch. With one arm I pulled in the rope and wound it around my arm, lifting Shelley up to me. She rose beside me, limp and inert in the water. I wrapped one arm around her chest and hauled myself in with the rope, towing her along, snatching each length of rope to draw us back to the boat. I reached the hull and we floated alongside until we came to the rope mesh hanging down.

Tangling my arm in the mesh I hung there sus-pended, pulling her cold body in beside me, supporting her, holding her face above the wash of the waves.

I needed to get us both out of the water.

I tugged the knot from my waist and wound the rope under her arms, two, three times, twisting and tying it with fumbling fingers. I leached what power I had left into my muscles and hauled myself up the mesh on to the rail. As I released my grip on the rope, she slipped away again, but then I had my hands free. Pulling the rope hand over hand, I dragged her back to me. Reach-ing down I caught hold of the rope around her chest and with a huge effort heaved her bodily from the waves, water streaming from her hair like a sodden rag-doll. I hauled her up to me, hugging her close, until she toppled over the rail on to the deck. Landing like a badly-netted catch, she sprawled across me.

I needed to lie there and breathe, but there was no time. Shelley lay across me, lifeless and limp. I pushed myself up and cradled her in my lap. In the harsh lights her face was ashen, her lips blue. I found myself suddenly wishing that I had done a first aid course or at least knew something medically useful. Wasn't there a position for recovery or a German manoeuvre I could do? Or was that choking? Surely the boat would have a medical kit, but looking down at her I couldn't help wondering if she was beyond that.

I rolled her on to her back and pulled apart her blouse, popping buttons with a bodice-ripping tug. I half-hoped she would open her eyes and slap my face for being so presumptuous, but she lay inert while I pressed my ear to her chest, listening for a heartbeat. Whatever faint pulse might be there, it was obscured by the rumble of diesel from the idling engines. I sat across her hips and pressed my hands, one on top of the other, on to her breast bone, gently at first, then harder. A gout of water spurted from her mouth. I quickly rolled her on to her side while she spasmed and coughed, retching. She subsided but did not stir, lying as flaccid and limp as she had before. I pressed my ear to her chest again, but could still hear nothing over the engine.

Leaving her momentarily I ran back to the cabin and switched off everything, plunging the boat into darkness and silence as the engine sputtered to a halt. I returned to Shelley and listened to her chest again. The heartbeat that sounded loudest was my own. I put my ear to her mouth, hoping for a breath, feeling only the water chilling on my skin.

I tried pumping her chest again, but nothing more came up. I desperately needed help. Even assuming I could pilot the boat back to shore, it would take too long when Shelley needed aid now. Would the men in the water know what to do? Would they help her if they could? Or would they be more interested in covering their tracks than saving their victim? They had brought three girls out here, trying to invoke a half-understood folktale. Two of the girls were already dead. I could not let that happen to the third.

At that moment, I suddenly saw the whole thing. I knew what they were trying to do. They had it all wrong, as I'd had it all wrong. My own failure to see what had been in front of me almost led me to understand their actions – not to forgive – but at least to understand. Of course there were maidens of the deep, I had seen them.

The spirit of the sea shall rise and claim his bride, taking her to him for life and love, so that the town may thrive once more.

I had seen them in the museum, the faces of the maidens captured in sepia, the Sea Queens of Ravensby. What had the man said? His grandmother lived till her nineties and beyond, was related to half the town through children and grandchildren. But there had been no mention of a father. The picture was alone, unaccompanied. Where was the husband?

A maiden shall walk among them, a queen, crowned of the deep, and she shall live long and happy and have many children to follow in his line.

And when that life was over, when the Sea Queens of Ravensby finally succumbed to age and ultimately death, their skulls would find their way to a cave on the beach where they would be honoured for long years to come. I had seen them, met them, all of them. I knew who the father was.

Even Greg Makepeace – I had wondered at that pulse of power when we first shook hands. I knew he had fey blood, but never asked where it came from. He told me anyway, when I asked him whether he had been called to work here.

Not sure you'd call it that. I was born here. Maybe I just came home.

A local lad with local blood and fey power running through his veins.

I found warm drops running down my cheeks. Brushing them away, I realised they were tears – hot tears of frustration. All the anger at having my daughter stolen from me, of having her life destroyed, just as this young girl's life was being destroyed, welled up in me. All the frustration at how people wreaked havoc upon each other's lives with half-understood ideas and wrong conclusions formed like a hard knot in my throat. Cradling her limp form in my arms, I stood and staggered forward with her to the bow. Shelley draped between my arms, her long hair dripping on to the deck. I lifted my face and screamed to the silent stars.

"No!"

The well of power within me pulsed in answer, responding to my need. It opened into a dark vortex, a whirling spiral inside me, sucking power from the air, the water, the boat, the waves, the wind. Everything chilled to bone-numbing cold. Frost rimed the rails of the boat, forming white and luminous on every surface. Ice crystals sparkled in Shelley's hair and eyebrows. Energy collapsed into me, faster and stronger, answering that single word of denial.

There was a single crack and the whole sky flashed white. A huge cloud formed visibly over me, a massive thunderhead built from the frozen air. Another flash, the answering boom only a second behind. For a microsecond I could see the whole coast outlined in stark contrast. Raffmir's words came back to me. *You can go there if you can see it. You can step behind the curtain of reality and push through.*

I fed my core with energy, pouring heat and warmth into it until my bones creaked and my joints ached. Waiting for the flash, I hugged Shelley tight to me, holding her cold wet form against my skin. I could feel the static building, a thread of tingling connection between the boat and the cloud above us. When the flash came, I kept my eyes open, letting the image of the coast and the beach burn into my retina. Then I stepped forward beyond the curtain of reality into my own flash.

The sea washed against the shingle beach, the soft hush and draw of the water on the stones telling me where we were, while my eyes still blinked luminous dots. I staggered forward as the rumble and boom of the thunder followed after me, echoing down the shore. Collapsing to my knees, I began to lower Shelley gently to the ground.

"Come!" I shouted, my voice cracking from salt and exhaustion. "I have brought her to you."

I could no longer support her weight and we sagged to the sand.

"Come," I repeated.

My eyes were closed but I felt his approach. The tingling that spread across my skin was no natural chill. Whether he came from the cave or the beach or somewhere else, I could not have said, but I knew he was there.

"You must help her," I said. "She needs you. You know the sea. You know its ways. She's been sorely used."

"This is not the way." His voice was wary, but did not hold the warning of our first meeting.

"You said… you said it must be soon. It's tonight, on a moon-dark solstice. It has to be tonight, doesn't it?"

362

"She must come willingly. She is not even conscious. Look at her."

"She will be willing. She will... once she knows. She wants to live. She wants it so badly. You must see that."

The lightning flashed out in the bay, the dark thunder rumbling behind only a second later. He waited until it had subsided.

"She's fading, give her to me."

He knelt in the sand opposite me, offering his arms. I lifted her, easing her into his embrace.

"How is she called?" He looked down into her pallid face, lit only by starlight.

"Her name's Shelley. It may be short for something. I don't know what."

He leaned down, his lips almost brushing hers, and spoke her name.

"Shelley."

Then he pressed his lips to hers in a slow gentle kiss, withdrawing slowly as he watched her face. She remained inert for a long moment and then jerked suddenly, coughing and retching in his embrace, spewing dark water over him from her mouth and nose, drawing great heaving raw breaths, struggling to be free while he held her gently, unconcerned with her wretched state.

Gradually she subsided, her breathing becoming regular and rhythmic, as she clung to him until she could open her eyes. She looked up into his face.

"Shelley," he said again.

She stared up at him. "I dreamed," she said slowly, her voice cracked from salt and coughing. "I dreamed you swam down for me."

He smiled down into her face and there was the hint of an answering smile there. He stood easily, lifting her in his arms like a child, holding her gently. "You are chilled through," he said. "Come. There is a warm pool. It will ease you."

He turned and walked away towards the gap in the cliff where the caves were. Neither of them acknowledged me in the slightest. I might as well not have existed. For a second I wondered whether I had done the right thing. I wondered whether this was really what Shelley needed, but then I realised that, more than anything else, Shelley needed a chance at life.

I picked myself up and brushed the shingle from my trousers. My jacket was already stiffening with sea-water and sweat. I would need to find Greg, but not until I had at least showered off the salt. I wondered whether my spare clothes had come back from the laundry yet. I trudged across the shingle, only noticing at the last minute the shadow that lingered near the bank up to the road.

"Why," I asked, "do you always turn up when I am soaking wet, cold and tired?"

Raffmir stepped forwards into the light and smiled. He wore a long Edwardian jacket and a white ruffled shirt, making him appear oddly out of time, but he wore it comfortably and easily.

"Perhaps that is the wrong question," he said. "Perhaps the question should be, why are you always tired, cold and wet whenever we meet? For the life of me, I cannot think of a good reason for it."

"If all you've come for is to gloat, Raffmir, you know where you can stuff it."

I climbed the bank up to the road, using tufts of coarse grass to pull myself up.

"Gloating is furthest from my mind, I assure you. I came for you."

I stopped and turned. He stepped lithely up the bank towards me. In his hand was the long black scabbard of a sword.

"You swore an oath not to harm me."

"So I did, and I intend to keep it." He held out the sword. "You will be needing this."

I turned away. "It's a bit late for that now."

"On the contrary, it is exactly the time for it. Come, we must depart immediately. We cannot be late."

"Late? What for?"

"We have an appointment that must be kept or all will come awry."

"Raffmir, I'm cold and wet. I need a shower. I need fresh clothes and dry boots and some hot food inside me. After that you can tell me about appointments. OK?"

"No. Now is the moment of choice. The midnight of the solstice is upon us. There is barely enough time. Either you come with me now and I will keep my promise to return your daughter to you…"

The grin had gone. He held out the scabbard, hilt vertical, for me to take.

"…or your daughter will die tonight."

TWENTY-TWO

It was an unexpected kindness, Blackbird thought, for
Ben Highsmith to collect her from the station. It meant
she didn't have to bother with hitching a ride or finding
a late bus. She didn't usually carry more than coins,
having little use for money, and the train ticket had cost
her most of her reserves.

When she'd called from the payphone she'd been
worried she would run out of change, but Ben had insisted on calling her straight back and then said he would
collect her inside half an hour. She wondered what she
had done to deserve such good treatment, when she was
already feeling guilty at bringing them the trouble that
would surely follow. Still, once she had the broken Quick
Knife, the blade she and Niall had left in Ben's keeping
last year, she would be safe. No fey could stand against
it. They could barely abide its presence.

When she told Ben what she wanted on the phone,
he'd been reluctant to part with it, but had agreed to
collect her all the same. He said they could talk about it
over some tea.

The tea was on the table and the whole family gathered round, but the conversation still hadn't turned to

the knife. Lisa sat close to Ben, her grandfather, ever happy in his shadow. She was a little taller and if anything a little leaner than she had been when they'd been here last year. James, her older brother, had filled out since Blackbird had last seen him and lost some of his puppy fat. He still had the downturned mouth of his mother, but had acquired some of his father's bulk. Their parents, Jeff and Meg, sat across the table, steaming mugs of tea in their hands.

Jeff had barely spoken since her arrival. When he'd asked Ben where Blackbird was going to sleep, Ben had just shrugged and said, "You tell me."

It was one of the questions they hadn't yet addressed. This house was filled with iron. It was in the walls, nailed into the beams and built into the fabric. It was the safest place Blackbird could think of, given who was coming after her, but she wasn't comfortable here either. It wasn't her magic that was reacting – she knew it was dormant and would not return until the baby was born – but even so the house felt unwelcoming to her, as if it hummed a sour note. It made the ache in her back worse, the skin on her elbows itch. She wasn't sure if she could rest here.

She realised that she'd missed a question from Meg, but it didn't matter as she continued her monologue without need of confirmation.

"Running about in that condition, what's that man of yours thinking?" said Meg.

"It's not his fault." Blackbird defended Niall. "He's been sent away on business."

"A fine business that means leaving a pregnant woman to look after herself. Must be due any day, surely?"

"It certainly feels like it," she agreed.

Meg must have caught the fleeting expression of trepidation in her eyes because she reached across and patted her hand.

"It's always scary the first time. It'll be over before you know and you'll have the babe in your arms. A boy, you say? Did that show up on the scan?"

"Not exactly," said Blackbird.

She could see the questions forming on Meg's face – when was the scan? What had it shown, who was her doctor? All questions she couldn't answer.

Slam! The kitchen door rattled in its frame at some heavy impact.

The room went deathly quiet. Everyone stared at the door.

"What the hell…?" Ben and Jeff were on their feet.

"What was that?" said Lisa, sounding suddenly small and nervous.

"Jeff?" said Meg.

"Dunno," said Jeff. "The dogs are out, aren't they? They'd bark if someone came." He went to the door.

"Don't open it," said Meg.

"I agree with her," said Blackbird.

Jeff hooked an iron chain across the back of the door before cracking the door open. "Oh shit!"

He closed the door, slipped off the chain, then opened the door again. A body sprawled across the threshold, fur the colour of burnt toffee, eyes dark and open wide, neck at an odd angle.

"Oh shit! It's Topaz. Look what they've done to him!"

He picked the dog up, cradling it in his arms. "Look, Meg."

Lisa ran to her father, tears streaming down her face. Jeff kicked the door closed behind him and laid the dog on the kitchen table. A pink tongue lolled out between its teeth.

Lisa stroked the dog's ear back from over his eyes. "What happened to him, Dad? Who would do that?"

"It's Deefnir. He's here," said Blackbird. "Ben, get me the knife."

368

Meg interrupted, "Where's the other one? Where's Tasha?"

"Don't worry about the bloody dog," said Blackbird. "Get me the Quick Knife."

"What do you want with it?" asked Ben. "It won't save the dogs now."

Blackbird stood up. "It's a message, the oldest kind. He wants me, and he'll go through all of you to get me."

"What are you going to do?"

"I'm fed up with running. I'm done with hiding. If he wants me, he can come and get me. Get me the Quick Knife, Ben. I'm going to finish this."

"You can't fight anyone in your condition. You're crazy," said Ben.

"I can with the Quick Knife. It will give me the edge I need, in both senses. Bring it to me."

"You can't fight anyone in that condition," said Meg.

"You don't understand," said Blackbird, quietly. "This is only the beginning. It's the way it's been done since before there were towns or cities, before kings or queens. First the dogs, the guardians of the settlement. Then the old people, the experience, the knowledge. Next the children, the hope for the future, any chance of reprieve. Finally the adults, until there's only one left to carry the story. He'll make them run until they can't run any further, until their hearts burst and their bones are broken, until there's just enough life left to tell the tale. He'll kill all of you, every one, and he'll still come for me. Now get me the damned knife!"

"Call the police," said Meg. "Never mind, I'll do it." She reached for the phone.

The air chilled suddenly and the lights went out. In the sudden silence, the fridge stuttered to a halt. Over the doorways, the mistletoe hung there glowed green, flickering with pale fire.

"Oh shit," said James, "there goes the power."

369

In the dim light Ben went to the dresser and opened the drawer. He took out a hardwood box and laid it on the table next to the dog.

"I'll do it," said Jeff, reaching for the box.

"No," said Blackbird. "It's me he wants. If you challenge him, he will kill you first and still come after me. Give me the knife."

Ben opened the box. Blackbird's expression soured.

"Are you going to be able to do this?" asked Ben, holding the knife by the blade, offering the handle to Blackbird.

She reached out her hand, the distaste written plain on her face. The moment she touched it she gasped, dropping the knife with a clatter on to the tiles and crumpling over.

Meg was at her side, "Just breathe. Give it a second. In and out, that's it, one at a time."

"It's too much, even now," said Blackbird, shaking her head. "Get me a cloth. I'll hold it in a cloth."

"Put it away, Ben," said Meg. "Can't you see, it's upsetting the baby. Put it away, now!"

Ben recovered the knife and slotted it back into the box, closing the lid with a dull thud. Blackbird relaxed visibly.

"I need it," she said. "I need the knife. I have to finish this."

"You can't touch it, don't you see?" said Meg. "Even having it near is upsetting the babe. You'll do more harm than good with that and no mistake. It's not meant for your kind."

"Get me something else, something iron." whispered Blackbird. She sat on a chair, breathing slowly, bringing herself back under control.

Lisa ran upstairs.

"Where are you going? Come back down here right now!" said Meg.

By the time Meg had reached the bottom of the stairs, Lisa was on the way down again. She came back into the kitchen holding a long-bladed knife in her hand, its blade dark but for the bright metal at the edge, the wooden handle burnished to a dull gloss.

"I made it myself," she said, passing it carefully to Blackbird. "It's too soft to keep an edge properly, but it was the first one I made, wasn't it, Grampy?"

Blackbird tested the weight of it. The iron in it still made her bones ache, but it would do.

Lisa went back to her grandfather and eased in under his arm. Ben ruffled her hair. "The metal's a bit soft. It's hand-beaten, closer to wrought iron than steel, so it should serve your purpose well."

Lisa raised her chin. "Use it for Topaz." She stared at the body of the dog on the table, eyes dry.

Blackbird stood, easing the cramps from her back. She lifted her bag and took the horseshoe from it. "Might as well go for broke," she said.

She went to the kitchen door. "Once I'm outside, bolt and bar the door and don't let anyone in, not even if you think it's me." She paused and then said, "It won't be."

She looked around the room as if memorising the faces, then opened the door, stepped out into the darkness and closed the door behind her. Standing in the dark, she waited until she heard the bolts shoot home while her eyes adjusted. The sky had been clear black and starlit, a good night for a fight. Now a mist had risen, clinging to the ground, swirling around her ankles, rolling away as she moved into the open yard. She stood in the middle where she could see all around her.

"You're going to have to come and get me," she called out to the dark. "I'm not playing hide and seek."

The words sounded muted and close, making her seem small and frightened. She uncurled and curled her fingers on the handle of the iron knife.

Over the building to her left, something large sailed out of the night. It bounced once and landed in a floppy

371

bundle near her feet. It was the other dog, what was left of it.

"It's not my dog and I don't care," she called, the lie tasting bitter on her tongue.

The dog had come from the left. She watched the right carefully.

The minutes stretched out. She waited, feeling the sweat condensing cold and running down her spine. For a moment there was a shadow where there was no moonlight to cast one and then there he was, walking out of the mist into the yard, clothed in black silk, a long blade hanging easily from his right hand. His hair fell over his eyes in a way that was almost feminine. Dark eyes glinted from beneath his fringe. He stopped, some way away.

"You're going to have to get closer than that," she said, shaking her head.

She blinked and he was yards closer. She hadn't even seen him move. The damned mist hadn't even stirred.

"Closer than that," she said. "I have something for you." She tightened her grip on the horseshoe, setting her feet apart. The sword would give him reach. She wanted him in close where she could use the knife.

"Come to mommy," she said, bracing herself.

"I can taste your scent," he said. His voice was high and light. It added to the impression of delicacy.

"Good for you," she said. "But you can't smell me to death. Come closer."

He sighed, softly. "Not you," he said. "Them."

On either side of her two shapes coalesced out of the mist.

Amber held a long straight sword casually, allowing it to swing gently from her hand as she walked forward. Slimgrin stepped forward, circling the long double-ended spear around until it pointed directly at Deefnir's feet.

"You waited for your moment," said Blackbird.

372

"We wanted him to show himself," said Amber. "Time to go home, Deefnir. Your master is calling."

"And the others," said Deefnir. "Show yourselves."

From behind him, Tate and Garvin moved out of the shadows.

"We're not going to have any trouble, are we?" rumbled Tate.

Garvin spoke. "I think our visitor knows when he is outnumbered."

There was a strange mewing sound from Deefnir, prompting Amber to lift the tip of her blade. It resolved into tinkling laughter.

"There, you see? It wasn't that hard in the end." His amusement was at odds with the tension.

"We are arresting you in the name of the High Court of the Feyre," called Garvin. "You are charged by your Lord to return to the High Court peacefully and await his pleasure."

"Not before I complete my mission."

He blurred into motion. Blackbird flinched as she found him kneeling before her. Amber's blade was across his throat, the end of Slimgrin's spear pressing under his ear.

"For the runaround you've given me, I'd cheerfully kill you," said Amber. "Go ahead, give me an excuse."

Deefnir ignored the threats and reached towards Blackbird slowly and gently with his empty left hand. Blood ran down his throat where the pressure of Amber's blade increased.

"It is good fortune," remarked Deefnir, "to touch the place where the child rests; good both for the mother and for the one who touches."

"It won't be good luck for you," said Amber quietly. "I'll send you back to Altair in two pieces. Hear my words."

"I am charged by my Lord Altair," said Deefnir, "to bring to you, Blackbird, the felicitations of the Seventh Court."

"What?" said Blackbird.

"My Lord Altair sends his greetings. He would present them himself but he is otherwise engaged, so in his stead he sends me, his grandson, to carry his good wishes and congratulations to you for the coming of your child."

"One more move and you die, Deefnir," said Amber. "Stop playing games."

"I swear on my honour that I will not harm anyone here gathered, most particularly the half-breed Blackbird and her unborn child. Even if I wished to, I could not. It is foretold."

"What's this about, Deefnir?" Garvin stepped in, turning aside the blades, placing himself between Deefnir and Blackbird.

Deefnir remained kneeling. "The son will rise and they shall fall," he intoned.

"What? What is he talking about?" demanded Blackbird.

Garvin raised one eyebrow. "I'm not following this any more than you are."

"What are you saying?" Blackbird moved around Garvin, tightening her grip on the knife. Slimgrin stepped in close to her, his hand wrapping gently around her wrist where she held the iron knife, preventing her from using it.

Garvin glanced at the hand with the iron knife. He nodded to Slimgrin. "We don't want any accidents, do we?"

"He's talking about my baby, Garvin. I want to know what he means!" said Blackbird.

"Deefnir?" said Garvin. "You want to explain why we're running around the country so you can bring Blackbird a greeting?"

Deefnir smiled. "What hour is it?"

Garvin's expression darkened, "It's after midnight, why?"

Deefnir stood, slowly and cautiously, leaving the sword lying on the ground beside him. He opened his hands, showing he was unarmed.

"My tasks are complete. I have brought the felicitations of the Seventh Court to the mother and to the son, and brought the Warders to me. Four Warders here, Fellstamp and Fionh with Lord Altair and the High Court. That makes six."

"We are seven," said Garvin.

"Not for long."

"What do you mean?" asked Blackbird. "Where's Niall?"

"He's in Ravensby, in Yorkshire," said Garvin.

"Not any more," said Deefnir. "It is the solstice day. Your last Warder is far from there and beyond all aid."

Blackbird tried to wrench her wrist away from Slimgrin without success. "What have you done with him? What?"

"Calm yourself," said Deefnir quietly, "for he has chosen, and there is nowhere he would rather be. He is fulfilling his destiny."

Garvin turned to Amber and Tate. "Find Niall. Go."

They vanished into the mist.

"You have some explaining to do," said Garvin to Deefnir.

"My Lord Altair awaits your pleasure," said Deefnir with a smile.

"You can let go of me now." Blackbird tried to twist out of Slimgrin's long fingers.

"You'd better go tell the Highsmiths that you're alive," said Garvin. "We will accompany Deefnir back to the High Court."

"Where's Niall?" said Blackbird to Deefnir. "Where is he?"

"All in good time," said Deefnir.

"Don't worry," said Garvin. "We'll find him."

"You'd better," said Blackbird. "You'd bloody well better."

TWENTY-THREE

"If this is one of your games, Raffmir…"

"I swear by my life, the hour is upon us. Hear the truth in my voice. Your daughter is in gravest peril and will die without aid. I have made preparations, but what must be done cannot be done alone. If you would have your daughter back, it must be now, before midnight."

I stood and looked at him. I was dead tired, bruised from the jump to the boat, desperate for a change of clothes and a hot shower. Even so, the truth rang in his words. I sifted through them, searching for the double meaning, the lie within the truth that would give his plan away. I could find none.

He offered the sword again and I took it.

"Where is she?"

He squeezed my shoulder. I stared at his arm until he removed it.

"I will take you to her. Come, we must use the Ways."

He strode away towards the town, confident that I would follow. I trailed after, unwilling to catch up with him, but drawn along all the same. When he reached the road leading up the hill past the church he waited for me and then walked alongside. We passed the church, where the lights blazed inside through the great east window.

"Give me a moment," I said. "I need to deliver some news."

He grasped my arm and hauled me up the hill. "We do not have a moment, Dogstar. If you can travel faster then do so. Our time is slipping away and we have much to achieve before the night turns into tomorrow. We must go now."

I allowed him to draw me on, wondering why, after all these weeks, it was so critical now. The pace meant I felt every ache as we mounted the hill behind the town. We reached the Way-node and he barely hesitated before stepping on to it.

"Follow swiftly."

He vanished in a swirl of air and I stepped after him.

The Ways are dangerous when tired, they sap the will and divert the attention. It took every fibre of concentration to follow the path left by Raffmir. Gritting my teeth, I swerved around the nodes, whipping tight around the Way-points. I was only barely aware that we headed south, focusing only on the chill path left behind him. We veered past node after node. Then we were there.

I staggered forward on to solid ground, wrong-footed by the sudden return of gravity and space. Raffmir watched me, his smile loaded with mute sarcasm.

"If you say anything about style, I will kick you," I said.

"It never crossed my mind to comment." The lie was obvious in his voice, as he must have known it would be.

I looked around. We were in a forest on high ground. I could see distant lights through the trees, but there was no obvious sign of civilisation. We were in the middle of nowhere.

"My daughter is in the middle of a wood?"

In response, he caught my sleeve and, despite my efforts to shake him free, led me through the trees until we emerged on a clear hillside. Below us was a broad expanse of heath land scattered with small dark buildings and what looked like abandoned vehicles. Beyond the heath was a complex of buildings, white lights arrayed around them. They glowed with industrial brightness, stark against the neglected landscape.

"There," he said, "we will find your daughter."

I watched for a moment. There was no sign of occupation, no movement of people or vehicles. The place appeared deserted but at the same time lights blazed in all the offices. Didn't these people know how to switch a light off?

"Where are we?" I asked.

"Wiltshire."

"No, I meant, where in particular are we? What is that place?"

"That is where your daughter is being held. This is the facility in which she is imprisoned. Tonight we must break in to release her. I warn you, it is well guarded."

"You didn't answer my question."

"They call it after this heath on which we stand. It is called Porton Down."

I glanced at him, wondering whether this was some kind of wind-up. "Porton Down? That's the chemical warfare place. The one where they develop nerve gas."

"And for that reason alone, I would watch where you step. They test fire ordnance on this heath and you might lose a leg if you were to wander unwary, but chemical warfare is not the only thing they do here. There is research into all manner of things. It is true, though, that defence against chemical and biological weapons is their primary purpose. It is the biological aspect that concerns us. This is where they take the

378

dangerous mongrels, the half-breeds out of control, the ones that cannot be contained through other means."

"How do you know my daughter is in there?"

"Are you doubting me?"

"I'm asking how you know. You don't even live on this world. I've been trying to find her for weeks and yet you know where she is?"

"Ah well, there fortune has smiled upon me. It has gifted me the ability to grant you what no other can. Your daughter's location came to me by happenstance, one of those moments of chance when you know that fortune does indeed play dice, and she always wins."

"You came upon her by accident." I could not keep the sarcasm from my voice.

"Not an accident, but I swear that I did not seek her out. Her name came up in conversation with regard to other matters. I made the connection and once the connection was made, it was obvious what must be done."

"Which is?"

"That I must bring you here to release her, so that you may be reunited."

Once again I could hear the clear and perfect truth in his words and yet I felt that there was more that he was not telling me.

"Swear to me that you are not intending her harm."

He looked offended. "Have I not already sworn? Would you have me repeat my vow?"

"I would remind you of it."

"The reminder is unnecessary. I have already sworn not to harm your daughter or by my actions to allow either you or her to come to harm, but I face a dilemma. What we attempt is not without risk."

He gestured at the complex of buildings. "If we do not rescue your daughter then she will die tonight, but releasing her is not without danger for you and for her. We may attempt a rescue and in so doing put your life and hers in jeopardy, but without the attempt you will surely lose her. Do you see my quandary?"

"I understand, Raffmir. Though the question that remains is: what do you get out of this? The way I see it, you could stand aside and let matters take their course. If my daughter is dead, why do you care? Isn't that one less mongrel to pollute your precious bloodlines? With a free hand, you would kill her regardless, so why the effort to save her?"

"Is it not enough that I would see you unharmed?"

I thought for a moment. "No," I said. "I want to know why you're helping me."

At that he looked at his feet and then sidelong at me. "Then I must confess my unwitting involvement in the harm that may come to her."

"Unwitting?"

He threw his arms wide in a gesture of innocence. "I swear I did not know she would be part of what is done here. There was never any intention that she would become involved. She was brought here without my knowledge or approval and it was only after she was within the establishment that I discovered she was here."

"You? What would you be doing at Porton Down?"

"That I am not at liberty to divulge."

I turned to face him and poked him in the chest with my finger. "Oh no. You don't get out of it that easily. If you are involved, you can't just deny all knowledge and expect me to accept it."

"It is not my secret to tell." He looked down at my finger and it was my turn to remove it.

"But you know what's going on. Come on, Raffmir, what are you up to?"

He shrugged and turned to face the distant buildings.

I stepped into his line of sight, forcing him to look at me. "You've done something that caused my daughter to come to harm in direct contravention to the vow you made. Otherwise I would not be here. I think you'd better tell me what you've done. Either you explain it to me or I'm going for Garvin and the Warders."

"By the time you return she will be dead."

"And you knew that would be the case."

He sighed. "I suppose that one way or another it will be known tonight. By the time this night is over, what is done will be done."

I waited for an explanation.

"The Seventh Court have been funding research into a cure for the condition with which your daughter is afflicted."

"What do you mean, afflicted?"

"A way of reversing the effect of fey bloodlines, of returning those who have inherited fey abilities to a normal human life."

"It's not a disease, Raffmir."

"There are those who would disagree with you. Within this establishment there are a number of individuals who would gladly receive treatment if it would only reverse the changes visited upon them."

"And you have been funding this?"

"The Seventh Court has, through a network of foundations and trusts, yes."

"That's ridiculous. This is a defence establishment. Surely they check into the sources of their funding? Otherwise they could be infiltrated by spies or enemy agents."

"We are not spies, though, are we? And we are not foreign. The foundations of which we speak were established in this country hundreds of years ago and have been engaged in supporting research and building understanding for all of that time. There are no enemies here."

"But why would the Seventh Court get involved in human research?"

"Because if a treatment can be found then the mongrels can return to being human and the Feyre can

381

return to being fey. The reason for our exile becomes a moot point. You have not lost anything and we have everything to gain."

"But you would be forcing this treatment on the half-breeds?"

"It is a humane alternative to culling. You would live as long as you were ever going to. It is a compromise."

"This is what Altair's been discussing with the High Court?"

"No. We hoped to, but unfortunately it doesn't work. I will not say that I understand the science but whatever they are doing has the effect of removing the ability to contain the power without quenching it."

"I don't understand."

"Nor I, but the effect is simple. Once the treatment is applied, the magic is unleashed and it consumes the subject. They have lost every patient they have tested. Your daughter is the next test subject and they are planning to run the test tonight."

"My daughter!"

"I have tried to delay it. I have done everything in my power, I assure you, but she is next on the list. They are very hopeful for the results. Unfortunately I remain pessimistic."

"This is barbaric! They can't do this on human subjects."

"They have consent from the patients and from the families. They can do it, and they already have."

"They don't have Alex's consent. How can they? She's a child."

"They don't need hers. They have yours."

Of course they did. I had signed the papers myself. It hit me, then, what they were doing. They were waiting until families were in the position that Katherine and I had been in at the hospital and then putting forms in front of them.

What was the phrase?

We will do everything in our power to save your daughter.

This was what they meant.

"I know what I consented to, and I didn't mean this."

"It makes no difference. They have all the permission they need."

"It's immoral. It's wrong."

"They believe they are helping them."

"They're killing them!"

"In pursuit of a cure. If they can make it work they believe they will save far more than they harm."

"You know that's never going to work. You know what being fey is like. Once the magic is active, it's there forever. You can't just send it back."

"They think they can."

"That's ridiculous."

"So is putting a man on the moon. They did that."

I turned away, speechless at the obscenity of it.

"There is not time for this, Dogstar. If we are to rescue your daughter, it must be now."

I turned back. "You did this, Raffmir. You're responsible."

"Did I not bring you here in time to set things right? I am doing everything in my power, but without you tonight's endeavour may fail with tragic consequences. I need your help."

"Then let's go."

"This facility has been constructed to contain those with fey abilities, mongrels who have lost control and are capable of murder and worse. It will not be easy to get inside."

"But you know a way?"

"Fortunately it has been constructed to stop fey getting out, not to prevent them getting in. It has its weaknesses, but once we begin we cannot stop. There are no friends here, Dogstar, and no innocents. Everyone involved knows what transpires here. Because it is night, the staff is much reduced, but the facility runs continuously – there will be people there."

"I'm ready."

"We will go to the roof. They are not expecting us. Their strength is limited and we have the advantage. Once inside we cannot afford for them to organise resistance. We will need to be ruthless."

"You shouldn't have a problem with that."

"It is not me I'm concerned about."

"I can do my bit."

"Your resolve must be firm if you want to see your daughter again."

The memory of what a few misguided men had done to the missing girls on the boat returned to me, but in a form that was distilled and cold. It left me feeling empty and full at the same time.

"I have seen what people do to each other, Raffmir. I don't need a lecture."

In my mind, though, I began to wonder whether I would be able to contain the anger again, if it was once released. Raffmir watched me. Whatever he saw, it was enough.

"Come then," he said. "It is time I took you to your daughter."

He stood close, pointing across the heath to the cluster of buildings. "The building we need is the one at the back there, near the road. That is Bethlem Wing."

"What did you say?"

"Bethlem Wing. That's what it's called. Why do you ask?"

Another piece fell in to place for me. Bethlem Wing, Porton Down. The initials on the B files were BWPD. That was what it meant. He was right, this was where they had taken her.

"Never mind. How do we get in?"

"As I showed you on the hill, that day, we must travel to the roof of the building. Once we are there, you must not draw power unless absolutely necessary. The alarms are set to detect changes in temperature, so if you draw power for any reason you will alert them to our presence. Use glamour alone until I give the word."

"OK. How do we get inside?"

"I have a way. Once we are in the building we must try and avoid raising the alarm for as long as possible. The longer we have before the alert goes out, the better chance we have of getting in, finding your daughter and getting out."

"And how do we get out?"

"We make our escape route as we go in. All we have to do then is get back to the roof and we leave the way we came. The best outcome is they don't know we've been there until after we're gone."

"Is that likely?"

"If we draw power the alarms will trigger and they will assume there is a break-out in progress. They will not be expecting a break-in. We still have the advantage."

"Until we want to leave."

"Do not get trapped in there, Dogstar. The best of it is that they would break my vow for me. What they will do to you does not bear speaking of, and I would not be the cause of it."

"And yet you've been funding it, all this time."

"These are the depths we are driven to. I do not like it any more than you."

"And yet it continues."

"Do you wish to argue morality or rescue your daughter?"

I stared back across the expanse of rough grassland.

"Good," he said. "Follow me."

He stood apart, gathering energy until he was surrounded by a white aura of power. The warm night breeze chilled in response until he suddenly vanished. In the glare of the arc lights on the distant buildings I could not see him, but I knew where he'd gone. I stood in his

385

place, focusing on the roof of the building he'd shown me, until the energy thrummed through me and the shadow world was overlaid on to reality. Then I stepped behind the curtain of the world into the space beyond, emerging on to a rooftop surrounded by arc lights.

Raffmir waited next to a large concrete structure built into the rooftop. Around us, banks of air conditioner units whirred in an incessant breathy hum.

"Now what?"

"There'll be a moment or two, then someone will come to investigate."

"The alarms have gone off already?"

"No, but the cameras aren't working." He pointed to a pair of wall-mounted security cameras angled to scan the rooftop. Their bare wires hung from them like entrails where he had ripped them out.

"Why did you do that?"

"Because we need this door open without raising the alarm," he said, indicating a service door. "Stand over there, out of sight."

We waited for a few moments until there was the sound of movement from the door. Someone tried several different keys, then the door swung open.

"…but whichever one it is, they ain't working now."

From my position towards the side, I could see two security guards emerging. They wore uniforms, but were not military. As the second one emerged, Raffmir stepped out on the far side of them into their line of sight.

"Ah, I'm glad you've come. We're having some trouble with the cameras."

"Who the hell…"

As the first one spoke, Raffmir stepped forward. The security guard jerked and the bright point of a sword punched through the back of his uniform. He waved his arms ineffectually and sank to his knees. At the same time, his colleague went for the gun holstered at his waist, his scrabbling fingers clawing for the weapon, flipping open the holster. In a second I had my sword drawn, the edge bright against his throat, pressed into his windpipe.

"Drop the weapon," I told him.

He held the unholstered pistol out by two fingers and let it fall to the ground, where it clattered heavily.

Raffmir stepped forward, placed a boot on the shoulder of the kneeling man and pulled his sword free. The man toppled backwards with a final cough, his head lying in a growing pool of blood. Raffmir swept the sword up in an arc, sending a spray of blood across the air-conditioner units.

"Are you planning on keeping him as a pet?"

I pressed the sword upwards, keeping the man on tip-toe, not letting him gain balance and posture to fight back.

"Can we tie him up?"

Raffmir whirled on the spot. The man jerked in my hand as Raffmir's sword thumped into his chest. He jerked again and then collapsed forward on to the blade I held at his throat. I was forced to relax it or slice his neck through. He fell into a heap across his colleague.

"What did you do that for?" I demanded.

"We do not have time to take prisoners, Dogstar. There are no innocents here, remember?"

"He was helpless. You didn't have to kill him."

"What were you going to do? Take him with us? Leave him here to raise the alarm?"

At that moment the smell hit me, a mixture of shit and blood, the smell of death. My gorge rose and I turned away, spewing what remained in my stomach on to the concrete roof. Cold sweat covered my forehead. I leaned against an air conditioner and tried to wipe my forehead.

"Some Warder you make, throwing up at the first sight of blood." Raffmir was amused.

"I do what I have to," I told Raffmir, the taste of vomit still sour in my mouth. "But I don't kill for pleasure."

"Nor I. It is necessary, I assure you," he said. "They might raise the alarm otherwise and we cannot risk that."

"The alarm will be raised as soon as they miss these two," I pointed out.

At this one of the men's lapel radios chirped.

"Did you find the problem, Chris?" The voice was distorted by the radio.

"Now what are you going to do?" I asked Raffmir.

In response, he rolled the dead guard on top on to his back and unhooked the radio. He shifted his glamour into the image of the man on the floor, and clicked the button on the side of the radio.

"Looks like a problem with the wiring to me," he said, using a voice similar to the dead guard's and looking at the broken camera. "You should get someone up here to fix it."

"Right you are. I'll give the security firm a buzz."

"We're on our way down," Raffmir said.

The security guard that was Raffmir tossed the radio on to the bodies. "By the time they find the bodies, it will be too late. Take the form of the other one. It will avert their notice."

It made me feel sick again to take the form of a man I could see dead on the floor, as if I was somehow stealing his identity as well as his life. He had been going for his pistol, so I suppose that meant he wasn't innocent, but did that make it OK? My hands were slick with sweat and I wiped them on my trousers as I followed Raffmir through the access door into the building.

We dropped three flights of metal stairs before opening a service door on to a corridor brightly lit by lines of fluorescent tubes.

"This is the administration floor."

We passed glass-fronted offices, one after another, each with a symmetrical array of desks. Close to midnight, they were deserted.

"How do you know so much about this place?"

"I have seen plans for the building. We funded the construction, after all."

"You're in this up to your neck, aren't you?"

"In my experience, necessity is only the mother of further necessity. We do what we must."

"Which way?"

"Down, always down. The lower floors are the secure area, below ground is where we will find your daughter. There are no windows and fewer exits. It makes it easier to contain the inmates."

"Inmates? Is that what we're calling them?"

"Mongrels, half-breeds, gifted individuals, whatever you would like to call them, that's where they're held."

We pushed through a set of doors and went quickly down a double flight of stairs, exiting on to an identical corridor. As we opened the doors, there were two more security guards walking down the corridor towards us.

"Stay calm," said Raffmir quietly.

"Did you find the problem?" one of them asked.

"Looks like a wiring problem. We reported it and they're calling in the security company," said Raffmir, mimicking Chris.

"Right you are."

They walked past us, the one who had not spoken nodding to me as they did so. I gave him a nervous smile, saying nothing. We heard one of them speak into the radio as they walked on to the stairs we had just descended.

"Chris and Terry on their way down," he said.

We came to another double door and Raffmir thrust through them to the stairway. We descended two floors, passing double doors at each level.

"This is the end of the administration area," said Raffmir. "Beyond here is secure. Stay alert. They will be guarding more closely from here on."

We walked down a corridor lined with more offices. The windows to these were translucent but obscured with privacy film. We came to a double door with an electronic lock and a blank proximity reader showing a red light. Raffmir pushed the door. It rattled but did not yield.

"It's too early," he said.

"For what?"

"To use power. If we trigger the alarms now, by the time we get downstairs it will all be sealed. We'll have a much harder time getting in and out. Let's try the other end."

"It's just as likely to be locked," I pointed out.

As we turned to go back the way we had come, an Asian woman stepped out of the offices ahead of us."

"Chris? Terry? What are you doing? That's the restricted area. You can't go in there." Her accent was Indian, educated and resonant with authority.

"There's been a break-in upstairs. We're checking to see if the security doors are locked." Raffmir glanced at her and then at the security ID badge dangling on a lanyard around her neck.

"A break-in?" She looked around disbelievingly. "Why haven't the alarms gone off?"

Raffmir stepped up to her and grasped her head with both hands. She gave a strangled squeak as he lifted her on tip-toe. He jerked her head sideways and there was a wet snap. Her body went limp and fell to the floor.

"For God's sake, Raffmir! Do you have to kill everyone? What's the matter with you?"

"Check to see if the office is empty." He said, gathering her limp form under the arms.

I ran forward, leaned around the door and found the office from which she had emerged empty. I swung the door wide and Raffmir dragged in the body. He tugged at the ID card around her neck and pulled the lanyard free.

"How many of them are you planning to kill?" I asked, looking down at the woman. She looked strangely peaceful, though the angle of her neck was all wrong.

"As many as I have to. Remember, these people have been systematically killing your mongrel brethren. They have no scruples and there are few things indeed that they would not do."

"So you can just kill them."

"I don't have the attachment to them that you do, Dogstar. To me they are mere curs, yapping at the moon." He took the ID card and returned to the secure door. It beeped once as he presented the card and the door clicked open. He went through and I followed, closing it behind us.

The offices on the far side were identical, leaving me wondering what the extra security was for. We walked past an office where two men argued. They sounded tired and irritable, but they did not notice us. That probably saved them, though they did not know it.

Further down the corridor was another electronically controlled door. This one had a proximity reader, but also a numeric keypad. I glanced back to the office where the men still argued. Maybe they were not so safe after all.

"Remember why we are here," said Raffmir. "Do not be distracted by trivia. When the alarm signal is triggered their reaction will be swift. In and out. That's all that concerns us."

I nodded.

Raffmir placed his hand on the keypad and the light blinked green twice. The door clicked open. He strode through, his pace quickening.

"If it was that easy," I asked him, "why didn't we do that before? We didn't need to kill that woman.

We could have just locked her in her office or knocked her unconscious."

"We do not have time for that. The door will open to my command, but by which token I cannot know. The magic finds the easiest route, the path of least resistance. It's like water running through soil, it goes where it can."

"And why is that a problem, exactly?"

We passed the lifts and came to the double doors leading to the downward stairway. Raffmir placed his hand against the keypad again and the light blinked green.

"It will not last. The locks will open to a valid identity, but there is another system that monitors who has access and when they use it. It's part of the security system."

A loud siren suddenly started emitting a piercing whine. Red lights flashed down the corridor. The keypad on the door blinked red, but the door was already open.

"It has just worked out," said Raffmir, "that we shouldn't be here."

He led the way, descending three full levels before he halted. "Wait here," he said.

"What are you going to do?"

"Below us is the guard station for the secure levels. I will deal with the guards."

"Can't we..."

He literally vanished from sight in front of me, fading into the stairway as if he'd never been there. "Raffmir?" I was talking to the empty stairway.

I gritted my teeth. "You're enjoying this, aren't you?"

There was a series of staccato eruptions from below, followed by the dull boom of a shotgun in a confined space. Screams and shouts echoed up the stairway with the acrid smell of smoke and discharged gunpowder. There was a final percussive shot and then silence.

A breath of air below me turned back into Raffmir. "The way is clear. Come."

He led me down another level to a bend in the corridor which opened out into a space covered by guard posts on either side. One had the menacing muzzle of a machine gun poking from it while the other had thick glass, now smeared with a red stain. Dead bodies were strewn about the floor, blood pooling beneath them, their weapons lying with them where they'd fallen. The smell of blood and guts was mixed with acrid smoke, making me retch.

"How many did you kill?" I asked.

Raffmir shook his head. "Are you keeping score?"

"No, but I need to know what this has cost."

"Even if it were a hundred, would you not pay that price in battle to have your daughter back? Blood calls to blood, Dogstar. It always has."

A young soldier behind a barrier had been rammed into the concrete face first, leaving his features unidentifiable. "This wasn't a battle. You slaughtered them."

"They prepared to fight the fey – mongrels, half-breeds, the ill-bred and misfits. They have not faced the true fey for centuries. They have become arrogant and complacent. It is their weakness." I noticed then what had been bothering me. The whole area was peppered with iron. The guards had been using iron in their ammunition. Raffmir was right when he said that they had prepared.

Beyond the guard station was another set of double doors. He put his hand over the keypad, but it flashed red three times and the door didn't open.

"Now what?" I asked.

He took hold of the metal bars of the door handles. With alarming strength, he ripped the doors apart. Once he had a gap he used one to lever against the other until the frame screeched and the hinges buckled, leaving the doors hanging limply and leaving the way down open.

"Bloody hell," I said.

Raffmir grinned at me. "The strength of the true fey is something to behold. You begin to appreciate the differences between us." He stepped through the gap. "The system triggered the alarm, but they still don't know what they're dealing with. The cameras are useless to them, they will show them nothing. We still have the advantage of surprise."

I followed him through what remained of the doors. Beyond them was a reception area with comfortable leather chairs and a water cooler. A middle-aged woman in a white coat was trying to barricade herself into a glass-walled office by pushing a chair under the door handle. If she'd seen what Raffmir had just done to the security doors, she would not have bothered.

There were three sets of opaque glass doors arranged at each corner of the area, leading further into the complex. On each door was a letter – A, B and C. Raffmir ignored the woman in the room, who was now hiding under her desk, and went to the door marked B.

"This way."

As I followed there was the sharp double crack of pistol shots. The opaque glass door to the right shattered in a shower of glass. Alarmed, I leapt aside and pressed myself against the wall, out of the line of the ambush. Raffmir pushed through, there was a dull thud and then a man in a security uniform was hurled backwards through the other door, shattering that too. He bounced once on the floor and rolled across the carpet, groaned and lay still.

I stepped gingerly across the glass-covered carpet to where Raffmir was sweeping fragments of glass from his sleeve. The acrid smell of gunfire hung around him. There was a black pistol on the floor, and I reached for the gun.

"Leave it," he said. "Its sound will only betray our location. Your sword is cleaner and more certain."

"Were you hit?" I asked.

He shook his head, but the smile had gone. "The time has come," he said, "to show them what they are dealing with."

He shifted form back to the long coat and ruffled shirt. As he did so the air chilled suddenly and the lights flickered and dimmed.

"Do likewise," he instructed. "Take as much power as you can. Together we can absorb all they have. Without power or light they will be unable to respond."

The well of darkness within me dilated and I drew in power. The room temperature plummeted and the lights winked out. There was a crackling, splitting sound as the water in the cooler froze and split the container. My hands and fingers were outlined in a white nimbus. The sirens faltered and then subsided into a muted beeping. Emergency lights flickered on then faded to blue and died.

"Keep drawing power. They are not creatures of the dark like us. We will have the advantage as long as we can hold it. Together we can deny them light, while we can still see."

He gestured around him and I found I could indeed see, even beyond the faint outlines illuminated by our flickering nimbus. The real world was in darkness, but the shadow world overlaid upon it was like glowing smoke.

He walked on into that spectral dark, and I followed.

TWENTY-FOUR

I followed him into the shadows, seeing beyond the walls into offices and corridors. Shadows shifted in those spaces and I realised there were people, moving shadows of smoke within a misty framework of walls and doors.

Amidst the misty world were things that stood out, stark and grey. We approached a vertical rectangular grid. It resolved in the faint light of Raffmir's nimbus into a barrier of iron bars.

"The door is reinforced iron, designed to be proof against our power. The lock is iron too, so our kind cannot affect it."

"Can we get past it?"

He grinned and in answer his glow intensified for a moment and then he vanished. There was a moment of deeper darkness and then his glow reappeared on the other side of the door and he began drawing power once more.

"It seems," he said from the far side of the bars, "that there is a chink in their armour."

I followed his example and gathered power into me. I could see the iron bars of the door, the impervious nature of it, standing stark where all else was smoke. Between the bars, though, was space, and space was ours. I didn't go through the door, but simply stepped around it, moving from one side to the other without passing through the distance in between. Where we could see, we could go.

Beyond that door was a short corridor and then another door, identical to the first.

As we approached the second door there was the loud crack of another pistol shot. This time Raffmir jerked at the impact. Behind him, I dodged sideways, avoiding the line of fire as bullets sprayed into the space, showering us with chips of plaster and paint. The ringing of the pistol shots, the muzzle flash from the gun, the smell of cordite and gunpowder catching in my throat, made the confined space suddenly claustrophobic. Raffmir flattened himself against the wall.

"Are you hurt?" I asked.

He smiled grimly, then pressed his hand against his shoulder and opened it, showing me the blood.

In the darkness beyond the door, a man crossed the corridor, trying to gain a clear shot where I was pinned against the wall. I watched in slow motion as he raised the pistol and aimed at my head.

Instinct saved me as I slid behind the curtain of reality, emerging in the corridor behind them. The shot was still ringing in the corridor as I emerged.

"Shit!" The man said. "He vanished."

As I drew my sword, they realised at once that the danger was among them. There were three men. The first, the security guard who had aimed at me, turned to point his weapon. My sword arced down, blade flashing in the dark, severing the arm at the wrist. The weapon fell and bounced off the carpet, the hand still grasping it. The second guard raised his gun and my sword swept under his chin. He stopped and shuddered, and his head snapped back as a fountain of blood erupted from his neck. The third stepped back clear of his comrades, trying for a shot. I closed the distance in a single long thrust. The sword thudded under his breastbone. He jerked, the hand with the gun flailing, colliding with the wall. The gun clattered heavily to the floor. He gave a wet cough and slid backwards off the blade on to the floor, red blooming across the front of his white coat. He looked down at the spreading blood, his chin unshaven, his eyes wide with surprise. Then his head fell back and his eyes glazed.

Looking down at him while he died, I could see that he looked like a medic. I had just killed a doctor. What kind of doctor carried a pistol?

The fight was over so quickly. All those months of training, long hours of step and parry, turn and slice, and the real fight was over in seconds. It was unreal.

I was standing over him, trying to stop my hand from shaking, when Raffmir appeared beside me. I still held the sword in my hand, watching the blood drip from the end of the blade on to the medic's coat. I could feel my heart thumping now that the adrenalin had nowhere to go.

"That was nicely done," he said. It was the first compliment he had ever paid me.

He shrugged out of his coat and let it fall on the ground. Underneath, the blood was soaking into the shirt around the gory hole in his arm. He glanced down.

"Careless," he said, shaking his head gently. "More haste, less speed."

He went back to where the guard whose hand I'd severed was sitting, leaning against the wall, cradling the stump in his lap and rocking back and forth. Even in the faint light of the glow around Raffmir I could see the sweat beaded on the man's skin, the way his eyes were wide and staring at nothing.

Raffmir picked him up by the front of his uniform and held him one-handed against the wall.

"Does it hurt?"

The man's eyes were staring but seeing nothing. Raffmir smiled. "Not for long."

Dappled moonlight spilled out into the corridor.

"Raffmir, don't…" But it was already too late.

Black tendrils of power extended from Raffmir's outstretched hand into the guard's skin. His flesh sank against his bones and his eyes bulged as Raffmir consumed his life essence in front of me. For once I understood what Blackbird had meant when she said that such a thing was obscene. What was left of the guard fell through Raffmir's hand.

He glanced sideways at me. "Squeamish, cousin?"

"Was that necessary?"

In answer, he drew back the shirt from his arm where the blood caked the cloth, revealing a newly puckered scar where the gunshot wound had been.

He prodded it gently, checking for tenderness. "I do believe it was," he said.

He reached down and retrieved his coat, putting a finger through the hole that the bullet had made. He shrugged back into it, covering the blood-soaked shirt. His glamour shifted slightly and the hole in his coat also vanished.

He squared his shoulders. "Come," he said. "We are almost there."

Beyond the iron doors was different. Where before there had been offices and computers, carpets and corridors, this was more like a hospital than an office building. The floors were dark vinyl, the walls painted white without pictures or pattern, and the air smelled of antiseptic.

The beds in the wards were mostly empty. The few patients lay comatose, immune to gunfire and violence.

Beyond them I could see where people hid in the wards, concealing themselves behind curtains or beds, trying not to be noticed. When we came near, they scurried away into the dark and I could see that most of them were medical staff. Raffmir ignored them, though he was more cautious after the encounter with the guards.

As we continued, the wards gave way to rooms, each with a single occupant. The wall facing the corridors was glass, as were the doors, but the glass had a peculiarly solid quality. The locks on the doors stood out dark and cold, a simple key lock in each, but made of iron.

I halted. "What are these?" I asked Raffmir.

"We have reached the inmates' accommodation," he replied, walking on without pause. "This is where your daughter has been kept. I did try and use my influence to get her moved, but the staff here are a law unto themselves."

"These people are gifted?"

In the nimbus glow, flickering light illuminated the dark room. A young boy was curled in the centre of the room, arms wrapped around his knees. He appeared to be mumbling something to himself, again and again. I moved to the next. An old woman sat on the bed platform, staring at us through the glass. In the room opposite, a large man stood leaning against the glass, hands cupped over his eyes, trying to see out.

"Do not be distracted by trivia, Dogstar. We do not have time."

"But they're like me."

"After tonight, I doubt this facility will continue."

"What will happen to them, then?"

"Do you want your daughter or not?"

"What will happen to them?" I repeated.

"I don't know." His voice held a lie.

"Get me a key."

400

"We do not have time, Dogstar. Your daughter is this way." He gestured with his sword down the corridor.

As if in answer, there was a dull boom from the way we had come.

"What was that?" I asked him.

"They are rallying their defences. Because we have disabled the power, sealing the door locks, they are having to force their way into the building.

"Get me the key to these doors," I said.

"There's no time."

"If we let them out, anyone coming after us will be delayed, while they deal with the escapees," I pointed out.

He paused for a second and then strode back to the wards. Disappearing for a moment he returned with a young nurse, her arm twisted painfully behind her.

"Get me the key to these cells," he said, pushing her into the corridor.

"I don't know where it is," she lied.

His sword flashed once in the dark. There was the beginning of a startled shriek which fell abruptly silent. Her headless body fell to the floor. He kicked the head ahead of him, back into the ward. Marching after it, he re-entered the ward. There was a hail of protests before he dragged an older woman out into the corridor. She swatted at him with her hands, but he ignored her, propelling her forward. She stopped in front of the headless corpse, breathing hard.

"Your colleague said she didn't know where the key to the cells was." He nodded at the corpse, speaking calmly.

Without hesitating the woman pointed to where we had come in. "The guard station," she said, her voice quavering.

"Bring it to me," he said quietly.

She ran down the corridor towards the guard station.

"If you do not come back," he called after her, "I will come after you."

401

We waited in the dim light.

"Maybe she can't find it in the dark," I said.

"If your daughter is dead by the time we reach her, remember it is you who wanted a delay."

The nurse advanced towards us, holding the key out gingerly.

Raffmir's hand shot out and took her wrist, holding the key up. "Take it from her," he said.

"It's iron," I pointed out.

"I know that. You wanted the key, there it is."

She tried to pull away, but he held her easily, tightening his grip so she gasped.

"Take the key." I knelt down and drew the coat of the headless corpse towards me. The woman watched me, eyes wide. I ripped the pocket off the coat with one clean swipe, then used it to take the key from the woman's hand, wrapping the scrap around the key, so I didn't have to touch it. Even so, I could feel the iron through the material, a curious ache from having it so close.

Raffmir twisted the wrist, so that the woman lifted her chin in pain. The sword arced brightly and another head arced away into the dark to bounce wetly along the corridor. The body spurted blood as it fell, dribbling red down the glass wall of the nearest cell in sticky dribbles.

"Another corpse to your tally?" I asked him.

"If you had not wanted the key she would still be alive."

"Don't blame me for your actions."

"I do not blame you, but she knew how many we are, and that we are sensitive to iron. That is too much knowledge to fall into the hands of our enemies. Now hurry. We are late."

I went to the cell with the boy and used the key wrapped in the scrap of cloth to unlock the door. Close up, I could see that in the glass there was a fine mesh of iron layered into the glass. I pushed the door open.

"You're free to go." He did not move, but simply sat on the floor.

I went to the next cell. The woman watched me while I unlocked and opened the door, but did not move.

"Come on. You have a chance to escape. Get out while you can."

She stood calmly, brushing down her grey overall. Then came to the door. As she reached the door I stepped back, but she came close and pressed her hand to my cheek.

Her eyes glowed lilac, momentarily.

She shook her head. "So much brightness..." Then she jerked as if in spasm, her eyes opening wide so that the whites were exposed in a ring around the dark of the pupil. I tried to thrust her hand away, but it was as if it were welded to the skin.

She leaned close, whispering into my ear. "The sun will rise, and they shall fall."

"The what?"

She snatched her hand back and cradled it as if it had been burned. Then she slipped past me and ran into the dark.

"What did she say?" asked Raffmir?

"I'm not sure..."

The sun shall rise – I had heard that before somewhere. Where was it? Shaking my head, I went to the cell opposite and unlocked the door. I didn't open it, but moved to the next, unlocking each of them along one side and then back along the other so that they could all escape if they wished. When they were all unlocked, I dropped the key on the sticky headless corpses in the centre of the corridor.

"We've done what we can. Let's go."

Raffmir shook his head and strode away, illuminating each cell as he passed. As I followed after, people began hesitantly to leave their cells, slipping away into the dark, unsure of whether our intentions were friendly or not.

403

I wasn't sure of that myself.

As we passed further along the corridor, there was another block of cells, empty this time apart from two. In one a young woman sat staring at the blank wall opposite, while in the other the inmate, an old man, raged against the glass, hammering and banging, screaming incoherently. I watched for a moment as we passed. There were smears on the glass where the man's hands bled. I couldn't tell whether he was raging at us, at his imprisonment, or at something else. Either way, it was too late to return for the key.

"What will happen to the ones that do not escape?" I asked Raffmir. "Honestly?"

He continued walking.

"Raffmir?"

He didn't stop but continued to a set of double doors at the end of the corridor.

"There is a purge mechanism," he said. "It is a gas, a combination of nerve agents, iron... other things."

"Can they trigger it remotely?"

"I believe so, but it will only affect the cells that are occupied and locked. The gas affects fey and human alike. It is quick."

"And painless?"

"I did not ask about the pain," said Raffmir.

"It seems to me," I said, "that there are a lot of things you didn't ask about."

We passed through a further set of doors, not locked and freely swinging, into an open area. As we entered, a man retreated into one of the rooms leading off the open area. Each room had heavy glass walls facing the corridor so that what transpired there could be observed from outside the room. The glass did not have the reinforcement of iron used for containment. To our left and right were large rooms with complex overhead lighting and a central raised table. They looked like operating theatres. In the dim light, I could see three men conversing urgently in the theatre to our left. In the centre was a room fitted out as a laboratory, with fridges, shelves of chemicals, racks of test tubes, microscopes and other scientific apparatus. I turned back to the room that was occupied. I could hear urgent words being spoken. As one of the men moved aside, I could see there was a figure lying on the central table.

It was Alex.

Tightening my grip on the hilt of my sword, I made for the door. Raffmir slipped quickly in ahead of me. He swung open the door and entered slowly, relaxed and calm.

"Dr Watkins. So nice to see you again," he said.

There was uproar from the other two men as they questioned the gaunt figure between them. "You know him? But he's one of them! How could you know him?"

Dr Watkins held up his delicately thin-boned hand to quell the clamour, but it was Raffmir who spoke.

"To answer your questions, yes, I know him and he knows me. No, I'm not one of them, I am something else, and he knows me because I am a trustee of the foundation."

"A trustee?" The two men spoke together.

"Yes." Raffmir wandered around the room, picking up objects and examining them. "I must say that it is most interesting to see all this first-hand, after reading so many dull reports." He affected a yawn, raising his hand to his mouth airily.

Impatient with his games, I raised my sword and stepped forward into the room. The men retreated, and in the confusion there was the briefest of struggles around Raffmir. When it resolved, Raffmir held high the wrist of a pale bald man, showing a hypodermic syringe, the needle bright in the white glow of his aura.

405

"What have we here?" He twisted the man's arm, eliciting a gasp of pain, his cheeks flushing harsh red against the pale skin.

"It's only a sedative," said the man, the curl of a lie in his voice.

"Ah, well. Nothing to worry about then, Mr…" said Raffmir.

"Todren. I'm the consultant anaesthetist."

Raffmir spun easily, lifting the man under the chin against the wall, pinning him there while he seized the hand with the syringe. The other man began to step forward, but Raffmir glanced sideways, halting him.

Without effort, Raffmir twisted the hand holding the needle down so that it was over his thigh, while the man tried to jerk free.

"You may feel a prick," said Raffmir, and slowly pushed the needle into his thigh. The man struggled and yelled, but Raffmir steadily emptied the syringe into his leg. When it was done, he jerked it out and tossed it on to the floor, leaving the man standing, breathless.

"Fuck," said the man. Then his eyes rolled up into his head and he fell forward on to the floor. He jerked once, twice and then lay still.

"It appears that Mr Todren is having a nap," said Raffmir. "Any other bright ideas?"

The other two shook their heads and backed away, eyes wide. I raised the sword again and they reversed into the wall, their eyes focusing on the red smears down the blade. I reached Alex's side and placed my hand on her forehead. It was dry and warm. She was alive.

"What's wrong with her?" I asked Watkins.

He wrung his hands, "She has a rare genetic disorder, instability in the…"

"No, you fool, why isn't she awake?" I tried to keep the anger from my voice.

"Oh, she was given a pre-med by the nurses. We didn't want her to be distressed throughout the procedure."

I was tempted to kill him right then. He talked about the procedure as if he was removing an ingrowing toe-nail. Instead they had been planning to try an experimental drug that would end my daughter's life.

"Alex? Can you hear me, sweetheart?" I stroked back the dark curls from her face. There was no reaction. "How long until she wakes?"

"It was only a small dose. She is physically quite well, I assure you."

That left an open question. "And mentally?"

The other man spoke. "Mentally she is traumatised. Her recent experiences have left deep mental scars."

"And who are you?"

"I am Professor Petrokos – Alexandra's psychologist. She has been able to show some progress, but so far she's unable to come to terms with the violence of her actions. She claims that there's something inside her that made her do it. She's externalising the guilt, you see?"

"Or there really is something inside her?" I suggested.

He smiled, uncertain, and shook his head. "We've done full body scans of all the patients, and there's nothing inside them that shouldn't be there. It's some kind of common delusion, you see?"

"No, I think it's you who doesn't see."

"Come, Watkins, you can show me where the samples are," said Raffmir, "While my cousin revives his daughter."

"The samples? What do you want with the samples?"

"I am afraid that we will not be leaving your work intact. It has become… an embarrassment?" He echoed the tone of Petrokos' voice.

"But my work…?"

Raffmir put a hand half around his shoulder, pro-pelling him towards the side door into the central lab area. At the same moment there was another dull boom from within the building. "Hurry, we do not have much time." He prodded the doctor forward.

I returned to Alex's side, lifted her wrist and patted it, trying to encourage some kind of life into her. Her hand dangled at the end of her wrist as if connected by string. I pointed the sword at Petrokos.

"Get in the corner. Stand where I can see you."

He moved sideways slowly until he was pressed into the angle of the corner. I laid my sword between me and Alex's body and lifted her shoulders. Her head flopped to one side at what looked like a painful angle. I laid her back down, trying to figure out a way to lift her on to my shoulder and still keep my sword arm free.

Raffmir pushed Watkins back into the room. "You're sure the glass meets the specification?" he asked Watkins. They had left all the doors to the fridges and freezers open, the containers open on the benches.

"It was all built to the specifications you demanded," he said. "We have complied with the trust's every wish. All our experiments have been conducted within the ethical guidelines." It sounded like an excuse.

Raffmir stood in the open doorway. He raised his hands and cupped them. He appeared to breathe into his hands and within them a spark of light kindled. It glowed bright through his fingers and as he parted his hands it persisted, hanging in the air, like the arc of a welding torch, casting his stark shadow huge on the wall behind. The air smelled of thunderstorms and the hairs on the back of my neck lifted.

I had seen this before. In the tunnels below the streets of London, Raffmir sent a glowing spark up into the vaulted roof of the hall where the anvil stood to illuminate the scene where I had been subject to a trial by ordeal.

Now, though, I stood in two worlds. In the physical world I could see the light as it fizzed and crackled and then glowed, but in the shadow world that overlaid it, the spark looked entirely different. It was a distortion in space, a lensing of reality where everything collapsed into the spark. Space bent inwards around the star as matter collapsed into it, releasing fierce energy. Raffmir urged the star forward and it drifted into the lab, floating on the air like a feather on the breeze. He swung the door shut behind it and the star glowed brighter.

"Dogstar, shield your eyes and those of your daughter. He turned his back to the star as its brightness grew.

"My work," said Watkins. "All my work."

"I would advise you both to avert your eyes," said Raffmir. Petrokos turned his face into the corner, covering his eyes with his hands. Watkins continued to watch the lab.

I covered Alex's eyes with my hand, bowing over her and shielding my own eyes against the painful brightness. Even then I could see the bones in my hand when the flash came. There was a cracking, popping crescendo, the sound of tinkling glass from the lab, and it was dark again.

I blinked, lurid green spots obscuring my vision. There was a scuffling sound as Petrokos ran for the door. I grabbed the hilt of my sword and went after him, still blinking away the luminous afterglow. As I reached the doorway, Raffmir stopped me. "Let him go. His patients are waiting for him in the darkened corridors."

Raffmir caught Watkins by the scruff of the neck and dragged him forward. He stumbled, eyes staring sightlessly, still mumbling about his work.

"What, cousin, would you have me do with this?" He shook Watkins, but all resistance had left him.

Part of me still wanted revenge, but there had been enough death already to satisfy any lust for blood. "Let him go. He can find his fate with the other one." I nodded after Petrokos and the darkened corridor.

"But what of his reward?"

"Reward?"

"Indeed. You do not yet know the full enormity of the good doctor's work. Tell him, Watkins."

The doctor looked back towards the lab, though it was clear he was seeing nothing. Things smouldered on benches. There were scorch marks dimly visible on the fridges. He shook his head.

"Oh, come now. This is no time for false modesty." Raffmir turned to me, "Your daughter was to be only the beginning of this man's crowning achievement." He shook Watkins again. The man was a rag doll. If Raffmir hadn't been holding him up, I think he would have collapsed to his knees.

"Tell my cousin what you made," Raffmir insisted, and shook him again.

The sword appeared from nowhere in Raffmir's hand. Raffmir released him and Watkins wobbled on his feet, but he did not have a chance to fall. Raffmir whirled on the spot and the blade sliced in under his chin and his head snapped back, the blood spraying around the glass walls. It splattered over the floor, Raffmir and Alex and me, running down the glass in sticky rivulets.

"That seems a poor reward," I told him.

Raffmir leaned on the end of the central table and used the sleeve of his coat to wipe the blade.

He looked up. "The coat is ruined anyway," he said with a shrug.

The sound of repeated gunshots came from the corridor.

"We need to get out of here," I reminded him.

I made to move forward, but Raffmir lowered the sword point level with my chest. "Not quite yet."

"I thought you did not need to be reminded of your oath."

"I don't, but I must remind you of yours."

"Why?"

He held up two small glass vials in his free hand.

"This is the culmination of the good doctor's work," he said. "Twenty years' dedication." He looked down at the headless body. "No wonder he was upset."

"Souvenir?" I asked.

"There is not one sample here, but two. The first is the one intended for your daughter and would surely have killed her, though we can allow that the good doctor might finally have reached his goal and cured her – it remains untried, after all."

"She's not sick, Raffmir, she's fey."

"Half-fey, or a quarter, or a hundredth part, but not fey."

"Whatever."

"No, there is a difference, and that difference is everything. The second vial contains the weaponised version of the cure. A strange word, is it not? Weaponised? No, don't worry. I am not intending to use it on you, though if it got broken it would quickly be fatal for both you and your daughter. It would be a very unwise thing to attack me when I hold so delicate an object, Dogstar." He lowered the point of his sword, confident now that I would not fight him.

"What do you want with it, then?" I asked him.

"Fear. That's what drives them. They live such short and fragile lives that they are governed by fear; driven by it."

Gunfire stuttered in the corridor behind me. "We do not have time for this, Raffmir."

He stayed relaxed, ignoring the approaching sounds of conflict. "They fear not only us, but each other. What if another nation has fey? What if they are secretly coaching their own squads of half-breeds in the arts of intelligence gathering, assassination, insurrection?"

"There are no other fey. Are there?"

Raffmir smiled. "They don't know, and not knowing drives them. It's the fear of the possible. What if someone else has found a way to control it – indeed, to create

411

super-soldiers to use against them? Enormous strength, stealth, strange powers – it's a dream and a nightmare. That's what made it so easy to manipulate them, their fear and their greed. With a gift of funding and resources, they were easy to subvert. We are not their enemy, after all."

I glanced towards the corridor, expecting the sound of approaching feet at any moment.

"So in their search for a cure they discovered by accident a way to destroy the half-breeds: a manipulation of genes and viruses, a manufactured disease."

"The Feyre don't get sick, Raffmir, you know that."

"This is true. If I drank the serum, even if I used a hypodermic to inject it, there would be no effect on me whatsoever. I am fey and neither of these vials are intended for me." He smiled. "In one of the vials, though, is an agent, a viral contagion, cultured to be as infectious as a common cold and passed from human to human. They barely notice it, and the fey are immune to that too – the true fey, that is."

"I don't understand."

"The weapon is a contagion aimed at the mongrels. Its effect is the same as if your daughter had participated in the experiment. It releases the magic within so that it consumes the host. Any mongrel that contracts the disease will die quickly and cleanly. Once released, it will spread through the human population as no more than an inconvenience – a day in bed at worst – but it will wipe out any and all of the half-breeds like a virulent plague."

I shook my head, trying to understand the scope of such a thing. "A weapon against the half-breeds? Why would you need such a thing?"

"It is their safeguard against a mongrel army being pitched against them – a last line of defence, but it will serve the Seventh Court just as well."

Then I saw the flaw in his plan. "You can't use it – if you do then Alex or I might become infected. You have sworn by fey law to harm neither of us. You can't use it without breaking your vow, and you can't give it to anyone else to use, either. If you do, you are in violation of fey law and your life is forfeit, as is your honour."

"A prize almost worth dying for, were that necessary."

"Almost?"

"I am giving you notice to quit. You have forty-eight hours to leave this world."

"What are you talking about?"

"You have the means, Dogstar. We are not as ignorant as you think. You have the Dead Knife from the Quit Rents Ceremony, and with that you can cleave the gaps between the worlds. You can use it to travel across the cosmos as we did, when we were forced into exile. You can go as far away as you want, and take your daughter and that pregnant bitch with you."

"Leave the world? And go where?"

"I care not. The only place you cannot be is here."

"But I can't take the Dead Knife. It holds the barrier against the Seventh Court. It's needed here."

"Oh, come. What use is a barrier when there are no half-breeds to protect? What is the point of all the rituals and the protections when there is no one to defend? Once the half-breeds are gone or dead, the Seventh Court can return to the world and stand alongside their brethren on their own soil. No more exile – what would be the point?"

I suddenly realised what he was saying. I stepped towards him, reaching for the vials. The point of the sword rose level with my chest.

"No violence, Dogstar. If the vial is broken now, you will die along with every other mongrel. You have the chance to be their saviour. It is not so poor a fate. After all, I am only trading my exile for yours. The mongrels leave and the Seventh Court returns. What could be more just? It is a fair exchange."

Raffmir grinned.

"It was why I needed you here on the solstice, when the walls between the worlds are at their weakest, so that you could be the instrument of their exile and know the bitterness that comes from knowing that you will never be able to return. You will rid us of them, every one."

He grinned at me, relishing his victory.

"And you will never be able to return."

TWENTY-FIVE

Raffmir admired the vials in his hand. "Driven by fear, the power of human ingenuity knows no bounds. Such a shame – it will mean the end of the pact between the Feyre and humanity. This is more than we ever asked for and more than you deserve. I am giving you the chance to rescue as many of the mongrels as you are able and take them somewhere else. It doesn't matter where you take them. Take as many as you please or none at all, only do not return once the virus is in the human population. It will spread and every visit will carry greater risk. You only need to carry the contagion back into exile..." He left that thought unfinished.

"You are breaking your oath, Raffmir. You swore not to harm me or my daughter."

"On the contrary, my oath remains sound. I am saving you and granting you the opportunity to save as many others as you choose. There's nothing in my oath that says that I must remain in exile, nor that you must remain in this world. If I had released the virus without telling you, then I would be breaking my oath. As it is, I am giving you the chance to be their saviour. Without you, doubtless they will all die." He shook his head in mock sadness.

There was a dull boom, then another in quick succession. I raised my sword.

Raffmir stood. "Yes, let's settle it now, blade to blade – only mind that my grip does falter and dash these vials to the floor, and if by some mischance you should best me–" He grinned, acknowledging that we both knew he was the better swordsman. "–then the vials will fall and break and all will be lost."

He watched me doing the calculation, while the conflict approached behind me.

"I believe the phrase is 'check' and 'mate'." He grinned. He had me and he knew it.

The battle in the corridors grew ever nearer. Still I hesitated. There must be a way out. Once he left with the vials, there would be no way to stop him. All he would need to do is break the vial on a railway station, or an airport, or a busy supermarket. After that it would be simply a matter of time. There was no way to find all the part-fey humans within forty-eight hours, let alone persuade them to leave our world for an uncertain future, and his smile said that he already knew that.

"Move out of the way, Dogstar. You have your daughter to save and I have business elsewhere. I have kept my promise and brought you to her. It is time for me to…"

He shuddered and faltered. Then he coughed. Mucus leaked from his nose while his eyes bulged in their sockets. Perspiration beaded across his brow and then ran in droplets down his face. Sweat rained from his jawline as he hiccoughed and spewed. He coughed again, a belch of liquid welling up in him, running from his mouth.

Behind him, winding coils like the tentacles of a black anemone extended out behind his head, long delicate fingers slid gently under his chin, cupping it like a lover's caress. Tremors spread through his shoulders, arms, chest and hands.

Slowly Alex rose behind him on the bed, her hair a winding mass of tentacle curls, moving as if washed and tugged by an unseen swell. Her eyes glowed intensely with a blue so deep it was almost purple. Her hands clamped under his chin as she looked down on his head with an expression of feral hatred. He jerked and spasmed, his hands flicked open, and the sword flew out of one hand and the vials flew out of the other.

I dived. I couldn't know which vial had the serum and which the weapon, but I dropped the sword and dived. They were too far apart to catch both. My hand stretched out and reached the floor just before the first vial hit. It bounced on the flesh of my hand and rolled on to the floor intact. The second vial smashed with the tiniest sound of tinkling glass.

I held my breath. I dare not breathe. But then I realised that if I survived I would have to watch my daughter die before me. I blew out a long slow breath and inhaled.

Nothing happened. How long would it take? How long did I have to wait before I knew it was safe? My hand reached out and grasped the unbroken vial, wrapping my fingers around it, firmly enclosing it. I rolled on to my back. Above me, Raffmir was leaking fluid from every orifice. His eyes, his nose, his ears, all ran with clear liquid. He jerked and twisted, and then with a mighty effort he swung his arm around and smashed it into my daughter's side. She flew sideways like a discarded doll, arms flailing, crashing into the wall and sliding down out of sight.

Raffmir staggered forward, reaching down for his sword. I summoned gallowfyre, filling the room with dappled light, reaching into the core of power within me. I focused the power, determined to end this now, oath or no oath.

Beyond Raffmir, the glass wall exploded in a shower of scattering fragments. Bright shards hailed all around, forcing me to shield my eyes from the glass. There was another boom, and another. Shotgun blasts echoed in the confined space. Plaster dust and concrete fragments ricocheted off me amid a stuttered cadence of dull reports. I was deaf and blind. There was a screaming, screeching sound, a series of yells and cries and then a deathly quiet punctuated by falling fragments of glass and the moans of the injured.

Emergency lights flickered into dim illumination. In their dubious light I dragged myself from the floor, stung by the fragments of iron from the dispersed shot. All that remained of the glass wall was limp crazed fragments hanging from the walls. Across the floor were the remains of bodies in combat uniforms, hacked to pieces or simply flung up into unnatural poses from which they would not recover. Some stirred vainly, but did not rise. I searched the carnage. None of the bodies was Raffmir.

Back in the room I found a small plastic container. I wrapped the vial with cloth, made sure that the top was tightly secured, placed it inside the container and capped it. Only then did I slip it into my inside jacket pocket.

From down the corridor came another series of dull reports, more shotguns. There was a bright flash, illuminating the scene in sudden and awful colour, then fading, bleaching everything back to a merciful monochrome – Raffmir.

I went to where Alex had been thrown against the wall. Her body lay sprawled at the bottom, unmoving.

Kneeling down beside her, I could see her pale cheeks dusted with plaster, her eyelashes sparkling with glass fragments. I lifted her gently and moved my leg under to rest her head in my lap.

"Sweetheart?"

She looked so small, so fragile, amid the destruction. My gut twisted at having come so far and failed. What kind of world would put such a gentle soul in such a place? I bent over her and placed a kiss on her forehead, brushing debris from her skin.

She was warm.

Of course she wasn't dead; what was I thinking? If she had been dead then her fey power would be released and it would consume her body, just as it would have done had the drug been administered to her.

I held her hand between mine, rubbing it firmly. "Come on, Alex, come back to me. I need you awake, now. Come on, sweetheart."

In response, her eyelids fluttered and then she began coughing, then rolled over on to her side and retched. I held her and stroked her back until the fit subsided.

"Are you with me now?"

She lay in my lap for a moment, just breathing. "Dad?"

"It's me, honey."

She raised herself on her elbows. "What happened?" She sat gingerly and began brushing dust and debris from her clothes. I got up with her and stood between her and the room. She peered sideways and I leaned to block her view.

"Is that Doctor Watkins?" It was impossible to keep her from seeing so much carnage.

"It was, sweetheart. Try not to look."

A slow smile spread across her face.

"I need to get you out of here."

I took her hand, brought her to her feet and led her carefully out between the bodies. None looked as if they were recovering. Weapons were scattered over the floor amid severed limbs and broken bodies. The stench of iron was over them all where it had been blasted into the walls and ceiling.

Where the corridor narrowed, the double doors were hanging askew from the hinges. I stood to the side, pressing Alex into the wall behind me, and leaned around the doorway. In the corridor, a black cat the size of a tiger was chewing on something that looked as if it might once have been human.

"Wait here," I said.

Walking forward slowly I edged along the corridor. The cat looked up at me, its eyes gleaming momentarily red in the dark. It growled softly, almost below the level of human hearing, and then resumed its meal. The cell with the blood smeared on the glass and the one with the young woman in it were empty, the doors wide. Had someone let them out? Beyond, the corridor was dark and appeared empty.

I went back to Alex. When I reached the place, she was stepping back over the bodies.

"What were you doing?" I asked her.

"Nothing." I could hear the lie clear in her voice.

I grabbed her hand. It was sticky and wet. Lifting both her hands in the dimness, I could see they were slick and black with blood.

"I'll ask you again. What have you been doing?"

She looked away, not meeting my eyes. It brought to mind, then, what Garvin had said: *The person you get back may not be your daughter.*

I had to know.

She dragged along behind me back to the room, not pulling away, but not going willingly either. When I reached it I saw what she had done. In the centre of the medical table, on the spot where she had been laid, was the head of Doctor Watkins. Sticking out of it, cleaving it partly in two, was my sword. It wasn't a clean cut the way a Warder would have done it. It had taken her several attempts. There were fragments of bloody bone and a wicked gash where an earlier attempt had failed.

I looked at it. "Why, Alex?"

420

She stood there, bloody hands in front of her, a defiant expression on her face.

"I asked you…" I stopped and took a deep breath, realising I was shouting.

Calming my voice, I tried again. "I asked you, why?"

She turned away and would have left the room.

"Sweetheart, I'm asking because I need to know you're OK."

She stopped, her back to me still.

"I need to know you're going to make it. So tell me, why?"

She turned slowly. In her eyes, blue fire glowed. There was a latency, a sense of something being held back, something huge. A tiny tinkling sound started, spreading through the fragments of glass until the whole area echoed with it.

"Don't tell me what to do," she said quietly.

"I'm not telling you, I'm asking you."

"You don't know. You'll never know what it was like."

"I need to know."

She stood there and slowly the tide withdrew. She bottled it up and pressed it down. The shine on her cheeks and the beads of sweat across her forehead told me what it had cost her, but the tinkling sound ceased. Then, when the glow finally faded from her eyes, she spoke.

"He would sit outside the glass and watch while they poke and prod you, trying to get a rise out of you." She shook her head, denying the memory. "They don't stop, no matter what you say, no matter how you plead."

She was breathing hard now.

"They keep going and going until you well and truly lose it and you scream and it boils up out of you."

She was gabbling, her eyes wide and unfocused, and I knew it wasn't me she was seeing.

"Or if they can't do that, they drug you so you piss

421

and shit yourself, until you can no longer hold it, and then, when finally you let loose, they shoot you up with stuff that burns through your veins until you scream and scream. That's when they dump you back in the goldfish bowls and watch while you squirm."

She was breathing hard.

"Then, when the heat has finally gone from your veins, when the burning stops... that's when he–" She stabbed a finger at the mutilated head "–would tell them to do it all over again."

She walked over to the head and spat wetly on to the dead doctor's face. She grabbed the end of the bloody sword hilt and levered the blade out by sawing it up and down. She pried loose the blade and then hacked it down again in a heavy wet slap. Tears were running down her cheeks, but her grip was firm.

"I'm only sorry I couldn't do that to him while he was alive," she said, and hacked at it again.

I laid my hand on top of hers, "Enough, Alex. That's enough."

"It's never enough!" she shouted, her voice cracking. "Don't tell me it's enough!"

"He's dead, Alex. He can't feel anything."

"No," she said. "But I can." She let out a scream and hacked down again, and this time the head split, leaking gore on to the table, the two halves wobbling crazily, one eye staring askew out of each half.

I waited while the heavy blade swung from her hand, watching her breathe, waiting for the focus to come back into her eyes. Kneeling gently beside the rest of Watkins's body, I ripped the tail from his lab-coat. I stood and offered the blood-spattered rag to Alex.

"Wipe your hands."

She dropped the blade with a heavy clatter on the metal table and opened her palms and looked at them, smeared with gore. She did not take the rag.

"Alex, you've done what you meant to do. Wipe your hands."

She looked up, horror on her face, whether at what she had done or at what she remembered, I didn't know. Edging forward, I moved the sword out of her reach, then did my best to gently wipe what was left of Doctor Watkins off her hands. She stood there while I cleaned one hand and then the other, eyes screwed shut, tears leaking from them down her cheeks.

The sound of automatic gunfire brought her back to me. Her head jerked around at the sound.

"We have to go," I told her, picking up my sword and wiping the hilt with the remains of the rag.

She let me take her hand and lead her through the debris and bodies and out into the corridor. The big cat had gone, along with whatever it had been eating. I opened the well of power within me and wrapped us in glamour, turning eyes away and avoiding notice, extending it as far as I could to include both of us.

The corridors were strewn with slashed and broken uniformed bodies. Many of them appeared burned, with blistered faces and blackened hands. It looked as if a group of soldiers had tried to ambush Raffmir. It had clearly not gone as planned, though there was none of the finesse that Raffmir had shown before. He had simply hacked his way through them and left them to die.

Beyond them the iron gate was wide open, the lock blown where they had broken in to reach the labs.

It was only when we pushed past the shattered doors into the office area, the glass scraping and crunching under our feet, that I heard the 'chink-chunk' sound of a shotgun reload. I shoved Alex backwards, dodging away from the noise.

A boom sounded far too loud echoing inside my head. I spun around as if I had been sideswiped by a truck. My shoulder went numb, my arm slapping uselessly against

423

the wall, the sword flailing from my hand. I collided with the wall and rolled to the floor, scattering shattered glass. In slow motion I heard the chink-chunk of the shotgun reloading.

Alex shrieked, "Dad!'

At the sound, the figure in the darkness twisted towards Alex as I got my feet under me and kicked off, launching myself at the shooter. As the shotgun swept around, my wounded shoulder collided with his torso in a jolt of searing pain. He careened backwards and there was a bright flash and another boom as the shotgun erupted in a hail of broken glass, falling plaster and smoke.

The man went down beneath me, landing heavily on his side. He tried to roll away as I crawled up him one-handed. He shouted and screamed, trying to beat me back with the butt of the shotgun. Flickering moonlight washed out into the room as the well of power opened up within me, sending out prickling sparkles of refracted moonlight from glass fragments. With a hand as black as empty night, I wrenched the gun from him and tossed it away. He beat at my head with gloved fists but my fingers found his throat.

Power surged in me, making the nerves in my shoulder sing in agony from the iron embedded in it. Black tendrils sank into him while he thrashed and bucked beneath me; they sucked the life from him until he kicked and struggled no more. I straddled him, draining the last dregs of life from him while his corpse withered beneath me. Under my shirt there was heat in the wound and a sense of wriggling, squelching life as the shoulder knit back together. As I watched, little black specks of shot were squeezed to the surface and popped out of the wound, smarting where they touched my skin and falling like patters of rain. Some fell inside the ripped shirt, and I had to wriggle out of the jacket and shirt to get rid of them, shaking the tattered remnants of the shirt to free them.

I looked up. My daughter stood among the debris, watching me, her face intent, her eyes bright, an expression of curiosity and horror on her face. As she watched, the red gore on my shoulder rippled into smooth lightless black while the ribcage beneath me crumbled, no longer able to support my weight.

I staggered to my feet.

Alex shook her head. "I don't understand. Where does the light go?" She stepped forward and reached out a hand to touch.

"Don't!"

She snapped her hand back.

"Don't touch me. I don't know what will happen."

"Nothing will happen."

She sounded certain, reaching out again and placing her hand gently where the wound had been. "Does it hurt?" she asked.

I shook my head, quelling the gallowfyre, calling the power back within me. The moonlight faded and the emergency lights paled back into dim illumination. My skin paled to normal under her hand. When she removed it, there was not even a scar.

"I'm sorry you had to see that," I said, looking down at the corpse where it lay like a desiccated mummy in uniform.

"I'm not."

I looked at her.

She hugged her arms around herself. "It means you're like me."

I thought about that for a moment. "I guess it does. A daddy's girl after all." I stepped forward and hugged her to me. She unwrapped her arms and clung for a moment, her hands cold against my bare skin. She stepped back, disengaging herself so that I could slip back into the ragged shirt and pull on my jacket. I reached into the inside pocket, reassuring myself that the vial of serum had not been broken in the fight. It crossed my mind that I should have destroyed it, but it was the only evidence remaining of what had been done here.

Alex collected the discarded shotgun from the floor, the weight of it clearly more than she was expecting.

"Do you know how to use that?"

She shook her head. "I've seen it done," she said, "and I can learn." She pumped the reload, chambering a round and resting the butt against her thigh, pointing it at the ceiling.

I pressed the barrel aside, gently. "Leave it. It will only weigh you down."

She appeared to consider for a moment and then dropped it on the corpse. "Didn't do him any good," she said.

I bent down and retrieved my sword.

"Do you know how to use that?" she asked.

It was a cheeky question, one that would have drawn a rebuke from me only a short while ago. I looked at my daughter and for the first time I realised that whatever had happened to her in this place, it had changed her. She had been on her own, beyond rescue or reprieve, and she had endured. The little girl I lost could not have done that. She had been forced to become something else.

Garvin said that the person I got back might not be the person I knew and maybe he was right. It didn't mean she was mad, though the incident with Watkins's severed head left me wondering, but it did mean that things would never be as they were. My little girl had gone, and I was going to have to find out what had replaced her. There would be time for that later. Her challenge remained, though.

"I'm told that I am competent with it," I said. "Though probably no more than that."

She must have heard the truth in my words, because she raised one eyebrow very slightly.

"I've been having lessons."

That was another thing. We routinely lie to our children. We tell them what's good for them, what we need them to know, and what it suits us to tell them. I was going to have to get used to not lying to my daughter. She would know as soon as I did.

I wrapped the glamour around us again, this time being careful to dampen any sound. We established a rhythm: me moving forward, then Alex following when I had established that all was clear. We found a trail of bodies. Raffmir had been busy. Most of them were in military uniform. The soldiers must have been moving the staff and patients out as they worked their way down. The place was deserted.

Once we were past the doors to the stairs there was less debris and fewer bodies. I retraced our route, passing up through the building, taking one stair flight at a time with Alex following. As far as I could tell, the building was deserted. We were the only living things left, which left me wondering what they planned to do next. Alex and I needed to be out, and quickly.

As we rose through the building a pervading vibration turned into a persistent thudding. By the time we reached the stairs to the rooftop and our escape route, I realised they had a helicopter circling the building. As we climbed the stairs its noise became a voice-drowning clatter. I had to shout to be heard.

"Wait here until I shout for you. I'm going up to get a clear view of our way out. When I shout, come up and grab tight hold of me. Don't hesitate. We won't have long."

She nodded her understanding and I took the steps up to the roof access. As I emerged on to the roof, the helicopter swung around the building, a huge thing with twin rotors which thudded through the air as if it was eating it in gulps. From a hatch in the side, a long gun swung sideways, aiming straight at me. I threw myself backwards.

The gun erupted in flame, sending a stream of bright fire in an arc across the access door. As I fell backwards through the hatch, the door was carved in two, sending splinters flying like needles through the air. I tumbled back down the stairs into Alex, rolling into her, the deafening roar of the gunfire rattling in my ears. Then it ceased.

I found myself lying head down on the steps, looking up into my daughter's face.

"Are you hurt?" she shouted.

I shuffled around, so I could sit, patting myself down, looking for fresh wounds. The only blood was where I had taken the shotgun blast. My instinctive reaction to throw myself backwards down the stairwell had saved me.

"No, I'm OK. I can't get to the roof, though. We can't leave if we can't see where we're going."

"Back down," she said. "We can break the windows in the offices below. They can't cover all of them."

It was my turn to nod. I led the way back down the stairwell. At the bottom I heard shouts. As I thrust the door open, gunfire echoed in the corridor. I slammed the door shut again. It was not built to withstand an assault, but it would slow them down. Placing my hand on it, I used my magic to seal it shut. It was the first trick I ever learned, and they would not get through it easily. I propelled Alex back up the stairs ahead of me. Within seconds a burst of bullets pierced the door below us, ricocheting off the metal steps.

"We're trapped," shouted Alex over the thudding of the helicopter.

She was right.

The noise from below as the men in the corridor tried to break through the door was almost drowned out by the helicopter circling above the roof. Even though I had sealed the lower door with magic, it would not take them long to break through it. They only needed a small hole and they could toss through a hand-grenade. In the confined space of the stairwell, the blast would kill us both. We had no time and nowhere to go.

"We're going up," I shouted to Alex, leading her away from the banging at the doorway. Thankfully the door was delaying them longer than I had hoped.

"What about the helicopter?"

I looked up the stairwell. Every thirty seconds or so, the helicopter circled around. Whatever I did would have to be done in that time.

I looked down the steps, wondering how much time we had. Not long.

"Get down on to the middle steps," I shouted to Alex. "Be ready to come up when I call you."

"You're mad! You can't go up there!" shouted Alex. She grabbed my arm, her fingers clinging to the jacket sleeve.

"No. Trust me. Shield your eyes."

"My eyes?"

"Just do as you're told for once, will you?"

She looked up at me and I could see the words forming on her lips: *Don't tell me what to do.*

Instead, she nodded and released my sleeve.

I leaned down and kissed her forehead, then took the steps up as far as I dared. I could hear the giant helicopter, the rhythmic thudding of the twin rotors, the whistle of the engines. I waited until I had the cycle in my head and then drew all the power I could.

The air chilled instantly, frost riming on the rails for the stairs. I heard the chopper engines falter and then whine with renewed force as the helicopter swept past the open doorway. I opened the dark well of power within me, feeling the prickle as white fingers of light crept around my hands. The world fell into a smoky veil. I could see through the walls of the small stair enclosure to the dark blocks of the air conditioners arrayed around the roof. I could see the insubstantial shape of the helicopter, wheeling around above me, its rotors too fast to perceive, the heavy steel of the machine gun poking inelegantly from its side.

The light from my aura must have attracted their attention, because another burst of fire swept across the open doorway above my head in a rattling crescendo, peppering me with brick fragments and concrete shards. I did my best to ignore it.

I cupped my hands in front of me. I had seen this done only once, but I thought I knew how it worked. The space between my hands was empty and not empty. It contained only air. I was a creature of the void. Blackbird could do things with air and fire, but that was not my element. My element was the void, the space between things. It was what kept matter from collapsing in on itself. It was what kept everything apart from everything else.

What happened, though, when it didn't? What happened when the space between things contracted, so that they came together in ways they were weren't supposed to?

I took the tiniest part of space and pulled the void from it. There was a fizzle and a pop.

Concentrating, I tried again. I reached in with my will, keeping it small, drawing the void into itself from the area between my hands. A spark fizzed into life and then crackled with energy. As the space around it bent, it grew brighter until it threw my shadows on to all the walls.

Another burst of gunfire hit the access, showering me with dust and brick chips. Where they fell into the spark, they vanished and it grew.

Opening my hands slowly, I allowed it to float, splitting my concentration between maintaining the spark and timing the helicopter's circles. If this was to work, I would have to get it right. Its noise grew as it thudded past the open doorway and then circled away.

I walked up the steps.

The helicopter circled round behind me, its view momentarily blocked. My spine itched with tension as I lifted my hands and let the spark rise and grow. I concentrated on feeding it, collapsing it into itself, seeing it brighten into an arc-light and then into a tiny star.

The chopper thudded into view. I heard the motor of the machine gun whine up to speed. If I left it any later I would be sliced in half.

I sent the star arcing into the sky into the path of the helicopter. The reaction was instant. The chopper tipped sideways and banked hard, klaxons screaming raucously from the open hatchway, The machine gun sent a stream of tracer out into the empty sky as it tipped wildly. Flares streamed out in pulses, bursting from the sides, aiming to distract a heat-seeker from its target.

This was no heat-seeker. The star rose ever brighter, unerringly following as the helicopter banked hard, the rotors chopping into the air. Everything stood out in harsh brightness, walls bleached of colour, shadows etched in black, sliding over surfaces as the star flew, chasing its target. The helicopter tipped and banked again, aiming to turn away. The star buried itself deep into it.

There was a flash, brighter than daylight, brighter than anything. It streamed from every doorway, every pinprick hole in the helicopter, outlining it against the blistering light. I covered my eyes with my hands, clearly seeing the bones outlined through them. A screaming, squealing, grinding clash of metal echoed across the sky.

The chopper exploded.

The shockwave thudded through me, a low pulse of destruction. Fire and metal rained down. Chunks of fuselage, scything lengths of rotor, metres long, strewed themselves out. The sky filled with a boiling cloud of thunderous fire, rolling ponderously upwards.

I was thrown backwards, sliding down the metal stairs, sheltering in the access as fragments rained down. When I opened my eyes, Alex was standing over me, looking down. I could not interpret her expression. It might have been fear.

There was a dull thud from below. The doorway had finally given way. I got to my feet. Opening the well of darkness within me, I drew energy into me until I glowed with an aura of white fire. I tugged my daughter out on to a rooftop scattered with burning debris, acrid with smoke and burning oil. Focusing on the distant hill, I hugged her close to me, pressing her skin to mine. The world faded before me and I stepped behind it, emerging through the flash on to the distant hilltop.

Looking back, we could see the plume of black smoke rising over the buildings and drifting out across the darkened moorland. Sirens wailed and blue and red lights flickered. Tiny figures ran around, shots echoed out, but there was no one left to fight.

We were free.

TWENTY-SIX

When Blackbird first showed me the Ways, the means to travel far across country on a wave of power, I was blown away by it. I was expecting the same reaction from Alex.

All she said was, "S'OK."

We travelled slowly, one Way-node at a time, in the knowledge that both of us were exhausted, both emotionally and physically. I shepherded her through each point until we arrived at the High Courts of the Feyre, not knowing what to expect when we reached our destination. Where else could I go?

I couldn't return to the guest house with my daughter in tow, not without first establishing what had happened after I left. Had they found the boat? Was Shelley OK? What about the missing men? Were the police involved? I needed somewhere safe, not an inquisition.

The house in the woods had burned and there was no way I could take Alex back to her mother, even if her house wasn't still being watched. There were too many questions to answer there too. We would have to answer them in due course, but not now, not tonight.

The High Courts had once said that they would accept my daughter if she inherited my fey bloodline.

That was a promise and the Feyre kept their promises.

I was relying on it.

We arrived at the Way-node under the High Courts of the Feyre, not knowing what welcome we would receive, whether I was still a Warder and if I had any right to be there at all.

Unsure what reception I would receive from the other Warders when they found out where I had been and what I had done, we arrived cautiously, first me, then Alex. I caught her as she stumbled into me off the node, the rush of adrenalin finally drained from her, her knees shaking from exhaustion.

Slimgrin and Amber were guarding the node.

Slimgrin immediately disappeared upstairs while Amber took the sword from me and simply guided us to the floor against the wall where we could rest, our backs against the stone. It was only then that I noticed that Alex was still wearing the open-backed hospital gown from the test lab. She was practically naked. I put my arm around her and she collapsed across me, her head resting on my chest, her dark curls winding under my hand as I stroked her hair. I could feel her trembling as she breathed.

They could do what they liked. I wasn't moving for anyone.

Then people started arriving. Everyone talked at once. They were all asking me questions. I couldn't hear them, or if I could hear them I didn't know which one to answer first. Was I hurt? Was Alex hurt? Did I know that Altair had gone and taken Raffmir with him? Where had the blood come from? Why hadn't I told them what I intended to do?

"Silence!" Garvin's voice cut across the mayhem.

In the quiet that followed, one figure crept between them, inserting herself under my other arm and resting against me.

Blackbird.

I kissed her head and stroked her shoulder while Garvin gave orders. Rooms were to be prepared, clothes to be provided, food was summoned, Amber was to carry Alex while Tate helped me to my feet.

"No." I held my daughter close as Amber tried to collect the sleeping Alex from me like a floppy child. "Don't take her from me."

Alex's eyes opened suddenly and she grabbed my arm, suddenly aware that we were being separated. Her eyes had a corona of lavender fire and there was a low rumbling from beneath the ground.

"Fionh!" Garvin's voice cut across the murmurs. "Damp it down!"

"I'm trying," said Fionh. "She's strong."

"Ah!" Blackbird wrapped her arms around the bump, curling around it protectively. "The baby! She's hurting the baby!"

The rumbling died in an instant. The look on Alex's face was as if she had been slapped.

"I didn't mean..." she faltered.

Silence filled the gap as I looked from one to the other. Alex looked shocked at what she'd done, but Blackbird looked accusingly at her.

"I wouldn't hurt you or the baby," Alex said.

Garvin's voice cut across it all. "Amber, take Blackbird up to her room. Fionh, take Niall and Alex up to the west wing and find them a suite as far from Blackbird as possible. Slimgrin, go with them."

Blackbird was led away by Amber, while we were half-carried and half-guided along the hall in the other direction and up the stairs to a suite of rooms. Stewards ran around turning back sheets, running baths, bringing towels. We were the centre of a vortex of activity, everything whirling around us.

Garvin told Fionh to take Alex and get her showered and cleaned up.

"Bathroom, Alex," Fionh told her, gently.

Alex stared at her. "Don't..."

"Alex, please," I interjected. "You're covered in blood and dust. No more tonight. Go and get cleaned up. Fionh will help you. She'll look after you."

Alex looked at me and must have seen how close to exhaustion I really was. She lowered her eyes and went with Fionh.

"She's not crazy," I told Garvin.

"She's not in control, either," he answered. "Her emotions are driving her power, making her unpredictable and dangerous. She can't be allowed near Blackbird. Think about it. The baby is floating in water, near enough. It's too dangerous."

"She didn't mean to hurt anyone."

"She doesn't have to mean it."

"She's exhausted. So am I. She'll be better in the morning."

"I've seen this before, Niall, though not with anyone that strong. She has no brakes, no limits. It's all or nothing. Fionh was having trouble damping it down. That's Fionh we're talking about."

"It'll be better tomorrow," I insisted.

"You'd better tell me what happened."

It took several attempts. I kept missing pieces out; the mess with the girls and the boat, finding out that Greg was fey. It was all jumbled up in my head and even when I thought I'd told it all I wasn't sure it made sense.

"Where is the vial now?" asked Garvin.

I pointed to my jacket. "Inside pocket, double wrapped, plastic container."

Tate searched my jacket and came back with the container. He handed it to Garvin who held it up to the light to view the vial of liquid inside.

"Tate, go to Kimlesh and tell her that on the authority of the Warders I seek an immediate audience with the

High Court. Get them assembled as soon as possible. Slimgrin, guard these two with Fionh while they get some rest. No one goes in or out without my say-so. Fellstamp, close the Way. No one in or out."

He turned to the diminutive figure of Mullbrook, who had been directing operations among the stewards.

"Mullbrook, if you could get some food inside these people and get Alex some rest. I need Niall dressed and presentable inside twenty minutes. Can you do it?"

"If I have Mr Dogstar's co-operation, that is quite possible," he said, nodding once, slowly.

Garvin glanced at me and I nodded.

"Do it. Get to it, people." He strode out of the room.

Under Mullbrook's supervision, I was taken through a connecting door to another suite, where I showered and then had the multiple slashes and cuts I had acquired when the helicopter exploded cleaned and dressed. My clothes were laid out for me while I wolfed down a freshly cut sandwich of cheddar cheese, black sticky onion chutney and pale green lettuce layered into crusty white bread and washed down with ice-cold water. It was just enough to revive me.

I returned, dressed in new and presentable grey, just in time to kiss my daughter on the forehead as she tucked into the meal of golden breaded chicken, sliced fried potatoes and corncakes in batter, with a side order of chocolate cake. She looked pink and scrubbed and more like herself, but there were dark rings under her eyes. She looked about her warily as if someone might come and take the food away at any moment.

"Don't eat too much, or you won't sleep."

"Dad? Stop nagging me. I'm starving." She stabbed a chip with a fork and devoured it in two bites.

"Fionh, don't let her stuff herself stupid, will you?"

Fionh shrugged, but kept a wary eye on Alex.

"Dad! Leave it, OK?"

"OK. I'll be back in a while. I expect to find you in bed, young lady."

She mumbled something through a mouthful that might have been, "Don't tell me what to do."

"I'm simply stating what I expect to find," I told her.

"Whatever." She waved her hand airily, then collected a second piece of chicken.

I was saved from the debate by the return of Garvin. He looked me up and down.

"You'll do. Come."

With Garvin before me and Slimgrin behind, I was escorted down to the main chamber of the High Court of the Feyre. Tate and Fellstamp were waiting and the Lords and Ladies were already gathered. I was brought before them with minimal formality.

"Tell us," said Krane, leaning forward from his huge dark-wood chair, "about this." He held up the plastic bottle containing the serum.

I made a better job of describing what had happened this time, from the half-breed fey imprisoned in glass-walled cells, to the shotguns loaded with iron shot. The only thing I left out was what my daughter had done to Doctor Watkins's severed head. That was probably better left unreported.

"And you say that Altair was funding this facility?" Teoth asked.

"Yes, my Lord. Raffmir told me the Seventh Court had approved plans and funded it through a series of trusts and foundations."

"Was there any sign of direct involvement from the Seventh Court, or any other Court, for that matter?" asked Barthia.

"What are you implying, Barthia? asked Yonna. "You know none of us had anything to do with this."

"I'm simply asking if there was any sign of direct fey involvement," stated the Ogre.

"None that I saw, my Lady. Everything appears to have been done from a distance."

"I see." She sat back, crossing her massive arms in front of her.

"Are there any more questions for the Warders?" asked Krane.

A slow ripple of shaking heads travelled around the room.

"Very well. Will you leave Fellstamp with us, please, Garvin?" said Krane.

"Yes, my Lord."

I followed Garvin back through the double doors. He closed them gently behind us. Tate was waiting outside. He handed me my sword, sheathed in a new polished scabbard.

I looked at Garvin. "I'm not being kicked out of the Warders, then?"

"Kicked out?" asked Garvin. "Why would you be kicked out?"

"You did tell me not to go after Alex," I admitted.

"I told you not to go until you were ready, but I also gave you Warder's discretion." He guided me down the corridor away from the chamber, flanked by Tate.

"There is no test for becoming a Warder. You train until you're ready and then you're in, straight into the crucible, no rehearsal, no safety net. You act with the full authority of the High Court and, for that reason alone, judgement is paramount."

"But I made such a mess of the situation in Ravensby. I'm still not sure I did the right thing."

"Where there is a clear course of action, where right and wrong are easily established, where the will of the courts is clear, the Warders are almost never needed. All we do is deliver the will of the Courts and they sort it out amongst themselves."

He stopped and turned to face me.

"The Warders are called in when it's messy, when there is no clear solution, or when there are too many solutions, all competing for attention. We are needed when there is no right, only a choice between multiple wrongs; where there is no justice, merely closure. We are called to act when no one else will, when it's already too late. That's what being a Warder means."

"You make it sound so attractive."

"Most Warders are chosen. They do not choose themselves."

"So how did you become a Warder?"

Garvin looked me in the eye and for a moment, I thought I saw a shadow there. Then it was gone.

"That," he said, "is a story for another day." He squeezed my shoulder. "You have done well, and the job is not over yet. The High Court has heard your testimony and must decide what action is merited. Get some rest while you can. I will have someone wake you as soon as I have news."

He gently propelled me towards the stairs and I used the momentum to keep going. There was no resistance left in me. As I mounted the staircase, I found that Tate had detached from Garvin and shadowed me.

When I raised an eyebrow at him he simply said, "The Warders look after each other."

I let him follow me back to the suite where Slimgrin paced the hallway. I found my daughter in bed and already asleep, despite her protests. She was curled under the covers so only her hair restlessly stirred as she slept. I stroked her head and the curls coiled around my fingers and relaxed. winding and unwinding as she breathed.

"She didn't eat much in the end," said Fionh. "I think it was only a show for you."

"How long has she been asleep?" I asked.

Fionh looked at her. "Don't worry, I can handle it. She'll sleep for hours yet, probably well into tomorrow.

440

She is a teenager, after all. Go and check on Blackbird. I can see you want to."

I thanked her and left, Tate falling into step beside me.

"Are you going to follow me everywhere?" I asked him.

"Just until you get where you need to be."

"I'm not sure I know where I need to be any more."

"You'll figure it out."

When we arrived at Blackbird's door, Amber let me in and then left with Tate. Blackbird was in bed, propped up on pillows.

"Is she sleeping?" she asked.

"Yes. It'll be quiet for a while now." I went over and sat on the bed beside her, taking her hand.

"I overreacted," said Blackbird. "She didn't mean to hurt anyone."

"Garvin says she's not in control of her power. I'm inclined to agree. She's going to have to learn to control her temper or she'll end up hurting someone, herself even."

She pulled the quilt back and shuffled to the side of the bed.

"Wouldn't you be better staying where you are?" I asked.

"My back aches wherever I am. It does me good to move around a little." She rolled upright and stood, helping me ease out of my Warder greys, draping them over a chair so I could dress if I needed to, inspecting the gashes and scrapes I had acquired, issuing a gentle rebuke.

"Next time, duck faster."

I smiled as she stroked the knotted muscles in my shoulders and guided me into bed. She prodded me gently across the bed until she could slide in beside me and nestle into my shoulder, resting her belly against my flank. The bump gave a desultory kick, a token protest, but then moved and settled against me.

Blackbird stroked my chest and hushed me when I tried to speak, pressing her fingertips against my lips to silence me. In the quiet grace of her comfort, I rested, and slept.

The hand that shook me awake was calloused and not nearly as soft as Blackbird's. Tate's grizzled face looked down at me.

"You awake?"

"Sure, I'm awake. What's up?"

"I've been shaking you for two minutes." The lie was obvious.

"I thought you were rocking me in my sleep."

He grinned. "You're awake. Get dressed. Garvin wants you downstairs. Five minutes."

"Five?"

"He said two, but I'm stretching the point since you already slept through those."

"OK. Five minutes." I yawned.

Tate left and I extracted myself gently from Blackbird's sleeping form. She mumbled in her sleep, but did not wake. I slipped into my greys, the familiarity of the uniform bringing its own comfort. Taking the pad on the dresser, I scrawled a simple note.

Garvin called. Back Later.

I collected my sword. Slimgrin was standing by the door when I left. He closed the door gently behind me and fell in beside me as we descended the stairs. I glanced sideways at him and he nodded.

"All OK?" I asked him.

He made the signs for sleeping, working and fighting: the fey equivalent of "no rest for the wicked".

Garvin was waiting for us. He made no remark as to whether it had been two minutes or five. As soon as he joined us, he nodded to Fellstamp, who held a door open so that Krane could join us.

"Is everything prepared?" Krane asked Garvin.

"Tate has gone ahead. He will let us know if it's clear."

"Very well. We should go."

Garvin led the way down to the Way-node, while I walked alongside Krane, with Slimgrin and Fellstamp flanking us.

Tate was waiting at the Way. "They have their cordon set up. We've been around their security. It's OK as far as it goes."

"Did they see you?" asked Garvin.

Tate grinned.

"Good. I'll follow you in two minutes. Dogstar, you're next. Then you, Lord Krane. Slimgrin and Fellstamp, bring up the rear."

Tate vanished in a swirl and we waited the full two minutes. Then Garvin stepped forward and whirled away. I followed close behind, using the trail he left to guide me as I slipped around the nodes to our destination. I stepped into a damp dawn of muted birdsong and the smell of mown grass. Overhead, the sky was tinted pink as the sun tried to break through the grey clinging damply to the trees. I stepped off the Way-node where Garvin was waiting. There was the prickle of magic all around us as Garvin turned away curious eyes.

"We're here as Lord Krane's escort. Just act natural. Let him do the talking."

We'd arrived on an open lawn with strange rectangular mounds set into it, like low walls that were knocked down long ago so that the foundations were now subsumed into the grass. Ahead was a large building of toffee-coloured stone with a high pointed roof and tall leaded-glass windows. Through the mist in front of the hall I could see three large black cars. I counted five police officers carrying machine guns. There were more stationed further away at the gate in the high stone wall.

"Are we expecting a fight?" I asked.

Garvin shook his head as Krane arrived and stepped easily sideways. Slimgrin and Fellstamp slipped in behind him. Slimgrin walked away, melting into the mist. Garvin led the way, Krane came behind and I brought up the rear. As we approached the cars, Garvin let the glamour slip away. We were immediately noticed.

The police angled their weapons across their chests in a kind of salute, demonstrating readiness without obvious threat. Krane simply nodded acknowledgment as if it were his due.

A dark-suited man emerged. He ignored Garvin and me.

"Lord Krane, delighted that you could join us." He bowed slightly. "Please come this way."

He walked through an arched set of double doors into a high-arched open hall, with dark ancient beams rising over us and high stone pillars supporting the roof. It was impressive if it was half as old as I thought. What was remarkable about it, though, was not the hall itself but the walls. They were covered in horseshoes of every size and shape. Some were three or four feet across while others looked as if they might genuinely have shod horses. All four walls were adorned in this way, making the room smaller and somehow more intimate.

The man withdrew, closing the double doors behind him. Fellstamp stayed at the doorway.

In the centre of the hall was a modern french-polished table with three matching high-backed chairs arranged along either side. They looked out of place in the ancient setting. Three men were waiting on the opposite side of the room. Two wore dark suits, the other a light-grey suit: two heavies and a bank manager.

The bank manager stepped forward. "In the name of Queen Elizabeth the Second, I bid you welcome to Oakham Castle, Lord Krane, and thank you for coming at such short notice. I am Secretary Carler and I greet you here in good faith."

"Your welcome is appreciated, Secretary Carler. I bring you the felicitations of the Seven Courts and the wish for a speedy resolution to our current troubles, also in good faith."

"The wish for a speedy resolution is reciprocated, I assure you." He smiled the bank manager smile, gesturing to the seats. Carler and Krane sat. The rest of us stood, facing each other.

"I trust the arrangements are satisfactory?" asked the bank manager.

"They are as we expected," said Krane, smiling.

There was something wrong with the sound in the room. I looked about me, searching for the source. It was a kind of hollow reverse echo that preceded anything that was said. Then I realised. I couldn't hear the truth in the words that were being spoken. Something about the horseshoes, or the building itself, prevented me from discerning the truth. I raised an eyebrow at Garvin. He shook his head minutely.

"If it is acceptable, we will get straight down to business," said Carler.

When Krane didn't object, he picked up a sheet of paper from the table.

"Last night there was a serious incident involving considerable loss of life and the destruction of buildings and equipment at Porton Down Research Facility in Wiltshire. We believe one or more of the Feyre were responsible for the incident. Do you dispute this assessment?"

I noticed that his hands were shaking very slightly where he held the paper.

"I don't dispute that there was an incident," said Krane.

"Do you dispute that the Feyre were responsible?"

"Responsibility can be difficult to assign. Is the sword responsible for the cut, or the swordsman?"

"The swordsman," said the bank manager, without hesitation.

"And yet," said Krane, "if the sword cuts out a cancer then the swordsman may be revealed as a surgeon, may he not?"

"You don't remove a cancer with a sword, Lord Krane. You use a scalpel."

Krane clasped his hands together on the table. "Just so."

"Thirty-seven people are dead after last night. Thirty-seven deaths to explain to the families, and that's assuming the remaining victims survive. The destruction of a Crown facility on a high-security site, unexplained lights in the night sky, exploding aircraft, radiation burns – how are we supposed to keep this quiet?"

"That is not our concern," said Krane, quietly.

"It may become your concern."

"I do not think so."

"The Prime Minister is demanding an explanation from the Security Services and the Ministry of Defence. He's demanding full disclosure."

"I trust that you can come up with an explanation that will… satisfy him."

"My colleagues in Defence are demanding an inquiry."

"That would not be wise."

"I'm not sure if we can turn them down. This is getting beyond my ability to contain."

"It has been beyond your ability to contain for some time."

That prompted a sharp intake of breath. "Are you questioning my competence?"

"No, I am questioning your control." Krane reached into his pocket and produced the plastic container with the vial inside. He placed it carefully on the table between them. His hands did not shake. He clasped his hands again and placed them on the table.

"What's that?"

"I believe the term is: a biological weapon."

"Where did you get it?"

"It originated at Porton Down."

"Is that what you were after?"

"No. Truly, we did not know it existed. Apparently, neither did you."

"Then who made it?"

"Perhaps," said Krane, "that should be the subject of your inquiry."

The bank manager reached forward.

"If you touch it," Krane said, "we will kill all of you." The hand halted in mid-air. "We are not in the habit of allowing weapons aimed against us to fall into hostile hands."

The heavies reached inside their jackets. My hand and Garvin's dropped in perfect time to the hilts of our swords.

"Your men will never draw their weapons in time," said Krane, quietly.

The bank manager withdrew his hand slowly from the table and replaced it in his lap. The heavies slowly drew their hands back too, and Garvin and I lifted ours slowly from our swords. Everyone watched everyone else.

"Perhaps it would be better if you retrieved your sample," said Carler.

Krane reached forward, took the plastic container and returned it to his coat.

Carler put as much conviction into his voice as he could muster. "We did not, and have not, sanctioned the development of a biological weapon to be used against the Feyre."

"That you know of," said Krane. "Nevertheless, one has been created."

"I can assure you that we had no knowledge of this."

"We have a treaty, Secretary Carler. The treaty was made long before you were born. Guillaume was both clever and capable, and when he sealed our bargain he got more than he hoped for. Since that time your kind

447

have spread and become far more numerous than even we expected. Regardless, we gave our word and we will keep it–"

"That's good to hear–" began Carler.

"–as long as you keep your side of the bargain," said Krane.

"We have acted in good faith–"

"The hoarding of weapons against the Feyre is specifically prohibited in the treaty."

"Our understanding is that the research was for medical purposes."

"Nevertheless," Krane repeated, "a weapon was created. We are not so naive as to suppose that this–" He touched his jacket over the pocket where the vial rested "–is the only example of it, or that the research that created it was destroyed along with the facility."

"I can assure you that all the research associated with this project will be destroyed and that any records will be eliminated."

"Let us imagine for a moment," said Krane, "that through circumstances beyond your control this weapon was deployed. Let us imagine that it got out into the human population. The Gifted, those who share the bloodlines of both our races, would fall like blossom in a hailstorm. Our hope of renewal and strength would fail."

"That would be most unfortunate," agreed Carler.

"Under such circumstances, our treaty would be annulled, the purpose of the Seventh Court's exile would become moot and the peaceful coexistence that we have all worked so hard to preserve would be… unsustainable."

"I'm quite sure that would never happen," said Carler. Sweat beaded on his forehead.

Krane continued his quiet musing. "The lights in the sky over Porton Down might be a foretaste of what would follow… over London, Manchester, Belfast, Birmingham, Bristol."

"You are talking about open warfare."

"Teoth believes that the weapon can be altered. He believes that, given encouragement, it would develop and grow. He thinks the sample can be used to create a weapon that would be effective against humanity. Do you remember the Black Death, Secretary Carler? Do you know of it?"

"The plague? I read about it."

"A dark time for humanity. During that time the human population diminished. Nature reasserted herself. Forests grew back, meadows flowered. It was a good time for the Feyre."

"Is that a threat, Lord Krane?"

"Teoth says that the serum would make a disease such as you have not known, enhanced to spread through power, seeded on the wind, flowing in the water, immune to fire or acid, lethal in hours but able to lie dormant in the earth for centuries to come... The Feyre would be immune to it, of course, though the Gifted would suffer along with humanity."

"Why would you create such a thing?"

"We would not. We did not create this abomination. You did. We would simply be turning it to our purpose."

"But the Gifted would die along with everyone else."

"Those that remained, yes. It would be a tragedy for all of us. Still, it is only speculation. We have a treaty, after all."

"I do not believe that these threats are helping us, Lord Krane."

"Threats? No, I am simply speculating on a chain of events arising as a consequence of activities of which you had no knowledge or oversight."

"Quite so," said Carler. There was a long pause. "What would the Seven Courts have us do, Lord Krane? What assurances do you require?"

"You cannot assure us of things of which you have no knowledge, and therefore any assurance is only as good as the oversight which supports it. It is a weakness, but

I wanted you to be aware of the consequences, should that oversight fail us. It is in your interests, Secretary Carler, and the interests of humanity, to ensure that your oversight extends as far as needed. Beyond that we only require that you abide by the treaty to the fullest extent. We, in turn, will do the same."

"May that long continue to be the case," said Carler.

"Indeed so," said Krane.

Carler cleared his throat. "We continue to have a live situation in progress. We can deal with Porton Down and the inquiry. The helicopter crash is an unfortunate accident, a sad and regrettable loss of life. I'm sure that the inquiry will conclude that a combination of a failure in navigation systems and pilot error was to blame. The radiation will be harder to explain, but we will think of something."

"That sounds acceptable."

"In the meantime, several dangerous individuals have escaped the facility. Some of them are dangerously psychotic. None of them are harmless. We can't just ignore them."

"The Warders will take responsibility for the escapees. Garvin, I believe this falls to you."

"I have someone in mind for the job, my Lord," said Garvin. He looked meaningfully at me.

"It would be embarrassing for any of this to come into the public domain," said Carler.

"The Warders are the soul of discretion," smiled Krane.

There was a lull. Then Carler said, "If you would like us to dispose of the sample safely for you, Lord Krane, I'm sure that can be arranged."

"There is no need. Destruction of the sample is well within our capability. It will allow you to concentrate your efforts on making sure that the research developed at Porton Down is properly contained and the records disposed of in a suitable manner, for the benefit of us all."

"For the benefit of us all. Indeed."

Krane stood. "If that concludes our discussions, I will leave you to make the appropriate arrangements. I'm sure there is much to do."

"Certainly, of course." Carler looked relieved.

We turned to the doorway. Fellstamp opened the door and the dark-suited man ushered us out. As we exited the building, Tate was waiting for us, watched warily by the policemen. He leaned close to Garvin and spoke briefly.

Garvin nodded and then drew Krane aside for a moment. Krane looked up at Tate and then spoke briefly with Garvin in low tones. Garvin nodded. Fellstamp and Tate faded into the mist as they escorted Krane across the grass back to the Way-node, while Garvin and I lingered by the doorway. After a moment the first of the two dark-suited figures emerged.

Garvin addressed him. "We meet here in good faith."

"That's right." The accent was Scottish, the voice low and hoarse. He looked tired.

"By tradition, he who calls the meeting secures the ground. That would be your responsibility, would it?"

"Security, aye." He took a cigarette from a packet, lit it, dragged heavily on it and blew smoke out to merge with the mist.

"I assume the two snipers are yours, then?" asked Garvin.

"Two, you say?"

"Two. They are unharmed, but you might need a ladder."

"And why would I need a ladder?"

"To get them down from the trees." Garvin turned and walked away, and I followed.

As we walked into the mist, he called after us. "What if there were three snipers?"

Garvin continued walking without looking back. As we reached the Way-node, Tate materialised out of the fog.

"Security is suggesting that there are three snipers," Garvin said quietly to him.

"Nope," said Tate. "And their recording devices weren't very well hidden either."

He placed two tiny tape recorders in Garvin's open hand.

"Is that all of them?"

"Hard to tell if they have anything remote. They're getting clever. That's all that was inside the grounds."

"Safer to assume the meeting was recorded, then. No problem. Nothing was said that can't be repeated elsewhere. Good work."

"It was fun. They're good." Tate grinned.

"We're better," said Garvin. "Keep an eye on them until they leave, just in case."

Garvin stepped on to the Way-node and vanished. I heard one of the cars rumble into life back at the hall.

"Good meeting?" asked Tate.

"I think it served its purpose. Are you gonna check there isn't a third sniper?"

"No. If there had been they would never have mentioned him. I'll join you in a while."

Tate slipped away, merging with the fog. I looked around and wondered if it would dissipate, now the meeting was over. Maybe later, when Tate left.

I stepped on to the Way and followed Garvin.

TWENTY-SEVEN

Waiting in the church gave me time to think. I'd let myself in and locked the door after me in case anyone else came by. Greg had a key and if it wasn't him, the sound of the door unlocking would give me time to conceal myself. I had an idea he was expecting me in any case.

Blackbird's advice was to let matters take their course and intervene no further, but for me it left too much unresolved. I needed to know what happened, and there were things Greg needed to know too.

I sat where the sunlight poured through the great east window and waited for him.

The pinboard with the photos was still there. No one had removed the pictures of Gillian and Trudy. I guessed that Greg was still working on a way to break the news to the parents. Whether I should explain to Greg exactly what had happened to them was a dilemma. I tried to feel anger at the men who had taken two girls out to sea and then forced them off the boat into the water. I tried to see them as murderers, as monsters. The problem was that they weren't really any different to anyone else. They were just men.

They had tried to save their livelihood, their families and their community. Wasn't that all anybody did? They had got close to the truth. They had found the records, searched the archives and pieced the puzzle together. That's all I had done. The only difference was that the picture they ended up with had interpreted the role of the girls as a literal sacrifice to the sea. The actual sacrifice was much more subtle, a life given in service to the community in return for... what? What was the link between the cave on the beach and the girls in the town? What did the women get out of it? A longer life? A better life?

My train of thought was interrupted by the sound of heavy footsteps and the turn of a key in a lock. I didn't wrap myself in glamour; there was no need. The man I had come to see let himself in.

He didn't acknowledge me at first. I figured he'd been expecting me sooner or later so my presence in a locked church was no surprise. Instead he marched up the aisle and knelt before the altar in the flood of light under the window. I sat in silence and let him commune with his Maker.

Presently he rose and bowed, then went to either side of the altar, moving this and that, checking things were as they should be. When he returned to me he didn't slide into the pew beside me but chose the one in front, sitting sideways so he could see my face. It was some time before he spoke.

"Questions, or answers?" he said.

"Both."

"Shelley is back with her folks. Artist feller says he found her on the beach, wet, freezing cold, totally out of it. He picked her up, took care of her, brought her home."

"An artist."

"Is that a question or an answer?"

"A question. Is he local?"

Greg smiled. "Aye. He designed that." He gestured at the main east window. "He calls it Flowing Sealight. Told me that glass isn't solid, that it stays liquid even while it's up there, that if you wait long enough it will flow down and pool at the bottom, like water."

I looked again into the flood of light from the window, noting how the shape of the cross emerged at random from the arrangement of the fragments, how some of the panes were thicker than others, so that they refracted the light in all directions, into every corner. It really was a thing of beauty.

"He's got a real talent for it."

"He's taken a liking to Shelley. Think she's a bit young for him, personally."

"How old is he?"

"Hard to say. She's just a kid, though."

"She'll grow."

"Aye, she will now. Where did you go?"

"When?"

"When Shelley disappeared. We were searching the waterfront. There was that van. You ran down the harbour and then... where did you go?"

"I had a hunch."

"I found the mirror, what was left of it. You weren't with it."

I wanted to answer. I wanted to explain, but I couldn't find the words. Instead I just shrugged. "What does Shelley say?"

"She says she went swimming. Says she got out of her depth, that she couldn't get out. The tide was too strong. Says she nearly drowned. Doesn't know how she made it out of the water."

"I expect that's right, then."

"Avesham says when he found her, she was near frozen to death."

"Avesham?"

"The artist. Says he was out on the beach, watching the storm. Saw her on the shingle. Says it was destiny."

"Does he?"

"Artists. They say things like that." He paused, waiting for some comment or confirmation from me. "Storm appeared out of nowhere."

"That can happen," I said.

"One of the boats was washed ashore. A lobster boat."

"That can happen too."

"Three men drowned. The boat was salvaged, but the men weren't on it. No lifebelts used, flares all accounted for."

"It's a dangerous occupation. There's a book in the Maritime Museum, it's full of the names of good men."

"Aye, it is." There was another long pause. "Helen came to see me."

"That's good."

"Brought the baby with her. Wants him christened in the church."

"That's a lovely idea."

"She said a man came to her in a dream and told her I wanted to know whether it was a boy or a girl. She described the man. He looked a lot like you."

"It's probably better that we don't meet then, isn't it? That might freak her out a little."

"Aye. Probably. Don't know whether her parents will come to the christening."

"If they love their daughter then they'll come. It's not every day you become a grandparent."

"And you, Neal. What about you? Did you find your story?"

"If there is a story, I am not sure where it begins or how it ends. Maybe I will write it, one day."

"Some stories are better left untold."

"I'm glad you see it that way."

I offered him my hand and he took it. The pulse of power passed between us.

"Static," I said. He smiled, wryly.

I left him in the church. He still had the task of taking bad news to the parents of Gillian and Trudy and I did not envy him that, but with the christening to look forward to, there might be some compensation.

I walked down to the High Street and bought a nice mirror from an antique shop, then took it to the Dolphin and presented it to Martha as a replacement for the one I had broken. She was full of reprimands until she unwrapped it, and then embarrassed that it was really rather better than the one it replaced. I collected my things and left, climbing past the church until I stood on the hill looking down on the town. Would it prosper now? Only time would tell.

Concealing myself, I turned to the Way-node and stepped forward, leaving the town far behind.

When I got back to the High Courts, Blackbird was going through her wardrobe, laying out the contents of her drawers and examining them all with a critical eye. She had amassed three piles – one for the charity shops, one to go back in the cupboards and a last one with an uncertain future.

"Do you think I'll ever wear this again? She held up a sundress with a blue floral design.

"I don't know. Do we have to decide right now?" I asked.

She surveyed the piles. "You're right. I'll keep that one but not this one. This one goes, right?"

She held up a yellow sun-top that faded into orange.

"Whatever you think's best. I'd better go and see how Alex is getting on."

I escaped into the hallway and met Tate as I walked through the house. He turned and fell into step with me.

"How's she doing?" I asked him.

"She's upsetting the stewards," he said. "Eating like a horse, and she's driving Fionh crazy. "

"I thought they'd get on OK."

"It's a long time since Fionh was a teenager. She's been trying to teach Alex to use her magic in a more controlled fashion, but she has no attention span. They just get started and she wants to eat again, or drink, or take a shower."

"She's only fifteen, Garvin."

"That may be true, but in fey terms she's a woman. The Feyre consider that once you come into your power you are responsible for yourself, an adult."

"She's not ready for adulthood."

"She has power, she's of an age to bear children. Those are all the qualifications you need."

"She'll need some time to adjust," I insisted.

"Stop babying her, Niall. You're making it worse."

We'd reached the suite which Alex and I had been assigned. Alex was reorganising it to her tastes, moving furniture while Fionh watched her from the sofa. I looked at Fionh. She shrugged.

"Sweetheart, what are you doing?" I called after Alex.

"Do you mind if you have my bedroom and I have yours?" she called, walking into another room. "You won't be sleeping in there anyway, will you?"

Tate touched my arm. "I'll see you later." He made a strategic withdrawal.

"I'm not sure..." I said. "We're not staying here, Alex. This is only temporary until we can find somewhere else."

She came back in carrying a set of bedding. When she had gone into the room her hair had been dark. Now it was blonde. She tossed the bedding on to the other bed and went back for more.

"What's with the hair?" I asked Fionh.

"Oh, that. I showed her glamour and she hasn't managed to be stable for more than two minutes since. Her mind's a butterfly. She can't concentrate on anything.

458

One moment she's a redhead, then a blonde, five minutes ago she had long hair, now it's short."

She appeared in the doorway. "You need to take me shopping," she said. Her hair was jet-black.

"There'll be time for that later."

"You always say that. I don't have any clothes. I haven't even got any bras." She looked down and her chest visibly swelled inside her jumper. She looked up at me innocently.

"How am I supposed to buy you new clothes if you keep changing size?" I asked.

"Maybe I need different sizes for different days," she said. "Maybe I need a lot of new clothes."

"Maybe you can have jeans and a T-shirt and you do the rest with glamour?" I suggested.

"Oh, Dad! I have nothing to wear. Literally nothing!" Her clothes switched back to the hospital gown. I was sure it was more transparent than it had been originally.

I was rescued by Garvin. He peeked around the door and raised his eyebrow at the jumble that our living space had become.

"I have business," I told her. "Can you just put things back the way they were, please?"

"If I can't have any proper clothes, I'll just wear this then, shall I?" She followed me to the door.

I held up my hand. "We'll talk about this later."

"Humph!" She screwed her hands into fists and stomped off into the other room. The water pipes in the bathroom gurgled in response until Fionh glanced sharply at the bathroom, whereupon the gurgling ceased.

When I stepped outside, Garvin was leaning against the wall.

"You wanted her back," he said.

I sighed. "At least it's normal. I caught her this morning curled up in bed, sobbing. When I asked her what

459

she was crying about she wouldn't tell me. She wouldn't even let me touch her."

"It's going to take time, and it's going to leave scars," he said.

"On all of us."

"You can't stay here forever. You do know that?" He pushed off from the wall and we walked slowly down the hallway.

"I know. Allowing her to rearrange the rooms does give her some sense of security, though. She needs the illusion of permanence."

"Mullbrook is making arrangements for another house. He was suggesting somewhere well-built, relatively fireproof, near a lake, or perhaps the sea?"

"Steward's humour? I think I've seen enough of the sea for a while."

"I think he was serious. With water and fire under the same roof, you could have some interesting times ahead."

"Tell me about it."

"We need to think about the future. You can't continue as Niall and Alex Petersen. You'll need new identities for a new life."

"I can't do that, Garvin. What about Katherine? I have to tell her something. What about my parents? They just lost their granddaughter. They can't lose their son as well. It would kill my mother. I have to think of something else."

"Perhaps it would be best to let things take their course. Alex can't go back, you know, even if she wants to. They will be looking for her and for anyone else who escaped from Porton Down. She's going to need to keep a low profile."

"Try telling her that."

On cue her head appeared around the doorway. "Can I go out?"

"Out where, sweetheart?"

"Just out. Am I a prisoner here? Fionh says I'm not a prisoner but she won't let me go anywhere."

"Where do you want to go?"

"Just out. Somewhere with people, shops, music. I'm fed up of being in one room."

"Technically it's three rooms."

She sighed. "Can I go out?"

"It's more complicated than that. What about your appearance? You need to be able to handle your power – so things don't get out of control."

"I'm fed up with being controlled!" That caused a growl from the plumbing.

"And that's exactly what I'm talking about," I reminded her.

Amber ran up the stairway and stopped. "I think you'd better come." She paused, waiting for me. I watched her expression.

"When can I go out?" asked Alex.

"Not now, sweetheart."

"You always say that. I'll be stuck in here forever. You got me out of one prison to put me in another. I'm supposed to be an adult. Why can't I do what I want?"

"It's time," said Amber.

"Alex, go back in your room and stay there until I get back. I have to go now."

"How come you can go and I can't? It's not fair!"

"No," I told her. "It's not fair. It isn't good and it isn't nice. Things are difficult, life is hard and the sooner you get used to it, the better. But right now I need to be with Blackbird, OK?"

"Why? What makes her so special? I'm supposed to be your daughter."

I hurried away, but then stopped and turned back to her.

"You are my daughter. I love you and I want you to

461

remember that, but you're about to become a sister. Now do as you're told."

I watched her face change as she grasped the implications of what I'd just said.

Then I ran.

ACKNOWLEDGMENTS

I am grateful that so many people will give up their time to read and comment, and point out where I have written something that doesn't make sense or backed myself into a corner. Indeed, so many people have contributed ideas or made suggestions that I'm sure I will miss someone in these acknowledgements, so if that is you, please accept my apologies and my thanks.

I am particularly grateful to Peter for wading through the early drafts and providing a wealth of questions, challenges and ideas, and to Geri, for resisting the temptation to read *Sixty-One Nails* so that she could read this book first and check that it made sense for a new reader. Once again I am indebted to the Roses, especially Jo and Simon, and to Ameen, Lauri, Rachel, Bob and Tina, who took the time to read, review and provide feedback, and to Jules for such interesting research material and providing continuing support and encouragement. A special mention also for Jenny, who as well as providing comments, looked beyond the story and asked the questions that really needed to be answered.

The Wellie Writers, Joy and Andrew, also have my gratitude, for their continued support and encouragement in developing my writing, for their honesty and integrity, and for their dedication to the mutual blood-sports which are our monthly critique sessions, long may they continue.

My thanks also go to the professionals, to Jennifer Jackson, my agent, whose comments always go right to the heart of things and whose advice and guidance I value immensely, and to the Angry Robot team, Marc Gascoigne and Lee Harris, who have shaped the concepts, tuned the output and provided huge amounts of encouragement and professional help. You are a pleasure to work with.

My gratitude also extends to the countless people who have fielded odd questions, bounced back ideas, and humoured the strange bloke with an uncommon curiosity as to how this or that came to be. Please continue to humour me, as it almost always leads somewhere interesting and you never know, the conversation may end up in a book.

It is generally considered a bad idea for an author to comment on reviews of their work. However, I do want to thank all the people who read *Sixty-One Nails* and then took the time to marshall their thoughts and put together a review. I have been delighted with the response and I hope this book lives up to your expectations. Also to the people who met me at conventions, stopped me in the street or sent their comments through email or via the website, thank you for your kindness. Your comments are much appreciated.

I would like to thank my whole family for being so spectacularly supportive, not just of my writing, but of everything I do, and for continuing to put up with me. Your encouragement, kindness and love is what keeps me going.

Finally, to my wife, Sue, and my son, Leo, who enduringly suffer the eccentricities of my writing, are my first and last critics, and can be relied upon to come up with the most obscure, bizarre and wonderful material. You always encourage me to be the best that I can be, you are always there for me when I stumble or fall, and without you I could not have done any of this. You make me proud and immensely grateful.

Thank you.

Mike Shevdon,
Bedford, UK 2010

ABOUT THE AUTHOR

Mike Shevdon's love of Fantasy & SF started in the 1970s with CS Lewis, Robert Heinlein and Isaac Asimov, and continued through Alan Garner, Ursula Le Guin and Barbara Hambly. More recent influences include Mike Carey, Phil Rickman, Neil Gaiman and Robert Crais, among many others.

He has studied martial arts for many years, aikido and archery mainly. Friends have sometimes remarked that his pastimes always seem to involve something sharp or pointy. The pen should therefore be no surprise, though he's still trying to figure out how to get an edge on a laptop.

Mike lives in Bedfordshire, England, with his wife and son, where he pursues the various masteries of weapons, technology, and cookery.

www.shevdon.com

THE WINDING WAY TO BEDLAM

Those of you who have read *Sixty-One Nails* will know that I like to incorporate real places and events into my stories and in this, *The Road to Bedlam* is no exception. However, I will admit straight away that Ravensby does not exist.

I knew from the beginning that the part of the story that fell within the fishing town would be set in North Yorkshire. I was born not far from there and I knew that the particular feel of that coast was what I needed for this book. When I came to select a town, though, I could not find all that I needed in one place. I will also confess that I did not want to lay the dark events that unfolded there on the warm-hearted people of one Yorkshire town.

So that's how Ravensby came to be. It is a composite place which takes elements from Staithes, Whitby, Robin Hood's Bay and Ravenscar, following down the coast to Scarborough, Filey and Bridlington. The story is no reflection on the kind and welcoming Yorkshire folk, and I thoroughly recommend a visit to the area to sample its delights for yourself.

The Sea Queens are also fictional, though further up the coast they crown a Herring Queen in Eyemouth in

July each year. That tradition extends only back until the 1930s, though, and whether such traditions were more prevalent in earlier times when the herring stocks were more substantial, I do not know.

While Ravensby is fictional, the storm of 10th February 1871 is not. It happened much as described in the book, with the weather turning overnight from the clear calm day on the 9th to hurricane-force snow and sleet the following morning. The lifeboats rowed out time and again to save men from ships that were either being overtaken by the waves or driven onto the rocks, until one of the lifeboats was also wrecked. By nightfall over thirty ships had been lost and seventy sailors had died, some drowned within sight of their loved ones. Reading the accounts left me in awe of the lifeboatmen, the sailors and those who risked their lives to rescue the drowning men, and full of respect for the men who, once the storm had calmed and the cost was counted, continued to go out to sea knowing full well the danger. Even with modern technology it continues to be a hazardous occupation.

The stones that form the Way-points that Niall follows to reach North Yorkshire are also real. The Devil's Arrows are three millstone grit monoliths, over twenty feet tall which stand in a near-straight line crossing Roecliffe Lane at Boroughbridge in Yorkshire, near the A1 motorway. The Devil is supposed to have cast the arrows from a nearby hill at the village of Aldborough, but they fell short. There used to be four, but one of them is now believed to form part of a bridge over a nearby stream.

The other Way-point is the Rudston Monolith and is the largest of its kind in the United Kingdom at over twenty-five feet high. It used to be taller, but the churchyard it stands in was levelled around it and it lost almost five feet in the process. Dating from approximately

1600 BC, it is far older than the Norman church which stands beside it and the site was probably sacred long before Christianity arrived in Britain.

It is not known why the asylum at Charing Cross was originally called the Stone House, but it was rumoured to contain both the dangerously mad and political prisoners. In the 1370s, it was closed down by King Richard II because the cries of anguish from its inmates were upsetting his falcons in the nearby mews.

The inmates were moved to a hospital founded by Simon FitzMary in 1247 dedicated to the Order of the Star of Bethlehem. Simon had a particular affinity for the star, for when he was in the crusades he became lost behind enemy lines and was afraid he would stumble into Saladin's lines, but then he saw a star over Bethlehem, just like the one that had guided the three wise men, and so he navigated back to his own lines and safety. The Star of Bethlehem is still the symbol of the hospital today, and of course, Bedlam is a corruption of Bethlem, which is what the people of Shoreditch called the hospital.

The original hospital had room for about twenty people, and in 1674, it was recorded that the "hospital house was old, weak, ruinous and so small and strait for keeping the great number applying for admission that it ought to be removed and rebuilt elsewhere on some site grantable by the city". London was overflowing Bedlam and so it was decreed that it be moved to a "Palace Beautiful" at Moorfields which was built for the purpose.

Then followed the period in which the mad were exhibited. In 1753, the newspaper *The World* reported that "It was in the Easter week, when, to my great surprise, I found a hundred people at least, who, having paid their two-pence apiece, were suffered, unattended, to run rioting up and down the wards, making sport and diversion of the miserable inhabitants."

Sixty years later, the Palace Beautiful had been subsumed in the urban sprawl of London. The roof leaked, the cellars were unwholesome and the whole edifice was in danger of collapse due to subsidence.

In 1815, the hospital was rebuilt once again, this time at St George's Fields, the building now used for The Imperial War Museum. There it housed the artists Louis Wain and Richard Dadd, among others. It saw action during the First World War as a respite for shell-shocked soldiers – 80,000 recorded cases, of whom 30,000 ended up in institutions – and they were the lucky ones. Finally, in 1930 it was moved to Monks Orchard, where it is today. I am indebted to Catherine Arnold and her Excellent book, *Bedlam – London and its Mad* (Simon and Schuster 2008), for much of the background and history of Bedlam.

I previously mentioned that Richard Dadd (1817-1886) was an inmate at Bedlam. In 1843, Dadd, convinced that his father was the Devil, killed him with a knife. He was imprisoned in the criminal wing at Bedlam for twenty years and then transferred in 1864 to Broadmoor. His painting, *The Fairy Feller's Master-Stroke* is in the Tate Gallery's collection, though it is not always on show. It was executed in minute and exquisite detail – prints and pictures of it cannot render the texture, which has an almost three-dimensional quality. It is well worth seeing if you get opportunity, as is Patricia Alldridge's book on *Richard Dadd* (Academy Editions, 1974).

Porton Down is the 7,000 acre home to the Defence Science and Technology Laboratory and is one of the most secret facilities in the UK. Its primary role is defence against CBRN threats, which are Chemical. Biological, Radiological and Nuclear. It should be noted that it is not part of Porton Down's remit to develop weapons, but rather to develop defences against weapons that may be used against the UK or its armed forces.

However, it has a chequered and controversial history. In the 1950s Porton Down was involved with the development of the riot control agent, CS gas, and testing of the nerve agent, Sarin. There are alleged deaths associated with this testing. In 1961, a Land Rover vehicle was driven by scientists from Porton Down, from the village of Ilchester through Wedmore and into the outskirts of Bristol. They sprayed Zinc Calcium Sulphide into the air from the vehicle to simulate a germ warfare attack. The spread and concentration of the cloud was monitored at stations through Wiltshire and Somerset.

Clearly, the defence against germ warfare, nerve agents and dirty bombs has to be carefully considered and appropriate preparations made if the threat from rogue states and terrorist agents is to be countered or mitigated. The facilities at Porton Down are an essential part of these preparations, but if there was government sponsored research into paranormal creatures, then it seemed to me that Porton Down is where it would take place.

The high-tech, high-security facilities of Porton Down are in marked contrast to Oakham Castle, found just off the market square in Oakham, the county town of Rutland. Although hardly secure by modern standards, the castle does have one unique quality. Inside the main hall the walls are completely covered with horseshoes. It is not known how the practice started, but since the fifteenth century, any peer of the realm, no matter what their rank, has been obliged to present a horseshoe to Oakham Castle or to pay a forfeit in its place. The earliest record is from 1470, when Edward IV commanded that a horseshoe be put up in the hall and that shoe is still there.

Interestingly, the family to whom the castle belonged were called the Ferrers. These were descendents of Henry de Ferrers, Lord of Ferrieres in Normandy (an area known for its iron workings) who came to England with William I in 1066 or very soon after.

The Ferrers were a prestigious family and were granted land including Rutland, which itself is rich in iron deposits. Ferrer is also the Norman French word for a smith, from which we derive the word *farrier*, still in use today.

SIXTY-ONE NAILS

MIKE SHEVDON

THE COURTS OF THE FEYRE, VOL. I

ANGRY
ROBOT

Teenage serial killers
Zombie detectives
The grim reaper in love
Howling axes **Vampire
hordes** Dead men's clones
The Black Hand
Death by cellphone
Gangster shamen
Steampunk swordfights
Sex-crazed bloodsuckers
Murderous gods
Riots **Quests Discovery**
Death

**Prepare
to welcome
your new
Robot overlords.**

angryrobotbooks.com

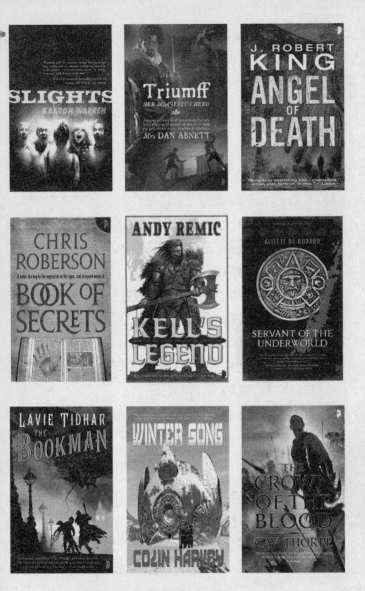